Praise for Domnica Radulescu's Fiction:

"Domnica Radulescu is a remarkable writer enriching American letters with her perspective. We are lucky to call her ours."

— Sandra Cisneros, international best-selling author of
The House on Mango Street and *Caramelo*
(referring to Radulescu's first novel *Train to Trieste*)

"My Father's Orchards is a historical novel, and its issues—race, immigration, violence, prejudice, persecution—could not be timelier. A native of Romania, Radulescu brings to the table a wealth of personal stories as well a keen awareness of historical, social, and cultural events."

— Lisa Spaar, award winning poet, Guggenheim Fellowship recipient

A poignant story — this paternal orchard that surrounds a family home, a microcosm of a country, Romania where the exiled narrator Corina returns in 2015 to explore family secrets buried in the home of her grandparents. The book reads like a thriller about a house haunted by the spirits of the half-dead whose murky existence continues to haunt the living. A powerful, abundant, moving novel which succeeds in reconciling, in the immense metaphor of the paternal orchard, the history of a people and the memory of those who constituted it.

— Michèle Sarde, Professor Emerita, Georgetown University and writer, author of *Returning from Silence* (2022), winner of the Grand Prix Wizzo, finalist for the Goncourt Prize for *Histoire d' Eurydice pendant la remontée.*

Weaving together poetry, fantasy, folklore, and brutally realistic images of war, Domnica Radulescu explores her native Romania's complex contemporary history through the search of her protagonist Corina, now living in the U.S., for her roots. Despite the horrors of the Nazi and Communist occupations, devastating pogroms, callous land grabs, and ruthless murders, love and joy persistently shine through this extraordinary narrative in the memory of the family's orchards—an idyllic Eden lush with cherries and plums. A brilliant novel, and now, in this time of rising antisemitism, timelier than ever.

— Bárbara Mujica, bestselling author of *Frida* and *Miss del Río*

"Domnica Radulescu is one of those remarkable writers born in Eastern Europe who made a transition from one language to another, conscious of what it means to translate oneself and to see how this transformation is essential to so much of our discussion about our world now. I look eagerly forward to her next book."

— Andrei Codrescu, bestselling author of *The Blood Countess*, NPR commentator

My Father's ORCHARDS

Domnica Radulescu

My Father's ORCHARDS

Histria Fiction

Las Vegas ◊ Chicago ◊ Palm Beach

Published in the United States of America by
Histria Books
7181 N. Hualapai Way, Ste. 130-86
Las Vegas, NV 89166 USA
HistriaBooks.com

Histria Fiction is an imprint of Histria Books. Titles published under the imprints of Histria Books are distributed worldwide. We appreciate your support of copyright by purchasing an authorized edition of this book and for respecting intellectual property laws by not reproducing, scanning, or otherwise distributing any part of it by any means without permission. You are supporting authors and enabling Histria Books to continue publishing books for everyone.

All rights reserved. No part of this book may be reprinted or reproduced or utilized in any form or by any electronic, mechanical or other means, now known or hereafter invented, including photocopying and recording, or in any information storage or retrieval system, without the permission in writing from the Publisher. No part of this book may be used or reproduced in any manner for the purpose of training artificial intelligence technologies or systems.

Certain characters in this work are historical figures, and certain events portrayed did take place. However, this is a work of fiction. Names, characters, places, and incidents are either the product of the author's imagination or are used fictitiously. Any resemblance to actual persons, living or dead, is entirely coincidental.

First Edition

Library of Congress Control Number: 2024953107

ISBN 978-1-59211-591-4 (softbound)
ISBN 978-1-59211-585-3 (eBook)

Copyright © 2025 by Domnica Radulescu

For the memory of my father, Gheorghe Radulescu (1926-2000)

For my mother, Stella Vinitchi Radulescu

"My Mother's Garden. Summer of 1944"
From Florin's Diary

When the Russian tanks drove into our town in Northern Moldavia in August of 1944, my mother was digging for roots in our back yard. The drought that came after the floods brought with it famine and epidemics. The earth cracked open, and vultures circled the houses in hopes of fresh corpses. My mother used to say while laughing that "disaster loved our country." She never lost her sense of humor even when death was a blink away. My father had died of pneumonia the week before, and my sister came down with scarlet fever right after that. Death was lingering on our doorsteps without shame and the bombs crackling their explosions in the sky lit up our nights with impunity. The house we had left in good shape the year before when we took whatever we could in large sacks and got on the crowded train filled with refugees, soldiers, and demented fowl had been ransacked, the furniture pillaged, and our family dog cut to pieces and left to rot in the front yard. The Russians had come and gone and were now back again, driving their tanks through the thick darkened air of that endless summer like kings of the world.

My mother would dig for roots in our backyard for hours every day to make food for us and to save my sister from dying of scarlet fever. She kept saying we were lucky to be alive and that we had each other. We still had the house, pillaged and ransacked as it had been. There were those whose houses had been bombed out of existence and returned to a pile of bricks. We were manifold lucky. She would wipe the sweat off her face with the back of her hand and try to smile to lift my spirits and convince me that we were lucky. There were never tears in her eyes, just a fierce glint of an irrepressible will to survive. My sister's moans as she lay unconscious with burning fever broke the silence all hours of the day and night. She sounded like a dying bird, almost beautiful.

I was fourteen and did not want to survive. When my father died, I wanted to be buried alive next to him or die of starvation first and then be buried next to him. I was already weak and dizzy from hunger, and death seemed just like a peaceful sleep, a happy alternative. I had lost my appetite for food and just wanted cigarettes. That week of the return of the Russians, I was capable of anything. Mostly bad things. I had begged one of our only surviving neighbors on the street, an old man who had worked for the railroad before the war, for a few cigarettes, and when he wasn't looking, I ran away with his entire pack. He called out after me and called me names like "scum of the earth" and "bad weed." It was the first time in a long while that something made me laugh and I ran home with the stolen pack of cigarettes laughing at the insults Mr. Gogu had thrown at me. He could have done much better, I thought, he could have hurled some real obscenities, instead of the almost poetic "bad weed." I thought I had done Mr. Gogu a big favor to steal his cigarettes, since he was always hacking and getting red and swollen in the face like a balloon ready to explode, and then he smoked some more.

Throughout the German occupation, he would just sit on the stoop in front of his house swearing in Romanian at the soldiers who paced up and down with their green uniforms and spewed harsh consonants in the form of speech. Now with the Russians' arrival he hurled the same invectives at their soldiers and added a few new ones such as "motherfucking animals" and "two legged pigs, may you rot in fucking hell and may your dicks fry!" Mr. Gogu knew how to swear like no one else in town but for some reason he went easy on me when I stole his cigarettes. It must have been out of pity that I had just lost my father, and the sound of my cries had reached him all the way from the other end of the street. The sounds of me saying: "No, no, I want to be buried too, please bury me too."

My sister said to me through her tears at the funeral that took place in our own back yard: "They can't bury you alive you have to die first, stupid!" So, I wanted to die first and be buried with my father afterwards. Only that would have killed my mother too, and what would have happened to my sister left all alone? She probably would have died too, as the present scarlet fever was there to prove it, and so our entire family would have been erased from the face of the earth. That was a sad thought, and it would have made my father very sad from beyond the grave to know we were all gone, since on his death bed he talked about all the grand things my sister and I would do later in life, when the war was over. He said it twice: "when the war is over, when the war ends." He had also looked at me straight in the eyes as he always did with both infinite love and harshness and said: "You are the man of the family now and you must take care of your mother and sister. Your sister is fragile, you know. Promise me you will look after her." I promised all that, I would have promised anything to please my father on his death bed in some hope that the more I promised, the more time I bought for him on earth.

But it didn't work like that. My father died that evening. He breathed his last breath while I was looking away following the flight of a swallow outside our window. I was thinking it was nice to see a swallow instead of a vulture, maybe things were looking up. Mother was sitting on the bed next to him and my sister was sitting on the floor at the foot of the bed, holding her doll Mitzi and talking to her in whispers as she always did. I heard my mother produce a tiny sob and when I turned my head, he was dead. Lila told her doll Mitzi that our father was dead, and they both cried. At least Lila kept saying that Mitzi was crying too. My mother held my father's hand crying in silence for a little while and then got up, wiped her tears and told us to come help her, there was so much to do, so much to do. That was when I clung to my father's body and did not want to let go and howled that I wanted to be buried next to him. That was when my world collapsed and fell with a deafening crash on my head like the American bombs that kept coming down during the German occupation. I had to be a man and had no idea what that meant.

That was also when I saw her cross the room silently with a sad smile and glassy eyes. Lila had been telling me about the strigoi girl that lived in our house, and I never believed her until then. She crossed the room once, twice, and the third time she vanished. There was a yellowness left after her in the room. Something sour and yellow, like a wet wind with taste and color. I had heard people in our town talk about the strigoi creatures that haunted some houses since the war, because there were so many dead and there was so much hunger and sorrow dripping everywhere like rain from the trees. Liquid sorrow dripping everywhere you turned. So much sorrow that you wanted to laugh at sorrow and spite it. Like Mr. Gogu who swore and laughed. And sometimes my mother too, laughed disaster in the face. Not a sardonic or wicked laugh, just a full laugh as if something was funny. That transparent yellow sour smelling girl haunting our house and circling around the body of my father did not scare me. Nothing scared me anymore after my father died. If it hadn't been so strange I could have almost thought the strigoi girl was comforting. Like the swallow darting by our window the split second my father took his last breath.

The day after the funeral my sister got sick with scarlet fever. The doctor couldn't keep up with all the people dying and getting sick and after he diagnosed Lila, he told my mother to keep cold compresses on her forehead and chest. My mother stayed up with my sister night after night putting cold compresses on her head and chest and making her drink beet juice. She found beets among the roots she was digging out of the ground and boiled them for hours. She gave me the other roots she had found such as parsnips and turnips, the white roots instead of the red ones; we were lucky that there were all kinds of good roots in the ground. The red beet juice trickled down my sister's face and looked like blood. "It's good for her, it will cure her," my mother said turning to me. I saw two huge tears sparkling in her eyes and hanging on her eyelashes. It should have been me, I thought, I should have gotten scarlet fever, not Lila. I told my mother it should have been me, and she said harshly: "Don't talk nonsense. Everybody with their own fate! It would have been just as bad if it had been you, I love you both just the same, stupid boy!"

The day when the Russian tanks drove into our town my sister started getting better, the fever went down, and she opened her eyes. They were glassy and blank like she was returning from the dead, which maybe she was. The doctor stopped by that day to tell us the Russians were back, everything was going to get bad for us and for everybody else. But my mother didn't care about the Russians, she would have welcomed extraterrestrials now that her Lila was back in the world of the living. The doctor said to make sure Lila rested a lot— her heart was weakened from the fever, she would always have a weak heart from now on, he said. My mother just smiled and nodded. Of course she would rest a lot, what else was Lila going to do but rest? She wasn't listening to the doctor anymore, all that she cared about was that Lila was going to live. If she survived this, she would survive anything, she said. The doctor left wishing us well and stirring the dust on the pathway to the street. The dust seemed thicker that day, the heat more unbearable, something wicked seemed to be floating in the air. There were no more roots in our garden, so starvation set in. How was Lila ever going to get better if we all starved to death? But my mother didn't think that way. We would manage somehow, she kept saying. I was almost enjoying the lightheaded feeling of starvation, except when my stomach wrenched in pain. Lila was still full of beet juice and feeble and wasn't feeling hungry yet.

The girl appeared again in the following days, hovering around the house. Our furniture was slashed and ransacked from the previous passage of the Russians, but the gliding of the unearthly girl between pieces of broken furniture gave everything a glow as if things weren't what they appeared to be. Here was this pillaged old house with chairs and upholstery all busted up, feathers from pillows and cushions lying everywhere, quivering from the palpable heat. Here was my father's walnut desk with the glass top smashed to smithereens and our beloved dog, Girl, cut to pieces in the front yard. And yet there was something else too, the promise of a song, the possibility of a cooler day with food and flowers and swallows darting around the house. Maybe a light dance in the afternoon to the sound of an old violin. The strigoi girl's smile was so sad it almost looked happy. It went to the other side of sadness and became happiness. I wanted to talk to her and ask her questions, like how did she become a strigoi, was it true what they said about the strigoi that they were undead children who became evil if the parents didn't remove some kind of crown or bonnet off the top of their head at birth? I always found the bonnet part slightly funny and much less worthy of respect or fear than that whole universe of other worldly creatures from our folklore. And what kind of evil was inside of them? What could be more evil than all the evils we had already endured?

My mother laughed wholeheartedly at such stories and said they were stupid superstitions of stupid people. But for some reason I wanted to believe in those stories at that point in my life. The girl gliding around the busted furniture seemed as real as the dust and the heat and the hunger. I welcomed her and was not afraid. I wanted to ask her how she got there, had she been living in our house for a long time, what was her story? She reminded me of someone I knew. A girl in another life. The yellow sour wind that came with her was almost pleasant and it soothed my hunger. Her colorless, glassy eyes didn't scare me, nothing scared me. I welcomed scary things like one who welcomes rest and food and peace. Just when I reached out towards her and wanted to talk, she vanished again. The glow lingered for a while, the sour yellowness. A yearning for something that couldn't be and that was forever lost quivered in the air and fluttered against the busted furniture.

Then we heard the Gypsy violinist down the street playing the Kreutzer sonata, my father's favorite piece of music. What a miracle, how was the violinist still alive in times like these? He used to pass by in the afternoon playing the two pieces of music that he knew: the Kreutzer sonata and a folkloric love song. I thought I was hallucinating now, but it turned out he was really playing outside our house. My mother came into the living room looking for me. My sister walked in her long white nightgown from her bedroom to the middle of the living room and stood there looking like a ghost, smiling to the sound of the music. She was holding her doll Mitzi as always. "Papa's favorite," she whispered. It was the first time I had heard her speak in a week and her voice sounded funny. My mother's face was flushed from the digging in the garden, and she was holding roots in both hands. She had found some more right behind the house after all. Tata had planted things all around the house. There were even potatoes. My sister said: "No more beets!" and she gave out a squeaky laugh. We all burst out laughing and my mother placed the roots like trophies on the floor in front of us and held us next to her. She had gotten so skinny that I could feel her bones when I put my arm around her. We were a family of emaciated ghosts living on roots. The strigoi girl wasn't any more of a phantom than we were. The notes of the violin spun a bridge of glowing sorrow and absurd happiness, a palpable bridge of feeling that kept us immobile and full to excess. Our eyes were dry like the dusty cracked earth, even though we heard sobs filling the heavy air. Our own dry sobs mixed with our laughter. The violin notes rose and crackled and devastated our hearts until we felt spent and sat on the busted sofa in a cloud of dust and feathers.

From then on things got better and worse. That is, good became the source of our demise. The Russians took over the town, the country, our entire part of the world from the river Dniester to the Danube, and distributed food in small packages wrapped in brown paper tied with rope. They threw them on the steps of houses from their tanks. It started with food, "you feed the people, and you have their souls," my father used to say. We were too weak to refuse the food packages and if we did, they might have shot us. You didn't refuse food or anything from the Russians, even if it was poisoned. They might have cut off your arms or legs as they had done to Girl and to people in our town who disobeyed their orders.

We were no longer starving to the degree we had been before, but we lived in fear and dreaded the future. We had heard of Stalin's camps and his reign of terror. My father had always predicted that the Germans were going to lose the war, and that the Russians would take over our part of the world. "They are both bad," my father would say, "Hitler and Stalin are the same — two criminals in charge of the world." How did he know it, how could he have been so right? I kept asking myself. My father must have been a wizard, a saint, and I had lost him forever. The Russians ruled us from every direction even though the war wasn't over yet, and the Germans hadn't yet lost the war.

The doctor still stopped by occasionally to check on Lila's progress and to give us news from the other ends of town. My mother never went anywhere now, she didn't care to see anyone in town. She just agonized over food. She stretched a few grams of flour for days and used every grain of it to make bread, dumplings, or thicken the soup. I was not eating much more than before when we were starving and barely surviving on roots. I didn't want the Russians' food. I knew it came with a price. I knew they wanted our souls in exchange for some rotten bread. I missed the boiled roots with desperation and yearned for purity and cleanliness amidst all the filth. Lila was gaining weight though and regaining color in her cheeks which made my mother beside herself with happiness.

The Doctor told us that the Russians were starting to round up people. My mother didn't understand what that meant, so the doctor whispered to her, and my mother became pale. Lila played with Mitzi on the floor and operated on her belly. She was explaining to Mitzi that she had to cut her belly open to perform the operation and it was going to hurt, but that she would feel much better afterwards. Mitzi had gotten sick of the scarlet fever too, Lila explained. The dry hot wind swept through our open windows bringing with it more yellow dust.

There had to be some way out, I kept thinking, some way to escape the Russians, the heat, the war. There had to be a place of comfort somewhere in our country or in the world, somewhere safe where we could all hide. Lila's mindless, rapid dialogues with Mitzi in which she was both the doctor and the patient, the mother and the child gave me the illusion occasionally that there might be such a place. "The war will be over, and the Russians will go away," my mother said. I let myself starve in expectation of something better, something saner. I stole cigarettes from Mr. Gogu and read the books in my father's library indiscriminately: Thomas Mann's *The Magic Mountain*, Tolstoy's *War and Peace*, or the *Arabian Nights*. Anything to escape the fear of the Russians and the indomitable heat, the yearning for my father and the despair about the future.

I searched for the strigoi girl around our house and in the garden, in our dried-up orchard, in the attic of the house. She appeared at the most unexpected moments and places and sometimes she even brought with her a memory of the Kreutzer sonata. I had a feeling that she was a carrier of memory. She gave the illusion you relived things and moments as if through a fog, or in a dream. A cluster of notes, a feeling of song that seemed to linger and get wrapped up in the yellow wind, carried along like a weightless child. She carried memories of happy days before the war as if she was the memory, the experience itself: a summer day sprinkled with flowers and a dance in the moonlight. She left me torn by unbearable yearnings.

I withdrew more and more into my own world in the company of the stirigoi girl and my father's books. I only looked at my mother when she came over to stroke my forehead with concern, as if checking to see if I had a fever. She came after me with pieces of food and I ate a little in front of her, but as soon as she turned around, I gave my food to Lila. Unlike me, my sister ate and ate and packed down every bit of food that my mother put in front of her and asked for more. Then she always gave some to Mitzi, but she ate it herself saying Mitzi didn't want any, she was a bad girl and didn't eat her food.

The days rolled by in a blur of bad news from the war front and the sound of Russian boots marching at night, for the rest of the summer and into the hot fall. It seemed that all the seasons were summer, the heat and the dust and the draught would never end, and we would just dry up eventually like the leaves on the trees around the house. We became nostalgic for the flood days; we even became nostalgic for the days of the Germans because their soldiers were more civilized than the Russians. Evil but civilized. Why was our country so special to deserve of the attention of the two worst and cruelest armies of that war, why couldn't we be occupied by the Italians or the French for a change?

One time, through some miracle, Mr. Gogu got a hold of a pack of American cigarettes, and he gave me one. He was so excited about it that he felt he had to share his tobacco joys with me. They were unfiltered Marlboro and so tasty you wanted to eat them. Mr. Gogu and I sat on the stoop in front of his house smoking the American cigarettes and enjoyed a moment of tranquility and contentment. "It's going to be so bad that we won't know what hit us," he whispered to me through the circles of American smoke. I said I didn't really know how it could get worse than it already was, and he said we were a cursed country, and the times will only get worse after the war.

How come everybody knew so much about what would happen to us? It was the first time I dared to think contrary to what my father always said. It just irritated me that Mr. Gogu had to say something like my father's thoughts. Maybe he had heard my father say it and decided he was going to be the town's prophet of doom sitting on his stoop, smoking and swearing all day. I decided I was going to listen to my mother's more optimistic views that the war was soon going to be over, the Russians were going to go back to their Russian homes, and life was going to get better. I was exhausted from doom and draught and hunger. That day of the American cigarette I wanted to eat my mother's thin potato stew but, because of how I had starved myself, the food wouldn't pass my throat and whatever I did, I regurgitated everything back. My mother said I had to eat in small bites, and Lila took the food off my plate and ate it right away. Her eyes were still glassy from the scarlet fever that had burned through her small body, but she had her mischievous smile back. My mother said nothing, just looked at us with love and worry. She looked exhausted like I had never seen her. The weeks of digging for roots and worrying about food, the loss of my father, Lila's illness, and the devastation of the house had drained and emaciated her. I felt tears choke me and left the table to not upset my sister who now had a weak heart.

I didn't recognize the face I saw in the mirror hanging in my room as my own — a gaunt yellow face with eyes that glinted with a crazed look like someone who was up to something bad, something irreversible. Just then she glided by me, forming herself out of thin air as she usually did. I felt her presence before I saw her. The mirror became foggy, and a heaviness set in the air. I thought maybe she would speak to me this time, my strigoi friend, as I delighted more and more in my dealings with the otherworldly creature. They made me feel closer to my father. the lines of separation between worlds melted reality lost its edges and its weight.

I thought of the story my father used to tell me when I was a child about the man who left his village and his family in search of "life without death and youth without old age." It wasn't just that I remembered the story, but also my father, who whispered it to me in his usual calm voice as I stared at my gaunt face in the mirror. The only unusual thing was that my father was whispering, which he never did when he was alive. It was probably the tiredness of being dead that made him whisper. The man who left in search of life everlasting and never-ending youth and whose name was Fat Frumos, Beautiful Child, returned home after what he thought had been only a year, but it had in fact been several hundred years, and his village had turned to dust and everybody he knew was long dead and gone. All he could find in the place of his native village was a desert of ruins and skeletons, where his mother and father and sister and bride had once lived and loved him. He was a foolish man to have gone in search of life everlasting and leave behind all those he loved and lose everything only to return to a pile of dust and bones. And once back in his village he immediately turned into an old man ready to die, because he could only reach immortality in the special realm of the magic fountain of youth. He had lost everything and everybody and never experienced the steady passage of time, having children, aging a bit more every day, seeing his children grow up and the hair of his beloved bride turn white, or burying his parents. The only eternity he had gained was a long frozen second without movement and without the usual bubbling of molecules. In exchange for that long second, which lasted several centuries, he missed out on the very life he was trying to prolong. All he got was a desert of skeletons and he was no longer Beautiful Child.

That's exactly how we were then in the summer and fall of 1944, a desert of skeletons. without even having been on any supernatural adventure in search of life everlasting. Everything turned from throbbing life to a desert of skeletons faster than we could grow one crop of wheat or than the fruit in the orchard could reach full ripeness. Once in the middle of the day when the dryness, the heat, and the hunger reached their peak, I saw my mother cross a desert all strewn with skeletons. She walked towards me and my sister carrying a large bag of beets on her back. A Russian soldier walked side by side with her carrying an enormous machine gun and it looked as if he was protecting her. But in fact, he was rounding her up and taking her to Siberia via a desert of skeletons — apparently a faster but more challenging route. At some point he tried to take her bag of beets away from her and she would not give it to him for dear life. She said she needed it to feed her starving children, and he would have to kill her first before she would give up the bag of beets. I heard her words like an echo that reverberated across the scorching desert. But suddenly the soldier stumbled over his own huge machine gun and fell in the dust. My mother picked up the gun and shot him without mercy. The entire desert became a red sea, and my mother traversed it with her ankles deep in blood and her bag of beets untouched still on her back. A big white pelican emerged from the dead soldier's body, and I saw my mother smile from a distance at the sight of the formidable bird. She started waving to me and said to come join her, that we were going to go to the Danube Delta to take refuge from the Russian soldiers. The Delta was still a free zone with lots of tame pelicans roaming around and lots of water and fish that we could eat. My mother put her hands into a cone in front of her mouth and shouted slowly so I could understand her from a distance: "Take your sister with you, we are going to the Danube, don't forget your sister. We won't starve anymore, we will eat lots of fish, take care of your sister."

A loud banging on the front door boomed through the house. Sounds of angry voices spitting Russian and rough steps were heard outside on the veranda in front of the house. All our invaders throughout the war spoke such ugly languages, was all I could think. First it was the Germans with their truncated chunky syllables, then the Russians with their heavy globs of consonants ruthlessly stepping on our language and everything else, just like their boots. My mother entered my room with a crazed look and whispered to me to follow her, she had to hide me, because a group of Russian soldiers and Romanian soldiers converted to Russian communism were at the door, probably to round up all young men. Everything was about rounding up those days. I was so tired and hungry I didn't care if they "rounded me up" to walk to Siberia. But my mother slapped me out of my sleepy state and forced me to stand up. She took me to my father's old room and there she took a tiny key like no other I had seen out of her apron pocket, removed the golden icon of Mary Magdalene that hung above the bed where my father died, and with that key opened a secret door that completely blended into the wall. She pushed me inside the space between the bed and the wall and then inside the compartment behind the wall.

I had never known of any such door and space in our house. I didn't know whether I was more shocked by the discovery of such a space, or the incredible strength that my mother, now all skin and bones, displayed by pushing me into the secret room like I was still a toddler. Then I thought, if she just killed a Russian soldier with a huge Russian machine gun while being deported to Siberia, pushing me around from place to place in our house (in the state of emaciation I also inhabited) was a small thing. I was weightless and insignificant like I had already died. I had never felt so much love for my mother as I did in those moments. The love that I felt for her reassured me that I wasn't dead yet.

The last thing I said before letting her close the secret door was: "The snake in the wall is going to bite and kill me, mama!" "No, it won't," she said with extreme firmness, almost like she was mad at me, "it's a good snake, better spend your night next to the house snake than on the way to Siberia." I found myself in the small space behind the wall, a room the size of a wardrobe with a large cushion on the floor, like the Turkish cushions you saw in the bazaars before the war. The existence of such an object in that space made no sense. I also noticed that I was holding a bag with dried fruit, a piece of cheese pie, and my father's flask, which sometimes had a bit of cognac he would serve to guests since he never drank himself. Now it was filled with water. I felt peaceful and hopeful for the first time since my father died. I didn't feel trapped but as if only then, alone with my own thoughts, I could be free. The only thoughts that tormented me were: where did my mother find this food in these times of famine when a piece of dry bread is a luxury? Is it from the Russian packages, one of my mother's secret food miracles when she came up with a real meal out of a handful of flour and two dried up vegetables, or has she stolen it from somewhere? And how did she have it all prepared for me at the exact moment when the Russian soldiers were at our door?

I sat down on the cushion holding my knees for a while without thinking of anything, without feeling anything, with just an airy pocket of nothingness sitting on my heart. I touched the floor around me in the dark and it felt smooth and cool like a foreign space. Then my hand touched a soft silky material that felt like an item of female clothing. My heart twitched. I let my hand examine the silky material for a long time, smelled it, put it over my face. A sash from a silk dress. I kept passing my fingers along the sash hoping I might distinguish the color by touch. At some point in the oily darkness, I thought I felt blue at my fingertips. A memory of blue and happiness in our orchard, on a spring day, long ago, centuries ago colored with girlish laughter and the glow of twilight! A girl with heavy blonde reddish curls, two girls with sparks in their eyes and silk dresses tied with white sashes, with blue sashes, an overabundance of blue somewhere centuries ago.

I fell asleep on the soft Turkish cushion without eating any of the food and holding the silky sash in utter puzzlement. Was it blue, or was it white? I was never going to go in search of life everlasting and youth without old age. I remembered that the reason why Beautiful Child in the story wanted so much to go back to his home, his village, his parents was that one day, as he was riding across luminous pastures and meadows on his immortal horse, he crossed by mistake into the Valley of Tears and was struck by insupportable longing, the famous dor, for his home. Not any of the tears and pleading of his immortal bride could deter him from returning to his place of birth. Longing for home was stronger than the threat of death and the allure of immortality. I, on the contrary, was going to live every single wretched moment of our lives, one after the other, no matter how miserable, rather than return after five hundred years to a deserted village and a house turned to dust. I heard loud Russian words behind the secret closet where I hid and sounds of furniture being pushed around the room.

"I Love You More than Plums"
Summer of 2015, Northern Moldavia

"Maybe you're a spy!"

"No, I assure you, I'm not a spy, I live in the United States, and I just …"

"Oh, you live in the United States, I see … well, what of it! You can still be a spy, I don't know, I have no idea who you are …"

In the incandescent June air, the linden fragrance is heavy and sweet all around us. It's the first day of the celebrations of the forest fairies, the sanziene, adorned with wreaths of tiny yellow flowers. Fairies and flowers carry the same name. I have never been called a spy before, and it makes me laugh. The man who calls me a spy is sweaty, smells of the Romanian drink called rachiu and has a long white beard like an orthodox priest. The odors and the words emitted by this bearded man are out of sync with the image I have of legendary celebrations of ethereal maidens dancing the hora across meadows of golden flowers. The orchards are nowhere to be seen, just an overabundance of linden trees from which the locals make a special kind of honey. Maybe they make honey instead of jam preserves because the fruit trees are all gone.

The wife is kinder and has a rosy complexion like she's been working outside all day. She asks me to come in, even though the bearded husband seems annoyed by her hospitality. A few names are passed back and forth between them, former owners of the property: Cosoiu, Badescu, Marinescu. They mean nothing to me, all I care about is the orchards, the veranda, the mythic fireplace, where are they? He always spoke of the luscious orchards — a paradise of pastels in bloom in the spring. The veranda — he used to play there with his sister Lila and the doll Mitzi. The fireplace — their parents read by the fire in the winter and the wood crackled and sparked on snowy winter nights. They had supper every evening at the oval oak table in the dining room. Mitzi the maid served them three-course dinners that he could never finish for some reason or another. After dinner, his father went to work in his study at the walnut desk with the glass top, the only thing they saved from the house after the war.

I always thought it funny that the doll and the maid were both called Mitzi and wondered if the doll had been called after the maid or vice versa. Mitzi seemed an implausible name in times of war, famine, and devastation. But so did many other things from my father's stories from before, during, and after the war. Before, during and after -- the three pillars of his youth: the before was idyllic under a good king and economic plenty with braided loaves of golden bread, scrumptious fruit from the local orchards, and exotic dried fruit from Turkey. The during was atrocious, reeked of corpses and bombs, wet trenches, death trains and cattle trains. The after was a different kind of atrocious and smelled of concentration camps, shared bathrooms in the houses divvied up by the Russian troops and desolate poverty wrapped up in red flags.

We had the walnut desk in the Bucharest apartment where I grew up and it felt important and majestic to do my homework on it, even though our place was tiny and had no kitchen. We lived in a drab doll house with an inappropriately huge walnut desk from before World War II. When the original large apartment was divided by the communist "liberators," and a wall was built to separate it into two parts, they left the kitchen in one of the miniaturized apartments and the bathroom in the other. My parents were ecstatic to have been given the section with the bathroom, it was easier to improvise cooking than to share a bathroom with five other families in the hallway. My mother cooked on a hot plate and washed the dishes in a basin on the edge of the bathtub.

The house of my father's childhood, of the before times, with its fizzy lush, rosy orchards all in wild bloom in the spring, the fancy fireplace, the oval oak dining table and the walnut desk with the heavy glass top and the doll and maid both called Mitzi, took shape every evening at dinner time and replaced our drab kitchen-less minuscule apartment with color and magic. The story of the house with the orchards and the beautifully carved wood furniture before the war was my father's way of surviving communism. It was "all lost, lost, lost, destroyed, only the walnut desk here remained," he always said. My father would stare wildly into space or maybe at one of the two thousand volumes crammed in the bookcases that occupied almost our entire living space. Since we had so little of it, we might as well fill it with food for the mind and pretend we lived in a palace, was my father's philosophy.

The bearded man with the plum brandy stench and visions of espionage tries to block my way into the living room. His wife wipes her hands on the apron and invites me in, while he follows my every move making sure I take no pictures on my phone. There are cross currents coming from each of the unwilling hosts, one in a timid attempt at hospitality, the other in a hostile lack of it. I feel dizzy from the confusion and yet almost without realizing it, I find myself in the middle of the living room area that is rather small, and decorated with an overabundance of traditional tapestries, blankets, rugs, wall hangings, icons of Jesus Christ and Virgin Mary, pictures of Elvis Presley, Christmas tree-shaped car fresheners, reproductions of still lives with grapes and slaughtered chickens bleeding on a kitchen table, glass ornaments, and glossy lacquered furniture that you can see your face in. An overpowering current enters me and gives me a feeling of vertigo: raw emotion, confusion, disappointment, fear and longing, and something else heavy and sour moving through the air, maybe from my startled hosts, or from the heat and lack of air in the room or maybe from the sum of the breaths and lives that have passed through this room over the last one hundred years.

This room is small and improbable. It couldn't have been the elegant living room my father used to talk about. It lacks everything and it's worse than if it had been completely empty. The bearded man tries to take my phone away thinking I'm taking pictures of the room as part of an American espionage project, while his wife stares at me with a pained look resembling the grieving Virgin Mary on the icon in pastel colors on the wall. There is something in the room that keeps me glued to the floor, a centrifugal force that makes it impossible for me to move. The linden smell and another smell that comes from the kitchen blend with one another and turn to gooey air, almost palpable.

As I'm protecting my phone while stuck to the floor in the middle of the room stuffed with the most incongruous conglomerate of objects, I remember the story about the snake that lived in the walls of the house for years. It lived there in the walls of the house and announced its existence with a ticking sound that it produced throughout the day, like a nervous clock. When my grandfather died, the snake went quiet, and the ticking stopped. It appeared that the snake was very fond of and loyal to my grandfather and decided to stop living and ticking in simultaneity with his master. "It was not an evil snake," "my father always specified," "it was a benevolent snake that watched over the house and brought us luck." Once my father's father and the snake died, their luck ended too and the long period of ordeals, disasters, and unstoppable catastrophes started. There is no ticking anywhere around me, just the sound of cars passing in the street and the remote sound of a lawnmower, an object unknown to my father at the time he lived here.

"Most Americans are spies," says the man as he tries to push me out of the house, sending a nauseating smell of badly digested food and Romanian aged plum brandy in my direction. I don't know what to say to that. I'm pleased he used the qualifier "most" and didn't just say "all Americans" as many of my compatriots tend to talk about other peoples and nations. I sort of feel proud to be thought of as a spy, and just when I feel liberated from the centrifugal force keeping me stuck to the middle of the floor facing the adjoining pictures of Virgin Mary and Elvis Presley, I say in great earnestness:

"There was a snake living inside the walls of this house in my father's time, have you heard of that?"

A sonorous silence follows my statement during which the sound of the lawnmower becomes louder, the thick air heavier, and the woman crosses herself as she turns towards the icon of the Virgin, though it looks like she is crossing herself in front of the picture of Elvis Presley.

"I haven't heard any of this nonsense," says the man regaining composure. "There is none of them snakes in these walls, the wood was all rotted when we bought the house. We rebuilt everything from the bottom up. No snakes, just a whole bunch of roaches and mice when we first looked at the house."

"All of it? You rebuilt the whole house from the ground up?" I ask petrified.

"It was just the skeleton, that's all, the wood was all rotted, with the veranda and all, only the foundations and the walls ..."

"Oh, the skeleton, at least that was left, so you built around that," I console myself.

A young woman with a bouncy ponytail appears from the back of the house, probably the daughter of the bearded man and the rosy cheeked woman. She greets me in a friendly manner as she goes out through the front door. I am dying of curiosity to see the back room from where she emerged, maybe my father's room, or my grandparents' bedroom, or the study with the walnut desk. But as I move towards the back of the house a neighbor comes in and whispers something to the bearded man. He tells his wife they have to leave immediately and I'm sure this is a ploy to get me out of their house.

A feeling of emptiness ravages through me as I step backwards across the threshold of what might have been my father's glorious childhood house. It's bad luck to step backwards across the threshold of a house. Virgin Mary and Elvis Presley and Jesus Christ on the cross, paper portraits of Romanian medieval kings, folkloric music celebrities and bleeding fowl amidst still lives of grape clusters stare at me impassively as I almost trip across the doorway. Bye-bye Romanian American spy, good riddance, don't disturb us again, they all seem to say. I wish I knew how to cast a bad spell on all of them, animate beings and inanimate objects alike, and curse their kitschy tacky post-communist Balkan capitalist lives out of existence and bring back the luminous living room, the veranda, the orchards, revive the skeleton of the house from its new stone walls with the ticking good luck snake and all.

Good and bad spells were once cast amid aristocratic furniture and the transitory passage of maids and dolls with vaudeville names during the idealized times of a prewar monarchy, the gory times of a war bifurcated into the two axes of evil, and the inconsolable dreariness of the post war abyss: all the regimes and governments pasted on top of one another like the stupefying collection of ornaments and reproductions gathered inside the confines of this reconstructed house with no orchards and no idyllic veranda. Fascism, communism, monarchy, the cult of Stalin, Russian tanks this and Russian tanks that, bad food, no food, lines, and rations for basic staples. All that spilled into our communist doll house in indiscriminate order day after day during the times of the much-hated modern dictator with a mechanical hand wave and bad grammar. "With the money my mother got on the house, I bought myself a winter coat," my father would say bitterly and then laugh at the absurdity of it all. A house in exchange for a coat, that was how devalued everything was after the war and how desperate he was for a winter coat.

The street is quiet and I'm looking for orchards like mad. Maybe they are hidden among the row of houses with tile roofs and iron fences, stone houses with reconstructed walls and exuberant flower gardens. Nothing in the back, but more houses and sheds and garages built in between small yards in a maze of fences and vegetable gardens. Occasionally, someone comes out on their front porches or verandas to stare at me, the word has probably already gone out that such and such a woman, the daughter of such and such a man who lived there during the war is snooping around, spying with American spying techniques, and trying to reclaim the family house, throw the good family at number 18 out of their hard won and abundantly renovated property. An American spy, that's all she is, I seem to hear whispers from behind fences, between rows of marigolds and tomatoes, from behind windows with thickly embroidered curtains.

I turn the corner at the end of the street and then turn again on a side alley, a dirt road that goes behind the row of houses on each side of the one at number 18. A postcard dated from May 1938 clearly showed the number 18 of this avenue, street, named after an important Romanian king who brought about an important national unification. "Greetings from enchanting Arges Monastery. I am having dinner with the nuns as I write to you. I am sending you best wishes of prosperity and good health and the nuns are also greeting you," signed Lila, and addressed to Mr. and Mrs. Angelescu on the 12th of May 1938. The writing on it is calligraphic yet childish. The ceremonious way of writing to her own parents at seven years old is endearing.

My aunt was traveling with a relative on their mother's side and spending her vacation with the nuns at the famous Arges Monastery which, according to legend, was built around the body of a living woman named Ana. She was the wife of the master builder who was ordered by some angels that had appeared to him in a dream to bury his wife Ana in the wall of the monastery to prevent it from crumbling. Lila and her doll Mitzi were having grownup vacations in the secluded quiet of a monastery while my father, two years older, stayed home, gorged on fruit from the orchard and ran through the neighborhood with his favorite dog. 1938 was still the prosperous before, with the good king, the braided bread, and the Turkish sweets.

I take the dirt road and somehow the thought of Romania as a monarchy seems profoundly comical as I step around potholes and stray chickens clucking with vehemence and a rusty Dacia car from the times of the dictator and then walk by a shiny silver Mercedes minivan and then run into more clucking chickens. The newly rich, the formerly poor, the sophisticated urban and the age old rural, all mixed up in a tiny dirt alley in a small town in the Northern province of Moldavia. Thinking of the woman Ana who was built alive in the walls of the famous monastery and the benevolent ticking snake in my father's old house and of stories of secret places inside the walls of old houses used for hiding people during the war, it strikes me that there seems to be an alternative life and death cycle going on inside the walls of Romanian abodes and monuments from this region.

A scrawny old man smoking and leaning on his wrought iron fence of the stone house next to the one I had just visited, greets me. His accent is soft with sweetened vowels like my father's used to be, with elongated and meandering syllables that he holds on to with each word he pronounces. Someone kind and welcoming finally. I have an impulse to run to him and hug him like he was a lost grandfather. I greet him back and ask him if he has lived here for a long time. "Long as I can remember," he smiles revealing a toothless mouth with rosy gums. A small boy runs to him from behind the house and holds on to his leg. A small boy with light chestnut hair, almost blonde, and impossibly blue eyes, deep and watery that you see occasionally only in this region of the country among mostly dark haired, dark eyed and swarthy looking people. He is laughing in irrepressible peals like he owns the whole world. Ancestries of Slavs and Dacians, Turks and Greeks and God knows what other invaders had passed through here centuries ago before and during the time of the important king who unified the provinces and gave the name to the street that my father used to live on. The blonde, blue-eyed people were a rarity and came from one of those strains of invaders, or so I had heard. Or from the first inhabitants, before the Romans, nobody is sure. Apparently, it was such a strain I had inherited from my father.

Maybe this boy and I are related, I think to myself laughing, the great-grandchild of an illegitimate son or daughter in another family that my father had never talked about. I want to know how you reconstruct an entire lineage of people, the texture of a family from stories told at the dinner table in times of dictatorship and a postcard from before World War II. I only know about the house and the orchards and something terribly bad that happened during the war.

I ask about the house at number 18, the family living there now, the previous owners, the orchards, was there ever a large property behind the house with cherry, apricot, apple, and plum orchards? The sun is so hot and the air so dry that we seem suspended in a mirage, a sweet state of immobility as if we were frozen in the heat. I drink from my bottled water without being able to quench my thirst. "Boy, go get the lady some cherries from the tree yonder," the old man orders the blue-eyed boy without answering any of my questions and gently dropping his elongated vowels to quiver in the air between us. Things normally invisible and impalpable, now take shape and acquire flesh in the fragrant dry heat: vowels, consonants, sounds of laughter, steps, the sound of a cuckoo bird calling for a mate and a feeling of eternal laziness and indifference. The boy's squeal of joy as he picks up a handful of cherries from the lower branches of a tree hidden behind a newly built shed breaks the spell like ripples on a still water surface.

I notice one heavy branch hanging low from behind the pointless unattractive shed, dark red cherries hanging in shiny clusters. The boy gives me his handful of fruit, I could swear he is a relative from the blue-eyed side of my family. He doesn't have many words, just a liquid energy that interrupts the sticky laziness of the place and turns it into thirst quenching fluid. He drops the cherries in my palm one after the other without touching my hand as if he was playing a game with cherries. I reach out to touch his arm in gratitude, but he slides away like a sleek shadow. At first the cherries are not as sweet as I had imagined, slightly tart with a tinge of bitterness but then they unfold into an unimaginable juiciness and the sweet comes only at the end like a surprise. The man unhinges a metal lock of the gate in the middle of the fence, moves towards me with a limping step, and leads me towards the cherry tree and the boy who is back under it in utter contentment and balance with the universe around him. Behind the shed, a thick cluster of trees standing on a small patch of earth opens in a startling vision of color and petulant beauty. Despite his age, he also moves with smooth steps almost like dancing or like gliding on ice.

"They done cut down most of them trees, it was the most coveted orchard in town until a man, Cosoiu, bought the property and chopped it up for profit. They say he was secret police and a bad man he was, with a missing leg from a car accident when he was driving drunk. He disappeared after the revolution of '89 and I bought up this here piece of land with the last trees left on the property." His mouth opens wide in a beautifully rounded toothless smile. "No other trees in town here make cherries and plums like these ones. It's the good snakes in the ground and the worms and the spirits that settled around this place. They like it here, the sun shines at a special angle because of the inclination of the earth, don't you see that? I reckon you had a relative living here long time ago before them cursed communists?"

"Yes, my father," I whisper meekly, "he was born and grew up here in the house at number 18." I can't say anything anymore because I'm choking with sobs. Images of my father throughout the different periods of his life and in all the different stages of the after times rush at me in a demented wave. I can't contain them, nor can I control the ridiculous sobbing that takes over me. The young boy hands me a handful of plums this time and says: "This make you feel better." I start eating a plum, dark violet and perfectly plump, swallowing my tears together with its juicy flesh. After the man's talk of snakes and the garden spirits I feel like I'm eating a supernatural fruit that is going to make me grow into something else or that will pop up into a lively creature as soon as I'm about to swallow it fully and ask me to spare it in exchange for something important like eternal life or the ability to make myself invisible or a magical mirror in which I can see my future. The plum has blended layers of sweetness and tartness and it makes you feel sorry when you have finished it. You know you could eat this fruit until the entire tree is barren and until you die underneath the ravaged tree in the shape of a human plum.

Only now do I fully understand why my father always said that all fruit and tomatoes in America were insipid and lacked everything that fruit should have, such as, for example, a taste. And then he would go back to the orchards again. Once I thought he should have become an orchard keeper instead of the impassioned teacher he was. Only you couldn't own personal property during the regime, it all belonged to the "people" when in fact all private properties were taken away by the cooperatives and the party members. Or maybe it was because of the fruit he had eaten during his formative years that my father had gotten all the irrepressible sass, madness and kindness, unassuaged melancholy and volcanic passion all mixed and sucked up from the substance of that special earth behind his house with ticking snakes, beneficial worms and a whole bunch of kind spirits rambling around the place. How could anything that came afterwards measure up to that? Only she measured up to it when he ran into her in the street one day, in the summer in the big city where he had moved a few years after the war, with two shirts, one hundred books, an emaciated body torn by tuberculosis and an irrepressible love of goodness and poetry as his only possessions. She was his protean, unparalleled star, a luminous creature amidst a sea of deadening uniformity, humiliating shortages, and secret agents.

The old man's name is Manole, and the funny thing is it's the same name as the master builder who stuck his own wife inside the scaffolding of the renowned Arges monastery and neatly put bricks and mortar around her as her wailing was heard from miles away. This Manole though is wrecked with age and seems kind, he most likely has never buried anyone in the walls of a building. He sees I am distraught and weakened by the weight of the unravelling story of the house at number 18 and asks me to sit down in the shade on the wooden bench right under the crowns of the fruit laden trees. The blonde boy sits right next to me as if I were an aunt visiting for the afternoon and Manole sits down on the other side of the bench. Between the benevolent old age and the blonde youth, I feel renewed and hopeful. Manole is staring in front of him peacefully and the young boy cuddles next to me in the most familiar way. For a few moments we all sit in silence and listen to the rustle of the light breeze passing through the heavy foliage around and above us, the distracted drop of one or two fruits on the ground and a cuckoo bird still calling for his mate.

Though I have never visited this place before, an overwhelming familiarity with it envelops me. I could have been sitting here on this bench under the canopy of cherry and plum trees for centuries with these two people on each side of me who could be my own son or grandson and my own grandfather. Kings and wars and vicious governments, pogroms and revolutions have passed by in demented bloody swirls and we have been sitting on this wooden bench in the shade wrapped up in a cocoon of quiet and gentle murmurs forever. I'm not sure any more about my family history or whether it really matters to dig into it, I'm not sure whether I even have a family or in what part of the globe I belong. America seems like a different planet: a bad joke with tasteless fruit.

"There was people buried in here during the war, there was ... and people hiding here, what have you ..." Manole says like an afterthought as if continuing the conversation, as if we had never stopped talking at all. The moments of quiet and repose from only a minute ago now seem like a dream. Passage of time here seems whimsical and unreal, long stretches of seconds that you almost see flickering around you, with tantalizing interruptions like butterflies, with tiny jolts in the flutter of eyelashes, you bat your lids, and an eternity has passed or the other way around, you think a moment has passed and in fact it's a whole century, just like waking up from a hundred yearlong slumber. Time is on its own around here, careless, reckless, and bouncing at will in all directions with no scheduled activities to contain it, to speed it up or slow it down. I want to ask him whether he was here during the war, whether he saw everything, whether he knew the family in the house at number 18 with the unparalleled orchard, but I can't bring myself to utter a word.

The laziness of the place has taken over me, the rambling spirits, the calls of the cuckoo bird, the fragrance of the ripening fruit have enveloped me with shrouds of delicious indifference. Through this glimmering hazy shroud, a thought lingers on me like a butterfly in repose: whatever Manole might have seen of my father's house and family was from the back of the house. The back door, the back windows, the door to the cellar, the rush of the children into the orchards in the morning, after dinner, at night under the moonlight in a forbidden escapade, all through the back door of the house. The front of the house is the bad side, the back side is the good one, just as simple as that. The front of the house was skinned alive to the bone by bestial Russian soldiers, greedy communists and even greedier post communists with a Virgin Mary and Elvis Presley fetish and was wrapped up in stone cut illegally from some nearby ravine, while the back of the house was saved by Manole and his love of fruit.

I try my hardest to stay awake and engage Manole in a productive conversation about my family's past and the people buried under this fertile soil. I look at the small blonde boy sitting next to me on the bench in a peculiar way as if he were also far away, I remember I too have a blonde son far away on planet America who once wrote me a poem titled "I love you more than plums." If by some miracle of global economy, one of these magnificent plums got mixed in with the tasteless ones we might have bought in the local supermarket, and my far away blonde son was the one to eat it, then his poem acquires an entirely new meaning, and the childish expression of his love appears in its full splendor. If I don't stay awake it will all dissipate though: my memory of everything, my entire family history, the one of the past as well as the one forming itself in the future and I will end up floating aimlessly in the universe with no place to belong. Everything hangs on this moment right here and right now, on my astuteness to stay awake, to hold on to this last patch of prolific orchard and good earth.

"My name is Lulu," the little boy says joyously. His voice pulls me out of the bad spell of laziness and replaces it with a luminous precision of place, shapes, and sounds. Time ticks now at a steadier, recognizable pace in which we care again about noon and night and dawn and two o'clock and ten o'clock.

"That's a sweet, beautiful name," I say, and I really mean it as I can't imagine a more appropriate name for this wonder boy out here in this back yard on this side of the planet. I remember also that my aunt's name was Lila, and I find the parallelism of this abundance of liquid consonants entirely comforting and the danger of my slipping off of the edge of history with no trace and no roots at least temporarily diverted. As long as I keep the conversation going and I stay fully awake everything will be all right.

"What's your name?" Comes the prompt retort from Lulu.

This takes me by surprise.

"My name is Corina Roxana Angelescu." I utter my own name fully including the middle name, a rare occurrence for me. Where I live nobody even knows I am also called Roxana which my father chose because of its meaning "dawn." He thought it was a good omen in life, to always look towards the beginning of the day and the coming of light. My mother wanted Corina because it meant "maiden", but Corina was also a famous Roman courtesan and the lover of the famous poet Ovid. So, between the maiden's candor and the courtesan's boldness, my mother thought I would have just the right amount of female sophistication and sass. The sophistication was also supposed to counteract the roots of our family name, Angelescu, which came from the too obvious "angel," which made my mother scrunch her nose in disdain. Lulu repeats my name with perfect enunciation and for the first time it sounds truly right, like I couldn't have possibly been named by any other name like Constanta or Margareta. I feel deliciously settled in my onomastic identity. I don't think I'll ever be lost, homeless, country less and nameless after all.

"I knew the Angelescu family right well … A decent good family it was, but bad luck struck them really bad, they were hard hit by destiny during those years." Manole speaks again like he has been continuing the same conversation, answering my unasked questions, or weaving his own memories suddenly awoken by my unexpected visit in his neighborhood. I look at my watch and realize it is only three in the afternoon and only a little bit more than an hour has passed since I have met Manole and Lulu. I am puzzled again by the slowness of time in this yard and wonder what we are going to do for the rest of the afternoon. I also realize I include

Manole and Lulu in my plans for the immediate future as if we were family and that an hour ago, I had no idea who these people were and how they were going to enter my life, even change it. Or at least change my perception of time and the weight of every second passing, the lightness of hours.

"Orchards are a big deal in this part of the country," I hear myself say.

"Indeed, they are, you have no idea the value of orchards and fruit trees in this town of ours, it's one of our biggest riches, or at least was until the evil communists started their deforestations and cooperative politics. Then everybody grabbed whatever they could of their properties and trees. I was lucky to keep these ones over here. The year when the man from the cooperative came to measure the property and count the trees, it happened that we had a bad drought just like the year when the Russians came, and the trees all looked dead. But I know trees because I talk to them, and sometimes when they are too sad about what is going on around them, they die for a year or two and then when the yearning for life comes back to them, their trunks fill up with sap again and they come back to life. I told the nasty cooperative man they were all dead; they would be no good to him or to anybody else and I could use the wood for fire during the winter. I'm telling you Miss, it was the good spirits living here that saved these trees."

We sit quietly again for a while, and I am completely relieved when I understand the rhythms of this conversation and that there is no pressure to answer or say anything in response. There is no rush and no ambition to get to a particular point in the story or to make a point or prove a point, it all just flows and quivers naturally together with the calls of the cuckoo bird, the breeze, the fruit dropping on the ground, or the passage of the clouds above us.

"I even used to teach the play titled *The Cherry Orchard*. Your father loved it, he thought it was the most beautiful piece of literature in the world."

The news that Manole might have been a schoolteacher once and had taught my father celebrated works of world literature seeps into my brain slowly and methodically, as I sit on the bench for another indiscriminate number of minutes I also realize that throughout the course of the afternoon and our conversation, Manole's speech had evolved from a simple brand of Romanian even letting in erroneous grammar occasionally, to a complex and educated brand. I like the older, simpler, and more peasant brand of his speaking more, but I get used to the new brand and liken it even more to my father's speech.

"You taught my father?" I ask slowly and notice I am starting to acquire myself the accent of the place, the elongated vowels and softened consonants, trying to match my speech to the rhythm of the time here, the distinctive rolling of the seconds moving towards a glowing twilight.

"He was an unusual child, he was, brilliant and melancholy with outbursts of joyousness and intense passions. He was funny too when he had the mood for clowning, he would bring all his classmates rolling on the floor with laughter. And then he would fall back into a spell of melancholy. He wrote the most beautiful pages of prose you could expect from a teenager growing up in times of war." Manole pulls out a pipe from his pocket and prepares it for smoking. I understand from the way he settles into smoking his pipe that he will stop there for now and this meandering conversation has arrived at an end. Lulu has had enough of sitting on the bench and starts kicking a deflated ball against the back wall of the next-door neighbor's house.

Suddenly it's five o'clock as if time decided to speed up and the seconds tumble hurriedly towards the end of the day. I feel nervous about what is going to happen for the rest of the evening, and my brain is in a state of disarray from the chaotic bits of information I gathered today about my father's years of growing up in this oasis where time moves in disordered leaps and the trees have a mind and emotions of their own. A dog starts barking in one of the neighboring yards and I remember there was always also a story about a dog. The dog that ran with him through the orchards and followed him everywhere, the dog that was cut to pieces by the Russian soldiers when they came through and pillaged the town and their house. He always had tears in his eyes when he told the story and said with unforgiving irony: "they were the liberators of our country, the Russians were." Manole gets up slowly from the bench straightening his back and tells me to follow him inside the house, he will show me something. For an inexplicable reason, my heart starts pounding in agitation as if I am on the verge of something momentous that I am not yet ready for.

Everything speeds up suddenly. I stare at the trees that apparently have the extraordinary ability to die and resurrect at will depending on circumstances. I hesitate to go into the house after Manole. I have the feeling that once I do, everything will be different, memory and time will get all jumbled up. I will be swallowed in a swirl of old history and family secrets, a vertiginous slide into the past from where I will never emerge again.

I know there is something more than plums out there in the world and that I have to keep remembering that other side of my life, the blonde son who loves me more than plums and needs me on another continent, the birth continent of Elvis Presley with his sultry look next to Virgin Mary on the wall in the front of the house on the front side of the street, the bad side with the greedy post-communist people who put stone around the wooden skeleton and buried all the ticking life inside of it. And yet it's not all that clear cut, the front and the back of the house merge somewhere in the middle and the good and the bad blend into one another, the post revolution new capitalist tackiness and the pre-revolution, pre-war fairy tale, and the war and post war horror tales. Somewhere in the middle of the house is a zone of neutral life and monotonous history with dreams of prosperity and health just like the wishes in the postcard of 1938.

I follow Manole to the back door of his house and notice his step speeding up as if he has grown younger. To my great surprise as we get closer there are sounds of voices chattering, laughter and music as if from a raucous party. This seems so wrong and more incongruous than any of the assortments of objects and ornaments in the restored version of what might have been my father's old living room. Lulu is still playing ball against the wall that is the back of the house as if he had forgotten himself in that mode and is going to kick the ball for the next decade. I am at the crossroads of two equally powerful temptations. The one to spend the rest of the evening under the plentiful trees in a state of bottomless contemplation, to mull over all the events and happenings of the day until I finally do fall into a rosy but deceptive slumber or to follow Manole into his house and find myself facing an incomprehensible gathering of unleashed hedonism and unfamiliar individuals. Everything is rushing in an unstoppable fall down a steep slope and it's up to me to slow things down to a bearable rhythm. It's up to me to shape this turn of events into a tellable slice of history straddling across continents, regimes, and horticultural mysteries.

The sounds of the party are getting louder and more raucous, out of place and out of time. I have stepped into a universe of layered and coexisting worlds all severely different from one another, neighboring each other in a small and crowded space and with fragile boundaries between them: cheap reproductions of still lives with slaughtered chicken, real life chickens clucking and trotting aimlessly in the dust of the back alley, a shiny Mercedes minivan most likely owned by a rising Mafia youth who fell into pits of money by means of shady business, walls decorated with car fresheners and cutouts from magazines, sublime patches of fertile earth and fruit like in the garden of Eden. Amidst all this reigns a toothless sage as old as Father time with bottomless knowledge about everything from world literature, to the mysteries of fruit trees and their souls, from the souls of the living and the dead to national and local politics, the corruption of the old cooperatives and the evil doings of maimed secret agents, but most importantly he holds priceless knowledge of the history of my own family and past, about secret graves dug in the space of that back yard during the war. Next to him, reigns Lulu the blonde chubby boy with a mellow temperament and bold curiosity. He fills the space of the garden with joyfulness and imparts heavenly fruit to unexpected visitors.

This is only the surface of the place, for there is yet another full layer of the unknown and the unspoken or of what is only obliquely referred to. There are the lives and movements hidden between walls, the psychology of trees, the energies pulsating under the wildly fertile earth and the dead buried there, the unfinished lives of humans and benevolent beasts, remainders and shreds of history, yearning souls, and murmuring spirits. Manole knows everything about the before, the during and the after. Lulu knows everything about the now. I want to absorb the sap from the substance of all these places in time, because here time is also place. But the centrifugal force created by the meeting of all these waves keeps me rotating in place and soft with indecision like a piece of clay molded in the rapid swirls of a potter's wheel. I look at Manole and then at Lulu and I know I must choose soon before something is too late. I notice suddenly that the residents of my father's old house are peeking from behind their intricately wrought iron fence that separates them from Manole's property. They are not even peeking but standing like statues behind the fence, staring at us with shameless curiosity. They are now wearing traditional costumes typical of the Moldavian region and look like oversized dolls in the museum of village life.

Manole waves to them and they wave right back. "Tonight, we celebrate Noptile de Sanziene," says Manole and stands sideways in front of the entrance to the back of his house waving his arm in a welcoming gesture. "The Sanziene are …" "I know what they are," I jump in abruptly. It's imperative to know about the

Sanziene women, the fairy maidens who dance the hora naked in the moonlight on earth and in the air during the summer solstice and wear crowns of bright yellow flowers. If you don't know about them and you don't celebrate them properly, they turn you mute or give you a crooked mouth for life. As I get closer to the entrance, the noise of the party subsides and seems faraway. The voices, the laughter, and the music are getting dimmer and become almost inaudible, but not completely. The sound of Lulu's ball prevails above all other sounds, a stubborn counting of tangible seconds. I want to get off this set desperately and jump out into the street where there are cars and lawnmowers.

"Come in Corina, come celebrate with us," says Manole in a melodious voice with no trace of old age. I want to delay as much as possible the entry into the room, but the sound of my name in Manole's mouth is irresistible. Corina the maiden, Corina the courtesan, I must choose which one to be, I have to choose a costume, a character, and the lines for the opera. I want to be Roxana and look towards dawn and the freshness of a new day. But I don't know this opera and I forgot all my lines. I try to buy time just as you would in a store with the new Romanian currency, and I blurt out hurriedly: "Manole, I don't know what the spirits are. What do you mean exactly by the spirits, the good spirits of the garden, the bad spirits tra-la-la?" I fidget, I look in my purse searching for something, maybe I'm looking for the postcard from 1938 which I brought with me all the way from the United States to prove I had family living at the house of number 18. It's a postcard that crossed the Atlantic twice, the first time when I left the country a long time ago and the second time when I came back to my country just a few days ago. This postcard will be handed down to my son who loves me so much in the United States. Manole answers calmly: "They are whatever you want them to be." I feel relieved and start laughing. I feel like playing: "Can they be a whale, a chimney, a plum? "Yes, they can be a plum," Manole says with absolute certainty. I walk with him into the party room.

The Movie
Summer of 2015, Northern Moldavia

There are no spirits of any kind in the room and the sounds of the party are coming from a recording. Now they are loud again. Everything edible on the table is made of plums and guests eat and drink in silence around the table. Manole asks me to sit down at the head of the table on a chair that is left empty as if waiting for me. I can't hear his voice asking me to sit down but I can guess from the movement of his lips and his ceremonious gesture of showing me the chair. There is plum brandy and plum marmalade, plum stew, and plum pie placed on the long dining room table in an orderly way. Everything is plums in a room of dead people eating in silence. I can't guess where the recording with the sounds of the raucous party is coming from, but instead I see a large plasma TV that is on in mute mode in a corner of the room. The images on the screen are showing a film of Hitler and Stalin dancing together a dance that looks like the tango, but nobody is watching. I imagine the plasma of the TV pouring out of the screen like lava with Hitler and Stalin melting to a hot goo in their tango position. I remember I live in the United States and have a house and children there but cannot remember any of the details of my life as if it has all been put in a bottle, sent to the ocean, and lost forever among its waves. Maybe one day someone will find my life in a bottle on a distant shore and save it.

The people sitting around the table are all wearing crowns of yellow flowers for the sanziene celebrations and I realize they are all women of different ages, from a teenage girl to an old grandmother and they each have a name tag on their chests as if they were statues or paintings in a museum: "Girl with grapes," "woman with red drapes," "looking towards the sun, portrait of girl with ponytail," "peasant woman with harp," "woman with hourglass." All the women are dressed in the style of the nineteen forties and eat daintily from the various plum courses in front of them.

"It's a reenactment," Manole explains in my ear so I can understand despite the recorded sounds of the party. "They are doing a World War II reenactment. An avant-garde Romanian director is making a movie here in town. This place played an important role in the war, you know, the town, these houses ... so they decided to film it here for authenticity."

Nothing seems authentic to me in this room of simulacra, and I feel tricked by Manole and his invitation to join a sanziene party. "Didn't you say it was a party, Manole?" I scream almost on the verge of tears, while I also try to remember the details of my life in America now floating randomly in the Atlantic. I feel a reverse pain: the grief and longing that the people who love me in my faraway home are experiencing for me right now from missing me too much.

"Of course, it's a party Corina, and you are the guest of honor. The director just wants to shoot this one scene and then the party will resume. You'll see, it will be fun," says Manole with a huge smile and I notice he is now wearing a perfect set of dentures that make his smile more grotesque that when he exposed his bare gums. I muster up enough courage to say: "I'm sorry Manole, but I need to leave, I have things to do, thanks for inviting me." I move towards the door and have the uncanny feeling that all the women sitting around the table with yellow crowns of sanziene on their heads slowly turn their gaze in my direction and follow my every move. I catch the woman whose name tag says "looking towards the sun, girl with ponytail" staring at me and I realize she is the girl who walked by me while I stood in the middle of the living room of the house at number 18 and I stared in disbelief at the atrocious wall decorations.

"Please stay," Manole pleads gently tapping me on the shoulder, "you won't regret it, you'll see, it interests you too. You know what they say, that 'the whole world's a movie set." Manole laughs impishly in his beard. His laugh makes me feel lonely. I am seized by unbearable longing for my father, for my childhood, for everything I lost when I left long time ago added to the grief experienced by the longing of the people in my family in faraway America who love and miss me and have no idea what I'm up to and what mysterious tunnel of Romanian weirdness I've been sucked up into. I am torn by a bifurcated transatlantic yearning of something on this side of the world and the yearning of someone else from the other side of the world. I hear myself saying: "mi-e dor, mi-e dor, mi-e asa de dor," the Romanian untranslatable expression for yearning for something impossible to attain, a yearning so deep that you want to die or cry for a hundred years in the valley of tears. I've been translating everything that has been happening to me on this day back into English. I can't translate this one expression though and instead of my transnational inner dialogue I've been carrying with myself since I got to this spooked street with its spooked houses, I'm now stuck fully in my original national identity. I'm falling in the swirl of bottomless yearning and nativeness.

"What's the name of the movie they are making?" I ask, trying to overcome my emotional meltdown.

"The Abridged and Combined History of Fascism and Communism as Seen through the Experience of One Family in Northern Moldavia" says Manole in one breath loudly in my ear.

The party sounds are turned off and replaced by sentimental music from the forties, a Romanian tango sang by a scratchy voice like that produced by a Victrola. I feel like fainting because they are stealing my story and are going to make some tacky avantgarde movie with clever close ups and slow takes of some second-rate Romanian actors running through a fake orchard and looking tragic. There is no such thing as the abridged history of fascism and communism combined in one family story. There is only this one flesh and blood story of my father by the name of Florin Angelescu and his sister Lila and his mother Victoria and his father Tudor who owned and lived in the house at number 18 with unparalleled orchards and good snakes living in the walls. And there is a story of twin girls who were taken in by the family and hidden in a secret compartment inside the walls, as well as the Russian soldiers who came after the Germans tearing through the house with their heavy dirty boots leaving mud and blood streaks behind them. And there is also the postcard of May 1938 that crossed the Atlantic twice and was sent by Lila from the famous monastery built around the martyred Ana. I remember a conversation about the twin girls, someone asking: "were they both Jewish?" and someone else answering: "no, no, one was Jewish, and the other one was something else." "Something else what? A Turk, a Gypsy, an Armenian, what?" "No, none of that, just something else." I'm not sure when and where this conversation took place, but it's imbedded in my conscience from long ago when I was a small moody girl going to communist school and listening to the whispered conversations going on at night in our miniature apartment with no kitchen of its own. And if they were twin girls, how could one be Jewish and the other something else, how did two different creatures grow inside one womb?

I see more actors come in, all dressed in forties clothing, one man who looks like an impersonation of my grandfather from a family photograph in sepia that I carried in my purse when I crossed the Atlantic the first time. He opens a secret door behind a red velvet curtain. Two small girls dressed in ragged white lace dresses with blue sashes appear from behind another door that opens in the opposite wall and the man that looks like my grandfather waves to them with agitated gestures to move quickly, he directs them both inside a compartment in the wall camouflaged behind a set of blood red drapes. The red drapes of course only make the hiding place more obvious, but the grandfather character doesn't seem to believe so because he does everything in full earnestness. He closes the secret door, pulls the red drapes over the door and sits in an armchair in the opposite corner of the room, reading a newspaper with the date of June 22, 1941, which is the date of the breaking of the Ribbentrop-Molotov pact and the day when Romania joined Germany in the invasion of Russia. Three SS soldiers barge into the room, overturn chairs and furniture, push dishes and glasses off the table, try some of the plum pudding from one of the bowls and go "zer gut," roughly push some of the women quietly eating at the table off their chairs and onto the floor, look under the table, pull the red drapes aside without seeing the secret door, pull the embroidered curtains off the window, loudly chatter some more in what sounds like a made up version of German and leave the room. The red drapes trick worked wonders because they didn't find the secret compartment hidden behind them. The sentimental Romanian tango fades out and the other tango music to which Hitler and Stalin were dancing initially, becomes louder and it turns out it's the Paloma Blanca tune. "They've got the dates all wrong," I want to scream, "the people, the events, the music, this is not how it was, this is just a masquerade of history and of my family story. Give me back my story!" I yell. "And it wasn't the German soldiers who killed the Jews around here, it was the Romanian Iron Guard, you Romanians are always lying about your history, always covering up for your crimes and blaming others." My heart is pounding and aching like mad, I am going to be obliterated into nonexistence and my entire family on both sides of the Atlantic miniaturized to the size of a tacky movie stuck in a bottle and sent down the voracious waves of that ocean with all its manufactured histories inside it.

"There is no such thing as the fucking abridged history of anything," I hear myself scream over the fake sounds of the party. "And when the fuck is the real party going to start?" The music stops abruptly, and my voice resonates stridently in the small room with the fictional women pretending to eat plum products around the dinner table. They all stare embarrassed at their dishes. A short man with round glasses, a paunch belly and a camera hanging around his neck barges in through a side door. He yells "cut" and everybody relaxes. The actor impersonating my grandfather puts the newspaper from June 22, 1941, on the table, takes off his forties blazer and lights a cigarette. The short stalky man with round spectacles draws everybody's attention by clapping his hands: "All right! Great job everybody!" Then he turns to me as if he knew me and says with a smile: "Thank you Corina, that was very real, beautiful."

"I'm not in this movie," I scream. "You are now!" the short spectacled man says with a grin. I look at Manole hoping for an explanation, but he is laughing with his shiny dentures as if he is in on the whole big joke. The plasma TV now shows a commercial about toothpaste, an American Colgate commercial dubbed in Romanian. The women with artistic name tags hanging from their necks get up and start cleaning up everything. It all speeds up and before I know it, table with plum dishes, period chairs around it, handwoven rugs with folkloric motifs, it all gets folded up, rolled up, pushed against the wall, leaving the middle of the room empty and useless. The girl with the name tag "looking towards the sun, girl with ponytail" crosses the room swaying her shoulders in the rhythm of the toothpaste commercial music.

"We are waiting for the Elvis impersonator so the party can start," says the man who seems to be the director of the ridiculous avant-garde movie and the leader of the entire team of pathetic actors. The Elvis impersonator walks in with a guitar hanging on his hips and dark glasses and starts singing Hound Dog. The women slip out of their forties costumes and appear dressed in the now fashionable torn up jeans, rearrange their yellow flower sanziene crowns on their heads and start dancing the swing and the rock and roll with each other. This is no longer the movie scene but an actual moment in real time and space. I realize the breaking of the Ribbentrop Molotov pact coincides with the beginning of the sanziene holidays both right after the summer solstice and I am thinking that these two events cancel each other out and that the Elvis Impersonator's show cancels both of them out and yet they all seem to coexist in a game of simulacra in this crowded and foldable room.

The German soldiers come in wearing their SS uniforms and after them appear the Russian soldiers who are supposed to be in the next scene of the movie, where they break into each house on the street, ransack and pillage furniture and cut to pieces my father's dog named Girl. I know this because it is written on a sheet of paper posted on the wall with the secret door covered by the red drapes. It's a list of the scenes of the movie in the order in which they will be filmed. I tear it off the wall and scrunch it furiously in my hand which gives me a feeling of satisfaction as if I have cracked the film into a million pieces. Everybody dances the swing and the rock and roll with each other, Nazis, Stalinists, the girls with museum labels and yellow crowns, the movie director, and even Manole, though he dances the tango cheek to cheek with the older woman titled "peasant woman with hourglass." One of the Nazi soldiers asks me in English if I want to dance with him. I say I speak Romanian, and he says he doesn't. It turns out they are also using British actors in this New Wave movie that might just win a prize at the Cannes film festival, says the young movie star. "This Romanian director's movies always win prizes at Cannes," he says very seriously. We speak over the Elvis song, and it feels like we are living in an oversized Tupperware container, so vacuous and artificial is the conversation. "So, this Sanziene celebration is the Moldavian equivalent of a Dracula cult for you people?" He grins. I want to call onto all the Romanian superstitions from the last one thousand years to strike this moronic British actor out of existence: the monstrous gigantic bat that turns a cadaver into an undead blood sucking creature, nightly witches that turn you into a mute or disfigure your mouth and put it on the other side of your head, the plum spirits and the wall snakes and the wicked well fairies and the freaky babies born on the wrong side of life with evil bonnets stuck to their heads, and the undying ghost of Nicolae Ceausescu. I want them to strike him to a mute pile of rubbish sitting in the middle of this empty room with a green ribbon around it in memory of the fact he had played a Nazi soldier. "Yes," I say, "Dracula is due any moment now, I heard this Moldavian version goes after British actors posing as Nazi soldiers and slashes their throat with a steel toothpick, it's very painful."

I burst out of the room through the back yard into a glowing violet dusk. A flock of swallows darts out towards sunset. A blonde plump boy is playing ball against the back door of a house. An old man sits on the bench under the branches of a tiny orchard smoking a pipe. Someone once told me a story about the house at number 18, the resplendent orchards that gave the best fruit in the region and the family that owned them. The father hid two fugitive sisters inside a crack in the wall, in the hollow inside the trunk of a tree, in a secret place where no one could find them, and only one of them survived. The other one became a magic plum, a benevolent snake, a crown of yellow flowers, a girl with harp, a girl with ponytail, on and on, until she got tired and died forever. The other one became me.

"Don't Stop the Music!"
From Florin's Diary, 1939-1940, Northern Moldavia

They were named Zoe and Carolina and lived with us for a year during the war. One day, our father told us that the two sisters were going to stay with us for a few months while their mother and father went on vacation. Who takes month long vacations in times of war, I thought then but trusted my father too much to question anything he said or did. They ended up staying with us for a whole year because their parents never came back after them. At the end of the year, someone came looking for them, but Father said no such two girls ever stayed with us. It was the first time I had heard our father say something so contrary to the truth. After that, they disappeared altogether.

Zoe and Carolina's parents were an elegant couple, friends of my father and were occasionally invited for dinner on Sundays. I never knew their last name, but my father called them Gabi and Frida which to me had the alluring luster of slightly foreign names just like their daughters' names. Not altogether foreign like some of the names my parents mentioned at the dinner table when referring to celebrities they were reading about in a French magazine with pictures they subscribed to, but not altogether autochthonous either. Gabi was a book editor and a poet, and Frida was an actress and a singer in the local theater of our town. Occasionally, our parents took Lila and me to a performance that Frida was acting in and we sat mesmerized in the soft red velvet chairs of the theater. We watched the bizarre actions of the people on stage but mostly we watched Frida in a variety of colorful, silky dresses that swayed and flowed alluringly when she moved across the stage. Lila, who always carried the doll Mitzi with her everywhere she went, described everything that went on stage in detail for Mitzi, to our father and other spectators' exasperation. Our mother on the other hand was always amused by Lila's whispered renditions of the show which she thought were a sign of her daughter's imagination. I usually found Lila's attachment to her Mitzi doll endearing and was amused by her endless conversations or rather monologues except for the times we went to the theater and her endless chatter became irritating as it prevented me from following the dialogues spoken on stage. But I could never stay angry with Lila for more than a few minutes.

There was an unforgettable time in the summer of 1939 in the company of Gabi and Frida and their two diaphanous daughters Zoe and Carolina. A day that deserved to be written up in the book of unparalleled days with golden letters. A summer June day with songs, laughter, and silk dresses despite the impending war. Hitler's troops were advancing throughout a terrified Europe, but our country was still in its position of neutrality and our town suspended in its last glow of peace and prosperity. My parents were happy with each other, and Lila was always up to a new prank with Mitzi that was an inseparable presence. My father suggested we spend the day in the municipal park and have a picnic with Gabi, Frida, and the girls. My mother put on a shimmering gauzy dress with white lace trim that brought out her olive complexion and she combed her hair in braids that she rolled around her head like a crown. She looked like queen Maria of Romania, whose death a year earlier she mourned passionately. Many women tried to imitate Maria's style or look like her, but my mother really did, not even as much out of vanity, but out of the endless admiration she had for the queen.

After her death, Maria's heart was according to her own wishes, put in a box and kept in the Bran castle in Northern Transylvania and my mother often spoke of going to the castle to see the box with the queen's heart in it. Then it was transported to the town of Balchik on the shore of the Black Sea that now belonged to Bulgaria and where the queen used to spend her vacations and paint landscapes of the sea. My mother always regretted not having taken that trip to the castle to see the box with the queen's heart in it. My father kissed Mama on both cheeks and on her beautifully rolled braids and she blushed, which made her look even more beautiful.

Gabi and Frida were elegant as always, he in a white summer suit, she in a delicate peach colored chiffon dress that matched her reddish hair. Zoe and Carolina who were identical twins, looked like otherworldly creatures in their simple white cotton dresses with silk and lace trims around the neck and the hem. Zoe also wore a light blue sash tied around her waist which matched her cerulean blue eyes. Since I always stayed next to my mother on the floor while she was making her and Lila's outfits with the sewing machine, I knew more about girls and women's clothes than men's clothes and sometimes I wore my sister's dresses around the house. My mother let me wear whatever I wanted and kissed me saying I was as pretty as a girl anyways. For our special outing I wore the grey summer pants my mother had sewn for me and a blue shirt that my father had brought me from a trip to Greece.

When we arrived at the park, an orchestra was playing in the kiosk and couples were dancing in a dreamy glide. The air was electric, past, present and future melted in the summer pastels and an illusion of everlasting happiness rose from the sentimental violins, rested on the swirling couples in the perfumed afternoon and became palpable like some fruit you could touch and eat. My entire life up to that point seemed to have been aimed at that enchanted afternoon. Gabi and Frida started dancing; my parents joined the dancing couples. I took Lila's hand and swayed her and the doll Mitzi in the rhythm of the music, a song of carefree love. I had never seen my parents dance before, and the sight made me dizzy with happiness. I remember thinking: "Mama and Tata will live forever, and they won't have any worries again. If they are dancing, they have no worries. They need to dance every day."

Next to Lila and me, the twin sisters danced with each other and giggled. Zoe's eyes sparkled, and yellow linden flowers had fallen on her reddish curls. Something blue and whimsical entered my heart at the sight of her glowing face, a vague craving that was not for food. There couldn't be anything wrong with the world, life was light as a feather and full of tasty rhythms, it swirled, and it glowed, and Zoe filled my universe with irrepressible color. It was an iridescent moment in time that carried the full weight of its ephemerality and of the losses to come, yet still innocent in its carefree exuberance. I looked at Gabi and Frida in their graceful dance. They were enveloped in a different kind of light that exuded sadness, a knowledge that life will never be like that again and that the moment was tinged with the gloom of an unknown future. I thought I heard one of the violins screech. The picture of our happiness melted, the pastels cried and liquefied in chaotic streaks, turning black and white.

A picture in sepia, taken by the park photographer has survived as proof of that day. Frida, Gabi, and my parents standing in their elegant clothes, and the four of us, Lila and me, Zoe and Carolina, lined up on the ground in front of them, obedient and innocent. Nobody smiles in the photograph, though I could swear everybody was smiling and glowing when the photograph was taken. Maybe the photographer missed the exact moment when we all smiled, still suspended in the shimmer of our ephemeral happiness, still giddy from the dance. A second too late and our smiles were gone, the sepia photograph snapped in the aftermath of our last happiness. Instead, a yellowish sadness enveloped us as we stood unmoved for the photograph, which did not lack beauty but lacked color and the glow of our joyfulness of a moment earlier.

Lila and I laughed for hours when we looked at the face of Mitzi captured for the first time in a photograph, with her black hair all ruffled up, one eye closed and one eye open. Even my mother laughed heartily when she saw the picture and said: "that was such a beautiful day." Frida and Gabi looked straight at the camera as if wanting to be remembered. My mother and father looked slightly askance as if not quite ready for the camera and only Zoe's eyes contained the possibility of a smile, while Carolina seemed surprised by the very act of being photographed. Lila and I had our eyes wide open, eager to be memorialized. I said to my parents "don't stop the music," as if they were responsible for the music being played by the orchestra in the kiosk. I knew that once the photograph was going to be taken, the music and the dancing were going to stop, and the worries were going to return. When the war started that fall, I had the crazy idea that if only the photographer could have seized the perfect harmony of a second earlier, the war wouldn't have started. I called it "the photograph of a second too late."

The rest of the summer tumbled in a mad rush towards the fall when the war started in Europe. Nothing compared to the day of music and dancing in the park at the beginning of the summer, though my parents tried to prolong the illusion for us that we could still laugh, and we could still be children and carefree in the brilliant summer days. I never saw my parents dance again, though they always looked happy with each other even when they were worried about something.

There were good words and bad words that summer being passed around during the dinner conversations and repeated incessantly. "Neutrality" was a good word, and Ribbentrop-Molotov was a pair of bad, bad words that sounded like a whole army of soldiers marching through town and they scared Lila and Mitzi beyond comprehension. My parents talked of the possibility of us having to leave the house and the town and flee into refuge because of annexations of Romanian territories in the north to Russia. "Annexations" was a terribly bad word that sent shivers down my spine. Every time one of my parents said Ribbentrop-Molotov,

Lila started crying and covered Mitzi's ears saying it gave Mitzi nightmares to hear those words. Our maid Mitzi crossed herself at the sound of the menacing names and that summer she got pregnant. She said the father of the child was an Italian soldier. Nobody understood how Mitzi the maid was able to find an Italian soldier in our small town, nor did anyone believe her until one evening when we heard a man's voice in our front yard speak in a language that sounded like the operas my father listened to on the Victrola occasionally.

He was an Italian soldier indeed who with a group of others from his battalion decided to flee Mussolini's troops to Romania sensing the impending war and Italy's role in it. He ran into our maid Mitzi one day in the market and she became pregnant. I didn't yet understand by what procedure Mitzi became pregnant by associating with the Italian soldier by the name of Gino Farinelli but Lila was quick to show me on her doll how they were going to cut up the belly of Mitzi the maid with the biggest pair of scissors and bring out the Italian baby. It was the first time I had heard my mother use an insulting word towards anybody when she called Mitzi the maid "an idiot for copulating with a fascist soldier." Mitzi, who had no idea what a fascist soldier meant any more than my sister's doll, cried for two days after my mother's outburst. "Copulating" also sounded like a bad word to me in those days, though not of the same nature of badness as "Molotov- Ribbentrop" and almost a good word by comparison.

Although everything fell short of the enchanted June day in the municipal park for the rest of the summer and the fall of that year, our lives did not lack richness and excitement, at least not for Lila and me who played with a vengeance in our magnificent orchards until dusk caught us perched in one of our fruit trees gorging on dark cherries, sugary plums, and tart apples. Our dog, Girl, was always with us as our most loyal protector from other animals and observer of our pranks as was Mitzi the doll with her unmoved stare.

The association between Mitzi and Gino the Italian deserter soldier did not seem to us anything as bad as it appeared to have been for my parents particularly after Gino bought a newer Victrola and played Italian music on it until late at night under the orange moon of those fragrance filled nights. It was a different kind of music than the one my father would listen to, more like the one played in the kiosk in the municipal park and for that reason it had a bittersweet taste for Lila and me. On some nights Mitzi and Gino danced in the backyard like the couples in the park. Their shadows projected on the back wall of our house ridiculously shaped and huge, were funny and frightening at once. Gabi and Frida had stopped visiting us for occasional dinners and we stopped going to the theater to see Frida in her glamorous roles.

On the first day of September that year, my father listened carefully to his radio for longer than I had ever seen him do it in the past and announced at dinner that Germany invaded Poland, and the war had started in Europe. A controlled panic entered our house at that moment. Mitzi the maid fainted in the kitchen breaking the Venetian porcelain bowl with the steaming polenta meal in it. My mother sat between Lila and me at the dinner table and held us in her arms kissing our heads for a long moment. A rush of bad words burst into the room and made a deafening clamor. The Iron Guard and General Antonescu were the ultimate bad words with the repeated word of "neutrality" being the only good word that might have stood a chance in the face of the onslaught of frightening vocabulary. And the word "King" was a good word that brought glimmers of hope in my parents' eyes.

If our parents were alive and healthy and we had our house, we could only guess the badness of what was happening in the world from the sonority and tone of words exchanged during dinner or in the afternoon at the time when everybody rested in the living room. Our lives were not going to be affected for a while if the word "neutrality" still held true. That was all Lila and I cared about, although the number and weight of bad words multiplying in our house started to affect my parents' mood and to instill growing fears in the two of us. Christmas was not as joyous and abundant as in past years and the snow climbed all the way to our windows that winter which to our great delight allowed Lila and me to easily climb all the way to the roof and then swish down into the street.

One morning when it was so cold that not even Girl who loved the snow wanted to go outside, Zoe and Carolina came to visit and play with us. I didn't see their parents stop by to chat with my parents as they used to do. The girls just seemed to appear out of nowhere on our veranda. We all went to the frozen pond at the end of our street with ice skates and skated on the sparkling ice. Zoe and Carolina were gliding effortlessly holding hands, their cheeks flushed from the cold and locks of reddish blonde hair framing their faces from under their white fur caps.

I was flying on my wooden skates watching Lila skate with Mitzi tucked inside her oversized white wool coat when I heard a scream and then another. The second scream emerged right from the first one but was different, a knife through the heart. When I turned my head, I saw Carolina half sunk in a hole in the middle of the pond with a purple face like raw flesh and Zoe lying on her belly trying to pull out her sister. Her face was shining as if the sun had exploded on it. I don't remember having jumped in, only the burning of the ice on my body and thinking that I couldn't swim and that it didn't matter whether I knew how to swim or not. I remember pushing Carolina upwards and Zoe and Lila pulling her arms and yelling "push." Then Lila and Zoe pulled me from the hole in the ice with the exploded sun on their faces. A million shards of the sun spread all over Lila and Zoe's faces. I remember pushing my skate into a rock under the water and hoisting myself on top of the ice with the girls' help and feeling an overpowering jolt of life through my body, like my blood had exploded in my veins. A bubble of blue ice contained me. Zoe was both the blue of the ice and the white of the snow, she expanded into infinite blue matter around me. She was living ice and throbbing blue. Mr. Gogu must have heard our screams and called my parents because in what seemed like another moment, they were right in front of us taking turns slapping Carolina and me. I wouldn't have felt anything if I had been beaten with a wooden stick, but it turned out the slapping was to keep our blood moving and our limbs from freezing and turning to dead flesh.

That evening by the fire, I traversed distant and fantastical lands, the burning wood crackling in the chimney, a constant fuss of people around me, teas, compresses, whispers, Mitzi holding me to warm me up, my mother lying on top of Carolina to warm her up. Mitzi's baby moved while she was holding me, and I thought a bird flew right through me. Mother thought it was lucky and life giving to be close to a living unborn baby to infuse me with life while I was a block of blue ice. German soldiers were marching on top of me with hard steps and heavy artillery as they were carrying the heart of Queen Maria, which had become a block of blue ice kept in an iron box. Red had disappeared, there was only blue in the world. They were stealing the blue block of Royal heart from the castle in Transylvania. Someone in a black cloak was also carrying my frozen heart in a box and taking it to the land of life without death and of youth without old age, tearing it out of my chest with a violent yank, while the rest of my body was left to age and turn to dust without a heart in it. Lila and her doll Mitzi were the only immortal creatures in a desert of skeletons and bones, and Mama was sewing silk dresses in the middle of the desert though she was not immortal, and she was going to die and turn to dust as soon as she finished sewing the dresses. She had to keep sewing dresses to stay alive and the entire population of Romanian women were wearing my mother's silk dresses which were made in the style of those worn by Queen Maria. I cried for Carolina and Zoe and asked if they were alive, I asked for plums and apples from the orchard, wasn't it the season of plums and marmalade? And who was playing a sad song on the Victrola over and over and again and dancing the tango on the roof of our house?

When I came out of my delirium, the girls were gone and Lila, Mama, Tata, Mitzi the maid and Mitzi the doll were all sitting on my bed smiling like they were having a party. Lila said I had been a hero and saved Carolina's life, and I could have died. I was lucky they didn't have to amputate my legs because of the frostbite. What was I going to do without legs for the rest of my life? She asked. It was Mitzi's unborn baby that saved me. It made me laugh that I was saved by an unborn baby. Where were Carolina and Zoe? I asked. They went to their home, and they were fine, my father said, and a sadness seemed to envelop his face like a thin veil. Something did not feel fine in the air, something dark and many headed was hovering above us, around us, crawling into all the empty spaces and demanding our hearts. I asked for food and my mother gave me lentil soup and corn mush. I slept for a long time, maybe days. I was only woken when my mother returned to feed me more soup and corn mush.

It seemed like spring came the next day and the orchards started to bloom in a wild outburst of rosy flowers as if they were blooming for the last time. Life had an appearance of normality with family dinners and siestas. I started playing with Lila in our back yard again and running with the dog in the orchards.

One night, as Lila and I were lying in our beds unable to sleep, she suddenly started to cry. She often cried for various and sometimes what I thought were insignificant reasons, but this time her cries sounded more like a wail and carried an ominous streak. "Mitzi told me that Hitler and Stalin are going to take our house and kill all of us and burn Frida and Gabi and the girls alive," she said in between sobs squeezing Mitzi at her chest. I knew that when Lila said that Mitzi told her something, she meant the doll and not the maid. Every time she heard something and reported it, Lila said it was Mitzi the doll who told her. And most of the time that she heard something my parents talked about in secret from us, was because she had eavesdropped which Lila did often. Hitler and Stalin seemed like ogres with bad mustaches to us and we couldn't understand why nobody good and strong and with no mustache in the whole world could kill these two ogres and rid the world of both. We had seen pictures of them in the newspapers that my father read, and they didn't seem as frightening to us as everybody claimed. Hitler looked sort of funny to us and reminded Lila and me of some of the bad characters in the movies with Charlie Chaplin that our parents took us to once a month in the local cinema. Those bad men with absurd mustaches were always punished in the movies.

"Where did Mitzi hear about this, Lila?" "From Gino, that's where, he knows because he's a soldier and he met Hitler," Lila said and wiped her tears with the sleeve of her nightgown. I was sure she was going to say from Mama and Papa, because Lila often tiptoed to the door of their bedroom and eavesdropped after we all went to bed and the house was quiet. She took Mitzi with her and then reported on what she had heard. But this time her report seemed more terrifying because it was coming from a stranger who had been in the Italian army. "How did Mitzi understand Italian, Lila? Doesn't Gino speak Italian?" Lila stopped crying and thought for a minute, then said confidently: "Mitzi can understand and speak Italian, didn't you know that?" I burst out laughing and was sorry for it the next second because I knew Lila was going to cry again saying I never believed what she said. Only that this time she burst out laughing too. She was relieved to hear me laugh because those meant things weren't that bad after all if I could still laugh at the news. She needed my laughter to calm her fears which must have been awoken indeed by something she had heard in the house.

"Maybe Mitzi misunderstood Gino's Italian, it's easy to misunderstand people who speak foreign languages," I said. "Yes, you're right, I think she misunderstood, maybe Gino said that Stalin and Hitler are going to be killed," she said which surprised me since Lila hardly ever agreed with me about anything. She fell asleep soon after that, holding Mitzi as always and I stayed awake for a long time worrying about what our future was going to be, if the war that had started in Poland was going to come to our town and what were we all going to do if that happened.

The ticking of the wall snake started and though it always spooked me, I now found the sound reassuring. That night I dreamed of the afternoon in the park when we all danced to the music of the orchestra the women in pastel silk and lace dresses, my parents gliding smoothly on the dance floor under the canopy of trees and Zoe smiling at me with a playful spark in her eyes. But then in my dream everything suddenly stopped, the music, the dances, the laughter and when I looked around all the people were black and white figures in sepia like in the photograph, we took that afternoon only they didn't have a face; they were all cutout figures from a coloring book, without a face. The photographer looked like Hitler, and he was the only one with a face and was telling us to smile or else we would all be burned alive. We were all made of cardboard, and I tried my hardest to smile but my cardboard face wouldn't move. Then Gino and Mitzi appeared and started playing an Italian song on the Victrola that was called "Tango della gelosia." Gino was wearing a green soldier uniform and Mitzi's belly was huge with her Italian baby. They were not made of cardboard, and they danced to the tango until they became huge shadows on the back wall of our house. I believe I woke up crying from my dream, then fell back into a deep sleep.

At some point after dawn, I heard Girl barking which she never did in the middle of the night, and I thought I heard Frida and Gabi talking to my father in the hallway. I tried to listen like Lila would do but the voices were low, and I could not make out clear words. At some point I thought I heard Frida cry and the meek voices of the girls. They seemed to be crying too, but I thought it was still in my dream. Then I am pretty sure I heard Frida say: "we'll be back soon, don't worry," and then my father saying: "don't worry, we'll take good care of them." Frida cried again, though it also sounded like she was singing in one of her plays, a sad beautiful song.

When I finally woke up that morning, Lila was not in her bed with Mitzi. I heard voices and laughter in the dining room. It sounded like Zoe and Carolina's voices, and Lila telling everybody what Mitzi had dreamt of that night. My mother and the girls were laughing. I looked outside and it was a fiercely sunny and blue spring day, the orchard that we could see from our bedroom was aflame in its petulant blooming, on the cusp before the flowers turned to leaves and tiny fruit. If my mother and Zoe and Carolina were laughing and the orchards were bursting with color, things couldn't be that bad, the war wasn't going to come to our town after all. When I stepped into the dining room for breakfast that morning the spring light was shining onto everything with an almost cruel brightness. Our house looked unusually beautiful and melancholy almost like it was wrong to be in the spring. It looked both festive and sad like a farewell party.

My father clapped his hands to draw everybody's attention and said: "Zoe and Carolina are going to live with us for a little while. Mother will turn my study into a bedroom. They are our family now." I couldn't contain my joy and clapped my hands just like Father did and Lila shrieked with happiness, now that she had not one but two girls in the house to play with her and Mitzi. Then she blurted out: "So Hitler and Stalin aren't going to kill us all and take our house then, Tata?" For a second my parents remained unmoved, and I thought I noticed a grimace of pain on my mother's face. Then my father regained his composure and said: "Of course not Lila, whoever gave you that crazy idea?" I noticed that Zoe and Carolina were covered in a haze of gloominess after Lila's words, and I could have hit my sister that morning. Lila must have realized she had made a huge blunder to blurt out like that and started crying and holding on to Mitzi for dear life. Her way of asking for forgiveness and deflecting attention from the unease she had caused was by drawing attention to her dramatic tears. Zoe looked up at me from her plate just then and she was in fact smiling with a spark of joy in her eyes like the afternoon in the park when she was dancing with Carolina. The giddiness I had felt that day, entered me again and it made me dizzy as if I had been dancing. I didn't care about Hitler or Stalin and the war seemed unreal at that moment in my life.

I suddenly cared only about Zoe. About everything that was beautiful and right there in that moment: my mother's queenly presence, the morning light bathing the room and glazing our oak and walnut furniture with a mellow sheen, my father's resonant voice and stately stature, Mitzi's Italian baby growing inside her, Lila's whims and her dark braids that looked just like her doll's braids and the orchards ablaze in rosy blooms. I became overly bold and went to Carolina and Zoe, took them by the hand and asked them to go outside and play. My parents didn't object to my unusual and unruly behavior and even told Lila to go out and play with us too.

We spent the day climbing the trees in the orchard and making tree houses. Throughout the day I kept brushing by Zoe in our chases and pranks and every time I felt touched with liquid blue, a spark of color and perfume that made me think I was Beautiful Child from not just one but different fairytales, a compound hero of all the variants of that character: I had drunk the live water of the good fairies, I was omnipotent and could fly, I had killed a dragon and won a sack of magic golden apples. So emboldened was I that in one of my climbing acrobatics I fell from the tree and broke my leg. Nobody seemed to be shocked by it and acted like it was to be expected. My mother, usually so worried about any injury or illness of ours, this time sat calmly in the armchair and watched the doctor put my leg in a cast. Her gaze was elsewhere. At some point she said almost absent-mindedly that two bad accidents in one year were enough, I should just try to settle down. An angel of gloom was circling around our lives, but I was still up in the spheres of liquid blue dancing with Zoe above the ground, eating apples in a cloud.

That night, my father played a tango on the Victrola. I was groggy from the tea mixed with plum brandy that my mother made me drink to soothe the pain of the broken leg. I shivered with a bad foreboding when I recognized the tango as being the one in my dream, "Tango della gelosia," the one that Mitzi and Gino danced to as two ominous shadows climbing on our house. I thought I had a dream with music, which was strange because all dreams were silent, but mine had sound and smell. It must have been a sign. Mitzi really danced with Gino that night on the veranda, and she started having her baby while dancing. A huge commotion started in the house, the family doctor was back, only this time with different medical instruments and Mitzi's cries filled the house for a while. My mother kept heating water on the stove and Lila was cutting the belly of Mitzi the doll trying to bring out her baby. Carolina and Zoe watched all the people coming and going, dancing, giving birth, as they both sat in Father's velvet armchair and held hands like they were at the theater watching one of their mother's plays.

At some point Mitzi's cries were replaced by the whimpers of a baby who was a boy by the name of Gino. Mother called the four of us children to see the baby. She asked Mitzi if the baby was going to speak Italian and Mitzi answered that "I don't know, we'll just have to wait and see." In the entire chaos of that day full of so many major occurrences, my mother burst out laughing. Even my father laughed and decided to play another melody on the Victrola, this time an aria from a sad Italian opera called L'Elisir d'amore. My father sang along the sad words with the refrain "una furtive lagrima," and stressed the sad ending of the aria saying "si puo morir d'amor," "you could die of love." Gino translated the words for us in a whisper in the funny Romanian he had learned with Italian accent. At the end of that song Father told Gino he had to be a real man and marry Mitzi. Lila cried because of the sad words of the aria and reported that the doll Mitzi was crying profusely. Zoe and Carolina had fallen asleep in the same armchair holding hands, with their heads on each other's shoulders.

I perfectly understood the meaning of the last words of the song, "si puo morir d'amor." Mother went over to them, woke them up gently and helped them to bed in Father's studio. I also understood then that a certain danger was hovering around Zoe and Carolina and that our mother was not going to reveal anything else she might have known of the reasons they now lived with us and why their parents were going on a long vacation right at the beginning of the war. As I laid on the sofa in the living room groggy from my mother's tea and hurting from the broken leg I knew that a time of chaos was about to start for us all, where the happy and the sad mixed and leaked into one another: flaming orchards, birth, death, sad music for happy events and joyous music for heartbreak, a great confusion of feelings, hunger, pain, love, frozen faces in a sepia photograph and the trace of a breath on the surface of a mirror.

The Night of Sanziene Summer Fairies
June 2015, Northern Moldavia

"Which is better: to be burned alive or frozen to death, killed by a firing squad or by hanging, to be occupied by the Germans or the Russians, go to Auschwitz or to Siberia?" My father asked these questions in rushed handwriting and red fountain pen in a worn-out notebook bound in soft burgundy leather that must have once been a fancy diary and a birthday gift from his father. On the first page is a dedication from my grandfather, Tudor, written in beautifully rounded letters that says: "For my beloved son Florin, to write his thoughts, impressions, and ideas about life. Be kind, be brave, be knowledgeable!" It was dated May 12th, 1940, and signed: "Your father who loves you more than his own life."

That summer of 1940, Romania lost parts of northern Moldavia to Russia, parts of northern Transylvania to Hungary, and part of the southern Black Sea shore to Bulgaria. Everybody wanted a piece of our country, and everybody got one that summer. My father and his family all had to leave the house at number 18, gather valuables in suitcases and pillowcases and get on the train towards the southern part of the country with other hundreds of refugees, cattle, and fowl. That was their first refugee journey. They returned several months later when it was settled that no more annexations of Romanian territories to Russia would take place only to find Nazi soldiers walking up and down the streets of their town like they owned it. The first entry in the diary was dated August 30th, 1944, a week after King Michael turned arms against the Germans and joined the Red Army.

My father had waited four years to write his first "thoughts, impressions, and ideas about life," and had only done so after his father died that summer which was also when Russian troupes marched and drove their tanks into Romania. This notebook has also crossed the Atlantic once each way like the postcard of 1938 and like the star diamond earrings that belonged to my grandmother Victoria and which I wore on my escape trip out of Romania. I carried my father's diary in my purse and inside the diary, scattered between the pages, my favorite family photographs when we all left the country on a train to Vienna. I trembled with fear that the customs and secret police were going to stop us all at the border if they searched my purse. Instead, they searched my suitcase, every single item including my underwear and they got stuck on a stack of my handwritten stories that I wanted to take with me as proof that I had a thinking mind and the ambition to become a writer. They took the stories and let us go. I crossed the border without any of my writings, a suitcase full of ugly communist clothes and my grandmother's star diamond earring sparkling on my earlobes. In my purse I still had my father's diary from 1940, that he handed me the morning of our departure. "In case something happens, it's better that it's in your possession than mine," he said. "Put it in your purse, where it's most obvious, they are least likely to search in the more obvious places," he said full of confidence. He had been right.

My dearest mementos and objects are world travelers like me, they carry the stories of irremediable uprooting and losses in the molecules of their weathered material. I stroke the soft worn-out burgundy leather of my father's diary and think of the dedication left by my grandfather. The love that flowed from his hand to my father's heart to my own person in a fierce will to bequeath something durable and fragile, not life everlasting but the everlasting power of a heritage of love. The love that made me and then flowed into my own children who were born at the other end of the world. The continuity of love, and then the breaking of it, the dislocation of an entire lineage onto a distant land. The separation of lives and the separation of continents made in one leap, in one gesture that changed everything like an earthquake, like a drastic movement of tectonic plates after which mountains become plains or rise out of the sea, plains rise into crested peaks. A whole new geography came to life in the blink of an eye.

It is almost dark in the garden behind the house at number 18 and the party or movie shooting festivities are still going on in the house next door, but they sound like the noises on a departing ship. The lights in the windows are flickering like strobe lights. I don't want to go inside the house. Yet I feel almost jealous that I am not present at the party and that I'm an outsider. I have always loved a good party with dancing, but this party dislocated all sense of belonging anywhere in the world including in myself, as if I was my own foreign country. It reinforced the foreignness of my own nativeness as if I had not been born anywhere. As if I had been unborn. While I was in the room earlier that day, with the women actors who sat around the table eating plum pudding, with the Hitler-Stalin tango performed by two British actors and the cocky would-be movie director shouting orders at his cast, I kept telling myself you can't undo that you were born somewhere, here that is, in this country; this is your language, these are your people. And then I answered to myself that these clowns stealing your life story and the story of your family are not your people, they are simulacra people in a simulacrum space eating simulacrum plum food. I am not from this simulacrum plum country. I changed from the second to the first person in my inner conversation, from Romanian to English and back to Romanian struggling for the best phrasing, for a place inside myself. Then I gave up and hated everything and everybody in the fake party room even though I was fascinated by it and was dying to see where all the madness would to lead. I was able to tear myself away. I am good at tearing myself away from people and places and turning myself into my own ship floating on the ocean in an agony of homelessness.

I am starting to get used to the coexistence of universes that cancel each other out and that rotate their startling images in an ongoing carousel. I want to know what happened to the two girls hidden away by my grandfather. I want to know what the purpose of this movie project is all about, if it's even a real movie or a con operation or a mafia stunt or an imagined reality, a mirage. I want to know who all the dead are buried in the back yard and nourishing Manole's orchard, other than my own grandfather. "Kind, brave, and knowledgeable." The word "knowledgeable" always surprises me more than anything. Knowledge was more important than love for my grandfather. In a dedication to my children, I would have put: "be kind, be brave, be passionate," or "be loving, be strong, be yourself." So American, so cliché, even though I try to avoid cliches. Maybe knowledge leads to love. Maybe my grandfather understood and experienced love through knowledge and not through the worn-out heart symbolism and language. "I know, therefore I love" — a different model for traversing the world and building a family, a home.

Winds from the east, winds from the north, and winds from all directions stir the leaves at this confused hour of night leaking its oily darkness into the day. An owl calling, the crickets erupting their sonorous musings into the linden air and then another delicate sound like a sigh of the trees, a whisper of the flowers. One two three it's suddenly dark, as if someone played with the lights. I don't remember such darkness in recent times with no moon and no streetlights and only a tiny light coming from the house at number 18, my father's house, like a timid star in a starless night. Suddenly everything shifts and changes in this unforgiving darkness. The same image keeps passing in front of my eyes like a slide projection against the starless night: the children bursting out through the back door into the yard in the moonlight, darting through the orchards in bloom, through the orchards heavy with fruit, one jet of irrepressible youth into the night, a spring night, a summer night with June fairies and yellow flowers. I shift my position on the bench, and something shifts again. A reality that moves like gliding doors: a delicate song, a dance, a wreath of yellow flowers whispering little magic words in the impenetrable dark.

The tiny light coming from the back of the house at number 18 is irresistible. I'm in a night fever, a quiver of the soul and a lust for danger. I get up from the bench under the plum and cherry trees, they seem to sigh in distress that I am leaving them. They seem to warn me, saying things such as don't go any farther, don't attempt anything stupid, you know nothing of this place, nothing of the life unfolding here, the Sanziene that turn from good to bad in the blink of an eye, from beautiful to hideous in a millisecond. But since I don't believe in talking trees after all, I walk to the back of the house using the light of my cell phone which seems to ground me somewhat in the modern world of technology and annihilate superstition. I walk through bramble bushes and tall grass, poppies, and rose bushes that prickle and sting my calves and ankles to the point where I feel thin streaks of blood running down my legs and realize this was a stupid idea. As I lean over to touch my legs and verify how badly I am bleeding I drop my cellphone in the brambles and produce a scream. In my world it's worse to lose your cellphone than to bleed from any part of your body.

An owl screeches, startled birds dart out of their nests, a dog starts barking, on and on. It seems that I started a chain of life events in the dark, that I disturbed the sleep of creatures and the harmony of the darkness. Night is a dense velvety fold of swarming life all around me. In my panic I start calling to my father in my head, in actual words and prayer lines like Tata, protect and help me now, please, don't let me get hurt, and get me out of here alright? I'm too ashamed to ask him to help me find my cellphone, but suddenly I start believing in the spirits of the dead even though I don't believe in God and am fully aware this is only opportunistic circumstantial belief in the spirits of the dead and of the good snakes and whatever other beneficent and maleficent creatures, only because I am freaked out in the uncivilized darkness of this place. I am worried about the streaks of blood I feel running along my calves and the utter sense of existential confusion I experience. It's too far now to go back to the bench through the stupid bramble bushes so I advance towards the light which I realize is coming from a room that looks like a cellar, under the house but not in the actual house, somewhat away from it.

I know I am here for a visit searching my ancestry, but it still feels like a game, an adventure for my summer vacation. I have a feeling I once swam to America or sailed to America in a boat like some other refugees I know and since I survived that crossing everything seems possible now. I know I have a solid home, a solid life in America with a house and two children in it and that with that first crossing everything shifted in my sense of spatial belonging. I wonder why I should even care about any of this ancestry down here as if it mattered? Nobody even writes diaries in paper notebooks anymore like this leather bound seventy-year-old diary I am still holding. And how come I dropped the cellphone and not diary? My father carried that diary across the ocean and died of longing for this place right here.

By some good fortune I get out of the brambles and find myself in front of a small staircase leading to the cellar room that is lit up like a cheerful welcome. The light of the house cheers me up even though I feel so devastatingly alone like I have lost everybody on all sides of the Atlantic Ocean and all I have is a vague memory of my own life. As I go down the staircase, the cellar room looks like an attic, both suspended and buried, above and below, in a vertigo of perspective, of ground and air, earth and sky. Only my people can be so literally upside down in everything they do, including the reconstruction of a house, particularly the renovation of a house, of this house that once belonged to my family. I say my family to myself as I go down the attic cellar almost tripping on the steps, as if I had grown up in this house myself.

It is a suspended cellar on wooden poles yet lower than the main level of the house, with potted plants and flowers, crawling ivies, and exotic ferns. It must be the Moldavian miniature version of the suspended gardens of Babylon. There is no limit to how far I will go tonight inside the mysteries of my father's family and the secret compartments of this house. It's not clear yet how much of this space that is both airy and subterranean is the result of this present family's reconstructive fervor or of the work of my own ancestors, grandfather Tudor and grandmother Victoria.

I find myself inside the airy space with potted rhododendron and cacti, a grand piano and velvet armchair, Romanian hand-woven rugs in bright reds and yellows, Turkish cushions, and a subterranean tunnel extending from the room towards the back yard like a dragon's tail. The room is lit by crystal candelabra hanging from the low ceiling that you can almost touch, it is all within reach, floor and ceiling, rugs, and candelabra, like an airplane submarine kind of creation here in the back of my father's reconstructed house. Nothing looks like anything in the actual house with the world's tackiest decorations, this is vintage postmodern. Maybe I've moved into a state of semiconscious dreaming where the lower and higher levels of consciousness merge into something else like the airy subterranean architecture of the place. Somebody is playing the Kreutzer sonata on the grand piano that sounds far away although it is close. I can't see who it is, maybe a lost Gypsy musician from World War II.

A strawberry blonde girl is braiding the hair of a tiny doll dressed in traditional Romanian costume. The folkloric motifs are everywhere, we must be in the village museum. A special village museum built for night visitors coming from America. Romanians are such inventive people my father used to say, they invented the first airplane though nobody knows about it, and they invented the anarchic cultural movement of Dada, he also used to say. Why not invent upside down inside out subterranean suspended museums where everything comes to life for bored Americans and British actors with Dracula fantasies? I think in return. That would really boost tourism and make our country better known in the world, across the ocean where everything hip and modern and consumerist seems to come from.

I move through space like through water with gliding motions touching crystal candelabra and folkloric rugs, reaching out for a doll in traditional costume. I just keep going on and on and can't seem to be able to stop. I move through a flooded tunnel trying to keep my head above the water and waiting to get to the exit. It's not really water, but fluid air but I call it water in my head for lack of a better word. An oak table is floating in the water and on it is a round crystal paperweight that used to sit on the walnut desk with the glass top in our miniature Bucharest apartment with no kitchen and one long bathroom. It seems that certain objects indeed have a life of their own and have gotten transferred from house to house from period to period from one life to the next irrespective of their owners. It must have been the secret police who took everything that was left after our departure and sold it on the black market yet some of it still ended up here in its original space. Objects, like pets, always want to return to their original owners, someone said once in a Romanian folk tale.

An Italian fascist soldier dances the tango with a pregnant maid. My grandparents, Tudor and Victoria, are playing bridge at one end of the oval oak table and whispering to each other while the girl dressed in a white cotton dress with a blue sash keeps combing and braiding the doll's hair, braiding, and combing. The Kreutzer sonata clashes with the tango music and I'm dying to hear what my grandparents are whispering about. I know it's serious, life and death kind of serious and that it must concern two girls, twin sisters, their fate, and their future. And why is there only one if there were two? I heard twin siblings can't survive one without the other, what in the world happened to the other one and which is which?

"Please, Grandpa Tudor and Grandma Victoria, tell me what happened to one of the girls, to the other one of the girls?" Someone sitting in the corner of the room sewing uniforms for the Romanian soldiers, whispers to me to call them by the Romanian words for grandpa and grandma, *bunicul si bunica*, they don't like to be called by the American denominations. I don't recognize that person whispering such an order to me, a woman with bright red curls and a fancy hat with plums and feathers on it like a Romanian version of a Carmen Miranda hat. Romanians have their own versions of everything in the world.

Through the rectangular window that runs the length of this habitation which might as well be a converted bomb shelter or trenches from World War II, I see the sanziene fairies floating in an airy circle dance on and above the ground singing an atonal melody that neutralizes the tango and the Kreutzer sonata into one monotonous yet delicate chant. It should be interesting to compose the soundtrack for this movie. Maybe it should be the soundtrack to the movie they are making next door. But I'm pretty sure it's not a movie but a huge block party with the entire neighborhood of creatures, spirits, ancestors come from all over Romanian territories to welcome me and help weave my family story for the global posterity and for my offspring to know where they come from.

Time has become a place. Time is a gelatinous box taking the shape of events and situations in the years of 1941 and 1942, 1943 and 1944, which apparently were crucial and defining years for my family. It happens so with certain important years or periods: they morph into places and float like constellations until someone yearns for them with the force of a hurricane, calls for them or invokes them with certain unified cerebral powers and ancestral conjurations. *Bunicul* and *bunica* look at me with blank eyes, really with dead eyes who am I kidding! What are they doing here then, being dead and planning the lives of two girls? It's not like they are ghosts of the dead people or simulacra, or the living dead, or some other horror movie nonsense like that. Rather, it's that the sum of their molecules has reformulated itself into their essential selves that existed before during and after their lives and found its niche in the appropriate chamber of time. My time has caught up with theirs or the other way around and who knows what will happen from here on? Maybe new formulas for space and spatial temporal relations will be created. Maybe from now on a year will be a hundred acres and a decade will be a province, and half a century will be a full country. One day we will say things like several countries ago Corina looked for her father's life story and found it in a submarine attic on the day of the summer solstice.

In this fantastical journey through my family's history, Aunt Lila sits in a pink armchair in another corner of the room looking incredibly gaunt and pale. She died from a heart attack because her heart was week from her childhood wartime scarlet fever, and I never got to say goodbye to her before I left the country for good. I was smoking an American cigarette that bothered her and my parents, and I left the next day so the secret police wouldn't catch us. Regret for unfinished gestures and failed goodbyes is a gash in the soul. I don't think I believe in communication with the dead. I believe in the continuous recreation of those who disappeared from our lives, from the flesh and bones domain. Are the girls Jewish? One is Jewish, the other one is something else. What something else? That bit of conversation keeps coming back with a will of its own spoken by familiar voices. I know it's crucial for understanding all this messy operation between the living, the dead, the undead wanting to be fully dead, the unborn wanting to be born, and the forever young wishing for the transitory warmth of aging flesh.

In the meantime, I keep rolling in the waves of this watery air, holding a leather-bound diary above my head to save it. I have a few more questions before

I get to the exit such as who decorated this room so stylishly? And how do you keep the rhododendron alive through the decades, who takes care of them and what's the point of saving rhododendron when you can't save one little girl? And bunicu Tudor, what's better: dying in a flood or a fire, being burned alive or frozen to death, the nazis, the Stalinists, Auschwitz, Siberia, what? And why should these be the only choices? It seems that Grandma Victoria is answering something audible to me and she says starving to death is also pretty bad, as if continuing that line of questioning of having to choose between the world's worst evils. She wears Queen Maria's wedding dress and drinks beet borscht from a bowl. To dream about a wedding means death, I know that for sure, it's not a good sign to dream about anyone dressed in a wedding dress. But dreaming about a funeral on the other hand is a good sign, everything upside down. Leave it to the Romanians and their famous inventiveness, making the first airplanes and jet planes, to turn the world on its head and put the earth in the sky and make water out of the air.

I think I've reached the exit from the tunnel. It feels like I've been walking for years. Maybe it's dawn outside and maybe I'll find my cell phone. Bye bye everybody here in the suspended gardens of northern Moldavia, playing bridge and planning hiding places for two girls: one Jewish one something else, and dancing the tango. I wish I had met you all, I wish I had known you all. To know is to love. And to know is also sometimes to hate I add to myself at the end of my subterranean journey, some kind of modern Julles Vernes trip to the center of the earth and of Romanian history. It breaks my heart to leave everybody in this stylishly decorated room, but I must leave and find my other blood family waiting for me out there in America and eating bad fruit. I stretch across the Atlantic from one continent to another like an endless formidable beluga whale, my head on one shore, my tail on another shore, and the middle torn between the two shores and washed by the waves.

Dawn slices the eastern sky with delicate streaks of reds. The fragrances of linden, ripe fruit, and roses from a white rose bush nearby sway me in the early morning like a delicious cradle. It turns out I have slept on this soft piece of earth covered in leaves and petals at the other end of the back yard, at the other end of the orchard, next to an open crater like construction site where they are about to pour the foundation for a new house, at the end of an underground tunnel. I wasn't planning for this night of camping in the open, maybe it's the strong air out here, the spell of the sanziene night that laid an overpowering sleepiness over me, like the less resourceful princes in the fairy tale who fell asleep and were tricked by the evil dragon who took away all their prize golden apples. Or maybe I'm just permanently jet lagged, and reality isn't what it used to be.

Manole and Lulu are walking towards me cheerfully in the dawn light. "Lulu found your cell phone out there in the bushes. You should have said that you needed a place to stay for the night." "I have a place to stay for the night, I'm at the bed and breakfast right at the end of the street," I say puzzled. "We could have given you both bed and breakfast for a cheaper price," Manole brags and starts laughing showing his rosy gums. "Thank you Manole, maybe tomorrow I'll take you up on your invitation," I say weekly. "For now, I just need to go to my room and shower, rest, and think things over." I put my cell phone, my father's diary, and the postcard from 1938 back in my purse and start walking through the back alley, towards the main road, past clucking chickens just waking up, a proud rooster calling out the new day, the Mercedes silver van, the broken Dacia car, vegetable gardens and linden trees, lots of linden trees. Amidst them is a plum tree like the ones in Manole's orchard, a stray plum tree amidst all the linden ones, maybe the plum trees are self-pollinating and reaching out towards the surrounding hills. Maybe the orchards are coming back.

"The Day and Night of Sanziene"
June 1941, Florin's Diary

Terrible things can happen on a sunny day. Historical catastrophes, the loss of a beloved person, a gory action or a display of evil can all occur amidst the most heavenly of landscapes and atmospheric conditions. The blue sky has no bearing on human actions or cruel strikes of fate. The day of June 22nd in 1941 offered such an example of radical contradiction between the beauty of nature and the pain that our country, our town, and our family suffered. Romania had long lost its position of neutrality that had accounted for our temporary sense of safety and was now deep into the war on the side of Germany providing Nazi troops with more weapons and soldiers than any of its other allies. Our town became a shameful site of persecutions and cruelty as our Jewish neighbors were rounded up and stuck in a camp called The Green House where they were trapped like animals, beaten, and humiliated in exchange for their fortunes and goods. They were called the bad names of Jidan even by many of those whom we had thought to be good-hearted people and who now said things such as: serves them right, they are getting what they deserve, they are greedy dishonest people who are destroying our country and they crucified our lord Jesus Christ, and they are bringing us communism and the Russians.

Nazi soldiers marched up and down our streets day and night like they owned the town and the whole country, filling the air with acid German consonants and loud methodical marching. Our school was used for secret meetings of Iron Guard members and some of our teachers seemed to turn into entirely different beings. They became harsh and cruel and preached to us about the merits of Hitler and his politics instead of teaching us algebra, formation of glaciers, or literary devices used in romantic poetry. My mother started keeping Lila and me home from school more often, until we stopped going altogether, which was an unexpected and delicious gift for both of us. Nobody in our family ever went into town for any purpose anymore and only my mother and Mitzi ventured once a week to the market to buy our essential food supplies.

Zoe and Carolina who had been living with us for more than a year had become part of our family, though my parents now forbade them to ever leave the house or go outside through the front door. They were only allowed to go through the back door and play with us in our backyard and orchards. The baby Gino Farinelli was walking already and filled our house with little words in an unrecognizable language, possibly a combination of Romanian and Italian and periodically broke a precious crystal vase or porcelain object. My mother who used to be so protective of her beautiful collections of Bohemian crystal and Venetian porcelain ornaments didn't seem to care much about Gino's destructive pranks and dismissed them by saying "these are just things, objects, our lives don't depend on them." Gino the Italian soldier who had been "a real man" and married Mitzi as my father had ordered him to do, now lived with us in the cellar of our house and he never left the house anymore either, to Mitzi's great delight.

Earlier that month of June, Lila and I woke up one morning to a sinister silence whose source we couldn't discover yet. When we came down for our morning meal, we realized the silence was due to the absence of the girls. "Where are Zoe and Carolina, mama?" we asked almost in one breath. My father answered unphased with an almost exaggerated degree of confidence: "Their parents returned from their vacation and picked them up early this morning. They asked us to say good-bye to you and Lila, they didn't want to wake you." Something shifted and trembled in the room. The way the light came in through our windows seemed crooked. The silence weighed like a heavy cloud and the room darkened. Lila and I looked at each other and a strange current of understanding passed between us. Neither of us believed a word of what we were told, and we knew immediately that we were not going to see Zoe and Carolina again. The secrecy was palpable and smelled of raw danger that brings with it blood and suffering.

Despite the glaring lie about the reason for Zoe and Carolina's disappearance, both Lila and I felt like they were not fully gone, not far away from where we were. They were both absent and present. Our mother changed the subject with an abruptness that didn't resemble her and asked us to help her with the household chores that day, there was a lot to do, and Mitzi wasn't feeling too well. Even though Mitzi the servant seemed perfectly fine and was singing one of her shrill songs to Gino in the kitchen, we went along with the pretense and told our mother, yes of course mama, just tell us what to do. In the girls' absence my universe shrunk and darkened. I felt bereft with a gaping hole in my heart. It hurt and it bled but I knew I had to just learn to live with it like someone learns to live with a lost limb. A darkness like the wing of a huge bird covering the sun fell over all of us and we just accepted it as our new reality.

Our house had become a shelter of sorts for people in hiding, for people in danger of something that seemed unspeakably bad. Unknown people came and left or sometimes stayed for a week at a time after which they disappeared without a trace. My parents whispered to each other almost all the time. One evening while we were having dinner and a young couple I had never seen before in my life greedily ate my mother's stuffed cabbage rolls and Mitzi's mamaliga, two German soldiers and two Romanian men wearing green shirts of the Iron Guard knocked loudly at our door. Before Lila and I could count to five, the unknown couple, and Gino the soldier disappeared to the cellar. Mitzi went to answer the door holding the plumpish dark-haired Gino in her arms. The sound of the metallic heavy boots on our floors turned my stomach in fear. Our parents had never told us how to act, what to say or not to say in those times, they just trusted our instincts that we would do the right thing and act accordingly, which to Lila and me meant not to say anything about any of our guests and extended "family" living with us at that time, occupying every bit of above the ground or underground space in the house.

When we heard the German boots, both Lila and I took the empty plates of the secret guests and placed them under ours. Our math classes hadn't been lost on us even if we had stopped going to school. We understood immediately that if several people who had been eating at our table were now supposed to be inexistent, so should their used dishes be. In a few seconds my father put an Italian aria on the Victrola and by the time the two soldiers marched into our dining room we offered the serene scene of a Romanian Christian family happily enjoying their intimate supper. I also noticed that all while starting the victrola, with the other hand, my father moved the icon of Mary and Jesus he had as a gift from the Greek patriarch in Mount Athos on the highest shelf of the bookcase. Lila stuffed her face with the leftovers from our secret guests' plates and held Mitzi the doll close to her chest to calm her anxiety.

They came in with controlled fury because everything the German soldiers did was orderly and controlled no matter how awful. One of them was fat with red pimples on his face, the other one was tall and skinny with a mustache like the one we had seen in Hitler's photographs. At the sight of them Lila burst unexpectedly into laughter and whispered to me that they looked like Stanley and Laurel in German uniforms. Sometimes we used to see films of Stanley and Laurel with our mother in the local cinema, but that seemed like a lifetime ago. We called Stanley and Laurel by the Romanian names of Stan si Bran. I couldn't help laughing at Lila's comment. My mother started laughing too, which shocked me but then I understood she was doing it on purpose to show we were just a happy family caught in the middle of recounting a funny story or one of the kids had made a funny face or performed a comical trick.

There were unspoken currents of understanding lately between our parents, Lila and me and our actions seemed to be guided by a secret flow of knowledge and intuition about the world and the new situations it confronted us with. Even Mitzi the maid understood her part and played with Gino cooing to him in unbearably loud trills then laughing to herself to distract the soldiers and contribute to the overall symphony of clashing sounds. My father smiled, stood up and went to welcome the soldiers with the most natural demeanor in the world. I was shocked to hear him talk German to them, I had no idea he also spoke German. My father never ceased to awe me with his knowledge, wisdom and savvy about the world and any kind of situation that life presented us with. They spoke for a while in German and my father even laughed. Then one of the soldiers laughed. Lila and I were now pretending to play with the doll Mitzi and in the meantime, Gino started crying and Mitzi the maid started singing to him the "nani nani puiul mami" lullaby. The Italian tenor sang the heartbreaking Celeste Aida song on the Victrola and even our dog Girl appeared from the veranda where she always spent her evenings and started barking out of the blue as if sensing the evil floating in the room like an invisible rapacious bird.

The soldiers said Auf Wiedersehen, mein Herr while the Romanian men in the green uniforms turned towards my father and told him in a scratchy whisper that if he was thinking of hiding any of the "jidani" they saw frequenting our house, they would find them even in "gaura de șarpe," in "a snake's hole," and kill the "miscreants" together with our family. I immediately thought of Zoe and Carolina and about how they had just disappeared from our house, like they had never been there. Their disappearance coincided with the increased raids of the Nazi soldiers on the population. All along though I had a feeling they were not far away, and I knew our parents were hiding every bit of information from us. I became terrified that the soldiers barging into our house at that hour of the evening would storm the house and turn over every corner of every space and would find and kill them or take them away to an undisclosed location and then kill them. I prayed that my father would prevent the group of brutish soldiers and local militia men from taking one step inside our house.

My father remained calm and unmoved and told the men at the door we had no snakes' holes, but we had snakes hiding in our walls, good snakes, and if they were going to throw any more threats at him, he would release the snakes on them. He started getting up as if ready to do just that, and from the corner of my eye I saw one of the two Romanian men recoil towards the door by a few steps as if scared. "They are poisonous snakes, too," my father added, which left me aghast. "As poisonous as you, only the wall snakes are good to us, but not to enemies of the people like yourselves." One of the German soldiers started getting irritated by all the Romanian chatter and yelled: "Was ist das? Hör sofort auf und geh!" "What is this? Stop it and go!" The SS soldier pulled the Romanian one away and out the door almost by force. The German and Romanian soldiers left the house with a click of their boots and the Heil Hitler salutation. After they were gone and we could no longer hear the offensive sound of their boots on the pavement, my father went back to his chair at the head of the table, made the music of the Victrola stop and sighed, exhausted. My mother touched his hand in tenderness and Mitzi started crying louder then Gino. Lila and I held hands for a while without saying a word and we all sat around the table in the sounds of Mitzi and Gino's sobs for what seemed like a long time. It felt like they were crying for all of us.

June 22 was the summer solstice and the first day of the sanziene celebration. We woke up, the house was fragrant from the fresh air coming through the open windows. That night we were going to have a sanziene celebration in our orchards with music and dancing and special summer cakes that mama and Mitzi would bake. "War or no war, we have to go on living," my mother always said. Despite the summer breeze and the blindingly blue sky, I felt a heavy emptiness that morning, as if emptiness had a weight. Something broke in the course of the day, something felt like a torn page in a book. The accumulation of boots marching down our street, the explosions, the airplanes circling morbidly above the town. It felt like something in the world suddenly cracked with a deafening sound.

The pace in our house became demented and out of control. Lila and I were told to sit in our room and not to move. Sounds of furniture being moved abruptly across the floor in my parents' room scared Lila and me as we sat unmoved on my bed holding hands. I wanted to see Zoe and Carolina so badly, the worry about their lives choked me like a stronghold. Something irreparable was happening right then right there under our roof and we were told to sit quietly in our room. More airplanes roared above our heads, then we heard loud bangs at our front door almost like someone was trying to break in. There was so much noise for a while that my brain stopped working. Noise became time and time roared mercilessly. German soldiers marching everywhere, Iron Guard men bursting into people's houses, Russian planes dropping bombs, shots in our house and Gino the Italian deserter soldier was dead on the floor in the middle of our living room. Mitzi was howling and tearing her hair out while Gino the baby also howled and pulled at her skirt. I don't know how I ended up in the living room staring at Gino dead on the floor.

I wondered again where Zoe and Carolina had gone and where they could be hiding in that moment. I had not believed it for a second that their parents suddenly showed up from their so-called vacation and picked them up and I felt the danger hovering over their lives like a live creature. I had a bitter taste, a separate howling in my own head that didn't come from any of the outside noises but from deep inside me. When my brain became quiet and I could hear the outside noises again, I knew that Zoe and Carolina were gone forever. In the silence of my head a deep irreparable gulf of pain and longing opened. I realized German soldiers were rummaging through our house and yelling their offensive chunky words. One of them was the fat one with the pimples on his face that had come into our house a week earlier when we were having dinner. I remembered Lila bursting into her irrepressible contagious laughter when she saw him then. "Where is Lila mama, where is Lila?" I heard myself asking over and over again. My mother was leaning over Gino the soldier and checking his pulse, his jugular for signs of life repeatedly, trying to find a tiny sign of life in what looked like a lifeless body. I thought Mitzi was going to explode from her howling and grief. My father wasn't anywhere either and another plane roared over the house. My mother asked me to help her move Gino's body in the back hallway outside of the living room. Did we have a hallway, a living room, a house? I didn't understand words very well. She gently pushed

Mitzi and Gino out of the way, how could she have the power to still be gentle? She sat them in the armchair like they were crying dolls.

My father appeared from the back of the house like nothing was happening and the fat German soldier was following him. They moved as if through a fog, a rain, slowly and ominously. For a second, I thought I saw the soldier point his machine gun at my father's back but then I saw my father talk to him, maybe even smile. The words were inaudible, but I was sure they were in German because of how my father's lips moved in an abrupt way, almost a grimace on his beautiful face. Other soldiers moved past us in the opposite direction towards the back of the house. The back of the house seemed to be the Mecca for the German soldiers and the Iron Guard men that day, they were looking for something feverishly but were not able to find it.

There was an explosion like the sun had burst and lit up our house through all the windows. Lila finally appeared from our room holding Mitzi, her black eyes wide open. My mother moved through the sun explosion to get Lila, and she held her at one side and me at her other side for what seemed like a very long time. It felt like years of burning in the June sun and in the sound of planes, German or Russian. I didn't care a bit about the nationality of the planes. Suddenly there were no more soldiers, and my father was listening to the radio, holding his ear very close like he couldn't hear, although it was very loud. The radio was saying that the Romanian and German troupes had invaded Russia together, general Antonescu this and General Antonescu that. Romania was on the side of Germany, and then again Molotov-Ribbentrop this and that, the horrible sounding words. The sun explosion and the plane sounds had ceased and the sound of the words flying out of the radio box were now the only roaring sounds filling the air in our house. Various cataclysms swept through our house one after the other. Now it was the bad word cataclysm. Everything else was mute: Mitzi and Gino's cries which you could see but not hear like in the mute movies, Lila's cries right next to me, the barking of Girl, a long silent cry covered by a torrent of bad, bad deafening words. It was the sanziene day of June 22nd, the summer solstice, the longest day of the year, when the sun sets very late, maybe never. An endless day with blazing, unbearable burning light.

The silence that followed was a suffocating thick paste. There were things we had to do: prepare Gino's body for the funeral, feed baby Gino, calm down Mitzi whose looks were mad and astray, prepare food for all of us, repair the damages made by the German soldiers. If we were allies, why had they been so brutish? I wanted to ask my father, I wanted to ask my mother. I wanted to go outside and ask the neighbors, for instance, Mr. Gogu. Then a white shadow passed on the wall across from the window, a fleeting shape, a white bird in its shadow form. I thought I heard a bird calling outside, maybe a cuckoo bird, a black bird or a crow greedy for corpses, or just another plane. My hearing seemed out of sorts, and I still heard sounds from an hour earlier overlapped with the present sounds. The roaring of the planes finally stopped, the crying finally stopped, the pasty silence was flowing and leaking onto everything like poisoned milk, and the sun kept shining shamelessly. Lila went to a corner of the room and started telling her doll Mitzi everything that had happened that day in loud whispers that reached me to the other end of our living room. I sat in the pink chair that was Zoe and Carolina's favorite chair, where they often sat holding hands quietly with a smile, watching all the commotion in the house with curiosity. I now listened to Lila's rendition of the day's events, like a miniature version of a radio broadcast for children. Yet it sounded more real and more truthful than the shouted radio voices interrupted by roaring static. Everything was roaring that day, even silence.

"Mama where are Zoe and Carolina? Where have they been all this time? Are they safe?" I heard myself ask through the roaring silence. She didn't even look at me. "Florin, come help me clean up this mess," my mother answered, referring to a mound of broken glass and porcelain, shiny, colored crumbles touched by the irrepressible sun and sparkling with ridiculous self-assurance. I knew that from then on brokenness would be our wholeness, light would be our darkness on top of the darkness of the night, and silence would be our deafening clamor on top of the sounds of planes and guns and shouted voices amid radio static. But despite everything that had happened we had to eat, and mother prepared our dinner by herself in the kitchen without Mitzi who by evening was sitting in a state of stupor in the armchair next to my father, rocking herself and baby Gino into oblivion. My father was smoking a cigar which I had never seen him do in the past but that would be the last thing to surprise me that day. He looked distinguished and powerful smoking the cigar. When I looked at him closer though, his face was wrecked with sadness like he was dying of a terrible illness. It scared me. I moved farther away in the room not wanting to disturb him.

I went to a corner of the room, Mitzi was in another corner, we were corner children in times of war. I understood also that Mitzi sat next to my father because he was the only man in the house now and he had made Gino marry her. She considered him her godfather, a protective family member. We ate eggplant stew with cauliflower and roasted partridge. I remember thinking that my mother's eggplant stew was not as good as Mitzi's and that the dead didn't care about any of that. But then I thought what if they did. What if they craved everything we did and ate and felt and spent all of eternity in an agony of cravings? That notion spooked me even more as I kept thinking about Gino's body lying on a makeshift funeral table in the hallway and craving our food and the warmth of the sun and the fragrance of the linden flowers in the air. Mitzi didn't eat, she just stared out the window, my mother fed Gino, while Lila ate both hers and Mitzi's portions. I ate everything greedily like never before, thinking that if I died in this war, I didn't want to spend all of my death time pining for my mother's cooking. After supper, we all rushed into the cellar for the curfew.

A group of young Gypsy women with crowns of yellow flowers, sanziene, stopped at our door to sing and ask for money. Didn't they know a full war was blasting across the country, that Germany had invaded Russia as well as our very own country? A Gypsy man played a sad song on the accordion right outside our house. There was no stopping the Gypsies from singing and playing. I didn't understand why we had to hide in the cellar now that we survived the formidable explosions and bombings and German soldiers bursting into our house and killing Gino, and since the roars and the explosions had ended. "Because there might be more bombs and explosions, that's why," was my mother's firm answer.

Even though it was nighttime, the light had a hard time melting away into darkness. The sun had forgotten to set. In the cottony silence of the basement, I felt like the house itself was a live being, a dragon bird with scaly wings that spread across the western skies to cover up the sun that didn't want to set. The wall snake was ticking like mad, a rebellious ticking: he wanted to break through the wall and be free. Then the snake went completely quiet. In the cellar, Lila and Mitzi the maid and Mitzi the doll and baby Gino all sat in a corner on the floor almost like one body. They were sitting right next to the grand piano, which had been there forever, and I had no idea why because nobody ever played the piano. I sat with Mama and Tata on the low bench covered in rugs and Turkish cushions and wondered also why we kept Turkish cushions in the cellar. It was warm, summer warm in the cellar and it should have been completely dark but light stubbornly lingered and spread thin golden threads, spider webs across the cellar floors through the tiny windows that were close to the ground. We heard the Gypsies talk and sing and play their sad songs. They were almost next to the cellar windows on the back side of the house.

"Are they Hebraic? "What Hebraic? Who?" "You know, the Gemini girls. They been living in this house for a good year now." "One is Jewish, the other is something else." "What something else?" "You know, the creature with the veil on the head." The Gypsies laughed in loud peals, they didn't care about the war planes and the bombs. I knew they spoke about Zoe and Carolina, and I wanted to hear more. I left Mama and Tata and moved to the window, but the Gypsies also moved away near the orchard, and I could no longer hear their conversation. After a little while I didn't see Tata anymore and panicked. Mama said simply "don't worry, he went to get something, he'll be right back." That sounded like the strangest thing I had ever heard: that my father suddenly left the secure shelter to go "get something" in the middle of the air raids. What could have been so important that it was worth risking his life for? I went back to stare out of the tiny cellar window at the strange antics of the naked Sanziene Gypsies. Finally, night had mercifully seeped into the air and the Gypsy women were climbing trees and eating the fruit.

A wicked moon rose. The air felt scratchy like it had thorns, yet it was also painfully beautiful outside. I remembered Gino's body and wondered if it was still lying in the back hallway, it was bad to leave the dead lying around like that. I wanted to go outside and talk to the Gypsies, see if they knew anything about Zoe and Carolina. Mitzi suddenly said: "the Gypsies are pillaging the orchards," and it was the first I heard her talk since Gino's death. Her voice had changed like she had aged in three hours, it was low with no modulations of feeling. "They are eating some fruit Mitzi, they are hungry, that's all, let them be," my mother said. I looked outside and the Gypsies were now dancing naked in the moonlight and the accordion music was wailing an uninterrupted melody of endless sorrow and lust. Everything got mixed up during wartime: night and day and food and the cravings of the living and the dead, the presence of the absent, fruit and live bodies, heartbreak music, bottomless sorrow and even shameless laughter and naked bodies dancing in the moonlight. The naked sanziene dancing in the moonlight amid the orchard trees with the accordion music and ripe cherries hanging from their earlobes turned that day into a terrifying and beguiling carnival.

    I was eleven years old and could not think of what my life was going to be like from that day on. War entered our lives and our house with a blast and there was nowhere to hide from it. The cellar felt damp and full of shadows. A warm wind came and went. A live creature wanted to save us but was too tired and gave up, and a palpable sigh of unbearable sorrow covered it up. The house felt again like a dragon bird wanted to entrap us all under its enormous scaly wing. I wanted to be the Gypsies climbing the trees at night with no fear of anything, the snake in the wall, the white shadow of a bird, a fearless accordionist. I turned away from the window and was surprised to see my father was back, as if he had never left, and he was standing behind the grand piano as if hiding. I heard my mother cry in the dark, then Mitzi, then Lila, one after the other, a canon of cries, sobbing in rounds in the dark cellar, and then an explosion next door lit up the cellar windows with blinding light. In the eye of the explosion the orchards were in bloom, the violins were playing a waltz, Zoe and Carolina were dancing in white dresses, mother was holding the box with the heart of Queen Maria, and Mitzi held a plump Italian baby. The photographer said "one, two, three, smile everybody," and everybody smiled and melted into a sepia photograph.

"Summer Hell"
Northern Moldavia, Southern Moldavia, June 26-July 6th, 1941. From Florin's Diary

The night of June 26th we heard a loud knock on our front door. Three more knocks followed quickly, a miniature artillery. An owl shrieked as if knowledgeable of an ominous event. The moon shone violently in the window, bright red like an explosion. Lila woke up first. She came over to my bed to wake me up with a strong nudge. "I think Hitler and Stalin came to kill us, I told you it would happen," she said as if continuing our conversation of some time ago. We had buried Gino the day before and were all tired from the preparations and the grief, from preparing the dead body, placing him in a makeshift coffin that Mr. Gogu helped us make from some of our stove wood, from carrying the coffin with the body in it to our back yard, digging the grave, and putting Gino to rest inside it. My father and I did most of the cutting, hammering, and carrying. My mother prepared the foods, while Mitzi cried and mourned. Lila recounted everything to Mitzi the doll in detail. We all contributed and collaborated in Gino's last rites, it was a joint family project like building a tree house or going on a long journey. My mother said it didn't matter it was war, and we were under bombardments, we had to bury the dead properly. And so we did, and buried Gino in the back of the orchard, under one of the cherry trees. Father marked the tree with a cross, so we remembered where his grave was and officiated a small service, like a priest in a hurry, before the bombs started again. We were all many things in times of war, from midwife to grave diggers. My mother had delivered Mitzi's baby, and we all buried his father now.

Lila and I went to bed earlier than usual, particularly given the bombing curfew, so the knocks ripped us cruelly from a deep sleep. We heard our parents go downstairs with rushed steps. Lila whispered to me: "Let's go listen," and for the first time I did not hesitate at Lila's suggestions but tiptoed to the top of the stairs. Though it was the middle of the night, there was a strange light coming through the windows and the sky was lit up. Tiptoeing on the landing behind Lila, I noticed that the big pot with our Ficus tree was cracked, and the plant was almost collapsing to one side. The tree was one of our mother's great sources of pride in the house, that she had managed to keep and grow from when it was a tiny plant in a tiny pot that her mother had gotten from her father the day of her birth. During her lifetime, it had grown taller than my mother. Right underneath the window there was a tiny shiny object that drew my attention. I wanted to follow Lila, but I was dying to see what the tiny glittery thing was. I made one quick step toward it and almost fell from the surprise. The shiny object was none other than one of Zoe's earrings, a tiny emerald stone set on a thin golden ring. Or maybe it was Carolina's, I couldn't remember exactly. I knew it belonged to one of them, those little details of dress and accessory distinguished the girls from one another, but sometimes I mixed them up. Only their mother Frida never did. Was it Zoe that wore the emerald earrings and Carolina the sapphire ones, or the other way around? My thought clung to that little obsession, and I quietly sat down under the window holding the emerald earring in my palm like a priceless treasure. Lila was making desperate signs to me to follow her on the landing not wanting to risk making more noise. I sat there and told her in pantomime that I was going to remain unmoved and try to listen from where I was. My father answered the door, and I knew it was him who did so because he always opened the front door with a slow deliberate gesture which made the hinges squeak twice while my mother opened it at once with no hesitation or deliberation which made the door squeak only once. I heard the methodical ticking of the snake in the wall and this time it felt reassuring.

As soon as he opened the door my father asked in rushed worried whispers, which didn't sound like him: "What are you doing here, are you crazy to come back in these times?" The person at the door was a man and he answered that he had to come, he had heard what was happening and had to save the rest of his family, and my father was the only one who could help. And not to worry, Frida was fine, and still in hiding, he came alone. By the rhythm and intonation of the stranger's voice at the door in the dead of night and because of the mention of Frida I thought I recognized Gabi, Zoe and Carolina's father. I crawled to where Lila stood against the wall listening and holding Mitzi in her arms as always. The stranger that could have been Gabi was asking our father to go with him to Iasi, the big city a couple of hours away. The words killings, massacre, death trains,

Legionnaires kept coming up again and again and then a woman by the name of Sofia Kunovicis and her two sons were mentioned twice with great insistence. Apparently, this woman and her son were relatives of the man at the door who must have been Gabi, and were hiding in the basement of the millinery shop in Iasi after her husband and other son had been shot in front of the store by Iron Guard militias right after the latest bombardments by the Russians. "They are killing them in the street or loading them on trains, nobody knows where they are taking them. They say we are signaling to the Soviet airplanes where and when to throw the bombs," I heard. From the look on Lila's face, I knew she had heard the same thing.

Then I heard the man ask my father to "see them even if just for a second, can I please?" I knew he meant Zoe and Carolina. My curiosity became intense, and I crawled to where Lila was so I could hear better. My father didn't answer right away, and it seemed I heard not just silence but my father's silence, as if silence was also words. It felt glacial and scary. Then he said: "they are well hidden, they are sleeping, it's dangerous, don't worry, you'd better go." I had never heard my father talk in such rushed short sentences falling quickly one after the other like heavy pebbles in a river of silence and darkness. Then he repeated: "They are well, don't worry, please we'd better go right away before they catch you." I didn't understand why my father first said: "You'd better go" and then "we'd better go," as if "you and "we" were one and the same thing. Words were all mixed up and language seemed a messy puzzle with non-matching pieces, a hopeless mess. Tears fell along Lila's cheeks that fell onto Mitzi's cheeks, and she was wiping the doll's face but not her own, as if it was the doll who was crying, not her. I took Lila in my arms, and we remained unmoved at the top of the staircase, barely breathing, listening to my father getting ready to go.

My mother came out of her room and told him to be careful, as if he would ever be reckless! Words held no meaning any longer, they were empty shells, the wind of the night howled through them, and everything sounded hollow and dangerous. Then I heard my father hesitate for a few moments, as if he had second thoughts. He whispered to our mother to take good care of us in case of something happening, just in case, you know. Again, empty words, as if my mother would stop caring for us and leave us in the street if something happened to our father. My mind started racing with a will of its own, a wild horse in an empty field, with malice and irony even, a wild malicious horse crossing the hollowness of that quiet danger and whisper filled night in a savage flight. Then my mother answered that nothing was going to happen to him, and that he had to go and do what he had to do, help, any bit mattered, if he could save one life … She left her words hanging in the air.

My mother's words had more weight than my father's I realized. She never spoke like other women or wives, who would have said, things like "why are you going and leaving your family, it's too dangerous," on and on, useless questions. But then the last words Lila and I heard were those of our mother telling Gabi to not worry, the girls were fine, one day they will all be together again, "when all this is over." And then she sounded hollow too. I knew she lied; I knew the girls were not fine. I knew my parents were hiding that fact from Gabi. I knew everybody in the room that night knew the truth, including Gabi. I listened to the shuffling of partings and goodbyes, the preparations for my father's journey to the midst of a massive massacre operation by the German Nazis and the Romanian Iron Guard. Truth was a heavy glowing bomb that couldn't be touched in the contained horror of that night. Only weightless feathery lies could be exchanged among the three people whispering on the ground floor of our house that night. The door was closed quietly as if the people on both sides of it were making efforts to keep it from squeaking, crying, screeching in pain. There was pain in everything, even in the inanimate objects that seemed to sigh under the weight of desperate farewells.

The following morning, I woke up before Lila and had a moment of confusion as if I had woken up in a different time before the war when the days resembled one another and on a late summer day the fruit hung heavy in our orchard. My first thought was that the apricots were probably ripe by now, the cherries almost too ripe and the plums not yet ready to eat. Lila was sleeping peacefully in the bed next to me clutching Mitzi to her chest like a baby. Then the previous months and days exploded in my conscience with the sound of bombings, shots, airplane whizzing above us, the sight of blood and a dead body in our living room, the German soldiers marching up and down our street and somehow even worse than all of that, the sight of Romanian men, some of whom had even been neighbors, dressed in green shirts and walking side by side to the SS soldiers, hunting down people and barging into the houses of our town. Disparate scenes sliced through my brains in great disorder, sometimes overlapping each other: explosions lighting up the sky, us hiding in the basement and looking at naked Gypsy women dancing in the moonlight, my mother slapping my face when I am lying half frozen on the blue ice, a German and a Romanian soldier hovering above our dinner table and interrogating our father, Gino lying in his coffin in a navy blue suit I had never seen him in and that could have been my father's, his last gift to the Italian deserter who married our maid and played Italian sentimental songs on our father's Victrola. Zoe and Carolina sitting together in the pink armchair looking sad and puzzled, staring into thin air! I realized I was holding something in my palm and when I looked it was a tiny earring with an emerald stone.

The girls' absence was the worst image, a palpable visible hollowness, gray and endless, worse than the explosions and the dead body of Gino lying in our front room. I remembered the previous night, the whispered conversation at the door. I put the earring in a small wooden box that my father had given me to keep change from my savings, and where I sometimes put stolen cigarettes instead. I rushed downstairs and saw my mother standing in the kitchen holding baby Gino and looking out at the expanse of our orchard in the back as if everything was in its right place and nothing was wrong. She felt my presence and didn't turn around but just said: "The apricots should be ripe by now, it's their time, the cherries must be over. You kids should go outside this morning and see about the fruit, pick some. I'll make a pie." She spoke all that without looking at me, monotonously and her voice sounded hollow like the previous night when she was telling Gabi that the girls were fine, not to worry. I wanted so badly to hear the truth from her mouth, to hear her tell me where Father had gone, where Zoe and Carolina had disappeared overnight, and who was the man who had visited us the night before, was it really Gabi? Nothing came out of her mouth except for talk about fruit and pies and Gino who was soon going to turn one soon. She talked as if there was no war, as if there were no German soldiers patrolling all over our town, as if our father was just going to appear any minute from his study. As if we were still suspended in the June day of 1939 when we all danced in the park to the music of the orchestra in the pavilion and took the sepia photograph. I noticed also she braided her hair in the same style as that day, too, the style of Queen Mary with her heart placed in a box somewhere by the Black Sea in a Bulgarian town that presumably had once belonged to our country.

I understood my mother couldn't do otherwise but wrap herself in the slippery substance of deceit to protect us and to help her keep going through the hours of the day without collapsing from worry and grief. The same undercurrents of understanding that crossed us at the dinner table during the visit of the SS soldier and his Iron Guard buddy, tied us together now. Lila and I never asked my mother where Father had gone and even Mitzi kept quiet and allowed my mother to care for baby Gino throughout the day while she went around the house tidying and cleaning up and preparing our food. Overnight Mitzi became a mature woman wizened by grief and the absence of the loved one. She was singing an Italian song she had learned from Gino, "il tango della gelosia." Her voice cracked occasionally, but she kept going over the cracks, just like we all had to go on covering up the cracks and craters in our lives and hearts.

My father arrived three days later, on June 29th, accompanied by a woman dressed all in black and a boy a little bit older than myself. My father looked almost disfigured by something incomprehensible, as if he had come out at the other end of a tunnel of fire. His usually calm and peaceful expression was fierce, and his face carved by new wrinkles. His hair was whiter than usual, his skin burned by the sun, and I noticed traces of blood on his shirt. My mother touched his face with a feathery caress like I had never seen before, both of tenderness and fear of not hurting him. He was an open walking wound. My father whispered something to her, then went to his room. Everything seemed rushed like they were preparing for another journey. My mother attended to the woman whose face was slashed both by a deep cut and frozen in a grimace of grief. The son was very skinny and had dark reddish hair and green eyes. He had a particular beauty and sadness I hadn't seen in a child my age. A cuckoo bird sang a lonely call, and an airplane roared above us. Lila appeared downstairs in her nightgown holding Mitzi and giving her a rushed explanation of the scene in front of her. Lila's presence seemed to bring a slight solace to the woman's slashed face.

My mother attended to her wounds with alcohol and band-aids, and I asked the boy if he wanted any apricots from the garden. Neither of us had been prepared for any of what was happening. I felt clumsy and laden, and my words sounded fake. Only gestures helped, a touch, a light caress. Since the boy didn't seem to hear or move, I patted him gently on the back. He looked at me with puzzled eyes. I led him outside through the back of the house to the orchard and Lila followed us whispering to Mitzi that we were caring for the wounded people that my father had brought home from Iasi. I wondered why Lila had said wounded people, but then I noticed the boy was limping slightly, his shoes were torn and one of his toes poked through the broken shoe and bled. Everybody was wounded in our house at that hour of the morning of June 29th, in the year 1941, a year of human-made cataclysms like the ones my father had talked about earlier in my childhood.

Everything during the days that followed the arrival of the woman in black and her timid son carried the weight of deep secrecy and unbearable grief. And then one day they were both gone, and nobody ever mentioned them ever again. The woman, by the name of Sofia Kunovicis, the one mentioned in the middle of the night by the man who could have been Gabi, stayed mostly in the pink armchair in our front room staring out the window for hours. She wore a stylish pink straw hat even in the house and it was the only colorful thing on her. My mother brought her food throughout the day which she barely touched. Occasionally, she seemed to brighten up whenever Lila appeared unexpectedly in the living room, holding her doll. She was the only person with whom Sofia exchanged more than a handful of words. The boy, by the name of Sebastian, followed me everywhere I went in the house and out in our backyard or the orchard. He did what I did as if he was obligated to, absentmindedly. I didn't want to ask him anything about himself or his life, as I sensed he must have been carrying the burden of terrible events. Once he climbed up to the very top of one of our cherry trees and pretended to be a bird wanting to fly away. I asked him to please come down with no success until my father showed up and talked to him kindly asking him to please come down from the tree. Then he did so quickly and with great agility. It was one of the only times that I saw my father during those days as he seemed to always either be hiding in his study or whispering something to my mother.

Time flowed with incredible slowness, second after a second, gooey and heavy, stuck in a sticky corner with nowhere to move. Three days into the visit of our unexpected guests, my literature schoolteacher, Mister Manole Cojocaru appeared on our doorstep. My father greeted him as if he had been waiting for him for a long time. A large envelope was passed from Manole to my father to Sofia like a precious treasure. My father handed back to Manole a thick envelope which, from the size and shape of it, appeared to be banknotes.

I didn't understand any of what went on. However, through Lila's recounting of the day's events and actions to Mitzi the doll, I thought I caught some glimpses into the situation happening in our house. Lila had a manner of retelling events that was simple and astute with very few descriptions, no commentary of her own, just the main gestures and actions that took place with a few important details which allowed me to decipher some of the reasons behind the actions. Every so often she embellished the stories and exaggerated things in a way that seemed to illuminate the actions instead of obscuring them. And she always heard everything better than me from all the practice of eavesdropping. One evening before going to sleep she went on for a while telling Mitzi the events of the day: "Tata woke up early today and greeted someone new at the door, a man with a big hat who gave him a large envelope with important letters and papers about Hitler and Stalin so they don't kill everybody and especially, so they don't kill Sofia and Sebastian. Tata paid the man at the door with a big envelope that was thick but not long. He called him Manole like the man in the story about the woman who is buried in the walls of the church, only this Manole is a good Manole who helps people. Don't be afraid Mitzi, Hitler and Stalin are not going to take you away and kill you. Tata and mama and Manole are helping the good people. But first Sofia and Sebastian have to be safe. Sebastian is sad all the time because his dad and his brother were killed in the attacks by the iron people who are bad people who like Hitler. I think they are leaving tomorrow very early on a good train, not on the bad train where they put other people like them and send them to die." She recounted all this before bed one night and I had no idea how she was able to find out what had happened to Sofia and Sebastian, about the plan to help them escape, about the actions of the Iron Guard which she called the iron people and even what kind of train they were going to take. I only listened and didn't comment anything in response to her recounting hoping she would go on and I would find out more about what was going on. But she fell asleep right after she finished that part of the story. I had no idea what my literature teacher had to do with all this, except that I remembered Manole was the only one who stayed away from the other teachers' praising Hitler and he never mentioned anything about the war and the German soldiers in our town during our literature class, the way the other teachers did. He only taught the texts in our literature textbook as he was supposed to.

Lila had been right. The following morning, I woke up before dawn and tiptoed to the window. There was shuffling downstairs, and I saw Sofia and Sebastian walking through the back door towards the orchard. There they met a man wearing a hat and a trench coat, despite the fact it was almost July and quite hot. It started to rain softly. My father and mother embraced Sofia and Sebastian quickly then went back into the house. The three people tiptoed through the trees following the path that led to the back alley and into town, in the direction of the train station. Sebastian turned for a quick second and looked up towards our room. A sharp sting of pain went through my heart. I waved at him through the curtain, and they disappeared among the cherry and apricot trees. Girl, who always barked whenever anybody moved through the house at night, didn't make a sound.

It was dawn, and a red sliver of the sun pierced through the clouds. It was drizzling right above our house yet in the distance there were red streaks of light as if two kinds of weather were happening at the same time. I went to bed and fell back asleep wondering where Zoe and Carolina were, maybe they were on the same train as Sofia and Sebastian, maybe they were long gone, if they were still alive. I dreamed of the icy pond through which Carolina had fallen and almost died the previous winter. The ice was no longer blue but red, someone was bleeding over it.

strength in my lungs, and I fear any effort on my part will tip me over, a breeze, a butterfly sitting on me will tip me over, is tipping me over slowly, a long slow gooey flight. And it's not true you see your life pass before your eyes in the last breath you take. All I see is the stupid gray pavement smeared with hopscotch boxes, one two three, skip, yellow box, blue and red boxes, skip, skip, win the game, lose the game, it's all a matter of balance and skipping dexterity.

Once upon a time there was a blonde girl named Corina in a country of bad men, in a confused country with a dumb president. She liked vermilion chewy candy and the smell of petunias and linden flowers and playing with her doll Mitzi because all the dolls in her family have always been called Mitzi. The name was handed down from generations of Mitzi dolls. She once read the story of a French boy flying, holding a red balloon above Paris, only nobody flies in red balloons above Bucharest, people run away from the secret police in Bucharest. She didn't have a long life and didn't live through much of anything at all. And then one day she flew out the window of her poor apartment, because she lived in a tiny apartment like Tom Thumb, like a small creature from a fairy tale. And just when she was about to start flying all over the city or maybe just crash on the pavement, somebody pulled her back inside, grabbed her tipping, out of balance body, and held it in the warm circle of his arms.

"You almost fell out the window, do you know that? What did you think you were doing?" My father is glowing and smells of the outside air, he is worried, yet his energy fills the room and brings me down to earth. Literally down to earth. "Where is your mother, did she come home from work?" He always asks me about mother, it's his way of connecting the three of us, though he knows she's back home, and our apartment is too minuscule to not know when someone is home or not. My body is shaken by the nearness of its destruction, and dizzy from the vertigo, pleasantly dizzy. I could have been the boy with the red balloon. My father is looking for my mother like he lost her, it's what he always does. I grab this summer day when I almost died and eat it like candy, it's my favorite day in a long time, despite the slimy tormentor, the man who follows my father. It's the name we all use for him, and yet there are too many syllables to pronounce for a bad person that I dream of killing.

"Zoe, did you see what Corina was doing? She almost fell out the window." When my parents talk about me in my presence, I feel like there are two of us in the house, me and Corina, the girl they keep mentioning. And when I hear my father call my mother Zoe, it also feels like she's another person, a visitor, I'm always surprised. I wonder who we really are, and how we ended up in this place, in this life. Childhood doesn't agree with me, I've never really liked it, something is always amiss. I wish I were a grown up from the start, or that I had a childhood in a pretty garden instead of this lousy apartment.

"They came looking for you again," is all my mother says. Zoe, my beautiful mother with blonde reddish hair and blue eyes — both my father and I are crazy about her. She is what makes living under a stupid dictator bearable and even beautiful. I'm the girl who almost fell out the window, now I'm like everyone else in my family, someone who almost died and didn't care. When my parents talk to each other I always listen carefully, with fast heartbeats that cut my breath, always hoping for a secret to be broken, for something that is never spoken, to be whispered or finally revealed out loud. An event in the past, long, long ago, in a time that doesn't seem any more real to me than the fairy tales my mother used to read to me and now I can read by myself. I don't know who my mother is, only my father does. Maybe she fell from a magic tree, a different planet, or she emerged from a secret lake in a salt cave like the one we visited in the summer on one of our vacations. It was called the cave of the bride because a bride plunged in the salty water long ago and never came out, but a whole bunch of salty stalagmites and stalactites appeared in her stead.

"I know they did," my father says as if it's not a big deal that they keep coming after him, and I never understand why they refer to one slimy individual as "they." Maybe there were others like him who lurked around our street, and I didn't see them, maybe they multiply under your very eyes. "I saw the rat following me to school this morning and then lurking around the hallway to listen to my lecture, but I went out through the back door of the classroom and then out of the building through another back door and he never saw me." He laughs the way he laughs at many of his own jokes. The way my father tells a story sounds like fun even when it's tragic. It sounds adventurous and enviable, a chase, a ferocious game of hide and seek. When my mother tells the story it sounds frightening, she says my father will be killed one day, run over by a car, a black secret police car running him over at an intersection, there have been other stories. Or locked up in an institution for political detainees, an asylum for lunatics in strait jackets. I don't understand the word detainee, and I'm afraid to ask. My mother says my father talks too much, "he can't keep his mouth shut, and that will be the death of him." She says all that without seeming nervous or agitated, while ironing a dress or a shirt, while watching me eat or while smoking a cigarette. She stares at the wall or out the window as if she sees this big future danger threatening my father in the sky, in a cloud or hanging in the tree in front of our apartment.

My mother doesn't have a story of her own, she floats in the unknown. She has one picture of herself when she was two, dressed in a white dress, on an empty street in front of a house with a fence, like a lost baby child on an empty planet. Her eyes are closed, and she is smiling like she is having a beautiful dream; the picture is torn in half, as if there was another person or child right next to her. In that picture she looks like a miniature version of me. She never showed me the picture herself, but I found it inside a French grammar book that she was teaching from. She blushed when I asked her who was in that picture and said simply just "me" and nothing else. I asked her why it was torn, and she answered the way she often answers when she doesn't want to talk about something. She said: "it's torn, it's a torn picture can't you see that, Corina?" I asked her to please put the photo in a frame and leave it on our common desk, a huge desk with a glass top that my father is very fond of and that occupies half of our living room bedroom space. And surprisingly she listened to me. Whenever I'm confused about my mother, I look at the picture of her with eyes closed and smiling in the baby white dress on the empty street in an old city in a different part of our country and I feel better. I think my mother is from a different realm, she knows something that none of us do, and I should just enjoy every minute of her presence. It is also what I'm doing right now when I hear my parents talk in the conspiratorial way about mysterious things of the past and scary men in the present. I tell myself my mother is here with us by a miracle.

Suddenly the summer is too hot, the apartment too small, the cats fighting outside over scraps of garbage too loud. I want to run away but I don't know where. I want a life like the one of the boy in *The Story of San Michele*, a life with white balconies and red flowers above the sea, with no obscene men who follow you and no food lines. Everybody doesn't live like us, I'm sure of that. The phone rings again and there are hard knocks at the door. All at the same time as a conspiracy. Even when things are bad, it can always get worse and then compared to the worse, the bad becomes the good. The pounding on the door is rhythmic, my mother comes out of our closet sized kitchen flushed from the heat and cooking above the hot plate on an already hot day.

All our family history is about soldiers, secret police, regular police, bad men knocking, barging, marching into the house, apartment, room of one of us, from during the war, after the war and on and on. It's the same scene only the time and the habitation changes. The Nazis barged into the house with the orchards and killed someone during the war, the Russians barged into the house with the orchards, killed someone again and pillaged it during the same war. It's part of our family lineage to be assaulted in our own homes by brutal groups of men. We can't find safety anywhere. Now bad Romanians are trying to barge into our tiny apartment to look for something or someone. Probably my father. It's a different kind of war.

My mother answers the door, and she looks like she doesn't care again. I admire how pretty she is in the checkered dress that swirls from the waist. A man and a woman in dark suits enter our hallway. My father comes in from the bathroom tucking his shirt in his pants. He even looks happy as if he is receiving special guests. When I look at the man, I realize it's the same man that was marching up and down and round and round our building, street, neighborhood in a short-sleeved shirt. The woman wears a brown suit that seems too warm for the summer day, and she is abnormally skinny. She has dark lipstick and a slightly crooked mouth. My father goes directly to the man and I'm afraid he is going to attack him, choke him, or punch him. My mother sits down at the big oval desk and looks at everybody in the room like she is watching a movie. My father says almost yelling: "What do you want?" The man seems scared while the woman makes a grimace that could be a smile or an expression of disgust. The afternoon sun is shining on the glass top of the desk and makes a rainbow puddle on it. What a pity we are stuck in this apartment, in this country, with these ugly people interrogating my father. "We want to know what your relations with Mr. and Mrs. Bogdan Simionov are."

"What the fuck is it any of your business what my relations are with these people?" Asks my father. My mother blushes, she doesn't like obscenities. "It is our business because they were caught trying to cross the border clandestinely and they were carrying one of your books among other illegal objects and documents."

"Why are my books illegal?" asks my father, getting angrier.

I look in our bookcase and see the marble statue of a woman's head, a beautiful sad face carved in white marble, she seems sad at her own beauty. I remember when Simona and Bogdan Simionov brought her over to our apartment together with many other objects and works of art all scattered and crowded in that one room: a standing lamp with an enormous golden lampshade and black fringes at the edges, a dark blue vase about which my father always says "watch out for the cobalt vase, it's very precious," a painting of an old man with a cane crossing a white field covered in snow, which my father says is by a famous Romanian painter, "we are lucky to have such a painting, it's worth a lot of money." Simona and Bogdan were planning to escape the country and go to Africa where they wanted to hunt crocodiles for a living. They left their most valuable things with us for the unlikely time in the future when they would return with a lot of money from the sale of crocodile skins and take back their art objects. "Until then, you keep them, dear friends," Simona said when she and her husband brought everything over to our apartment. I was hoping they would never come back so we could keep all the nice things forever. But it's not going to be like that. Simona and Bogdan will be put in prison and the secret police will take all their nice objects from our apartment. My father yells at the man to "get the fuck out of my house," he is not afraid of anyone. After that it all gets muddled up in bad words, slaps, punches, my mother disappears in the kitchen. "Your book is reactionary," the woman screams with an angry face and a screechy voice like a rabid witch. "Your parents were reactionaries, enemies of the people," the man screams with foam around his mouth. People are turning into wild beasts foaming at the mouth. We live in a filthy zoo.

My father is panting, his face is disfigured by pain and hatred. The man jerks away from my father's punch and knocks over the shiny cobalt vase on the bookcase shelf. I am flying away to another country. I am falling out the window in a rapid glide towards the pavement. I don't die from the fall. Instead, I get up and start playing hopscotch. Then I fly to a rose and poppy flower garden in the Carpathians and start playing with my cousins. It all happens in the millisecond of a catastrophe in blue, of the breaking of the cobalt vase by the secret police who received a punch in the face from my father, and the blue orangey shards that fly around and fall on the floor in a mound of dark blue cobalt. I fly above it all in a red balloon. Everything is an explosion of bright colors. My mother reappears and her face is changed like she has taken a voyage to another country. My father is still panting and sits down in the upholstered mahogany chair by the huge walnut desk, and he looks exhausted. Even the secret policeman and woman look exhausted and slightly ashamed, almost human.

I wonder what their real jobs are and if they are ever going to leave our house. Some long difficult moments slowly pass during which my father stares at the shards of blue cobalt on the floor glinting under the afternoon sun rays and my mother smokes a cigarette and stares out the window like nothing has happened or changed. She is so absent from the scene that I almost expect her to set the table for everybody in the room including the Securitate couple and serve us all a dinner made of burnt cauliflower. Mercifully the frozen moment cracks open, and the two secret police people start walking backwards towards the door. "So long, Professor. I will write in the report that you know nothing about the attempted escape of the Simionovs. But we'll get you one of these days, don't you worry!" My father says nothing, he just sends daggers with his eyes in the direction of the ridiculous couple.

After they leave and close the door behind them, I feel lonely like after a party, as if the visit of the Securitate couple, the fight, the breaking of the priceless cobalt vase left in our care while Simona and Bogdan tried to escape the country for crocodile hunting in Africa, had been a welcome distraction. "I can't believe they were caught," whispers my father. "I wonder what happened with the stuff I gave them. If they really got it from them and they are not just bluffing, we are in trouble." The most important part of my parent's lives happens in the whispers between them, a world of secrets and mysteries that they try to protect me from. Things that happened during the war, after the war, in the times after the period after the war, in the times they keep calling the Stalinist period. There are curtains behind curtains that cover dark secrets of deaths and disappearances, letters, and people whose faces were ripped from photographs, like the photograph of my mother as a baby standing and smiling on a deserted street next to someone I will never know.

There are secrets hidden inside the box underneath our sofa bed, photographs and letters, stories, manuscripts, journals, an old doll with dark braids clothed in Romanian national costume, with one lazy eye that always stays closed. It was Aunt

Lila's doll from the house with the orchards from the time before the war. I ask my father why that doll has to live inside the sofa box. "Why can't I play with it?" "Because it's an heirloom doll, it's Aunt Lila's doll from when she was a child." "Then why doesn't Aunt Lila keep it inside her sofa box?" "Because it just so happened it ended up in our sofa box when we all moved, things got lost and destroyed and mixed up, such devastation, such chaos and destruction." My father could go on and on forever about the catastrophes of his youth. I know it's the famous Mitzi doll that Aunt Lila carried with her everywhere all the time. I have a strange notion that if I held it and played with it for a while, I could find out more secrets and mysteries from the doll herself, everything she had heard and seen from the times in the house with the orchards. For example, she might know who the people in the photograph with the elegant man and woman and the two girls in white dresses are, that look like my mother as a baby girl, in the torn photograph of her. Why is that large black and white photograph with three rows of people arranged symmetrically by height, with the children sitting on the ground in front of the adults also hidden in our sofa box instead of put in a frame on the walnut desk next to the photograph of Grandmother Victoria dressed and coiffed like the queen Maria of Romania? "You're too old to play with dolls, you should be writing in your journal instead," my mother always says. It's not really about the doll, but about why it can't come out of the sofa box. And I don't care to write in my journal, it's boring. I have no idea what to write about and what the point of writing in a journal is anyways. "So that you can know what you did and thought of as a child when you are all grown up," says my mother, and I know she doesn't fully believe that either, she just says so the way my mother often just says things while her mind is elsewhere.

The ugly visit that we just experienced is part of a family curse of unjust persecutions. I'm afraid there will be more. My family has a funny way of surviving though and even dancing between catastrophes. I know that there were dances even during the most frightful bombs, famines or droughts, a crazy streak of my ancestors and parents who all think that dancing through bombs, army or police raids is a matter of necessity. Sometimes my parents and some of their friends danced with coifs, sequined dresses and confetti at New Year's Eve's parties not caring about the Securitate and forgetting about war and post war catastrophes.

Later in the evening Aunt Lila comes over which is always so much fun because she has no children or husband and pays attention only to me and makes me laugh until I pee in my pants. After dinner, which consists mostly of my mother's breaded cauliflower, bread and a bit of cheese, my father makes Turkish coffee, and everybody drinks and turns their porcelain cups upside down so Aunt Lila can read our future. Then the man and woman with the schizophrenia disease who have been my father's friends forever stop by wearing winter coats even though it's hot June and they smell terribly of sweat. The schizophrenic woman asks to look at the coffee cups and then laughs saying everybody one day will go somewhere else in the world, in a plane or in a star or by camel because Bucharest will one day be the new Jerusalem, a place of pilgrimage for people all over the world. My mother rolls her eyes in utter exasperation as always and disappears to wash the dishes in the basin set the edge of the bathtub. I wonder if things would be better for us if my parents had been given the apartment with the kitchen instead of the one with the bathroom. I think it's better to have a nicer cooking place than a nicer place for our private needs, but my parents think a communal bathroom is the ultimate degree of communist degradation. A journey, a path, a train departing, it all appears in the coffee grains in the inside of my mother's cup. In my father's cup there is a libidinous man and woman riding an elevator after stealing important documents and Aunt Lila's cup shows a man and a heart which means she will meet a man for her lonely heart. I have no idea how she knows that the man and woman are in the elevator and are libidinous too, all I see are lines and circles and smudges and dots. But everybody's future is in those circles and smudges it appears. The schizophrenic couple get up to leave, they never even took off their coats. The woman laughs and looks at me saying I am an old child, I have the soul of an old person, and my mother says dismissively "yes, yes, sure," waiting for them to leave.

I am intrigued by the phrase "an old child" and I know it's true, because being a child often feels awkward and embarrassing to me, like I made a big irreparable mistake. I say, "mama I want to go out and play hopscotch, all right?" remembering how I almost fell and crushed my skull on the hopscotch squares only a few hours earlier. I could have been dead. "You are not going anywhere Corina," my mother says harshly, "it's getting dark and there are drunk people going by at this time." My father laughs and says: "Let her go, she hasn't been outside at all today.

The child needs to play." Even though I don't like it when they call me "the child." I am grateful to my father for taking my side not to mention for saving me from falling out the window.

I leave after the schizophrenic guests of my father who seem to float in their own separate world, and I go slowly down the dark staircase behind them listening to their incomprehensible conversation. Then suddenly it becomes comprehensible. They are whispering impressions about the visit at my parents, they talk about my mother and say, "she is strange, she doesn't like us." "I think she's just sad," the man says, "she will always be sad, after everything …" Then I don't hear anymore, then I tiptoe after them like a cat and she asks: "Were they Jewish?" "One was Jewish, the other one something else." "What something else?" "You know …." Then I can't hear anything anymore as if my head was suddenly wrapped in a shroud of silence that feels like cotton. I stand in the hallway and wait for them to go through the revolving door. I go outside and am grateful for the summer evening air, the linden flowers that grow wild at this time of the year. I breathe in the fragrances thirstily and I start skipping the hopscotch squares making the bet with myself that if I play the whole set of skips without a mistake, the secret police will die, and we will all leave the country for San Michele. The schizophrenic couple looks ghostly and creepy in their dark coats, walking slowly in the quiet street, in the afternoon orange light. Suddenly because of their slightly crooked hunched walk I feel terribly sorry for them. They will probably die soon, and I will never know what they meant in their whispered conversation. The street is quiet like everybody died and my childhood feels like a huge mistake again. I didn't win the hopscotch game with myself.

We will live and die in this apartment building on this street in this country. We are doomed for disaster because something got terribly twisted in my family along the way a long time ago. My father always says destiny, destiny, destiny, like a chant. The cats mew obscenely around the garbage cans in the back of our building, the old woman with the brightly died red hair on the second floor passes by me like a bad witch hissing an ugly word. Even though I'm only eleven years old, I want to say bad words and smoke cigarettes. I don't care, I almost fell out of my window this afternoon and died, crushed on this hopscotch pavement right here. Then something happens that lifts me away from the dark moment I am falling into. Suddenly I am not alone and a sweet presence, almost invisible but palpable shifts and glides around me. It's a girl like me, or like my mother, I'm not sure, though I'm pretty sure her smile is like the one my mother has in her baby picture on the deserted street in the deserted city. It's the smile of someone who has seen other things and has been to other places. Even though she looks terribly sad her presence makes me happy. Maybe I really did fall on the pavement and die, and this is what is happening to me now. I know I'm not dead though when I hear my mother calling me to come home, when I smell the linden tree flowers, when I skip on the hopscotch squares one more time and this time around, I win. I know I'm not dead when I hear the church bells for the evening service and the cats mewing and the Gypsy woman calling out to buy empty bottles, all at the same time. Too many sounds and smells for a dead person to hear and take in.

I think the girl visitor is dead though, a kind and mild kind of dead like in the strigoi stories my father and sometimes Aunt Lila tell me. I want to eat this day again like a piece of candy or an omelet, with all its good and bad people and the living and the dying, like the schizophrenia couple and the dead girl and all the rest, with the smells and the sounds and the coffee smudges that tell our future. I say goodbye to the weird transparent girl. Maybe I'll see her tomorrow all over again and again. I run upstairs to our tiny apartment imagining I am running up the white steps of a street in San Michele in the country of Italy.

"August 1941. Northern Moldavia and the Danube"
From Florin's Diary

The American bombs were lighting up the skies like gigantic fireflies. They lit up the night with ferocious yet almost beautiful sounds. We hid in the trenches that my father had built in the backyard and were grateful every night that our house was still intact. Not even the cellar that we used for a while as our shelter was safe any longer, only the trenches were. It felt so wrong to be an enemy of America and an ally of Nazi Germany, but then I would have rather died from an American bomb than a German one. There was no good way to be in that war for our country. Our next-door neighbors had been killed by Russian bombs two years earlier when Romania joined the German troupes and our neighbors across the street had been bombed and killed by Russian or American bombs, it wasn't clear which, on the Sanziene night of the first huge explosions in the sky. Our house and family still stood in the middle of the devastation like a sad ship. We were survivors from an ongoing wreck and could be like our homeless neighbors any day.

Our parents never let go of one another or of us or of Mitzi and her boy Gino or the house with the orchards. The house had become a living creature that moaned and creaked and swayed during the bomb raids and still held us like a magic cradle. Despite the bombs, we even danced sometimes, nothing mattered anymore, we might as well dance. Father would play a song on the Victrola after dinner sometimes and a current of inexplicable joy traversed through us for the simple reason of still being alive. Mitzi danced with baby Gino, and I danced with Lila. The occasional "visits" of German soldiers searching our yard or house for possible fugitives left us cold. They came, they left dirty boot marks on our floors, they left slamming the entrance door and swearing in harsh German words that only my father understood. My mother shrugged her shoulders as if it were no big deal and continued to do whatever she was doing. They mostly arrived at dinnertime. The worst was when the German soldiers were accompanied by an Iron

Guard man, or as Lila called them "the iron men in green shirts." For the rest of the month of July, they came almost every evening hoping one day they would surprise us and find who they were looking for. But my parents always acted in the same calm and undisturbed manner and in perfect synchronicity with each other, with an edge of indignation as if to say, how dare they suspect them of anything, how dare they question their word, why don't they just go and look, search the house on their own if they didn't believe them? Just go ahead. My father once threatened the Iron Guard man that he was going to complain to "the General," if they didn't stop harassing them. After which he turned his back on the inopportune "guests" and put a record on the Victrola leaving them looking like fools in the middle of our living room. The SS soldier and the man in the green shirt backed out into the street.

Very late one night, Lila and I heard someone knocking on the back door this time. Like we had done before, we tiptoed out of our room to the top of the staircase and listened. Girl barked only once as if woken up and then was quiet again. This time we heard Father talk to her quietly and tell her to be quiet; to not worry, it was friends. He talked to her like he talked to any of us in the house, gently but firmly. He opened the back door slowly and we thought we heard again my literature teacher Manole Cojocarou speak to our father. He whispered about another train that was going to pass that night, it was taking many of them, he said, it was full of them, women, and children too, he said. This one was going to a town called Podul Iloaiei, Manole said, and was passing through our train station. There were three families with children in the last car of the train, they were going to jump when the train slowed down near the station, where he would wait for them near the tracks and bring them over. My father said he would be waiting and then I thought I heard him ask Manole about Sofia and Sebastian. Had he heard from them? "They were able to cross over," I heard Manole say. I squeezed Lila's hand in the dark on the landing at the top of our staircase, feeling a great sense of relief about the grieving mother and her absent-minded son who had taken refuge in our house for those few days which now seemed like centuries ago. Every day seemed endless as they stretched from the blood red sunrises to the orange sunsets in the heavy heat that felt like melting metal dripping its poisonous substance over us. The nights, which brought some relief from the heat, seemed like a whole new day only in the dark, filled with whispers, tiptoed steps and doors whining in their hinges. The neighborhood roosters sang earlier than usual, the cuckoo birds called at odd hours, the owls sometimes forgot their calls, the creatures all seemed confused and all of nature yanked out of its normal course.

Lila and I spent the entire rest of that night till dawn at the top of the stairs, listening and waiting. Occasionally, Lila recounted to Mitzi what was going on in minuscule almost inaudible whispers which this time I could hear and understand perfectly as if my hearing had sharpened overnight. "Tata is talking to Mister Manole the teacher about the bad train passing through our town. Some people with children are going to jump from the train to run away from Hitler soldiers and Manole is bringing them to our house. Tata is going to hide them inside our house until a good train passes by so they can escape at night and go far from Hitler. You can't tell anyone about this Mitzi or Hitler will kill everybody and cut open our bellies and burn us to death." Lila's stories became gorier and scarier with each of our episodes of night watching and listening. And that night of the news of the train passing through it seemed I only heard what went on in the house through Lila's story to Mitzi. What she described was an unlikely story. "Manole left to the station to wait for the people and Tata is waiting in the back of the house for them. They are arriving with many children, and some are crying. Gino is up and crying very loudly and Mitzi and mama are not calming him down, so all our neighbors think the crying children from the train are all Gino who cries because he is sick and sad because his father was killed in the head. But it's easy to know there are more children crying, not just one. A woman is crying and then it's all quiet again like everybody went to sleep in the basement." In the morning, mama found Lila and me sleeping on the floor at the top of the staircase. She woke us up gently and led us to our beds. She never mentioned anything during the day as if she hadn't seen anything.

The days and the nights became separate realities in our house. The days were long and hot and filled with normal sounds and gestures of everyday living as usual. The nights quivered with clandestine journeys, dangerous hiding, the whistles of sinister trains, the heavy breathing of people running away from something dark and unspeakable. The roaring of the planes over our town in the morning was less frightening than the nightly whispers and steps, cries and whimpers, doors squeaking, trains whistling. The late evening bombs when we hid in the trenches were almost fun for Lila and me. The bombs were simple and clear, and you could see and hear them. They either fell on your house, or they didn't. What was hidden, whispered and secret was scarier.

I missed Zoe and Carolina fiercely again. I thought of Zoe more: her sparkling mischievous smile, the way I sometimes caught her looking at me and then bursting into laughter, her bouncy steps on our creaky wood floors. I missed the laughter and the times we chased each other among the orchard trees in the spring and summer. A luminous ease surrounded her and came from a different place, from something else than just her physical beauty. In my dreams she always appeared flushed and with a light on her face the way she was when Carolina fell in the pond through the crack in the ice. Her features were almost melting in the winter light, and she was begging me to save Carolina. I could never see Carolina's face in my dreams, she was either being swallowed in the hole in the ice or turning to a cardboard figure like in my dream where Hitler photographs our entire family and we all turn into cut out cardboard figures. Dreams merged into one another during that period and left me breathless from fear in the morning. The bombs multiplied.

Then one day that July, Father told us we were leaving our house to go into refuge in a village south of us, near the Danube. It wasn't safe anymore, we could be blown up any time just like our neighbors, or the Russians could occupy us any day and annex that whole northern part of the country to their other stolen territories. We were toys blown around the ruthless winds of an absurd history. That same day, I saw Carolina walking around our house like she was looking for something. I knew it wasn't really Carolina but more like an eerie replica of her, not dead but not truly alive either. I didn't mention it to anybody because she didn't seem to have made herself seen by anyone else and something in me told me I wasn't to betray her shadowy presence. She seemed to want to tell me or ask me something through a yellowish fog. It seemed like the most natural thing in the world, and I wasn't scared. I followed her to the back of the house and into the orchard where the cherries hung heavy on the branches: "Where have you gone? Where is Zoe?" I thought I heard myself pose that question several times repeatedly. Language spoke itself independently of my will.

I ate cherries to calm myself, she waved goodbye and walked through the trees. She swayed in the summer breeze, became one with the trees and the landscape, she melted into the green of the branches. But just when she was almost gone, she re-became in a terrifying shape glowing in brilliant shreds of clothes and skin, weeping blood tears, and swirling in a tornado of mud and palpable pain. She said words in a foreign language which oozed out of her like a different kind of blood. The words were live things, and they bled. I screamed "Carolina who are you, where are you, wake up!" and she turned back into the insubstantial girl made of yellowish fog of a few seconds earlier. I imagined that maybe you had to talk to her to take her out of her torment. She was hungry for fruit and for everything. She seemed to have slipped through a narrow crack between life and death, a moving hallway of the invisible world that shifted and showed itself for brief instances like a tease. Or a warning, a carnal and self-creating nightmare. She sang a devastating song of sorrow and eternal longing like a human violin. Memories came alive in flesh and blood and turned around me in a mad carousel.

The day at the municipal park with all of us dressed in light summer clothes, dancing under a shower of linden flowers, the waltz, the tango, all frozen in a yellowish photograph came to life. The dances to the music of Gino's Victrola and the arias on my father's Victrola, in a competition of the world's most sentimental tunes came to life. "Si puo morir d'amore." My father never played that record again, no more songs about dying of love when everybody around us was dying by American or Russian bombs. I held on to the trunk of a cherry tree and waited for everything to pass, for the storm that Carolina's absent presence had caused in the reality around me to fade. "I am one of the Sanziene girls now," I heard Carolina say, and there she was like a sanziana from the night when we all hid in the cellar during the first bombs and the Gypsy Sanziene danced naked in the moonlight. My quiet waiting paid off in the end. Carolina melted in the trees, her heartbreaking song quieted, the live memories went to sleep in the ground. Memories were buried too just like people. I carried out the funeral of beautiful memories before the war all by myself by stroking the earth, covering a patch of ground with petals and twigs, a tomb for happy past moments. So that they rest in peace.

That night, we were going to pack for our temporary refuge, make sanziene wreaths and light candles for all the whimsical forest fairies so they wouldn't take our speech, make our mouth crooked and give us more curses than we already had. I whispered goodbye to Carolina and a tiny note from her sad song trailed off among the cherry and plum trees. But then something else started. The plum trees were alive like people and the fairies were dressed in embroidered swirling Gypsy dresses. They appeared and disappeared like features made from smoke. I told myself I was going to forget everything, there was enough turmoil and catastrophe in our lives right then for me to burden anyone with my sanziene and strigoi stories. I waved goodbye to Carolina again and again, begging her to stay dead and stop tormenting me with her pretend aliveness. I said goodbye to the tomb of memories one more time, I asked about Zoe one more time and it was alright to leave the answer in the air. I didn't want a clear answer. I imagined that since she hadn't appeared as an in between person next to Carolina, she must have still been on our side of the living. She was the Jewish one, Carolina was the something else one. Or maybe it was the other way around and being identical twins maybe they had fooled me all along and the undead Carolina might have been Zoe, the one who was something else.

There were guests when I came back to the house and a chaotic caravan of people carrying sacks and luggage was passing on our street, an exodus. There was a woman with two small children, an old woman that seemed to be blind and a younger looking man who seemed to have escaped something ominous and was eating greedily the meal my mother had served him. The woman seemed to be a widow, as she was wearing a mourning dress and a scarf on her head, and she looked like a wailer from the funeral ceremonies in our town. They were all gathered on one side of the table crowding each other because the other half was full of packages that my mother was preparing for our refuge. My mother was feeding everybody a cabbage meal and beets from the garden while Mitzi pouted, slammed doors, and shouted at Gino to be quiet which is what she did whenever she was mad at my mother for feeding the entire town at our dinner table.

In the street there were people I had known for all my life mostly from the Jewish part of town, with German soldiers sternly surrounding them and shouting harsh orders to move faster, to drop some of their belongings. Occasionally they would hit a man with their rifles. A couple of the soldiers, young men from our town, were hitting some of the people in the crowd not only with their rifles but also with their boots. Some of the townspeople were throwing stones and spitting at people in the convoy. At the beginning of the war, I had heard my mother say that war was the best test of character, the truly good ones would have the chance to prove their character strength and the bad ones, who pretended to be good for the entirety of their lives under peace, would show their true colors and ugly sides.

My mother's words couldn't have proven truer than during that hour of the sinister convoy of families brutally pulled out of their houses and taken to God only knew what ominous locations and on what inescapable trains.

I saw Mr. Gogu approach a family with two children of the same ages as Lila and I, giving them each a package of food and a canister with water which everybody seemed to beg for in the overwhelming heat of that day. Several more times he went back into the house and came out with tin cans of water for several of the children in the convoy. One of them was a thin, terribly pale red-haired girl carrying a doll that looked like Mitzi and who for the span of a millisecond I thought was Zoe. I almost ran out into the street after her, if it hadn't been for my mother who pulled me back faster than I had time to catch my breath, whispering in my ear "it's not her." There was a strange smile on my mother's face which I didn't know whether to interpret as joy for the fact that Zoe or Carolina were not in the convoy because she and my father had hidden and saved them only several days earlier, or as a grimace of pain because they hadn't been able to save them in the end.

Mr. Gogu kept bringing small packages of food and tin cans with water for the people in the convoy until one of the SS soldiers hit him with his rifle and pushed him to the side of the road. Other neighbors, whom I had heard my parents say in the past were "good Christians", and "good neighbors" threw stones at the people in the convoy or buckets of filthy water. A woman from our street rushed to a mother in the convoy and tore off her neck a gold chain, then spit in her face calling her a "rotten communist Yid." The woman's house had been torn in half by one of the Russian bombs earlier that week and I admit in that moment I felt a sense of profound joy, almost like a pleasant rush at the thought that her house had been struck by a bomb. I thought she deserves it, she is an evil human being who deserves what she got, I wish it was her walking in that convoy. The next second though I saw my mother's look, her stare burning my face as if she had heard my thoughts and I felt ashamed of myself. That was how people became hateful and merciless, one spiteful thought led to another until we were all obliterated in our own burning cauldron of hate.

The air was hot and pasty, and the sky looked whitish like soup with swallows and crows rushing in all directions in chaotic circles until they were swallowed up in the soup of the sky. I couldn't breathe, the air had become an unbreathable substance. Amid the swarming of people with luggage and domestic animals in cages and fowl, a Gypsy man was playing a weepy song on his accordion, like a farewell. I had had it with sad songs for the day, accordions and violins and human singing voices, the whole heartbreak lot of them. Lila was standing on the veranda staring amused at the crowds in front of her like she was at the circus. I didn't understand why my mother had allowed her to leave the inside of the house and stand outside, as if she had a moment of absent-mindedness, having to care for all our refugee guests and acting as the guardian of my conscience. War was a dark circus and Lila seemed to almost enjoy it. Very soon she came back into the house, and I realized I had been wrong to think she was enjoying the spectacle. Lila's face was full of tears, and only then did I realize she wasn't holding her Mitzi doll. Maybe she was also crying because she couldn't find her companion and had no one to talk to about the horrifying spectacle and find consolation. I didn't want to ask her about Mitzi for fear she would break into unstoppable tears as she sometimes did.

Through the window to the veranda, I saw a man in a dark suit come up the steps and knock on our front door. He looked threatening even though he was wearing civilian clothes. My mother immediately moved towards the refugees at the table and made a sign for them to follow her. They noiselessly glided out of the room towards the back of the house faster than I would have imagined they could move. My father was intent on taking some books out of the bookcase, possibly to prepare for our temporary refuge. He turned around when he heard the knock and went directly towards the door holding one of the books. He opened the door and greeted the man without letting him in. I heard the man ask about "two Jewish girls by the name of Zoe and Carolina Abramovic," had he seen them, was he "harboring them in the house?" My heart stopped; my breathing stopped. I stood in place in the middle of the room halfway towards the door halfway towards the bookcase reading the titles in my father's bookcase, one after the other. Useless names and volumes from all over the world that hadn't saved anybody's life in times of war. Thomas Mann's *The Magic Mountain*, Leo Tolstoy's *The Resurrection*, Rilke's poems, *The Last of the Mohicans*, a huge history of Romanian literature, art books about Paris and Istanbul, the works of Karl Marx, the *Arabian Nights*. I was intent on reading every title carefully and tried to imagine what the book was all about if I hadn't read it already. It all seemed chaotic knowledge of no use but since all the books were so important to my father, I made them very important for me as well in those moments of utter catastrophe.

My father said quietly and calmly that he had no idea what girls the man was talking about. He didn't deny anything, he just said: "Who are these girls? Why are you asking me about these people?" The man seemed taken aback that my father answered with two questions in return to his and that he referred to the girls with the generic "people." "Why are you persecuting people in these times of hardship for everyone?" my father went on in a state of supreme calm. "Aren't we all on the same side?" I was confused out of my wits by my father's words but in a flash, I saw the man's face filled with shame and hatred and I understood exactly what my father was doing. The noise in the salon sounded faraway like the din on a departing ship: Gino's unintelligible words, Mitzi's out of tune singing, the clinking of plates and no music. For once no music. Carolina's "visit" of only minutes earlier with her forest fairy strigoi undead person tricks circulated through me like an electric current now. How funny, I thought, whoever they were looking for was no longer catchable, arrestable, and killable. Mister Nazi in civilian clothes could never catch Carolina no matter how hard he tried. But what about Zoe, where was she hiding?

The books in my father's bookcase stood still as if waiting to be of use and save someone. It turned out they did. I went to the bookcase and brought out a volume of plays by the German writer Schiller. I thought that I would distract the civilian Nazi, if indeed he was that, by showing him that my father read classical German literature in German. "Here Tata, the book you were looking for ...." My father had an imperceptible smile that only I could decipher, took the book from me allowing enough time for the officer to see the author and name of the book. He studied it carefully for a couple of seconds, then said something in German to the officer almost smiling, most likely referring to the author Schiller, then returned it to me together with his other book. "Just put these two books on the desk in my study, will you, and we'll read them together later on," my father said and turned back to the man without moving one muscle in his face. When I looked at the other book's title it turned out it was a book on German romanticism. Even I could understand the title, and in that moment, I was infinitely grateful to the German cultural heritage that could kill and save your life at the same time. The trick worked, from what I understood of the heavy German words he exchanged on the topic of Schiller and German romanticism. What killed you could also save you.

After speaking in German for a while, my father and the man searching for Zoe, Carolina, and their parents went back to speaking Romanian. The man spoke in intelligible but accented Romanian, and it turned out he was from the Romanian German minority now helping the Nazis as a secret agent. You saw everything in that war, brothers turned against one another and neighbors denouncing neighbors, Romanian soldiers on the eastern front deserting and defecting to the Russian side, Romanians from the Bessarabia regions deserting the Russian army and defecting to the Nazi side. A cruel upside-down circus of desperate choices and fanatic ideas dueling with each other.

My father said an abrupt Aufviederseen to the Romanian German Nazi undercover man as if he had bothered us enough, saying again he had no idea who those persons were and why us? Why was he interrogating us in those times of hardship and national catastrophe, didn't his superiors have anything better to do? He closed the door with a slam. For some reason baby Gino got down from his chair and ran to my father in a gesture of effusion. My father picked up Gino and kissed him on the forehead. It was unlike my father to have effusive gestures of affection and his attention to Gino warmed my heart as if it had been directed towards me. The crowd in the street seemed to have thinned out, and the caravan of refugees consisted of only a few tired old people, moving slowly through the haze and dust of that hot July afternoon. The spectacle was almost beautiful in its colorful chaos of rags and sacks filled with a lifetime's worth of belongings. The inside and the outside of our house now seemed to merge with another, it wasn't clear anymore whether we were living in the street, or the refugees were living in our house. Soon we were going to be them. During that same afternoon, another wave of people on the road passed our house. A scent of blood filled the air we breathed. We heard atrocious screams, and our parents practically forced us into the cellar where the group of refugees were hiding. We sat in silence on the damp ground of the cellar forgetting about time.

There was a train to the city of Bacau south of us that night transporting people and cattle, coming from north of us towards the capital. It wasn't the city of Orsova on the Danube, but on the smaller river of Bistrita and still in Moldavia. Though I had never been to Bacau I was happy we were not going to a city by the

Danube, that seemed too far away and terminal, like we were never going to be back. At the last minute when we were all packed and ready to go to the station Lila said she couldn't find Mitzi the doll. She must have gotten scared and hid somewhere, said Lila crying. And only then did I realize that we were going to leave our dear dog, Girl. Though my parents never said it, I felt it in the way they both avoided looking at her. That was when I threw myself on the floor and started screaming, saying I was not going to leave without Girl. Lila was in a frenzy of desperation and couldn't stand the idea she was going to lose both Mitzi and Girl. The dog was sitting quietly in her usual corner next to my father's velvet armchair near the large bookcase and looking at us with the most trusting eyes. Gino started screaming because Lila and I were crying. And Mitzi the maid was crossing herself with frenzy and muttering songs and prayers in an indiscriminate mixture to calm herself down.

It was the first time in my life I felt anger at my parents instead of the unconditional adoration I had always had for them. They seemed harsh and unfeeling to make us leave everything and the creatures and things we loved. My mother's persistent chant that we had each other, and we were still alive stopped making sense and seemed suspended in a hollow bubble floating aimlessly around the room. The train was leaving in an hour, and we had to walk to the station with all our belongings. Mr. Gogu came to our house with his blind mother, wanting to come with us, while the nameless widow with the two children moved to the veranda and waited. The children started playing hide and seek around their mother. They were all coming with us and had all their belongings in a couple of trunks and sacks that they dragged after them. My father pulled me up from the floor and slapped me. His hand on my face was heavy and hard like steel. It was the first time ever that my father or either of my parents ever laid a hand on me other than as an expression of tenderness. My shock was bigger than anything else we were going through right then, bigger than all the war horrors, the caravans of refugees, and our own fate suspended in a murky unknown. My mother looked away and held on to Lila who was crying her heart out and trying to escape from my mother's hold so she could look for Mitzi and take Girl away to a better place with sunny golden flowers and marzipan cakes.

I didn't care about the bombs. I didn't care about the war that was killing everybody. In that moment I hoped a bomb would fall on us and crush us into pieces and scatter us to the four winds. I called out to Carolina to take me away as if she was still part of the household. She was. She swept through the room in a green light. She had feathers instead of hair and she embodied all the beauty and ugliness of life at the same time. Get up, get up, Zoe is waiting for you, I heard her whisper, and she melted inside the wall. Maybe she lived with our serpent in the walls of our house. And once I thought that, I calmed down by miracle. If she lived inside the wall with our serpent, she would protect the house in our absence just like our serpent did. I was stunned by her mention of Zoe. Where is Zoe waiting, Carolina, what are you talking about? I heard myself ask in whispers. My parents stared at me now and waited for me to stop my conversation with the spirits, thinking I was delirious from the anguish I experienced. I got up from the floor and asked them directly with a confidence I hadn't dared before: "where are Zoe and Carolina? What happened to them? Why are there people looking for them?" Lila stopped her crying and stared at me. My parents looked at me without blinking, without saying a word, like clay statues, expressionless. For a few heavy moments it didn't feel they were my parents.

The July light was thickening into twilight like yellow gelatin. Girl was curled up in the same corner with an unmoved gaze directed towards all of us like a judgment and like a forgiveness. I went to her and embraced her for a long time whispering calmly in her ear all my love and promising her I would come back for her. I was sure she understood and believed me. Lila screamed again and Girl gave a tiny startle in my arms as if a current ran through her, like she was saying goodbye.

"What is Girl going to eat when we are gone, mama?" Lila asked amidst her irrepressible sobs. "I left lots of bones and dried up bread in the cellar for her, Lila." My mother had thought of everything after all. "And there are always the roots in the garden," she added showing signs of impatience. "And for water?" Lila went on stubbornly. "I filled several basins in the cellar too, and then there is the rain." Despite all the reassurances Lila was inconsolable and nothing was going to calm her down, particularly since she couldn't find Mitzi, her inseparable companion who offered her constant consolation. She was undone. She screamed and wouldn't budge, and the train was leaving in less than an hour.

"Why can't we take Girl with us if there are cows and chickens on the train?" I was amazed she could ask logical questions amid her agony and the overall chaos. A sharp ray of sun fell on my mother's face through the veranda windows, and she squinted her eyes. In that squinting she re-became my beloved mother. All her agony and the effort she made to keep calm and be strong so we wouldn't all completely collapse and disintegrate gathered in the tiny squint of her eyes where she also kept her tears from bursting into a flood. I felt she relied on me to calm down Lila, that her energy was spent. I embraced Lila in her violent agony of separation and whispered to her that we were going to be back by the end of the week, that Mitzi hid herself from us because she didn't want to travel on the cattle train, that Girl was going to enjoy herself with the house all to herself, and she and Mitzi and the wall serpent were going to protect the house in our absence. I didn't believe a word of it but wanted to and uttered it with conviction like a poem I recited in school. I almost added Carolina to the list but thought better of it, nobody but me had seen her I was sure of it, and it would only have added more worry to Lila's overwrought self. She melted in my arms, and I felt endless brotherly love for her. I was always going to protect my sister from all dangers, including her own stubborn whimsical self. We each picked up our suitcases and sacks and my father carried the biggest trunk filled with household items and bedding while Mitzi carried Gino in one arm and a sack flung over her other shoulder. I held Lila's hand and let her carry my school case filled with cakes for the road so her hands would be occupied, and she wouldn't miss Mitzi too much.

Our walk to the train station seemed endless and all our luggage weighed on us in the merciless heat of that July afternoon. I took one last look back at the house when we turned the corner off our street and the windows sparkled, the tile roofs glistened dark red in the twilight. I said goodbye in my head to our beloved house as if it was gone forever. Before I turned my gaze away, Carolina stood in the doorway, a creature of light and feathers, a young girl in a white dress, a Gypsy girl in a rainbow dress, a sanziana girl wrapped in garlands of yellow flowers, a bleeding shadow waving farewell and promising protection. She changed shapes many times like a cloud, and the air around her was on fire.

We barely made the train; people were almost stampeding each other. The wagons in the back had no compartments, they were just one long smelly space filled with cows and horses. The animals were crowded and looked terribly sad. The following car had compartments like a real train and by a miracle my father found us a free space. We all crowded inside it content we were able to sit down for the long overnight ride. Summer was shedding its light like it was winter and only the heat remained. People turned to shadows, mixed in with the cattle, melted in the dark heat, profiles were shrouded in the smoke of the train. Many seemed familiar and the familiar faces seemed foreign.

In the split second I was climbing the steps of the train car, I looked to my right, and I caught a glimpse of a couple embracing and parting on the steps of the train that looked like Frida and Gabi. The woman was leaving, and the man was staying, and they clung to each other with a desperation I hadn't seen before. The reddish curls, the elegant style of the dress stood out amid the chaos of that drab humanity. The man was wearing a beige straw hat like the one Gabi wore on the last happy June day in the municipal park. Just as I stepped inside the car, I realized their parting was a forced one as an SS officer stood right behind Gabi, grabbed him, and dragged him down onto the platform. I wanted to be able to run in between Gabi and the officer or scream and distract him so that Gabi could get on the train. The next second everything was swallowed up in the multicolored mass of refugees, soldiers, animals. The July light turned to gray, the heat, and the smells thick as glue on our sweaty bodies. We were crammed together in the train compartment, unwilling passengers, starting our journey towards an unknown city and future.

I didn't know if I was asleep or not. We were crossing the Danube or another big river by walking through water up to our hips. Frida and Gabi were always ahead of us in elegant clothes gliding through the thick gray waters, only our family was dressed in rags. "Ya vohl, ya vohl," a German soldier kept yelling, then "davai, davai" said a Russian soldier walking towards us through the waters. Russian and German words crashed into each other with an ugly clamor squishing the life out of our own melodious Romanian words. Languages were at war with each other too. My mother kept asking where are the girls, where are the girls, and I could see bodies that looked like those of Zoe and Carolina floating on the river in festive white dresses. It looked like they were buried in water and it reminded me of the time all four of us almost fell through the ice and died in the frigid water of the pond. Lila walked to them through the muddy river and asked them about her doll Mitzi, had they taken her doll, had they seen her doll anywhere in their travels. Zoe got mad and said we are not traveling, we are dead and floating on the river, can't you see that, don't disturb us, we don't care about your doll. They kept floating until they were swallowed up and pulled under the muddy waves. I was thankful Lila wasn't dead like them and grabbed her arm to make sure she stayed next to me. Neither of us knew how to swim, yet we had to survive that crossing by not drowning and not swimming. Lila looked at me with enormous trusting eyes as if she had no one left to hold on to but me.

A house with a thatched roof is waiting for us at the other side of the river," my mother said, we must get there before the Russians annex this side of the river. Rivers will also be cut in two, and annexed to the Russian Volga because the Russians are greedy people, and they want everybody's rivers to wash their dirty boots in. My mother was saying all this like a history lesson as she floated on the gray waters of the river herself. The Russian soldier didn't seem to see us even though he was walking towards us, maybe he was also dead. The dead and the living were all mixed up and you couldn't distinguish them from one another. Hurry up, hurry up, get to the other side of the river as quickly as you can, a familiar voice kept repeating, a voice surging out of the water with a life of its own. I wasn't sure at all whether I was still in my dream, or if we had actually arrived on the earth of our refuge.

In the morning, we arrived in Bacau, the city by the river Bistrita that was not only under water from flooding but seemingly under siege by the Germans even more than our own city in Moldavia. Why did we have to leave everything and Girl and our beloved house and orchards to live in a flooded city under German occupation? The Russians are even more dangerous, I heard my father say. He also said the Russians were after our land, the Germans were not occupying us, but were our allies, as bad as that may have been and sounded. Our country is screwed no matter what, I heard my father say too and was in shock to hear him curse, the world was indeed coming to an end.

And there it was: a house made of hardened mud with a thatched roof and one window in the middle with red geraniums on the sill. It looked real and I pinched myself just to make sure I was real. In the midst of a world war and catastrophic floods, somebody had the time to tend to a geranium plant on the windowsill of a one-eyed house. We arrived just before dawn, and it was still dark. The moon shone like a mad creature over the waters and the desolate fields with no flowers and no trees. We were strangers in a strange land. I missed the orchards, I missed the hills, I missed the winding streets of our Moldavian town. The order between dreams and reality was all mangled up and the nightmares on the train were no less real than our arrival in the flooded Bacau town and our steps into an atrociously smelly mud house with a thatch roof and a geranium flowerpot in the window. I went in and out of sleep that first night in our new abode by the water like the time I became delirious with fever after falling in the frozen pond. This time it was delirium from having been swallowed up in the darkness of a hot and airless summer and surviving a train ride like a journey into hell.

Bacau was a town under siege with a flooding river spilling its muddy water onto the streets and into people's houses. The German soldiers ruled the streets, the stores, filled the public gardens, whatever was left of them, always on the lookout for enemies, spies, Jews. Mitzi was in a state of utter confusion and stopped even caring for Gino and cooking for us. My mother did everything from the cooking and cleaning to caring for Gino, finding a kilo of flour from some unknown neighbor, a liter of oil at some dark store in an alley. She ran everywhere and strangely looked younger and more beautiful than ever. In the absence of her doll Mitzi, Lila played with Gino like a doll and talked to him about everything from trivial things like a lost item of clothing to the Germans and Russians who were all going to put us in a camp like the people with the yellow stars and kill us, or worse even send us on a train and sink the train in the Danube with us inside it. Gino howled in terror and kept running away from Lila like from a menace. There was no music, no dancing, and no story telling like in our town in the rolling hills of northern Moldavia. Just muddy water. No colors, no flowers by the side of the roads or in people's yards. I had no idea why we had moved there and why we were safer in that German studded town than at home. If there was a deep and dark reason like the murky waters around us, only my parents knew it.

After the Sanziene Night
Northern Moldavia, June 2015

The day after the journey in and out of my father's orchards, house, his slippery universe populated by the living and the dead, human, animal, and plant spirits, I stay in my room avidly reading my father's journal trying to pick up any clues and secret messages between the lines, the words, the yellowed pages. The previous day with the vertiginous rumbling of strange events and encounters rushing over me like the floods of 1941 seems partly unreal, partly sharp, neither fully real nor fully hallucinatory. Objects I carried with me are proof that the day had happened, that the people I met, particularly Manole and Lulu exist: a blue silk sash, the cover of an old record titled "L'Elisir d'amore," an old pipe. The pocket of the skirt I wore is stained with purplish reddish spots that could have been blood but come from a fistful of cherry and plum pits that I apparently carefully collected rather than spat on the ground. A feeling of treachery and trickery sways over me, a confusion in time and space as if they were one and I could walk into yesterday, or spring into tomorrow like into a vestibule if only I wanted to. I don't want to.

I stay put in my room and read my father's journal. Eat the food that my hostess has prepared for me in the morning and make sure I still taste, hear, see, and feel things like any other normal day. The material world around me seems transparent and squiggly like a live organism, memories and thoughts are heavy and carnal like a plum tree or a snake. Not my memories, but my father's. I can't even conjure up a coherent line of memories of my own, a stable picture that defines me fully. Only snippets and fragments dived between two worlds: the before and after, or the out there in America and the over here in Romania. A house over there, a house over here. Yet worlds apart, whole existences apart, disconnected. I have scratches on my knees and arms and remember a bramble bush taking possession of me like a living, desiring creature. I am constantly fighting an overpowering drowsiness and blame it on the troubled night.

Somewhere in the middle of the journal, my father changes the tone completely and starts spinning a strigoi story. Carolina, the twin girl, is the strigoi, not an evil one that rips you apart and eats your entrails but a sad and wailing presence that got caught in the house during the war, died inside the wall like the mythic Ana of the monastery and melted through the wall becoming a semi beneficent presence both a protector and an avid destructor. She feeds on human breath but also brings solace and forgetfulness in the unbearable episodes of his war riddled childhood. Sometimes the air became un-breathable, -- whenever she sucked up the air and the seconds of life to add them to her eternity of undeadness. She needed seconds like they needed air. "She was a thief of time," that was her problem says my father.

In Florin's journal, Carolina is a bird- ghost kind of creature. She smells sour and brings with her a yellow fog. My father writes about her with the same earnestness with which he writes about concrete aspects of the war, the behavior of the German or the Russian soldiers, the detailed description of their uniforms, the taste of the beets that he and his mother and sister survived on during the famine, his mother's emaciation, Lila's almost fatal scarlet fever and the shade of red of the beet juice that saved her life. The Kreutzer sonata rising from the street played by the blind Gypsy violin one famine stricken late summer afternoon and the restless eerie shuffles in the house that day. He never once uses the word ghost, that's only my assumption. Because what else can you really call the Carolina being? An un-being? He talks about her as you would about any other real person. He talks about the sanziene in the same assured tone, the summer forest fairies with crowns of yellow flowers who turn evil in the blink of an eye if you forget about them.

Memory is the key to everything in this story, the key to survival itself. I don't believe a word of the strigoi story, and I think my father must have been hallucinating through the whole period of the drought and the famine, but I am inescapably drawn into the story. Hardly anything is left from the world described in the journal, yet the small remainders are overpowering — the tiny orchard cared for by Manole, the basement of the house full of family objects, furniture and even some photographs, the eerie feeling in the back of the house and the back yard, a palpable heaviness that comes from something other than weather conditions or the material world. The familiar features on Lulu's face. A swaying between the visible and the unseen. Carolina is neither, she is the in between, a hiatus in the story of my family left untouched for decades, until her story was filled with spider webs and tears. She is a nomad of the afterlife.

By the middle of the day, I decide to go back to the house at number 18 and talk to Manole again. He holds impenetrable secrets of life and death like it's no big deal. And he owns part of my father's orchards like it is a big deal. The day is translucent quivering gelatin, not clear, not overcast either, just hazy hot. The heat is palpable, and I move through it with a dizzy head wondering where it will take me. Today I have no agenda to discover any big secrets and penetrate the history of some old piece of cloth or ornament left in a basement corner. I want to understand Manole and Lulu, their ties with my family and the magic plums. Lulu's blondness, Manole's love for my father. The spirits and the dead buried in the orchard a long time ago. And what is going on with the film team? Is it another masterpiece of Romanian cinema made at the expense of my father's history, full of erroneous facts and cheap sets?

Manole and Lulu aren't anywhere when I get to the house. I take the same back alleys, through the same potholes, passing the same clucking chickens and the dotted red and black rooster, only the silver Mercedes van is no longer there. Neither is the old Dacia. Somebody must have come and gone, decided to leave that morning and I realize with a nagging feeling of regret that I never bothered to check the license plates the day before, whether they were local or from elsewhere, the capital or abroad. The back yard is empty, and the earth looks moist like it had rained but I only remember dry heat since I arrived in town. Maybe somewhere in the vestibule between yesterday and today there was rain.

I go to the orchard patch afraid that too might have disappeared, plums and cherries all wiped out, stolen, and ingurgitated by a team of Romanian actors or a former cooperative leader turned newly elected official, turned mafia. The orchard is still there, and I am so happy to see it that I start consuming the fruit from the lower branches in a frenzy, then I am still not satisfied and start climbing the plum tree to reach the higher branches. I have an overpowering feeling that I am reliving my father's childhood, and I stepped even beyond the vestibule into the first room of the past, the one with the happy times of tree climbing and a dreamy white blossom filled dance in the municipal park. I hear a mad woodpecker in one of the linden trees in the very back of the yard and before I can put another plum in my mouth two policemen burst out of the back of the house at number 18, followed by the family who had reluctantly allowed me to visit their living room bazaar. I'm thinking it's still the Romanian movie thing, it keeps going and going, new turns of the plot and new sets. Oh yes, the bric-à-brac in the living room must have been a movie set.

It's a hot June day in a remote town in northern Moldavia and I am perched in a plum tree like a twelve-year-old. The childhood I never had but dreamed of while listening to my father's stories of his idyllic childhood, has come after me with a vengeance and is reclaiming my soul and my body. The police and the family come towards the tree with a fierce step and a German Shepard dog. They move through gelatinous air, through the heat, through time. For sure they are mistaken, they must think I'm someone else, or it's all part of the movie. The woman who sort of welcomed me in the house yesterday runs towards the tree tearing at her hair and screaming "it's her, yes that's her, she came into our house yesterday." At first, I didn't realize she is talking about me. But when I do it's too late, because I'm on the ground, in between the two policemen who hold me each by one arm, with hard unforgiving hands. It's a movie, a joke, a primitive land where they arrest foreigners just for being foreigners.

"What are you doing here, Mrs. ….?"

"Angelescu, Corina Roxana Angelescu," I say in a rush, when I find myself in an office that looks like a police station.

"And so, Mrs. Angelescu, you've come to our town here to pillage our gardens and trespass our properties, hm, is that what they teach you there in that America of yours?" The middle-aged policeman with a small forehead and pudgy hands is just like the secret police I ran away from a long, long time ago. An eternity ago, a young woman with all her belongings in a bag, running away with her parents on a night train. Running away from men like this one right here. There was a precious cobalt vase that smashed to smithereens two eternities ago, in a tiny half of a kitchen-less apartment by a man like this one here who holds me hostage in a stinking office in my father's hometown. I remember watching the American astronauts gliding on the moon surface on our tiny black and white TV screen in the doll house apartment. Now I am a citizen of the country with the astronauts, only I am trapped back in the country I left hoping I would never have to see or deal with men such as this one right here. There were shards of cobalt everywhere, almost beautiful, sparkling in the June sunlight that entered our tiny apartment, and a gooey cavernous silence followed the episode. "What were you doing pillaging the orchard of these good people here?"

"I was eating plums, that's what. And it's not these good people's orchard, this orchard belongs to their neighbor, Mr. Manole," I answer full of spunk and spiritedness I think I must have sucked up from the enormous quantity of plums ingested that afternoon.

The policeman with the pudgy face seems taken aback by my boldness and to my surprise changes his aggressive attitude, sits down in the chair across the desk, looks me straight in the eyes and asks: "Do you think I could find work if I come to America?"

"What kind of work?" I ask puzzled, thinking again that I must be part of a simulacrum situation, a show prepared by the townspeople especially for me in which I am both actor and spectator and I don't know it. The pudgy policeman melts into a scabrous laugh: "work, like work for money, you know, for dolari," he makes the sign of money and tries to get closer to me in a way that scares me.

I kick the pudgy short forehead policeman off his chair. Chaos starts in the office that seems unreal, people are moving and changing shape. Policemen become birds, birds turn into cherries, cherries become children, it's a wild merry go round of transformations and creatures. I once read *Alice Through the Looking Glass* and everybody turned into everybody else until there was a complete confusion of who was who, of matter and identity of nature and humans. Instead of policemen there are three women who look like Gypsy sanziene sitting in chairs and braiding yellow flowers into wreaths. The nature of the place has changed, it's no longer a police office, but an elegant room in someone's house, though it still feels like I'm kept a prisoner. Which maybe I am. A girl in a ragged lacy dress dances or rather floats around the room and she is either crying or laughing, I'm not sure. She finally sits in a pink armchair and starts telling a story in a high-pitched voice.

The girl in the torn lacey dress says she had a twin sister who stayed hidden in a compartment in the wall for weeks, they were hidden there together by the good family at number 18bis. She stresses the bis part and I realize the people with the bizarre living room and American spy ideas live at number 18. It is Manole's house that is the 18bis one, that was the actual house where my father grew up. I got emotional in the wrong house and thought I had felt God knows what kind of special vibe from the past. Wrong vibes in the wrong house, just my overly abundant imagination and emotionality playing tricks on me, that's all. The girl gets very agitated when she tells the story and glides effortlessly around the room, but in between parts of the story she sits down in the pink armchair and dozes off looking dead. Which she probably is, some kind of dead, an unusual kind of dead who roams around.

Their parents left the two sisters there with the family because they were running away from the Germans who put people like them in ghettos and cages and trains or downright massacred them in the very middle of the street. The father kept her and her sister in a secret compartment behind a door behind another door in his study and brought them food and water every day, while the mother emptied out their night pot and made sure they were still alive and healthy. The girl's voice is getting more plaintive and melodious at the same time, she spins her story like a wailing song while wrapping herself in a yellow fog. One night, the girl says with the most heartrending sigh I've ever heard, one night she couldn't breathe, one night when there were explosions outside or maybe inside the house, she couldn't breathe, she asked her sister to give her some of her air, which she did by putting her mouth next to hers, but she still couldn't breathe, and the explosions were getting louder. She stopped breathing and melted inside the secret compartment. Then she changes her story and says she was lying on the floor outside the secret compartment after Nazis barged in and did something … something … Then she doesn't say what the Nazis did. They were two, she says, there was two of them, she keeps repeating. I hear myself asking what did they do, what did the Nazis do, did they kill you? I surprise myself by realizing I am speaking to an undead person in my bed and breakfast room.

The airy girl in the lace dress of a century ago goes on and on, telling and retelling different versions of the moment of her death. She could hear her sister sobbing but couldn't move, couldn't feel her body. Her body transmigrated, she says, evaporated and melted inside the wall, slithered outside in its evaporated form, or maybe it was her soul that did that, and the body stayed in the secret compartment and rotted. She couldn't remember which part stayed and which slithered outside into the garden, coiling around the trees, and sucking their sap. Was it her body or her soul, she asks herself as she slowly dwindles to the size and consistency of a curl of smoke, to the form of a peal of laughter, or a tear, or was it the memory of a tear or of laughter?

The elegant room with the pink armchair re-becomes the police headquarters before I can blink twice and the two policemen are sitting and looking angrily at their desks, writing what appears to be a report. I think I've been here before. I've lived this scene before, long ago, during the dictatorship, I was being interrogated for something I had done or not done and threatened that my career was going to suffer. What career, I think, what had I done and what was the reason for the interrogation? The pudgy faced policeman lifts his dull face from his report and says: "you can go now Mrs. Angelescu, you're lucky we are letting you go this time, just stay away from people's properties, all right, no trespassing, all right, here you're not in that America of yours." I leave the police office in a daze wondering what just happened and through what rabbit hole might I have fallen. If I was dreaming or under the influence of a powerful hallucinogenic, then how was I ever going to return to reality and stay in control of my life and actions ever again?

It is twilight, and the street is empty and serene, strangely quiet like everybody has left town or died. I lean over and touch the pavement. I feel the heat emanating from its hard-grainy surface, almost like tar. I'm pretty sure it's the real thing and not a make-believe pavement that opens into a drab police office that gets taken over by an undead unbridled spirit from a different zone of existence. I know I have acquired some important information about my family history during these last few hours of overlapping universes. I wrack my brain trying to remember everything. It was about two sisters hidden in a secret compartment in my father's house. There was a mistake in the house number, that's why I got arrested. I had trespassed into the wrong house. But I have a feeling I'm in possession of an important family secret my father never revealed to me before dying. A secret that my mother glides around, hovers above, fiercely pretending there are no secrets, and that part of our history is not only irrelevant but nonexistent. Like she came from a different space, period, from a deserted street on another planet, and a picture of her standing on that planet has been handed down together with a handful of postcards and old pictures. So many things got lost in our passage from one continent to another, almost everything got lost, just a few scraps of memory survived the purge of our escape, immigration, translocation.

Northern Moldavia, April 1942
From Florin's Diary

We arrived at our house in the spring when the orchards were in the wild glory of their pastel blooms. We walked with our belongings from the station as we had walked to the station the previous summer: a caravan of ragged dusty refugees. The sight of the rosy and foaming white waves of flowers of our cherry, apple and plum trees flooded my heart. As we got closer to the house, something was crooked and dark. I stumbled and almost fell over my luggage. Lila laughed but it sounded like a scared laugh. Something felt out of place and out of sorts, the open front door, the missing fence, a mound of rubble across the street. The sojourn in Bacau in the mud house by the river had been an agony and a deeper descent into darkness. The river had stayed as unwelcoming and rough as when we first got there, and the German soldiers imprinted the sound of their angry steps my mind forever. The sight of their ruddy arrogance as they fished drowned fugitives from the shores just to make sure they were the kind of fugitives they had been hunting down haunted me and filled me with flaming anger. I still couldn't understand the reason for our refuge in that dreary watery town. Now our house greeted us with a mad appearance, the flowering orchards in contrast with the devastated entrance, a crooked light hovering over it like a dagger.

"I want to see Girl, mama, I wonder if she's waiting for us at the door," said Lila and rushed towards the entrance. Mother stretched her arms in a premonition wanting to stop her, but Lila was faster. The day rumbled and collapsed a minute later. Years and centuries passed over us and we sunk into the earth like into an endless crater.

Our dog, Girl, had been massacred and left to rot in the front yard and the house ransacked and pillaged with savage fury. I grew up to be an old man and lost all my innocence in a few seconds. Father kept saying "look, look they even took out the electric outlets," as if that was the most important thing, the electric outlets. Mother was making a strange face as if crying without sounds, just her chest was heaving as she held both Lila and me by our hands. From beneath a mound of torn books from Father's bookcase Lila found Mitzi and produced a squeal of joy.

"See, I told you mama that she wasn't lost." One of Mitzi's eyes wouldn't open anymore and that's when Lila started crying. She reported to Mitzi every bit of the disaster in front of us amid cries and we each sat down on a busted chair to listen to her story as if it was someone else's story. The mere spectacle of it took our breath away. Look Mitzi here is Tata's Victrola and collection of records all made into little pieces, the soldier people did that and also killed Girl and broke our furniture while we were gone and made dirt and brought mud on all our floors, they were dirty soldiers, like garbage people and like huge spiders with guns..." Gino sat in Lila's lap dazed from the vision of destruction in the house, though he seemed excited by the story. Yes, the story, as if it didn't concern us. Lila and Gino, the youngest among us, seemed to be the adults for a little while, as we all sat among the feathers and spun wool of the broken upholstery. The pink velvet armchair had all the upholstery taken out and was stained with dark reddish blotches that could have been dried blood. It was the chair Zoe and Carolina used to sit in together holding hands and watching us live, talk and go about our daily occupations like they were at the theater.

Only Mitzi the maid was going around in circles looking for something. Mother ordered her to sit down, that it made her dizzy to watch her go round and round and Mitzi went on walking as if she hadn't heard my mother. Then she said "Ma'am they killed the snake, it's bad sign, a bad, bad sign it is, the snake brought us luck before and now we lost all our luck." Mother actually laughed and said: "Well, Mitzi, if all our bad luck were only the death of the snake, we would be the happiest people on earth right now, for whoever came in here and did this was bad luck enough for sure. But the snake still brought us luck, dead or alive." We all looked at her and saw that her tears were dried up and she had a smile. "Think about it if we had been here when they came, what would have happened to us then? We are lucky to be alive. To be together still. Besides, how do you know the snake is dead, did you see its carcass anywhere yet? I think it must have slithered out of the walls and run into the garden when it saw what was going on here. Mitzi calmed down and sat in the broken pink armchair with a puzzled look as if she hadn't thought of any of that.

Was it the Germans or the Russians, did either of them do that to every family and every house on the street and in the town, or just to our house? My mind raced as I choked on the dusty air in the room. Had any part of our country been annexed, returned from an annexation, then unified? Why were the two largest opposing armies of that war fighting in our miserable part of the world? I understood nothing of the twisted politics but lived the full grim agony of it. The Russians were brutish, and the Germans were atrocious, which one to pick as your occupiers? Why couldn't it be the Americans? My mind reduced all politics to a flat card game of kings and queens, then smashed it all on purpose. A mound of useless playing cards lay on the busted sofa where father had sat down exhausted from going around the house and ascertaining the vicious damage done to it but mostly obsessing about the gouged electric outlets.

At twilight, mother started preparing some semblance of a dinner after practically forcing Mitzi out of her state of thick stupor and helped her clean the front rooms and the devastated kitchen. She was able to find preserves and pickled vegetables that she had hidden in the cellar in a secret compartment underneath the staircase. She found a bag of flour and oil in the same place that apparently remained undiscovered by the barbarians who had passed through our home. The smell of fresh bread baking in the oven spread through the house and gave us a temporary sense of solace. Maybe things were going to get better, maybe the war was going to come to a screeching halt, Hitler was going to be assassinated and Stalin poisoned by one of his men and American troupes would glide in on multicolored parachutes descending smoothly from their fighter planes onto our green pastures instead of bombing us.

As we sat down to dinner in the sound of Lila's sobbing the front door opened brusquely and a German soldier entered our house, rushed through the hallway leaving a trail of blood and fell on the busted pink armchair in the salon. Just like that, like a confused bird flying through an open window by mistake. Father got up from the table calmly and went to talk to the soldier. It almost seemed like he knew him. The pendulum clock struck seven and only then did I realize it had escaped the general pillage by some miracle I'd rather it hadn't. I'd rather it be crushed to pieces if it meant Girl would still be alive. The soldier produced heavy grunts and blood gushed from his side onto the floor. We sat quietly eating our pickles and fresh bread. It all suddenly tasted bitter. Mother stared at her plate without saying a word, as if it wasn't any big deal that a bleeding German soldier entered our house and sat down in the middle of our living room like he was walking into his own house. He couldn't talk or answer any of Father's questions, he could only moan, bleed, and stare into space.

Something strange passed through the room, like a burning whisper that you could touch with your fingertips, stranger than anything we had found out that day on our return from the city on the river. If that was even possible. It had to do with the bleeding German soldier and with the way father circled the busted armchair on which he had collapsed. With the way he talked to him with familiarity. Almost smiled. Looked at his wound. "It's a superficial wound, it barely missed his liver," he said looking at my mother. Mitzi was wildly confused and started moving around our dinner table like a lost hen. Mother asked her to sit and calm down and immediately turned to Father whispering "yes, we should call the doctor," and Father whispering right back "we can't call the doctor." I had no idea who they were whispering for. Who was sleeping? Maybe for the wounded German soldier. Maybe he was dying.

I remembered the death of Gino the Italian deserter right by the front door in the hallway. Why was our house a dying place for soldiers in the Axis armies? Lila was talking to doll Mitzi like a lunatic, repeating what everybody said in thick whispers with exaggerated gestures, like she was acting on a stage. She reminded me of Frida in one of the roles she played when we all used to go to the theater. That reminded me of Zoe and Carolina and the encounter with the embodied memory of Carolina with whom I had spent the most fantastical hours of my life the afternoon before we left our house to go to the river town.

The soldier groaned and seemed to be dying. A pink flutter that I knew was Carolina's spirit moved through the room. Memories were people again and they moved through our house in a dark circus in blazing colors. Our parents had no power over them, nobody did. But father seemed to move confidently through the convoy of memory people and sat down next to the bleeding soldier. Mother joined him and together they applied pressure on the bleeding side to stop the blood from gushing all over our floors and still didn't call the doctor. Mother tore a piece of her own skirt and tied it around the man's waist, like a full body tourniquet. She took his pulse and said it was regular, like she was a doctor. Memory people were moving through the room with impunity. The widow that had once sat at a corner of our table and ate cabbage and beets with her children during the exodus of people passing by our house, Frida and Gabi in their stylish attires, Gino the soldier, they were not ghosts but shapes of people once in our lives and now gone. Memories do come to life. There was no way of getting away from them.

Mitzi said he was a German soldier, why did my parents help him? Because he is a human being and a young man, my father said, that's why. Carolina flourished and swirled around creating a thick fog that was sometimes yellow sometimes pink, a spectacular blending of fluid colors like watercolors intermingling and bleeding into one another. She moved around the armchair with the German soldier bleeding in it. She moved like a bird in love with her prey, waiting for his soul to take its flight. I wasn't scared, just curious, almost excited. As always, she led the convoy of memories.

The German soldier didn't die, and Mitzi fell madly in love with him once he regained his consciousness which wasn't for several days as he lay delirious on the sofa in the salon under my parents' care. Mitzi needed to fall in love like some people need clothes or sleep and soldiers on the run seemed to hold a particular hold on her heart. It turned out he was a Romanian soldier fighting on the German side and wanting to desert his army. It turned out he had been to our house before, in one of the raids, searching for people in hiding, the months before we left into refuge. There was a strange familiarity between my father and him that escaped my understanding.

During the early summer months after our return, the Romanian German soldier whose name was Kosmin, settled in our house for a while, just as it had happened with Gino. Food became scarcer every day, but my mother and Mitzi did wonders preparing meals out of nothing, and prolonging a make-believe normality between air raids, and rabid searches by the remaining German soldiers looking for deserters. Every time we heard German boots at our doorstep, Kosmin disappeared miraculously like a bird. Until there were no more German soldiers in town. News of Russian armies heading our way again squeaked in threatening and broken announcements through the static on my father's radio. No music graced our house, just radio static and bits of news about Russian armies.

Over the months of April and May the Allies' bombardments have intensified, particularly over Bucharest and the city of Ploiesti. Between the periods of static, father was still able to catch bits of news, the destruction of the Bucharest

Atheneum and of railway stations and the deaths of hundreds of civilians. One morning we received a telegram announcing the death of one of my mother's cousins living in Bucharest, Mihai, whom we had visited a couple of times during one of Father's vacations. My mother seemed un phased and acted more upset about the destruction of the Atheneum than the death of her first cousin. She reminded us we had been to the Atheneum to listen to a Brahms concert on one of our trips to Bucharest. None of us could remember any of that, reactions to news and catastrophes seemed upside down and warped in my family at that point. My mother also said we should worry about the air raids in our area and over our town more than those in Bucharest.

Kosmin never said anything when those moments of bad war news entered our house. He sat quietly and acted like he hadn't heard any of it. I had no idea who he was although he lived in our house and now Mitzi was his lover like she had been the lover of the Italian Gino at the beginning of the war. Our house was still heavy with incomprehensible secrets. The same heavy yellow fog started dancing through it around twilight time. It seemed like a thickened but gauzy body, like a human presence but not quite. You expected it to talk and tell stories. Or sit in an armchair and stare at you for all eternity. I still didn't know what happened to Zoe and Carolina and no one ever responded to my queries about them. If I asked my mother where had the two girls disappeared, what had happened to Frida and Gabi, she pretended she was busy mending one of the busted upholstered chairs or looking for something under the sewing machine. If I asked my father that same question, he first looked at me as if he didn't understand the question and then slapped his forehead like he just remembered to look up a certain page in a certain book in our ravaged bookcase. Lila didn't care either way as long as she had her doll Mitzi to talk to and as long as there was enough bread which now, she ate all the time as if possessed by a continuous and insatiable hunger. And of course, she always told us she gave most of her food to Mitzi, but the doll didn't want it. It was as if she was storing for the weeks of hunger that would soon grip our house and the entire town in its unforgiving claws.

I started drawing my own conclusions and weaving my own stories to fill in the absence of the twin girls and explain the unnerving yet somewhat consoling "visits" of the new Carolina, in her eerie appearances, haunting flurries through the different indoor and outdoor spaces of our property at unexpected times and places. Since I couldn't accept the idea that Zoe might have died, I considered her alive but absent and since Carolina appeared to me in less than carnal yet occasionally visible form, I considered her to be the dead one. The absent sister was alive, the present one was dead, that was the only equation that made sense to me, and the one I wanted to hold as true. The presence of dead Carolina exhausted but excited me at the same time, I started to look forward to her visits and I missed them when she failed to appear, while the absence of the still living Zoe maddened me and kept me awake at night. Maybe she was being tortured by the Germans, maybe she was lost amid hostile strangers and hunted down by soldiers in some remote town of our messy ravaged country. I had a feeling the two of them had stayed hidden in our house long after we stopped seeing them around until one day when they were gone forever, each their separate ways. A day when the wall snake ticked like mad and then stopped, a day when the light seemed crooked and the air heavier than usual. It was the day when Gino the Italian soldier who had married Mitzi was killed in our house and we all hid in the basement during air raids and bombing, while naked sanziene Gypsies danced an unearthly hora in our orchards. That was the day that shifted everything in our family, and in the order between the living and the dead. Something shifted in the flow of history that was going to shake our world like never before, make it an ugly world with upturned graves, torn sepia photographs, uprooted trees and a bloody confusion between occupier and liberator.

Post-War Terror
Brasov, 1953

In the fall of 1953, Florin Angelescu was a young literature teacher bursting with enthusiasm for his profession and inexhaustible hatred for the communists. The Russians had won the war and installed their Stalinist type reign of terror with the help of many willing Romanian citizens, some out of fear, others out of real conviction. A thick desperation settled among the intellectuals and the educated Romanians, while many from the proletariat believed in the socialist dream of equality, "to each according to their needs, from each according to ability." At the height of that era of terror, of confusion and famine, Florin Angelescu taught at the boys' high school in Brasov, the Transylvanian city known for the natural beauty of its surroundings and the famous Black Church, the Gothic Lutheran cathedral that survived a wicked fire a century ago. He soon became the talk of the town for his effervescent and charismatic spirit, his good looks, and the belligerent courage with which he stood up to pressures and tendencies imposed by the communist party at a time when everybody trembled and kept silent for fear of being demoted, fired, or taken from their homes by a black van in the middle of the night, never to be seen again.

Florin owned one winter coat, one suit for all seasons and a handful of shirts that he had gotten out of the money his mother received on the sale of their house in northern Moldavia. Yet he always looked sharp and perfectly groomed, his shirts always starched, his one pair of shoes always shiny as he crossed the hallways of the high school like a bullet, to the admiration of all his students, from the most diligent to the weakest and most delinquent. Nobody would have guessed he lived in a tiny, rented room in the loft of one of the old buildings at the foot of the mountain, with no running water and lived on one meal a day and two packs of cigarettes. His fierce love of literature gave him wings and irrepressible energy. It also drove the girls from the Princess Maria high school to fall madly in love with him and frequently stalk him on his way to his room in the mansarda, the loft in the old stone house that touched the edge of the moody forest and the lower rocks of the mountains.

My father was also recovering from a bad case of tuberculosis that he had gotten during his even poorer years as a student at the University in Bucharest. He writes in one of his journals that he used to sell his food tickets to buy books and ate only occasionally, but smoked more. The reckless neglect of his health cost him the tuberculosis which almost killed him and forced him to interrupt his studies for a year while he stayed in a sanatorium in a remote Transylvanian town. He finished the following year first in his class and for once the communist authorities did him a favor and gave him the high school job in the coveted city of Brasov on the recommendations of his doctors.

In Brasov, he thrived on the luxurious regimen of one full meal a day, breathing the clean mountain air and teaching all the forbidden texts of Romanian literature. Despite the rampant poverty and the Stalinist terror the students gave raucous parties with French and Italian music and dancing, smoking Bulgarian cigarettes which were less disgusting than the Romanian ones and with the Romanian plum brandy tuica that burned your insides and made you forget even the worst of the communist inequities. He always refused their warm invitations to such parties with the excuse that he had to prepare his lesson plans, catch up on his readings, or that he was too tired.

One Saturday evening though a group of the more rambunctious seniors pleaded with him until he agreed to go. "There will be girls from Princess Maria too," one of them said mischievously with a wink. Florin wore his best shirt that night, the off-white with a thin stripe, and smoked all the way to the party which was taking place at the other side of town in one of the more elegant areas with the nineteenth century villas behind the municipal park. The panoramic view of the city from that side was breathtaking and as he was gasping for air between his cigarettes and the rapid walk uphill, he experienced for the first time since before his father had died, a feeling of exhilaration for being alive. An uncanny energy possessed him, and he became impatient to get to the party faster like he was late for an important encounter. It was early fall, and the city was glowing in the sunset, the Black Church stood majestically against the bluish forests and peaks behind it and its bells tolled for vespers. It all spoke of a history and nature that transcended regimes and parties, wars and governments and looked ironically at the turbulent waves of the centuries with all their useless battles.

When he walked into the first room of the spacious house where the party was there was a stir of excitement, some of the men in his class even applauded and rushed to greet him. A record with the Italian singer Domenico Modugno was playing and a group of girls were dancing with each other and giggling. A fleeting memory of a happy time, a sunny afternoon with music, the last he could remember fluttered through him. One of the girls in a red polka dot skirt and a simple white blouse was not dancing. She was looking out the window as if searching for something. Then she turned towards him, and their eyes met. He couldn't quite understand what happened. He suddenly felt lighter. He was back in time, and he could start everything all over again. No Germans, no Russians, no famines, no Stalinism, no secret police, a new page in history. He had another chance at happiness.

She had dark blonde hair with red tints, blue green eyes, and a dimple in her smile. Something that had already happened before was turning back, like a journey into the past. He went straight to her and asked her to dance without any introduction as if they knew each other. It was the first time he had done something like that, on an impulse. It was the first time he had danced since the afternoon in the municipal park on the cusp of World War II. She smelled of jasmine and was nimble without being too light. She was tied to the earth yet seemed to soar. Something seemed painfully familiar and refreshingly new. There was a slight clumsiness to her and a profound sadness that she tried to hide. The light was dim, and he couldn't quite distinguish her features with great precision. He thought she was luminous and asked her name as Domenico Modugno was pronouncing his "volare" refrain." "To fly, to fly in the sky painted blue," said the song. "Zoe, it's Zoe," she said with emphasis.

He knew it of course as soon as he looked at her. He staggered for a second and then recovered, took her hand in a ceremonious way, and kissed it. He held her tiny and extremely thin body almost fearfully lest it should break. He swirled around with her towards the middle of the room to the Italian tune. "Everybody knows you here," she said with a mischievous glimmer in her eyes. He experienced vertigo, a feeling of the unreal. Yet she gave no sign of recognition. "Are you …, aren't you…?" He started timidly with almost a stutter, as the volare song came to an end. She slid from under his loose grip around her waist and ran to the other end of the room joining a group of men engaged in a heated conversation.

From that point on, Florin was absent from the party. Memories he thought and wanted buried rose from the dead and circled him. The party was a faraway din with French and Italian music and jokes about the bad teachers from school. He pretended to care about the conversations his students were trying to include him in out of politeness. He finished his pack of cigarettes and left the party before anyone else. When he looked back at the room on his way out, she was again standing in front of the window by herself staring at the night.

He walked to his tiny attic room in a fury, running from his past, clinging to the image of the girl in the red polka dot skirt. Who even wore such bright stylish clothes in those times of utter poverty?! Maybe she was the daughter of a party member who happened to look like Zoe and Carolina, the twin girls who spent a year in his parents' house during the war. It must have been just a ridiculous coincidence, there were lots of girls named Zoe, it was a fashionable name after the war, like the character in a famous Romanian comedy. More than ten years had passed, who knew where the real Zoe and Carolina were, if they were still alive!

That night he had a dream about his parents' house and the orchards in the spring. A luminous day before they went into refuge. Everybody was getting ready to leave to a city by the Danube River and instead of getting ready for the trip and helping his mother he ran into the orchard. Zoe was crying and turning into a snake that slithered into the ground. Carolina appeared wrapped in a cloak of yellow sanziene flowers and danced around him, a mating dance, a macabre dance of life and death. Those twin girls were not human stock, a voice kept telling him in the dream, he should run away, go help his mother, but he loved them, he loved one of them more, he told the voice, he couldn't let go. Then Gino the Italian soldier came with a gun and shot the dancing Carolina and the snake slithering nearby that had been Zoe. And only a handful of the yellow flowers were left on the ground. He always knew Gino was a fascist at heart, with his Italian opera songs on the victrola and his many secrets about what he had done in the war. He woke up shaking from the dream, drowned in unbearable and unexpected longing, a deep sadness that he hadn't allowed himself to feel since the summer of 1945 when his father died, his sister Lila almost died of scarlet fever, and they all almost died of starvation. And then there was an afternoon when the spirit girl wrapped in a yellow cloud slid through all the spaces of their devastated house and through his heart and the blind Gypsy violinist passed by their house playing the Kreutzer sonata like a hymn to the world's greatest sadness. It was as if only now did he allow himself to grieve all the losses and devastation that swept through his life over the last decade.

The darkness that settled over the entire country since that summer kept him closed up and focused on his work, not a step in the wrong direction, not a moment of inattention while still keeping himself unsullied by contacts with the party and its armies of informers and secret agents. He didn't care about the food shortages and never complained. The summer of the famine and the Russian boots had taught him endurance and surviving on minute quantities of food, a couple of pieces of dry bread, a slice of salami, some potatoes and lots of cigarettes. But he did care about what he could or could not teach, speak, write, and did not hide his feelings. Eyes were on him all the time, shadows in the dark ready to pounce and annihilate him if he went too far. Or even if he didn't. And yet he managed to glide through the gauntlet, pass by the danger untouched, his blue eyes blazing with the intensity of his thoughts and always a cigarette at the corner of his mouth.

After meeting the girl in the red polka dot skirt named Zoe, something in him shifted. He wanted to see her again, ask her who she was, ask her to tell him the truth. Just as simple as that. "Are you Zoe, Carolina's sister who lived with us during the war?" After his classes he took the longer route to his apartment, passing by Princess Maria high school at the exact moment when the girls came out at the end of the day, hoping desperately to see her. But he never did. As if she had never existed. As if the encounter at the party had been a dream.

Then one day he was asked to substitute one of the Romanian literature classes at Princess Maria high school. He walked into the classroom with his usual confidence thinking of the texts he was going to teach, the poem by the famous romantic poet about the morning star who falls in love with a mortal girl and transforms himself into a man of extraordinary beauty, dashes down to earth, lands directly into her bedroom, then begs her to marry him and follow him to his cosmic magnificent kingdom in heaven. Only the girl refuses his proposal because he is too cold, and too immortal and she is in love with a boy in the neighborhood who is warm and oh so perfectly mortal. As he walked into the classroom, he saw her sitting in the first row, her dark blonde reddish hair pulled back, and her eyes fixated on her book.

He levitated his way through that lesson and was at his most brilliant, teaching only for her. In turn she caught his act and answered the most difficult questions, even argued with him: of course, the girl isn't going to marry the star, immortality is a burden, a mortal life is light even though interrupted by death, she argued. He noticed she had stressed "interrupted by death" as if talking about herself, as if she was the one whose life had been interrupted by death. Immortality was boring indeed, he said, "but how about resurrection? And how about the immortality achieved through art, through what remains behind?" "That doesn't matter," she said. "All that matters is here, and it's very short," she said. A shadow like the approach of death passed on her face and that was when he recognized her fully and he was terrified. The poem ends with the two mortal lovers kissing under a linden tree, covered in fragrant linden flowers. He left the classroom in a flurry, not even the cigarettes could calm him down. All that matters is here and now, he kept hearing her words in his head at all hours of the day and night and her face transfigured by an uncanny light as she uttered them appeared to him more frequently in his dreams like a sign.

Northern Moldavia, June 2015

I visit Manole and Lulu the day after the incident with the local police, which leaves my brain burning in puzzlement. Manole is not just a neighbor and is not just an enterprising gardener who bought and saved a patch of my father's orchards. I feel that he is directly connected to my father, my grandfather, and our entire family history. And though I always laughed off all notion of existences and presences from another realm, or of beings caught in an in between space that is also an in between time, with Manole there is a different kind of energy, an unseen quivering of souls. I always said, "I'm an atheist who believes in the soul," and during the past two days in my father's native town, that statement appeared to me stale and meaningless, pretentiously academic. I have felt the presences of my ancestors trembling around that plum orchard like one feels the wind or the warmth of the sun on your arms after a long winter. But mostly when Manole is around as if he were the one waking them up and troubling them. I want to know who is buried in the back yard and how they died. And I want to know who Lulu is. Manole owes me some explanations.

"He he he, look who's here!" Manole bursts out laughing when he sees me coming through the back of the yard towards the bench underneath the plum tree patch. "How has the bed and breakfast been treating you?" He says "bed and breakfast" in English with a heavy accent that sounds more German than Romanian. I am stunned to hear Manole pronounce even a syllable in English, he seemed so entrenched in an archaic Romanian universe of language. "He he, you didn't think old Manole could speak American, did you? How are you, how is it going?" Again, he utters the last question in English and this time I have to laugh because he is trying to speak in the way which Romanians who want to imitate the American accent adopt, moving his jaws in an exaggerated way as if chewing a big blob of chewing gum. I also notice he is wearing his teeth which make him look younger and almost handsome.

"No, I admit I never thought you could speak English, Manole, I'm quite impressed." I sit down next to him on the bench and wait for a while. Again, I have the feeling of time changing its course and its pace. I almost start dozing off as if captured in a magic gauze of slumber. I startle myself. "Manole, I was sort of arrested yesterday and interrogated by the police because I climbed up in that tree over there and started eating some plums. What's going on?" "Well what adult woman in her right mind spends her day perched in a tree eating plums?" I burst out laughing and am reminded again that communication with Manole defies certain conventional expectations of logic. "That's not the point, Manole, the point is that there wasn't enough reason to violently arrest someone and take them to police headquarters for interrogation as if I were a criminal, even if my sitting in the tree and eating plums might have seemed bizarre." "You weren't 'sort of arrested' my dear, you were really arrested. You were lucky the little peasants who work at that sorry police station know me and are afraid of me, otherwise you would have spent some time in the local jail yonder there at the edge of town. You were trespassing property, weren't you aware of that?"

I realize Manole knew of what had happened, small town, news travels fast. "And then some really weird stuff started happening, Manole, I don't even know whether it was real or whether I was hallucinating but …" "It was real," he says without equivocation. I am stunned. And there is that breeze again like a warm caress that transports you. Lulu comes out of the house bouncing his ball, his blonde hair glowing in the afternoon sun. The neighbors must be cooking grilled peppers and eggplant because the yard is suddenly filled with the fragrances of delicious summer foods that I always craved for and never had enough of growing up. The smell, the breeze, the light, all is acute and alive as if it were inhabited by living creatures. I know I'm falling under that same spell and can't fight it, but I must find out important truths about my family. My life will be forever stuck in this point and not move any farther unless I disentangle my family's past. I don't waste any time because time is treacherous in this garden. "Manole who is buried in the orchards?"

The summer breeze gets warmer and more persistent and envelops me in a strong embrace almost frightful, too tight for comfort though irresistibly pleasant. The fragrances become palpable tickling your fingertips, a mellow chaos of the senses takes over the garden. A sweet desire to join the dead, the undead, the unliving, everybody who is out there or down there or up there! "Come here Corina my dear, let me show you …" Manole takes my hand and leads me to the back of the garden, his words echo and resonate, they sound both close and faraway. I follow Manole and do everything he says, there is no resisting him. Behind the patch of the plum and cherry orchard there is a meadowy place covered in the sanziene flowers, an ethereal gauzy yellowish carpet that appears out of place and alive. I wonder why I didn't notice it when I came through the back of the house the first time. There is a cross carved on one of the cherry trees in the back, the carving looks almost fresh, lighter than the rest of the tree bark as if it had been done yesterday and yet it looks deep as if it went right to the core, to the heart of the tree.

Everything here lives in doubles and opposites. "Here, touch here, touch this dress of flowers here" urges Manole and I wonder why he calls the small patch of flowery growth a "dress." Everything has a life of its own. Death is not the ultimate finish line, the end of everything. There is an exhausting life of things and souls beyond that line. Or not even beyond, but right here, everything in a dizzying simultaneity, the past and the present inseparable and indistinguishable from one another. I touch the ground where Manole showed me and I feel a slight deviation in the flow of time, a screeching sound as if the space where we are contained resettles, finding its groove.

"The two girls stayed hidden in the secret chamber your grandfather had built for them, for weeks..." starts Manole, his voice echoing from afar even though he is standing right next to me. His voice gets lost in the rustle of leaves. Another voice takes over. Two girls younger than ten are breathing in unison inside a tiny compartment in the wall, behind a door, behind a bookcase. "I can't breathe," says one, it's not clear which of the two because they are twins, they are both dressed in white cotton dresses, only one has a blue sash around her waist. "Give me a little bit of your breath." The one with the blue silk sash gives the other her breath, slowly, steadily, two hearts that still beat in unison for a while. Outside there is a deafening roar, fire and bombs wreck furniture and flesh and the cosmic balance. But the heartbeats are louder. One two three breathe, one two three breathe. Stop. The one with no sash is limp, faint, breath-less. "It's so dark in here in this tomb. Help us. Help." One of the girls goes out for air. Two men enter the room at that exact same moment. They are ferocious men in their unleashed hatred. The girl should have never left the room. It's too late now, and all the air inside her is gone. The other girl comes out and breathes into the one lying on the floor. But no amount of breathing from her sister can give her back her own breath. The bombs are louder than the screams but not the heart beats. Everybody thinks the heartbeats are also bombs exploding. Everybody is hiding in the cellar.

The father opens the door to the study, moves the bookcase aside, opens the secret compartment. "Come quickly, there is no time." "Carolina is sick, Uncle Tudor, she fainted, please save her." The father picks her up and carries her, Zoe follows him through the smoke to the underground cellar. Now everybody is there cuddled together in a corner on one of the larger sofas, like one enormous body. An unearthly light is shining in the orchards, and naked gypsies are dancing a mad hora. They talk about the two girls, and they say that one is "Hebraic and the other is something else." The father gets one of the sisters from the secret chamber amid the explosions and the bombs. He only gets one and not the other. The mother keeps the family distracted in conversation, they even play cards and sing an old song while the father carries one of the girls in his arms while the other follows him. The rest of the family must not see them.

After the explosions and the air raids are over, the father takes one of the girls in the greatest secrecy to the train station. He hides her in blankets like a package. There he hands her to an unknown man who gets on the train and puts her on the luggage rack. The train crosses the border into southern Transylvania and the city of Brasov that evening and then farther into the country or maybe even outside the country. Why one sister and not both is the crucial question that quivers in the golden smoldering air of the afternoon and that is buried under the dress of yellow flowers. There is an absence like the shape of a body without the contents that pulsates underneath the humid soft earth dressed in yellow. There is a movement of the air that is not the wind, curtains of warm air that are trying to settle. Everything here is restless and trying to settle. We are in a chaotic pocket of time and space where the past keeps reliving itself, Carolina and Zoe's story keeps re-telling itself. The present and the past coexist and take turns with each other in a merry go round movement.

I am not any more present here in this heavily perfumed mini orchard than Carolina, the strange girl who lost her breath, who ran out of her secret chamber for breath, who lost her breath again at the hands of two Nazi soldiers. I am part of the merry go round of relived memories. One moment I glide to the foreground and see Manole sitting quietly on the bench under the plum tree, another moment

Carolina comes forward telling her own story. I can't catch up with her because we are on the same axis at opposite sides of the time carousel. I hear her story in truncated bits, sometime melodious, sometimes screechy. I hear "out of breath, breath, breath ...." Like a sad song. Then "carries me into the yard .... Sunrise..." it's all in the present. A screeching wheel that doesn't let you rest. Then she turns into a cloud of yellow fog that my father mentioned in his journal, and she is giggling an unearthly giggle. "Open the door so I can go out and then close it right back," now she talks like a real person. "I fall out of the picture, and nobody catches me." It's all in the present. There is a picture in sepia with two girls in white dresses, an elegant couple, my grandparents, my father, and aunt Lila, and suddenly I remember having seen it in the small apartment where I grew up with my parents in Bucharest. I had found it in the sofa box together with Mitzi the one-eyed doll dressed in Romanian folkloric dress that used to belong to Aunt Lila when she was a girl during the war. The picture is in the present too, it's all happening at once. I look at the picture carefully and I think I am melting into it. Carolina moves in and out of the picture like an image under water, she comes to the surface, and she melts back under the waves. Once she fell through the ice and almost died but my father saved her. Carolina is laughing a bell like laugh, crystalline and pure as she is flying on the carousel of time. She fell out of the picture and remained suspended forever on that carousel.

I touch the ground; its ethereal gauze of yellow flowers and I feel it pulsate under my hand. An unbearable longing fills me like poison. Manole pulls me out of it and before I can blink twice, we are sitting on the bench under the plum trees. "It will only stop when your mother returns, Corina," says Manole. "She has to face her history and put her sister's soul to peace."

"Carolina was one of those creatures, you know, she was born a certain way, and she was left unfinished."

"What creature, Manole, what are you talking about? What way was she born? How unfinished? And what did you just say? 'Her sister?' Carolina is my mother's sister? My mother Zoe is that Zoe of the twin girls that were hidden and then lost, saved, but not truly saved?"

"You are asking too many questions now. There were dark acts that happened here which dislocated the order of things. You can't know it all at once. You wouldn't be able to comprehend it. Bit by bit, it's the only way."

Manole is laughing wholeheartedly, and I don't find one single drop of humor in all this, let alone comprehend it. I realize I knew it long ago but never allowed myself to believe it. My mother is the Zoe of my father's childhood, the Zoe of the twins. I knew it from her eerie silences, the estranged look she acquired at times, the torn picture. From the whispers between my parents, from the way my father was always worried about my mother, that she might fall sick, that she might leave, that she might die or disappear. From the way he pronounced her name as if calling to her from the depths of time and history, embracing all her secrets and all her pain.

An Encounter like No Other
Bucharest, 1955

Florin settles in the capital as an assistant literature professor at the University of Bucharest, at the height of the communist purges. People are getting arrested for no reason left and right, some never to be seen again. It's always a black van, it always happens at night. Not him, although he remains as loud and belligerent as ever in his proud nonadherence to the party line. His theory is that they know what he's all about because he carries his heart on his sleeve therefore, he does not present a serious danger to the party. Just a big mouth, that's all, no reason to worry about him. Not yet. On the contrary, he says, they are allowing small windows open of freedom and belligerence to give the illusion of freedom, look, everybody can say everything they want, we are a free and open society. He mimics the would be lectures of an unknown party speaker, voice. I am the token dissident, he says laughing.

He lives with his mother in an apartment in the city center, with a shared kitchen and bathroom, the best anyone could get in those days, if one was not a party member. Now that he lives with his mother he eats better; she is an expert at making a meal out of nothing, like she did all throughout the famines during the war. The neighbors are envious of her cooking skills and curious how she does it, only she hates talking about the meals she cooks. "We don't eat that much anymore these days, we mostly sleep," she jokes to avoid recipe discussions. She is certain one of them must be an informer, one Securitate person per floor, so she stays mostly quiet while using the shared kitchen, better not to say anything these days, and most of all not to complain about any shortages.

On the table next to her bed that she was able to have transported from the house with the orchards, there are two photographs, one a portrait of herself in a white silk and lace dress and a hairstyle like that of Queen Maria, the other a group picture of a memorable summer day in 1939, on the cusp of World War II. In the background is a kiosk covered in ivy and tiny white flowers, and everybody is lined up in a symmetrical way, Florin and his sister Lila, two younger lovely girls in white dresses, an elegant couple both smiling sadly from under their white straw hats, and she and her husband also in festive attire. At first sight one might think it's a happy photograph and everybody is smiling normally. But at a closer look, you are bound to notice the slightly off smiles on everybody's faces, a twinge of melancholy seeping through the sepia shades seems to get deeper as one stares at the picture longer. It's a photograph with a life of its own. She only leaves it out on her night table when Florin is not home, then when she hears his steps, she hides it in the drawer. One day she forgets and leaves it out. Florin stares at it with a sigh of displeasure but instead of leaving the room as she had thought he would, he picks it up and stares at it for a few long moments. His eyes fill with tears.

"That was such a happy day, mama! Everybody was still alive!" Victoria keeps knitting a blue sweater dress she has been making for Lila as if she hadn't heard her son's comments. "I think I saw her in Brasov last year, mother, while I was teaching there."

The tiny metallic sound of the knitting needles touching each other is the only sound heard in the room for a while. A comforting luminous silence fills the room as the summer afternoon sun rays shine on the furniture: old pieces she could save from the old house, a pink velour armchair, a vanity table and chair, one of the bookcases with several of the old volumes of German and French philosophers that her husband Tudor used to read.

"Everybody was still alive," his words echo in a chant-like whisper in the room. "Are you sure it was her? It's hard to believe." There is a long pause, a sun-drenched silence that envelops them almost with tenderness. "We never heard anything about her since that night …"

The blue sweater dress seems to be knitting itself, growing smoothly out of the mother's intrepid small hands. Lila will look nice in it, he thinks, trying to distract himself from the thoughts that hurt and haunt him. "So what? It doesn't mean it couldn't have been her," he says with an almost irritated tone. "So many people disappeared and then resurfaced again. Maybe she was one of those that resurfaced …."

A long pause, a flutter of the curtains, children playing ball outside, people still have hope and make children, some still believe in the future, he thinks. He knows that his mother knows something that she had never shared with him, that she will take the full secret of the twins and their parents to the grave. "Nobody has eyes like that, mother, nobody," he leaves the room in a flurry, almost angry at his mother's stubborn silent knitting. The summer afternoon is so balmy and fragrant that it hurts to be alive.

In the fall of that same year, he runs into her in the street as he returns from one of his lectures. There is a humid smell of autumn and wet leaves in the air and the city feels more alive than usual. Or maybe it's just an illusion, he feels happy because of the success of his lecture that morning. He is walking fast with his head down, engrossed in his thoughts, but when he gets to the statue of Michael the Brave at his bus stop, he lifts his head up. He notices her gaze directed towards him as if she had been watching him for a while. She laughs a full laugh like he had only heard from one person in his whole lifetime. Time melts, space expands and in the same moment he finds himself in his father's orchard running among the cherry trees in bloom with Zoe and Carolina as well as in front of the majestic statue of Michael the Brave looking at the same Zoe only twelve years older. The two pages in his life overlap and become one. Because now he is certain that he is standing in front of the same Zoe. It feels like kinship. She is laughing because he had dropped all his papers, and they fly in all directions like the autumn leaves. She leans down to help him pick them up. "Oh, you are teaching Lucian Blaga, I love him! His poetry and philosophy, his theory of the Romanian soul in tune with the Romanian space! Isn't he a forbidden author?" She whispers and laughs at the same time. This way no secret police lurking by can imagine that they are talking about forbidden texts and authors. He is not afraid because he teaches such authors. In fact, he says he is not afraid of anyone but God. And that's forbidden too, because you're not supposed to mention God unless you deny its existence and quote Marx about religion being "the opium of the people."

They are standing and talking about forbidden ideas, authors and realities as the buses stop and pass one after the other. He asks her where she lives, can he accompany her home. She avoids answering. She is wearing a navy-blue taffeta dress and a blue sash around her waist. He refuses to notice and to think of the blue sash. Once upon a time, two girls were hidden in a secret chamber, one had a blue sash and the other didn't, one made it, the other didn't tra la la! A wicked riddle song buzzes in his head annoyingly. It wasn't from a fairy tale. Yet it didn't seem real either. The autumn colors explode around them like a surprise. "Instead, let's have a beer at Carul cu Bere," her syntax sounds deliciously out of order, and they start walking slowly in the direction of the famous restaurant, called the Beer Cart. She smokes, she drinks beer in the middle of the day, she speaks fast about many ideas at once, he loves it. It's a new page, the past doesn't matter. It's all here in the honey light of this golden Bucharest afternoon, communists or no communists, the fall colors are still there, the crimson leaves dance their delicate pirouettes on the grainy uneven sidewalks. "The past matters," she says crisply as if answering to his thoughts, "but we are not going to talk about the past now." Her laughter has remained the same, despite everything, despite everything …

Northern Moldavia, December 1947
From Florin's Diary

It was the hardest winter ever. Not just cold- that we would have put up with more easily. But gray and dark like no other winter until then. No hope, and Russians everywhere. The Romanian communists who were trained in Russian style communism multiplied like mushrooms. The house was almost buried in snow like the year during the war when Carolina and Zoe lived with us. We had to climb out through the windows to get to the street and enormous icicles were hanging from the roof like shiny spears. It was getting harder to get wood for the stoves and my mother started using old pieces of furniture gathered in the basement to make a fire. "What's the point of keeping a whole lot of furniture in the cellar if we are all going to freeze to death?" Lila thought it was the greatest thing that she could throw old chairs and table legs into the fire and hear it crackle and groan like an angry dragon. Or that's what Lila thought, that the crackling fire was in fact an angry dragon. She still held on to the world of fairy tales with a vengeance, to her doll Mitzi and to her universe of fantastical creatures, even though she was already fourteen. I didn't mind the snow at all, I loved it. I hated the shadows of soldiers and unknown men that passed by our house every night like signs of inevitable and unending doom. "The war was better," our neighbor Mr. Gogu said sometimes in low whispers, smoking the nasty Romanian cigarettes avidly, "because we knew it would end at some point, it wasn't going to last forever, but there is no end in sight to this doom."

On December 30th of the year 1947, we heard on my father's old radio which my mother had learned to operate quite well, that King Mihai had abdicated. "Was forced to abdicate," was my mother's interpretation. We all sat in silence for a while staring at the tiny Christmas tree that my mother had managed to get for us that winter "so we have one more Christmas together in this house." She knew the house wasn't going to be ours for much longer, we all knew it but pretended we didn't. Mihai's abdication was the last and final blow to the old world and the beginning of a world of fear and imprisonment. I remembered my father's vehement speeches about the atrocities that happened during the Bolshevik Revolution and that continued ever since: the purges, the camps, the whole dark spectacle of it. A couple of old chairs were crackling in the fireplace and Gino, now six years old was chattering happily with his mother Mitzi, happy beyond belief with his new toy, a tiny wooden train that my mother was able to get for him in the only general store left in town. With most of the Jewish population wiped out, deported, or exterminated, and with the Russian restrictions on everything from food to clothes, to household goods, we lived in a ghost town.

The German Romanian soldier who had barged into our living room in the spring of 1942 when we returned from the city by the Danube, bleeding and almost dying, was living with us too, as Mitzi's new husband. Unlike Gino the Italian soldier who brought in Italian operas in the victrola, dancing and delicious Italian conversations, Kosmin was morose and dark, hardly ever talked, and did very little to help around the house. My mother didn't seem to mind and let him do whatever he wanted. At times she acted like he didn't exist. There was an air of suffering and gloom hovering around him all the time. After he recovered from his wounds, and lived with us for almost a year, he disappeared and reemerged in the fall of 1945. He asked where Father was, and when he found out he had died that summer, he sat in the pink chair and cried for a long time. Mitzi was so happy to see him again that she never left his side until he married her. His presence was heavy and felt awkward, like a mistake.

Christmas passed and a deeper, thicker gloom settled in our house. The snow surrounded us like the walls of a tomb. Carolina's presence, wrapped in the yellow curl of fog slithered around in my room or in the living room at the most unexpected hours, sometimes at dawn, waking me up with a flutter and a tiny wail, at other times before or after dinner as I sat in front of the fireplace to warm up and watched the fierce flames consume pieces of our old furniture. I never talked about her to anyone but wondered desperately whether she graced anybody else with her whimsical presence. It didn't seem likely, but I never dared to ask. She had changed her behavior since the summer of my father's death. Then she was timid, with bursts of energy that were almost affectionate, her unctuous gliding around our busted furniture during the days of Lila's scarlet fever and her recovery brought me solace, a cooling of the soul. But now she almost taunted me with quick appearances and flights, tiny rattling sounds that could have been giggles or something deeper, a shifting of dead souls fighting for space in their graves. A call so deep that if you listened for too long you might have gone mad and wanted to follow her and pair up with the whole lot of hungry souls.

Whenever I wanted to get away from the wailing giggling curl of yellow smoke that was Carolina, I ran to my mother and helped her with whatever she was doing, clearing the table, or looking for broken furniture for the fire, or I played with Gino and his small pile of toys. I engaged in every family chore just to move away from her, only to regret it and feel like I had hurt her, wishing for her to return. I had established a relationship with Carolina that was like that with an annoying, yet indispensable sister. Someone I needed for my survival but who exhausted me out of my wits because of the unpredictable nature of her visits. Between Lila's constant storytelling and conversations with Mitzi, and Carolina's random appearances, I had enough sisterly comfort and annoyance for two lifetimes.

Around that same time, between Christmas and the New Year, the ticking in the wall restarted unexpectedly. "Ma'am the snake in the wall is back," shouted Mitzi with so much joy as if God in heavens had descended into our pathetic looking living room, to tell us that the endless series of unimaginable horrors and sufferings our family had endured for eight years since the start of the war to that wretched December of 1947, had only been a bad dream and we would all wake up to a new dawn, a happy time, that was much like the happy times before the war, only better. "Our luck is back, Ma'am," she yelled and picked up Gino in her arms with unparalleled effusion. Mother looked at her calmly, almost with irony and said: "We can only hope so, Mitzi. Let's wait and see how our luck turns. It can always be better, but it can be worse too.

It turned out it could indeed be worse. Several times that evening, we heard through the scratchy sound waves of my father's radio that King Michael had abdicated, as if the news needed to be repeated to dispel any disbelief that such an event might occur. All hope that the postwar darkness might be only temporary vanished forever. We were now going to be fully under Stalin's foot, with scary crowds of Romanians converted to the new regime enthusiastically cheering. The new snake in our wall ticked viciously all morning. "This must be our bad luck snake," said mother with a bitter smile. That same evening, a Russian officer accompanied by a Romanian policeman in civilian clothes knocked thunderously on our door and asked me to follow them. Piles of snow from the roof shifted and fell with a thick thud in front of our door. My mother, in whose eyes I saw for the first time since the war had started, a flash of terror, stood in front of them and said: "Why does he need to go with you? He hasn't done anything wrong. Where are you taking him?" "Don't worry comrade Angelescu, he'll be back soon, we just want to talk to him for a bit." "Why can't you talk here? I'll make you some tea and you can talk here in the living room all you want." I noticed my mother's voice was trembling. The Russian soldier didn't say anything, he just looked stern. Though he was the one in uniform, it was the Romanian civilian whose presence and self-important tone sent shivers throughout my entire being.

I remembered how during the German occupation, it was sometimes the Romanian civilians, the members of the Iron Guard, with their green shirts and hateful looks that were the more zealous ones in the work of deporting and massacring our Jewish neighbors than even the SS soldiers who acted on the command of Hitler himself. My people were an enthusiastic lot, I had that to be proud of, I thought to myself looking at the Romanian overzealous communist wearing some semblance of a Soviet type of uniform and recognizing him in the end as the son of one of my former high school teachers. Indeed, love your neighbor! What a joke that had been in our town of "good" people and "good" neighbors. The new snake in the wall must have indeed been our bad luck snake.

Then the enthusiastic Romanian communist accompanying the Soviet one looked around the room, measured it up and down, and said mockingly: "Nice house, you own it? Is the land in the back yours too?" We knew what that meant, everybody was losing their properties to the new State, some were turned into co-operatives, some were just taken over by the new communists and by the Russian troupes still living in our country. They had to be sure their system was well established in all areas of life, from the running of agriculture to school education, to the division of lands to the new language we had to speak. It was a dry language filled with formulae that extolled the virtues of the new world with each coma and each dotted "i." We also knew that the questions were superfluous, they knew everything about everybody, they knew of course that the land, the house, the orchards were all our property left to us by my father's father who had bought it and improved it between the two wars. My mother took a chance though. She no longer looked scared but fierce.

"It's a bad house, it's all rotten and it's full of snakes. The trees in the yard are rotten also, they don't give anything since the big drought. We can't wait to leave it and move in with my side of the family in Bucharest. Anybody whose lap this property falls into will just be getting a lot of trouble, that's all, nothing but trouble. If you want to have it after we leave, just go ahead, you'll inherit the bad snakes inside the walls too."

I couldn't remember hearing my mother speak for so long in years. She looked radiant at the end of her speech. Her hair was braided in the Queen Maria style, and she looked like a queen herself. A sad but defiant queen. She even winked at the man and invited him in. He was taken aback. The Russian soldier grunted and hollered something in Russian to him. I was myself taken aback, not just by my mother's cunning denigration of our house and orchards, but by the news we were going to move to Bucharest any time. When I looked around, everybody in our family stood in an unmoved pose, as if for a photograph, staring at the two men and making a human wall between them and the rest of the house. For a second the thought crossed my mind that the soldier standing proudly on the threshold of our front door might have been that very Russian soldier who three years earlier killed and cut our beloved Girl to pieces or gouged our electric outlets, or both. Or someone like him: beefy, well fed on food he took from the local population, with brazen eyes like everything were owed to him and wearing big heavy boots up to his knees. Even Mitzi looked stern and not scared the way she looked for most of the time since the occupation of Poland in 1939. Her usually panicked eyes now expressed disdain. Kosmin held her by the waist and looked straight at the two men. Lila was holding her one-eyed doll and staring at them too.

Gino went to the Romanian man and pulling him by the hem of his sheepskin coat asked shamelessly: "Are you a bad man?" The Russian soldier smiled at Gino, having no idea what he had said. Maybe children were his soft spot, maybe he had a wife and a couple of children himself and was not just a communist brute but had a human side despite his brutish appearance. The Romanian smiled at first and then displayed an embarrassed face. He didn't know what to say at first, but he recovered and answered, "No kid, of course I'm not a bad man, is that what your parents are teaching you?" Mitzi proved more presence of mind in that moment than in all the time I had known her and jumped in: "No, Sir..." "Comrade, there are no more sirs anymore," the man corrected her brusquely. "No, Mister

Comrade, he is just scared because we had a thief and a murderer come into our house some while ago, Mr. Comrade, and he's done scared witless ever since. He asks everybody who comes in that question, Mr. Comrade, please." I could only smile at Mitzi's outburst of unleashed imagination and storytelling talent at such a key moment in our lives, not to mention her mixture of forms of address. Twilight was falling and the snow shined in bluish tints through our front windows.

I thought of Carolina and wondered why she hadn't come to our rescue, like my father had once come to her and Zoe's rescue during the war. Maybe to her that wasn't a rescue at all since she never made it alive out of their hiding place. But just when I was thinking that thought, a breeze seemed to pass through that couldn't have come from outside because the two men had closed the door behind them. The snake in the wall started ticking like mad again and the two men touched their weapons at the sound, looking worried. Now they were our prisoners more than we were theirs. The air smelled of earth after rain and at first was hot like a mid-summer gust, then it acquired a more palpable consistency and turned to tongues that licked like a cool flame. It enveloped the two men from head to toes for the time of a blink and a chaotic agitation started in the room. Gino started screaming and running around, Mitzi ran after him knocking the last of my mother's precious Venetian vases down, Kosmin started looking for something under the sofa cushions, Lila was throwing a tantrum and yelling at her doll Mitzi, and my mother picked up the duster and furiously started dusting the furniture that hadn't yet ended into the fire. Everybody ignored the two men standing in the doorway, their boots dripping water from the melting snow. A huge pile of snow crashed from the higher to the lower veranda roof with another thud and the two men seemed dazed, as if ignoring their own presence in our house.

Then it all changed brusquely. The Russian soldier took out his gun, turned towards his Romanian comrade and asked him to put his hands up behind his head which he did instantaneously. A greenish blinding light shone on the two men standing in the doorway like an interrogation light. Carolina's yellow curl of smoke traversed the greenish light. Memory people emerged from everywhere: Gino the Italian soldier, the widow who had once sat at our table the day we went into refuge to the city by the water, Sofia and Sebastian who had stayed with us briefly after my father saved them from the big massacre in Iasi helping them escape on a late-night train in June of 1941. Unknown people, maybe from someone else's past, were all sitting around our dining room table and eating in silence. Never my father. Again, the past slid into the present through the opening that Carolina kept between their lives and ours. It wasn't that she was awakening ghosts, but she brought the past and the present together like two adjoining rooms. Life went on in each of the rooms unbeknownst to one another. Our room of life was swept with chaos by that closeness, while theirs stayed the same, unmoved across time. They didn't care about us, only we still cared about them.

While mother was sweeping and dusting furiously in our space of life, the Russian soldier guided the Romanian civilian police to open the front door and step outside into the snowy night. A small tunnel through the snow had been dug out by Kosmin that morning so we could go in and out without having to climb out the windows onto the roof. I pushed the door shut behind them. A deafening thud of snow, then a shot. I was pretty sure it was a gunshot. I had heard enough of them during the war not to recognize one.

The frenetic agitation in our house quieted. Only thin delicate shadows of the memory people could be discerned around our dining room table. Barely their contours, almost invisible yet still clinging to that moment of vicinity with the present and with our lives. I remembered the voracious hunger of the summer of 1945, devouring us like a beast of the apocalypse, unforgiving. It was more like the hunger remembered me; not just people, but events and feelings relived themselves in our overly charged, overly crowded present filled with all generations, still avid for life, fidgeting in the space of our dilapidated yet still beloved house that our mother had saved from the pillage of the new rulers in town for just a little bit longer. I thought I heard Carolina sob quietly in her smoke consistency, a sob that was almost a sigh of relief not necessarily of pain. I was pretty sure I understood that she had been watching over us for four years and had likely created a protective layer around us, that she wove around us, of energies that stood up to the ultimate obliteration of our family, house, lives, though still put us through unbearable tests.

Not all danger and suffering were staved off, but the biggest ones, the bombs during the war that obliterated many of our neighbors but not us, the German soldiers that executed many of the citizens in our town but not us, the Russian soldiers that crushed so many under their callous boots but left us alive. She did what she could, there was so much danger and evil that poured onto our country, our town, our neighborhood that some of it still seeped through Carolina's protective wall, like through a sieve. She made herself present to me, an undeserved gift I thought. Every time I wanted to ask her but how about Zoe, where did she go, with whom, is she with you or with us, Carolina? In which room does Zoe reside? And that was when I always lost Carolina, her disappearance a rebuke of my greed for knowledge and happiness still.

The following morning the winter sun, we called it sun with teeth, shone fiercely and coldly made the snow blindingly white almost blue. There were blotches of blood on the path leading from the front doorstep to the street that Mitzi tried to cover in the morning by throwing pails of cold water over them, she couldn't stand the sight of blood, she said. Only the water she threw froze instantaneously and the blood shone through a layer of ice. Mitzi didn't understand the laws of physics very well and marveled every time she saw that instantaneous transformation of water from one state to another. It baffled her and seeing her wonder I burst into laughter for the first time in months. I shook with irrepressible peals of laughter. I was a grown man now of seventeen, my sister Lila fourteen and we had both aged twice that amount during the war years, yet also were stunted in our physical growth.

Our childhood had been sliced short in its ripest years and sat smoldering somewhere inside us, erupting at its own will at the most unexpected times. Lila was so excited to hear me laugh that she rushed outside in the freezing air and started laughing just by seeing me laugh. Mitzi was puzzled and offended at our reaction, thinking we laughed at her, which we did. And so did my mother who watched the whole scene from the inside of our front room with her arms crossed. She was beautiful and young for one last time that frigid winter morning with fresh blood stains on our doorsteps and a mad reckless sun shining onto everything.

"Now they are killing each other among themselves," she said laughing. Lila and I were both pretty sure that she was referring to the Russian soldier shooting the Romanian civilian and found that even funnier. Mitzi who was about to start crying turned to laughter too. She might not understand that water turns to ice in an instant at the right temperature, but she understood the dark irony of my mother's statement. We didn't care about the Romanian civilian police, really, there was no use pretending we were still good Christians caring for our fellow men and women. We wanted those Romanian police communists dead, every one of them, and the Russian soldiers piling up on top of them, dead too.

The rest of the day we let the radio roar at will its news of the abdication of the King and the beginning of the new era of the Romanian Communist Party and the new Popular Republic of Romania. Toward evening, my mother, Mitzi, and Lila prepared New Year's cakes with walnut and poppy seeds from all the rations of flour, sugar and eggs and some preserves that my mother kept hidden in our cellar since before the war and had miraculously survived all the pillages and raids through our house. At midnight, some of the remaining neighborhood children sparked fireworks. A timid choir of young voices singing a traditional song trailed through the snowy silence of our street with bells and the bleating noises of the goat decorated for the New Year's celebration. They stopped at the remaining houses for good wishes and a few coins. We all came out on our veranda to greet them: they were neighborhood children claiming bits of their war childhoods and refusing the total obliteration of our customs.

I remembered how much my father used to like the Christmas and New Years' Eve caroling and the good-luck-decorated goat being walked through town for people to touch, the ringing of the bells strapped around her neck, the children's "sorcova," a stick ornate with pine branches, bells, and colored ribbons to chase evil spirits. It was hard to imagine how those kids were able to procure a live goat in those times of rabid poverty and devastation. Maybe everybody hid something or somebody in their cellars. Maybe every remaining household had their secret miracles like we did, their secret chambers of the living and the nonliving cohabiting and watching over them, the past and the present brushing by one another in unexpected flurries and mysterious dances. The stars shone fearlessly over the snow, making it glow with bluish streaks of light. There were things in the world that didn't care a bit about our wars and regimes. Stars, goats, the tree roots of our orchard sleeping and dreaming under the heavy snow didn't give a damn, the memory people were untouched by any of it, the children caroling with their dressed-up goat seemed to have little knowledge or worry about the forced abdication of the King. Gino's laughter of joy at the sight of the baby goat welcomed in the New Year. For that night we didn't care either. We followed the example of the snow, the tree roots, the stars, the goat, the singing children.

Bucharest, Summer 1956
From Florin's Diary

"There is no place to hide this summer, the Securitate move in on everybody who shows the slightest sign of refusal to embrace the party, the regime, the creed of happiness for all. They crawl in all corners like roaches, and when you least expect it, when you let your guard down and breathe for a brief moment thinking you are all right, they've forgotten about you, that's when they bite, emerge from black Russian Volga cars, black vans, the same dull hardened faces and greasy hair, small eyes filled with rancor and emptiness. Nothing, nimic, nichivo. A void of conscience and feeling. Hard to comprehend how they were all created from the same mold, in such a short time, to imagine who they were and what they did before the takeover, before the party and its cohorts of trained ideologues and killers appeared.

Even with the cohorts of human roaches, party killers and informers, still a stubborn life pulses in the streets, in tiny apartments made of appropriated divided properties, a stolen poem, a furtive smile, a warm handhold. A secret life unwinds between the cracks and refuses to be obliterated. It grows its secret crooked tendrils that thrust through the spaces between enemy footsteps, suspicious glances, malicious reports, and whispers. There are whispers underneath whispers, a battle for life and death between whisperers on two sides. An exhausting and inexhaustible chase, and often a maddening confusion between prey and predators. Sometimes the victims become executioners out of exhaustion, and confident executioners end up with a bullet in their head or bite into a poisoned apple. Arsenic for example is the poison of choice, tiny doses, undetectable, lousy meatballs, or lentil soup laced with the white powder cause virulent un-treatable cancers that look like natural deaths. They say Stalin was killed like that, by his own men. Whoever had the idea waited far too long to lace his Kremlin foods with arsenic."

These pages from my father's precious journal carried twice across the Atlantic in both directions are written in red pencil as if he were writing in it while correcting student papers. He took a break from correcting and with the same red pencil he jotted down his thoughts on an early June day in Bucharest of 1956 in his mother's apartment with the communal kitchen and one bathroom. This is how I imagine my father while he wrote this section of his journal. Sometimes I imagine the writer and focus on how he must have felt and what he must have been doing at that time. Other times I completely forget it was my father writing and get swept up by the story as if I am reading a novel written by an unknown author.

Florin and Zoe spend late evenings in the parks of Bucharest talking about all the writers and philosophers of world literature in the heavy fragrances of linden trees, under cascades of linden flowers, Bucharest at its most glorious time, Securitate or not. There are still trees, flowers, birds, all has not been eviscerated, it will take time before they can wipe out all nature and every inhabitable corner. Better make the most of every breath taken in the interstices between footsteps and whispers. Some are still unafraid and intimidate their predators with their unafraid stands. Like Florin and Zoe who walk arm in arm taking side streets to the university, the longest routes, and quietest alleys.

She never talks about what happened, about the war, as if it never existed. He has stopped bringing up the topic and broaching any topic from the past, before 1950. Anything before that year is taboo, a dark abyss. Even though he is by now sure she is the one, the Zoe he knew and played with in the same house during the years of 1939, 1940, and 1941, there are still times when she looks entirely foreign, unrecognizable, a glacial film casts over her green eyes, almost terrifying, sometimes she is completely absent. But there are times when she becomes overwhelmingly alive in the present moment, as if compensating for all the times when she is not. And then her sudden outbursts of laughter, the philosophical statements, ironic comments, bold retorts — it all blooms in a warm familiarity, fragrant and life affirming like the heavy clusters of linden flowers. A certain aura protects her and makes her both invisible and untouchable by the Securitate "roach" people. This is how Florin likes to call them, when he doesn't refer to them by the more formal term of vermin. He feels protected by the same aura, which, together with the shield of boldness he created during his years in Brasov, make him believe he is invincible.

"I'm not afraid of them," Florin keeps saying defiantly, brushing strands of dark blonde hair off his heated forehead. "Neither am I," she echoes and laughs an irreverent laughter. They drink beer at their favorite café in the park by the lake near the Arc of Triumph, he buys her daisies and roses from the Gypsy girl making the rounds in the neighborhood. She knows them and always comes to their table, an old Gypsy accordionist plays the same old song for them, over and over again until the summer moon comes out. Florin recites verses from the 99-strophe poem of the great romantic poet he had once taught in her high school class in Brasov. She picks up the verses, nothing escapes her, they argue about the choice of the young woman in the poem, did she want the cold immortal star or the warm mortal young man, until they both agree it wasn't a fair choice. "They should have both — immortality and warm love," she laughs wholeheartedly like there had never been a dark moment in her life. Maybe there hasn't, he consoles himself, maybe it was all a bad dream.

His memory never failed him though, and once the moments of magic dissipated into the grind of the everyday, he knew very well that it had all happened: the German raids in their house during the war, sweeping through like poisoned winds, harsh German words, merciless German boots, the Iron Guard men in their green shirts even more menacing and sinister than the Germans themselves, the daily shuffle in their old magnificent house with the orchards, hiding people in secret places, closets, cellars, every little space where a living creature could fit was filled with a breathing person that fit in it and that hid from a deadly enemy. The two girls he so adored, Carolina and Zoe, sitting quietly in the pink armchair holding hands, watching curiously the family animation around them, then one day disappearing. Both overnight! The American bombs, the Russian bombs, the German bombs, every nationality of bomb turning neighborhoods to smithereens, almost wiping out their family if they hadn't been "lucky."

He remembered his painful yearning for the twin girls who suddenly disappeared, even though he felt their presence, their aura and heard their breathing in the house for months on end, until he didn't. One night, the last night he heard Frida and Gabi's worried voices, his mother reassuring them, "we'll take good care of them don't worry." Then the night of the big bombs whistling and crashing into the neighbors' house, the family gathered on the old dusty sofas in the cellar, crazy Gypsies dancing naked in the moonlight, and then a formidable silence in which the irreversible absence of one of the girls felt painfully real. "Where are Carolina and Zoe, mama?" the echoes of the anguished questions from that period of this childhood still linger and toss in his brain at times. His mother's stubborn silence through the remaining years of the war, and the yellow foggy presence following him through their dilapidated house, confusing their enemies and protecting him and his family, haunting him through sweltering famine ridden summers and blood-stained snows. He remembered every terrifying bit of it and even if he tried, he couldn't forget it. But Zoe's impenetrable eyes that refused to give any of the secrets of the past made him doubt himself. Not for long though, not for long. He knew his childhood was all there wrapped carefully in a thin shroud of pretend oblivion, ready to awaken any minute. The restless flock of memories are swallows rushing to their nests at twilight.

The more Zoe let down her guard, the more he remembered. His mother warned him though as soon as he met her: "Don't trouble her Florin, let her be, she doesn't want to remember, go along with the pretense if you want to be with her." He followed his mother's advice for the most part. They walked their way through the linden filled early summer of 1956 as if they lived in a different country, then plunged into the July canicular days head on, unafraid, unmindful of the eyes watching them from hidden alleys and hallways. She studied for her exams in philosophy, he proctored his exams in literature. He waved and greeted the university informer warmly at the gate every morning, like a joke of defiance. She had moved in with him in his mother's apartment, happy in the one room put at their disposal by Victoria, despite the shared bathroom and kitchen and the suspicious looks of the neighbors. They weren't married, and they looked foreign, she with her polka dot skirts and silky blouses, he with his starched white shirts, a strikingly handsome couple dressed too well for the misery of the times. They refused to conform to the grayness of the times at all costs, even though it meant washing and ironing their one good set of clothes every single day. "It's not bad at all, compared to other places I've been," she said referring to the apartment the first time he took her to "meet" his mother, playing the game of not knowing and not remembering every step of the way because that's what she wanted and demanded.

Zoe always refused to let Florin get close to the street, alley, house where she lived. "Just a tiny mansarda, attic room, with a grouchy old lady who lets me have the room for practically nothing. It's dirty, smelly, maybe another time when she cleans the place," she always told him whenever he got too close. He didn't believe a word of it of course but went along with the game as his mother advised. One afternoon he walked her a little too far, a little too close, so he could see the house.

It was one of the old prewar houses of Bucharest with ornate architecture and wrought iron entrance gate, one of the few that had survived the bombs. She forgot herself talking heatedly about the French enlightenment, Diderot, her favorite, and before she knew it the house was in sight. She pretended it was not it, just a bit farther down. The glacial film spread over her face, she said goodbye like a stranger, and he thought he saw a familiar silhouette, a tall, slender, aged, slightly bent female silhouette whose sight pierced his memory chambers painfully. A pain so acute it felt like an ulcer. He had to hold on to the nearest fence, electric pole, anything that stood in the ground. He closed his eyes for a second to calm his pain and when he opened them, she was gone, the silhouette had disappeared, the wrought iron gate was shut like it had never been open.

The street was quiet as a tomb, an old street of old Bucharest. A cuckoo bird sang his tired afternoon call and there was a heavy smell of red and white mulberries filling the sidewalk, crushed under heavy steps, an overly sweet and heavy smell of summer. Not a soul or a sound in the street. Maybe everybody had died already, and he was the last one left alive to carry the memory of his family, his people, the whole lot of his miserable people. He had to carry this history like the heaviest of burdens, in a heavy iron box like the heart of Queen Mary of Romania hidden somewhere in a secret place by the Bulgarian seashore in a city with a funny Turkish name. Peoples, and borders, and historical periods, annexed and stolen territories, long painful journeys on smelly trains to somewhere by the Danube, a bunch of people sitting around the table in his parents' house eating in silence. A kaleidoscope of images, a wild burst of memory sweeps through his body weakened by exhaustion, too little food and too many cigarettes. Luckily a kind person passed him by as he was about to faint holding on to a newly installed telephone pole. Communication was easier and so was the surveillance, they listened to conversations here too, not just in the street, in line for bread or through thin walls.

There were still a few kind people left in the country it seemed, a tall gaunt man in a blue shirt helped him regain his balance, tapped him gently on his back. "Watch out professor, they are after you." Florin was pretty sure that the kind man helping him steady himself had said those words, whispered them, then asked loudly if he was all right, was he going to be all right? He thought he had recognized him too, his bold generous features, a familiar face from his recent past, he couldn't quite place him. Before he thought twice, the man was gone. He was alone in the dead silence of the street. The air was soaked in ripe mulberries smell. The cuckoo bird called again, maybe for his mate. He hurried home to his mother, he knew she was waiting for him with a dinner made of a handful of vegetables she had gotten at dawn from the local market, and the last rations of oil and flour for the month.

That night there were loud knocks on the door of his mother's apartment. He had a feeling before night fell. He didn't tell his mother but let her go to sleep and he put his clothes back on as if going out. Victoria was woken by the knocks, got out of bed, and answered herself. She knew it too and was trembling. The first time ever he saw his mother shaking with fear. For him not for herself. Two men in white shirts stepped right into the house uninvited, passed by her and went straight to him. They always sent them in pairs to barge into people's houses.

His mother stood shield between him and the two men and faced them boldly: "what do you want barging into people's houses in the dead of the night?" "We just want to have a few words with your son, comrade, that's all!" "Oh, yes? At this hour? Have a few words right here, why don't you?" He remembered another evening, the abdication of the King, the bluish snows big as the house, his mother doing the same thing then, making herself into a shield and asking the Russian soldier and the Romanian Securitate to leave her son alone, what had he done? The yellow smoky presence of Carolina swirling in and confusing everybody into a frenzy, the Russian soldier shooting the Romanian man. The red blotches in the snow the next morning, his mother and Kosmin shoveling snow over the blood as if nothing had happened. Carolina was nowhere to be seen or heard now, she had disappeared ever since, she hadn't come to him since he moved to Bucharest. Maybe she was just a spirit of the north, of the countryside and couldn't exist in urban areas. Or maybe she had finally melted back into the endless night of non-being. One of the two men who looked almost human was going to give in to Victoria's plea, but his comrade whispered something to him, threw him a harsh glance and turned to his mother: "Comrade Angelescu, we need to talk to your son at our office, he'll be back soon." Florin knew that soon could be anything from a week to five years or never. He leaned over and whispered in her ear, he didn't care, he was not afraid: "take care of Zoe, mama."

The night air was warm and fragrant, he crushed the mulberries on the sidewalk under his feet as he was walked to the black Volga van. When he lifted his head up towards the morning star, he saw his mother at the small balcony crossing herself, blowing him a kiss, holding her hands in a prayer. The morning star sparkled indifferently. They shoved him into the van. The driver was a tall slender man who looked back at him. Florin realized it was the same man who had warned him earlier in the street and said, "watch out professor, they are after you." He then remembered more: it was one of his former students from the high school in Brasov, the one who invited him to the party in the elegant villa behind the municipal park and where he met Zoe standing by the window in a red polka dot skirt and a white blouse.

Anything was possible in those times, and everybody could be anybody, like a grotesque circus, a wicked merry go round of saints, monsters and everything in between and you never knew who was who in the mad carousel. He wasn't sure in what category this tall former student of his fell, and he didn't care. He thought of Zoe and what she was going to think of his disappearance. She knew about disappearances better than anyone else. It so happened that she was not there that night as she had gone back to stay at her old apartment for a couple of days, the lady who rented her the room had fallen sick, and she wanted to care for her. So, she said, but he knew it wasn't really the truth.

The black Volga took off with a screech like a bad conscience, cut through back alleys and came out in the main boulevard by university square. A couple of drunks were leaning against the university walls, an empty trolley bus was dragging itself like a huge caterpillar on the empty boulevard. The night was littered with poverty and fear. Florin stared ahead of him in the back of the black Volga flanked by the two men who gave off a smell of rotten garlic and sweat, and for the first time since the war he prayed. Not for himself, but for Zoe.

June 1948, Northern Moldavia and Bucharest

My mother sold the house on June 1st, 1948, to a family of three who were relocating from northern Bessarabia, the area that had been entirely appropriated by the Soviet Union in 1945. A man and a woman in their thirties with a teenage daughter, shabby and tired like they had just escaped the war. They seemed to wear soviet style factory clothes, dusty overalls and blue shirts, and the daughter wore a type of uniform, drab and too small for her lanky growing body, with a red scarf tied around her head. An impenetrable sadness flowed from their eyes. Their movements were robotic, mechanical, and absent, as if they had forgotten something. As if they had forgotten how to live. They spoke with a softer accent, almost Russian, and paid on the spot the sum that Victoria had asked for, a derisory sum in devalued notes, a whole satchel of them that the woman carried in a bag hanging from her shoulder by a strap like a postal worker. Everything about them was off, a moment too late, their words out of sync with their gestures, their expressions vacant and askew. They asked in the same robotic manner when they could move in and my mother said by the end of the month, to which the woman asked in a surprisingly loud voice: "what day at the end of the month can we move in, comrade?"

Mother was slightly taken aback by her tone and answered almost irritated and formal: "As I said, the end of the month, that will be June 30th." "You will have to pay us rent for this month, comrade if that is the case," the woman replied. "Fine, here is another hundred lei," my mother said handing her the notes. The woman counted the notes meticulously and put them in the satchel from where she had taken the money to pay for the house. Lila, who was sitting on the sofa behind the couple, with Mitzi in her arms as usual, made faces at the family and Gino for some reason that morning was filled with irrepressible energy and ran around the room singing an old Romanian children's song at the top of his lungs. The woman asked out of nowhere: "Doesn't he know any songs of country and party?" To which Mitzi the maid burst out laughing and said: "No ma'am, we aren't done teaching him those songs yet, there is nothing wrong with this old song, is there? My mama used to sing it to me when I was a little girl." It was the first time Mitzi had mentioned anything about her childhood or family. I had always somehow assumed she was an orphan, and my parents had taken her in as a teenage girl from the orphanage at the edge of the town.

It felt as if we were all stuck in that awkward moment forever, and a whiff of a new and terrifying era of phoniness and lies was starting right there right then in our already sold living room. I prayed to Carolina, begging her to make an appearance and swirl around in one of her colored curls of fog, disrupting the order and pace of things, breaking the static stale air with her convoy of memory people. But Carolina had been silent and absent since the New Year's night when she saved me from being taken away by the Russian soldier and the Romanian Communist informer. My mother broke the awkwardness with an abrupt "goodbye comrades, we will vacate the house by June 30th. We will be out in the morning. Kindly if you excuse us now, we have to pack our things." She moved towards the front door, opened it and politely showed them out

We spent the remaining month of June packing up the house in a frenzy, big and small items, precious China, Venetian crystals, the few that had escaped Mitzi's carelessness and the various purges that swept through the house, my father's hundreds of books, leather bound editions of German and French poetry, philosophy, Romanian fairy tales and folklore, the entire universe my parents had so carefully crafted over decades and which Lila and I had grown up in, our only known world. Parts of it still held up, in small pieces. We had no idea what the future had in store for us, but it didn't feel like anything good was on the horizon. That June felt gooey and unkind, the orchard was hardly producing any fruit as if the trees had dried up in revolt against the violence and terror of that new era. The family that had bought our property didn't seem to care about the orchards and didn't even bother to look at them or ask about the fruit trees we grew.

I soon found out I did not need to worry about that -- a few days after the sale of the house, two men from the local party headquarters came to our house and asked to see the orchards. I had gotten used to the type of people who belonged to those rapidly growing ranks. They all seemed created by the same mold: short, stocky, small foreheads and tiny eyes, a new species born only for the needs of the sinister party that led us now. I wondered day and night where the party had found and co-opted these people. I had never seen them before anywhere in town.

Our neighbor Mr. Gogu said they were even bringing people by bus from remote areas of the country, rural areas forgotten by the world, feeding, clothing, and indoctrinating them to be loyal party people and informers. They were tabula rasa, Mr. Gogu said, "virgin clay," the party could mold them any way they wanted. Yes, but where had the original party people come from immediately after the abdication of the king in 1947? I asked. Mr. Gogu, who had lost one son and one brother in the war, wasn't afraid to say anything out loud. "What are they going to do to me? Arrest me? Kill me? Fine, let them go ahead, motherfuckers, I don't care, the only thing I can lose is my life, so what? Some of these people were brought from Russia, others from Bessarabia, others have existed all along among us, and we just didn't notice them. We were too busy protecting ourselves from outside forces while the monster was lying asleep among us all along." He dragged from his American unfiltered cigarette, and I was for the hundredth time amazed at Mr. Gogu's ability to obtain such luxuries during the darkest time. Nobody knew how he did it and he never revealed his secret. But as always, he shared one with me and I smoked it with delight.

The two Party men who came to look at our orchard were no exception to the rule, both wearing dark suits that were too tight, sweaty, and grim, walking with impunity through our house to the back door leading to the orchard as if they owned the house, the land, the country. Which really, they sort of did, together with others like them. I went after them walking behind my mother. I sensed the nervousness in her by the way she kept touching and fixing the braided chignon she was wearing that day. We found ourselves in the orchard with the two men who walked up and down the property, looking at the trees like they were people they hated, touching their trunks occasionally, shaking a branch for fruit here and there. A heavy stillness in the air settled over us and slowed everything down.

I sensed Carolina's presence sneaking around us, dancing and gliding through the trees and on the heels of the two suited party men. Tiny yellow flickers and threads of smoke played between the branches. I sensed the sudden weariness of the trees and heard their barely audible moans as if cracking under the burden of the heat and the heavy silence, the poisonous hatred exuding from the two men. The one wearing a straw fedora hat that made him look like a grotesque clown bent down and picked a ripe plum off the ground and tasted it. He grimaced in disgust and threw it back on the ground. The other one with a balding sweaty head picked a cherry off one of the branches hanging low. I thought I almost heard a tiny wail, a whine of pain. The trees were coming alive as they paradoxically dried up and poisoned their own fruit in a form of revolt against a greedy ruthless invader that swallowed our properties and tried to steal our souls and our lives. They couldn't steal the souls of the trees though.

The man who picked and ate the cherry seemed to become pale, greenish almost, and spat the contents on the ground. I almost laughed, but my mother held my hand and squeezed it as a warning. Just then Gino came out of the house running towards us and laughing. Mitzi was running after him, trying to catch him. Before she could catch him, he picked up a couple of fallen cherries from the ground and stuffed them in his mouth devouring them happily and spitting the pits on the ground. The two men looked at him puzzled, most likely wondering how the child could eat and apparently enjoy the fruit while they tasted bitter rotting fruit from the same trees. They didn't know the life of the trees, their souls. They didn't know Carolina, our beneficent protector, sometimes playful, other times vigilant and other times fiercely chasing away enemies and evil doers with her mysterious dances. I wondered if mother could feel Carolina's presence too. I had never dared to ask her. The last time I asked my parents where the two sisters had disappeared, they acted like they had no idea what and who I was talking about.

I knew now that Carolina was not a ghost, but a presence of a different kind, a being made of a different substance that was like the souls of the trees, a condensation of vapors, natural energy, molecules, an ethereal incarnation of memory with a mind and heart of her own. She could pass through you and leave you breathless like a free fall from a hundred meters, but you couldn't pass through her. She was immaterial yet opaque. And she had power over creatures that were alive, like these Party men who looked dizzy and confused after their attempts at tasting the fruit. They were moving with difficulty as if caught in a magnetic field that pulled them down into the earth. While Gino was giggling and gorging on ripe cherries the two men seemed to be made of lead and sink into the ground. They stumbled over a stump and preferred to crawl to the edge of the orchard instead of getting up to walk. They were both panting by the time they reached my mother, Mitzi and me and then they stood up.

The man with the fedora had a grimace of pain which was like a window into his humanity. It truly was a window. He was once a little boy in a sailor suit raised by a loving mother and father in the Ukraine when Russian soldiers came to his village and killed his family for owning property and selling their crops on the black market in the dreariest famine after World War I. Then they took the boy and raised him in Lenin's teaching and a red communist beret. I shook myself as if from a shiver and felt like I had fallen into a momentary slumber. The men said the orchard needed to be terminated, cut down, it was not valuable but poisonous. But the earth is plowable, they said, they will have to talk it over with their other comrades at the headquarters. What did plowable even mean? The important thing was that they were not going to take it away for now and re-appropriate it to one of the local recently developed cooperatives, but rather let it be until new orders came in from the party headquarters.

The new post-war language was flat and metallic with no color or depth. "It's not valuable property like they say about it in town," the fedora man said. I hadn't realized that our orchard was a topic of conversation for the townspeople. Only later did I realize that every bit of property owned by anybody in town and in the entire country was a topic of conversation for the intrepid and the rapidly growing communist party and its members. The moment they were about to leave, an image of the full entire person of Carolina with her greenish eyes, reddish curls in her white cotton dress passed by us in a floating step, circled around the party men once and then towards the orchards in a continuous flow, bluish light, a feather of life from somewhere else, a lost bird's feather floating in the air. The space around us was ticking like time, seconds and steps blended, the past paraded by us in dazzling colors and settled in for the space of a second. Frida, Gabi, Girl, Gino the father, moved with imperceptible steps within the time of a centimeter. An Italian aria rose from an old Victrola. Something had gotten stuck in time, a tune, a step, a feather of life, a whole group of lives with their dances and horrors quivering with such fast, tiny moves that it all looked immobile like a sepia photograph.

"We'll be back," the fedora man said in a squeaky voice, almost terrified.

"Yes, we'll be back with documents and papers for the property," the balding one added almost dizzy. They withdrew to the street walking backwards; they looked like people in one of the silent films we used to see before the war in the local theater that now was a Party building. Carolina and her visitors from the past melted into the thickness of the summer air. The Party clowns were out of sight, and we stood for a while looking at the fruit trees and their heavy branches, the fruit was always there, hanging in the air, sometimes dropping on the ground with a gentle thud, an embrace of the earth.

By the end of June, everything was packed for our move to Bucharest. The empty house resonated sadly like a huge bell from our last words and steps. On the day of the departure Mitzi cried incessantly, she was not coming to Bucharest but joining a remote relative that had found her, farther north in the country together with Gino and Kosmin. It wasn't clear what they were going to do and how they were going to survive, but Mitzi said between her sobs that she was going to work in a textile factory that had opened "up there." Private properties, maids, house cooks were disappearing by the day as an "obsolete remainder of bourgeois and capitalist exploitation, which had to be eradicated," according to the new Party language. And what was she going to do in the capital? That was for educated people, she said.

Mitzi, Kosmin, and Gino were going to stay in the house one more day until the new family who bought the house moved in. All our luggage stood in the street in front of the house while we took our goodbyes with tears and sighs. Mother moved around the house incessantly at the last minute without crying, picking up one more object she had forgotten, leaving another that she didn't think we needed after all: a clock instead of a crystal vase, a tablecloth instead of an embroidered cushion. Lila looked pale and almost faint from all the tears she had shed for leaving forever the house where she had spent her entire life. My mother kept saying "it's a house, it's only a house, we have each other," as she had always said throughout the war and the years after, with each departure, bomb, disaster, destruction, regime. "It's only a house, they are only things." But we knew that for her, as for each one of us standing there on that hot day in June, the house with its magical orchards had been our world, a part of who we were and who we had become. The walls held secrets, souls and creatures that had guarded us, its spacious rooms held stories of love and despair, Lila's cries and laughter and her many conversations with Mitzi, the dances to the music of the Victrola, pranks, births, deaths and murders, and the unfathomable presence of the twin sister Carolina who would be left alone roaming through the hallways and the orchard alleys in her yellow haze and timid wails.

Mr. Gogu came from across the street to say goodbye with tears in his eyes and a pack of American cigarettes for me. One of the local Party men was standing at the corner of the street taking note of the scene and smoking. Everything was under surveillance: conversations, encounters, separations of families with life and words throbbing inside them. Hardly anything happened anymore without it being recorded and interpreted for political reasons. We walked and carried our luggage to the train station wrapped in a thick silence and weighed down by the burden of our loss.

When we arrived in the Bucharest train station after a whole day and night of travel, sweaty, hungry, and exhausted, we were welcomed by one of my mother's cousins, the daughter of her only remaining sibling, Uncle Serafim who had lost a leg and a son during the war. Bucharest welcomed us with a maddening roar of cars and trams, thick dust, and unfriendly inhabitants. Lila liked the city as soon as she stepped outside the train station, while I started crying like a child horrified at the roar, crowds, and vehicles, with a gaping raw wound of longing for our town and the house in northern Moldavia, now forever gone and in the possession of a Soviet style Romanian family. We lived with my mother's cousin and his daughter for a few weeks until they found us an apartment near the center. Apartment was a generous term really, one entry hallway and bedroom combined that gave into a larger room, bedroom/living room. The bathroom and kitchen were shared, which at first, I didn't even truly understand, until I started meeting, one after another the neighbors that shared those spaces with us: curious, malicious faces sagging and pale from poverty and malnutrition, dressed in drab clothes like they had just arrived from a camp or a prison. Which most likely, some of them had.

"It's hard to get housing these days," said Serafim when we first walked into the so-called apartment, "the building is an old nice one and it's right in the center, great advantage." We were supposed to count our blessings, which my mother in fact did and reprimanded Lila and me for showing disappointment. "What do you want, it's how things are now, they took away all properties and parceled the apartments to house more people per square meter," he whispered as we went out into the hallway on our floor on the way to the bathroom and kitchen area. More neighbors opened their doors surreptitiously to see who the new tenants were, and a suspicious looking man appeared from a corner and took the stairs down to the lobby, casting several glances in our direction as if to relegate our faces to memory. A new world of fear, shortages, poverty, and shared efficiencies was to be our lot from now on. Maybe dying in the war under American bombs would have been better. As we crossed the hallway the thought of Carolina and Zoe took hold of me, a sharp memory of them graciously moving through our old house during the war, the way they sat and listened and watched us looking amused and curious in the pink armchair.

Then came an image from the afternoon we took the train to the Danube area in the summer of 1941 amid crowds of dislocated people, animals, German soldiers. The image was of the couple saying goodbye on the steps of the train, the officer who brutally pulled the man back off the train, the gesture of grief of the woman wiping tears as she watched the man being taken away. I achieved a sudden clarity about that scene and an assurance that, as I had thought then, the couple were indeed Frida and Gabi, the parents of Carolina and Zoe who were separated by a Nazi officer. A warm breeze passed in the chilly hallway and instilled a new clarity in my memory. I was now almost certain that Carolina would follow us, if she could cross the mysterious corridors between the living and the non-living, for sure she could cross the distance between northern Moldavia and Bucharest. All the doors in the hallways were now closed, the lives of our neighbors pulsated in the semidarkness. More secrets, new surroundings. A whole new grayness spread over our lives.

Marriage
Spring 1957, Bucharest

They released Florin on April 9th, his birthday, and the birthday of Charles Baudelaire, his favorite French poet. The one night they had taken him in for interrogation the previous summer turned into eight months of imprisonment. His mother and Zoe are waiting for him at the edge of town, in front of a gray cement building with a high wire fence and no name on the front. It doesn't look exactly like a prison, more like a factory. He is accompanied by a tall scrawny young man who leads him out of the main gate into the courtyard towards an iron gate and taps Florin gently on the back. "Take care Professor, so long." He doesn't look exhausted as they were expecting, just emaciated, which they did expect. His eyes are fiercer than ever, as if he has come from the battlefield.

Zoe embraces him first and holds his diminished body for a few seconds before she lets Victoria embrace him. "You're alive, it's what matters," she says, her usual chant after all catastrophes. "Barely," he says and smiles. He pulls Zoe to him and kisses her on the mouth. "It's already spring, April 9th, Baudelaire's birthday." Both Victoria and Zoe are surprised at his vivacity, almost optimism, after the eight months in prison. First, they didn't hear about or from him for almost a month, a time in which they knocked on all the doors of Party officials they knew, kept each other company at night and ate in silence, listening to the dreary communist programs on the radio just to have some contact with the outside world. Then the same tall scrawny individual who now accompanied him out of the prison knocked on the door of the apartment one evening and told them not to worry, he was being held for interrogations for a while. He wouldn't say more, but somewhat reassured them, just because he didn't talk or act like all the other party and Securitate people they had run into before, and he seemed to care about Florin.

Florin refuses to talk about anything that happened to him during the eight months in prison. The two women respect his silence and know they might never know. Anybody who is lucky enough to come out of the communist prisons is silent afterwards, they want to move on, to forget. They know Florin isn't really the type to keep silent for too long, he always needs to analyze, testify, tell the truth at the expense of his own safety. He mentions the tall man who escorted him out of the prison, "not all of them are rats, you know, some had no choice, others had real conviction at first, the guy who came out with me, you know, he was my student in Brasov, I would be dead without him." He laughs and picks a branch of bright yellow forsythia from one of the bushes in the street and hands it to Zoe. As she takes it and looks at him closely, she notices a bruise and a couple of scars, at the base of his neck and near his temple, partly covered by his wavy, already graying hair. "Both his parents died in the war," he goes on, "he was one of my best students, a little naive, and now he can't get out of it even if he wanted to, unless, you know…"

Victoria and Zoe don't really know, they have no idea. He leaves the sentence hanging, they hear steps behind them, they don't look back, just walk in silence to the apartment. It's all a continuous race of life and death, the stronger ones survive, and strength is measured differently now, not by character, not by muscle either, but a certain steely endurance of the nerves to keep going despite the web of fear, the labyrinth of suspicion, the steps. It's the footsteps that drive you crazy. A Gypsy girl is selling hyacinths at the corner of their street, Zoe buys a bouquet and inhales the fragrance, her favorite spring flowers. He has a memory of a Spring in his parents' orchard, running on the alleys between the cherry and plum trees in bloom and Zoe running ahead in the light between the trees, like a fire bird, like a dream.

He knows it's only a dream though and there is no use dwelling in the past, it will never come back. Months in prison have taught him the inevitability of the new regime, which is here to stay, maybe for the duration of their lives: gray, gloomy, unfolding under the shadow of ruthless governments installed by the Soviet Union with the very help of his compatriots, with food shortages and potholes, moral ambiguities and fear. He is prepared, lucid and unafraid as he is walking between his mother and his lover. He will not talk about the months spent in prison until much later in his life. For now, he is driven by a fierce will to survive without giving in to any outside pressures from the Party, or Securitate. The hell with the dumb secret police, they are mortal too, he doesn't give a damn about any of them. What more can they do to him? Arrest him again? Fine. Kill him? Let them. Though deep down he doesn't believe they will, he believes in his guiding star.

Florin and Zoe get married in May at the city hall in the center of Bucharest with Lila and Victoria as the only witnesses. Zoe is wearing a pink summer suit that she made herself out of old dresses and carries a bouquet of daisies that Florin bought for her from their favorite Gypsy seller in the University square. After the expedited wedding ceremony, they have a meager dinner at the restaurant of their first encounters in the park near the Arch of Triumph, Victoria even has a taste of the plum brandy. Florin doesn't dare to ask about Zoe's parents, he knows there is an untouchable nebula in that region of Zoe's life that he cannot penetrate and whose secrecy he has learned to respect. Zoe knows that he and Victoria know who she is. They all tiptoe around the untouchable domain of her past like walking around a minefield. There is no talking about it, the past was left behind but improperly buried during an explosion-lit night in June of 1941, when the earth opened in dark terrifying craters and then closed back with a dull thud and in the morning, everything was different, the light had a cruel glare, and the twin sisters were nowhere in sight.

Even though she lives with Florin at his mother's apartment, Zoe still goes away for days at a time every so often saying she must care for her old aunt. Once Florin follows her and realizes that she goes to her old apartment. He goes back ashamed of his mistrust and remembers the skinny woman he once had a fleeting glimpse of when he walked with Zoe after her courses. He has his suspicions but learns to accept Zoe's absences like a normal ritual, never asks where she is going and when she will come back. He knows she always returns, with her otherworldly yet irreverent allure, her cheeks framed by the crown of reddish curls that she sometimes ties with a blue ribbon.

Once there was a girl in a white dress tied with a blue sash at the waist, once in another world. But it wasn't her, that was a girl from a different story, he possibly forgot all the details of that story. There are no traces anywhere of that story from a war and a couple of governments ago. Only a picture on his mother's night table, a group picture of two families lined up against a background of flowering trees, four adults and four children. He is sure that there were four children in the sepia photograph on his mother's night table: he and Lila and two girls that looked alike, two girls in white dresses, one with…. Maybe not, he can no longer find the photograph, not on the night table, not inside the drawer of the night table. Sometimes he is not sure whether that was his past or someone else's past, there are hardly any traces of it, a few pieces of furniture that could have been anybody's. A mahogany desk with a glass top, a pink armchair, a few embroidered tablecloths that escaped, that escaped … so many armies and journeys… Lucky them, they escaped with their lives while others did not.

If it wasn't for Zoe's nightmares during which she sometimes cries or sits up and stares in the dark, and for Florin's brooding silences, one would say their lives were almost happy. Florin continues to teach the same authors, texts, and ideas he has always been teaching and which likely were the reason for his arrest, added to who knows what other illegal activities he might have been involved in. He refuses to talk to Zoe or to his mother about it, "Why worry uselessly?" He asks his mother once. "Why not, I'm your mother, we've been through so much together, it could make you feel better, freer." He laughs because nothing short of the total collapse and annihilation of the present government and the entire lot of Party and Securitate could make him feel even in the vicinity of better and freer. Victoria doesn't insist because she knows how stubborn he can be, she just gets more creative at cooking with the little she has, the tiny rations; she does wonders with a kilogram of flour, a bit of oil, a cup of sugar, a handful of green peas. Zoe and Florin have no idea where she possibly got an egg or two or even a cup of milk or dried fruit.

Sometimes Victoria leaves the house at dawn and returns with a bag of food. Maybe she gets it all on the black market, they wouldn't be surprised. The women in the shared kitchen stare at her with envy and try to find out her secret food sources and miraculous recipes. "No miracle at all, didn't you learn anything from the war, where were you then?" The women stare at her with their mouths open with no idea what she is talking about. "Well maybe you had a better time during the war than we did up there in the north of the country," Victoria laughs and goes on kneading her dough on the cool surface of the metal table. "These women neighbors aren't too smart, God bless them and their poor souls, the poor in spirit will inherit the kingdom of heaven indeed, everybody around us will go to heaven." Florin and Zoe laugh heartily when they hear her unforgiving sarcasm.

During one of their "copious" dinners there are knocks on the front door, they weren't expecting anyone. Lila is at the baths in northern Transylvania for her heart condition, and she would just come inside without knocking. It must be "them" again, some new version of "them," more considerate, who come earlier during the day instead of in the dead of night barging into people's lives like they owned them. Victoria gets up slowly, she is in no hurry, she has all the time in the world. On her way to the door, she takes down the small golden icon of Mary and baby Jesus that her husband brought from Mount Athos in Greece long before the war, in another universe, and hides it under the mattress of her bed. Icons are illegal, praying is illegal, breathing is practically illegal. Too much air, where did you get it, on the black market, from a capitalist source, or did you inherit it from your bourgeois reactionary relatives before the war? Give it back, it's confiscated, go to prison for life!

Florin sometimes had conversations like that in his head in an almost delicious reductio ad absurdum of their lives and Zoe, as if hearing his thoughts, which she probably did, would laugh out loud and say something even more ironic, imitating the voice of a Securitate man. Comrade, Professor Angelescu, because they are very polite people, they address you by all your titles. Why are you looking to the right, didn't you know you could only look to the left, to the left of capitalist bourgeois depravity, where our brothers and comrades of the Soviet Union shed their blood and gave their lives for our eternal socialist happiness? Sometimes they bounced off one another during their imitation act and could go on and on until they keeled over with laughter. Who said you couldn't laugh and be merry in the communist "paradise?"

Victoria opens the door, as she always does, since she is the main tenant on the lease, and Florin and Zoe stop their banter and listen intently. They hear the door open, they cannot see it from where they are sitting, for some reason they feel like laughing. They hear whispers, Victoria produces a long sigh then says in a louder voice "come in please, no bother, we were just having supper, why don't you sit down with us and have something to eat, you must be tired!"

June 1941 — Northern Moldavia and the Trains

On June 10th, 1941, an official communique was issued in the entire region of northern Moldavia announcing the forthcoming publication of another communique that would explain "the real causes" of the economic crisis. On June 16th, an official order was issued by the local government that all gatherings, meetings, written or oral communications of any kind among civilians or groups of civilians regarding the war, military operations, Romanian or German military hospitals were deemed illegal. The order also mentioned the establishment of "committees of citizens" formed of "prominent representatives" of Romanian society which were to act as militias and have the right to arrest those who disobeyed. The "committees of citizens" were expected to help establish the closest relations between the German and Romanian soldiers and supervise the growth of "admirational attitudes" of the Romanian population towards "the great German people and the Third Reich."

On June 24th, light air raids were conducted by the Soviet army over the city of Iasi and two days later, massive air raids took place killing several hundred people. The Jewish people in town were all blamed for presumably signaling to the Soviet planes the location of the headquarters of the Romanian army and collaborating with Soviet aviators, although many of the Jewish people in town were also killed in the raids. That was not a credible argument however, according to the Romanian and German authorities interrogating the prominent members of the Jewish community in town, because in their words, "Jews are all traitors, they would sell their own for a few coins, haven't they sold the Lord Jesus Christ for 13 golden coins? They are all Judas."

On June 27th, another order was issued that militias and local police should inform on any gatherings of citizens. In the order, the militias were summoned to prepare for any sacrifices, to carry flashlights, to confiscate any funds for the printing of manifestos, report any conflicts among the population, take away binoculars, photographic equipment, any accessories belonging to the Jewish population.

The orders also called for the arrest of more than 300 Jewish people and the arrest of a couple of hundred more who wore red clothing or accessories. Any "instigators" and anyone who initiated any breaking of the order, would be proposed for the camps.

On that same day of June 27th at noon, Frida and Gabi packed a small suitcase and left the tiny attic room where they had been hiding for several months in the town located between Iasi and Florin's hometown. A tall man in an elegant suit and a white fedora hat waited for them in front of their building and saluted them with an unconvincing "Heil Hitler" to which they answered back, equally unconvincing. He drove them in an elegant car to the nearest train station and before dropping them off handed them false identifications. Once out of the car they moved slowly towards the platforms; they were to take the train to the south. The crowds were enormous, men, women, children, old people, carrying their belongings any way they could, in enormous suitcases, or large bags improvised from bed sheets and tablecloths. Frida and Gabi became separated in the crowd for a few seconds, they found each other again and held hands desperately feeling that something ominous was upon them. Gabi whispered something in her ear, she whispered "not without you." Gabi whispered back "you have to, for the girls, they need you, they are fine, I saw them last night when I picked up Tudor at the house, they are fine ... when all this is over, we'll reunite. Tudor has already gotten Sofia and Sebastian out, but we must save the others ..."

On the train platform, just when they reached their train, a man in civilian clothes with a large golden cross on his neck grabbed Gabi and told him he was coming with him. Gabi tried to escape, looked around him and realized that lots of other men in civilian clothes, some Romanian, some German, were grabbing and arresting people. And a few steps behind there was a solid line of armed soldiers. Gabi begged the man to give him a minute, then he pushed Frida onto the steps of the train, they kissed and held hands for all of two seconds. The man grabbed Gabi back, the train started moving and the train doors closed. Frida's face was glued to the filthy train window where her tears left long streaks. Written grief on the train window.

When the train left the station and she saw Gabi being dragged by the two Nazis, Frida knew that was the last she would ever see of her husband. Against all her intuition though, for decades she kept hoping Gabi would miraculously return.

Years later, a man knocked at the door of her apartment in Bucharest. He told Frida that he had befriended Gabi on the train in the short time they spent together. He gave her Gabi's wedding band engraved with her name. He related that he and Gabi had vowed to one another that if by chance either of them was going to survive, the survivor would search for the other's widow and give her their wedding ring. The man said he wasn't sure who of the two of them had been the luckier one, at times he wished he had been the one who died. Gabi was a hero, a man like no one else, he said. He had given his last drink of water to a child on the train, then paid one of the guards all the money he had to get a glass of water for himself. The guard took the money, promised the glass of water, came back with one, Gabi drank it in a gulp, then fell dead on the spot. It turned out the guard was handing out glasses filled with lye. Several other people in that car had died the same way, the man said, maybe they were the lucky ones, they died on the spot. Frida stared at him without blinking and said your wife must consider herself lucky nevertheless, because you returned alive, and she wasn't just left with an empty ring. Now, after the end of the war, she lived in Bucharest with Zoe, her one girl that survived.

The train that Frida got on the night of June 27th, 1941, was going south towards the Black Sea. She had no idea where she was going and where she would get off. She stayed on it until the next day when she was brutally woken up by the train police asking for identification. She handed them her false documents half asleep and they let her be. She dozed off immediately. When she woke up again the compartment was empty, all the crowds had progressively left finding refuge with relatives in different cities along the way, as the train got closer to the Black Sea and then all the way to the port of Constanta, which was the end of the line. She smelled the salty air, saw the fierce blue line of the water cutting the full length of the horizon, felt the June sun on her face and for a second, she thought a new life had started, luminous and blue, and Gabi, Carolina and Zoe were waiting for her at the end of the line, on the platform. They were all going on a vacation to the beach. Then two soldiers passed on the corridor checking the compartments and yelled at her to get out, everybody out, it was the end of the line. She remembered. Gabi was gone. Judging from the way he had been dragged by the German soldier and his Iron Guard companion, most likely he had been put on one of the trains leaving from that same station never to return. Gabi had told her that the girls were fine, that he had seen them, but something in the way he looked away when he said that, made her believe he was lying to give her courage and hope. If the girls were also gone, what was she alive for? She picked up her tiny suitcase, got off onto the crowded platform, and looked around her. She had no idea where to go, what direction to take.

A lanky young blonde man in a white shirt got off the train at the same time as she did and stood on the platform at a distance. He looked at her and locked eyes with her as if delivering a message. Then he turned around, walked out of the station, and started walking on a rugged dirt road that seemed to stretch into nowhere right outside the station. Frida felt she had to follow him, that maybe he was part of the same group that had helped her and Gabi get false identifications. She followed him in what seemed the direction of the sea. She walked for a long time in a daze. Her face was flushed from the sun and her red hair blazed in the afternoon light like fire. From afar she looked unreal, a red-haired ghost gliding through the heated salty air of the town. She had never seen the sea. Gabi had promised her he was going to take her to the sea when the war was over. That was a long time from now, probably never. Gabi was going to get killed if he was not dead already. She had seen the trucks filled to the refuse with people mercilessly piled on top of each other like cattle meant for the slaughterhouse. She had seen them from the minuscule window of the attic room where she and Gabi hid for what seemed an indefinite amount of time, waiting for a sign, for their journey of escape.

When she reached a portion of beach, the lanky blonde man went in the opposite direction and disappeared. It seemed to her that before disappearing, he looked at her again and made a sign with his head as if to say straight ahead, go on. Or maybe she imagined it. She crossed through the dusty brush and thistles, then walked on the sand towards the sea like towards salvation. She wasn't sure whether she was hallucinating or whether it was real, but groups of people in colorful clothes were standing around a fire and making a racket, talking, maybe even singing. There were tents and naked children running around on the beach. Women in colorful skirts picked them up and carried them back into the tents. Some even laughed. It sounded to her like they were speaking a different language. Maybe she had reached another country, another zone, another life. She looked all around her again searching for the tall man who seemingly guided her all this way and was convinced he had disappeared. As if he had accomplished his mission of leading her to a safe place. She did not give it much thought, as she had gotten used to out-of-the-blue appearances and disappearances of people, some benefic, others horrific.

She walked at the same steady pace to the water, felt the coolness of the waves on her burning feet and legs like a deliverance. She moved through the waves with her suitcase until the water reached her waist, her elbows, then she let go of the suitcase and watched it float on the water for a second before disappearing underwater. She thought she heard someone calling for her, maybe they were going to put her on one of the trucks too, burn her alive. She'd better hurry before they got her like they got Gabi, like they probably got Zoe and Carolina. The water was up to her neck and then a wave covered her. Everything was all salty and refreshing, they couldn't burn her now, she got to the sea before Gabi, he was probably on his way, he was bringing the girls, they were all going to have a long vacation. Water filled her mouth, her eyes, her nostrils, algae, and jellyfish were gliding over her body like soothing hands. A cool green darkness set in.

The Russians and Corina's Grandmother
Bucharest, 1968

I met Frida one evening in August after the Russians invaded Czechoslovakia. I was sick with chicken pox and burning with high fever, itching all over my body from the red pustules when a thin red-haired woman that seemed more like a ghost than a real person entered my rubbing alcohol scented room and sat on my bed as if she had known me forever. She placed a cool compress on my forehead and her eyes shone with a strange light, a connection with other worlds, a lightness that seemed to make her unreal yet soothingly real. I wasn't sure whether it was the delirium of my fever or the encounter but whatever it was, I started feeling better. I also felt a strange familiarity with the red-haired ghostly woman.

I wondered where my mother was and why this stranger had entered my room and sat on my bed, but very soon her presence started feeling natural and beneficent. She asked me how old I was. I thought it was strange that it was the first question she asked. I told her I was six and she sighed, "oh six years old, I see," after which she seemed engulfed by a wave of melancholy. She sat by my side on the bed for what seemed like a long time, but it felt normal. She could have started to fly around the room, and it would have seemed normal. "You have such blonde hair," she said after a while, "just a tiny bit of red, like your mother." Then she sat in silence for a bit longer, while I heard my mother wash dishes, my father's attempts to get the radio free Europe station through the thick static, and a cuckoo bird outside calling his mate like an afterthought.

I knew something bad had happened that had to do with the Russians and that possibly meant we would all have to become Russian, but for the time that Frida sat on my bed wiping my forehead with a cool cloth asking sporadic questions about my age, school subjects or favorite dolls, I felt calm and unafraid. When my mother entered the room with tea and medication I had to take, Frida looked at her and smiled with almost happiness on her face. My mother gave Frida the cup of tea and medication and asked her to administer them to me. My father came in too and told us some more things about Russian tanks and a student burning alive in a place called Prague. My mother insisted he not talk about those things now and in front of me, to not upset me when I was sick with the chicken pox. She called the red-haired woman sitting on my bed Frida and I thought it was a magical name. I had never heard such a name before, I wished I had been called Frida.

There seemed to be an understanding between my mother Zoe and Frida as if they had known each other for a long time. My father left the room, and my mother and Frida looked at each other for a little bit, then my mother sat right next to her as if needing to rest. It felt like something important had been put into place for the first time. My mother seemed unusually calm, and I noticed that I wasn't burning anymore, and my body no longer itched. With Frida in the room, we were not alone. The space was filled to its fullest with a quivering presence, a fluttering that made everything both immaterial and surprisingly alive, like you had just discovered life for the first time. Frida held my hand for a long time, and my fever left me like a wing that flew away. My mother said look she is already feeling better, the treatment is working, I told you so. Nobody ever contradicted my mother, but she often acted as if she was being contradicted or had to prove her point to the world.

My father walked into the room and announced that see, what did I tell you, he is giving a big speech in the Piata Palatului to say we are not beholden to the Russians. Turn on the TV, he ordered. With my father everything always turned to politics. We lived in the regime, it was always about the regime and my mother never cared about the regime, its growth, existence, or collapse if that were ever to happen. The TV showed the leader gesticulating to a huge mass of people and screaming in his usual style of broken sentences how we, Romanians from the entire country, were never going to allow foreign aggression, invasion, we were sovereign and on and on. Static from Radio Free Europe covered the speech, and my father said it was bullshit, just for show, just for show, the Russians had us, owned us no matter what.

I was only interested in Frida and the fullness she brought to the room. She sat quietly, she looked straight in front of her, held my hand, stroked my forehead, it all flowed smoothly like a dance. My mother sat down next to her on the bed and my father's words, the leader gesticulating on the TV, the Radio Free Europe static interrupted by far away voices speaking a foreign sounding Romanian, all filtered through a haze, became muffled to almost inaudible. It all became insignificant. I remember asking my mother who is Frida, can she live with us? And my mother saying Frida is your grandmother, she lives nearby, and me not understanding the word grandmother and asking her again who Frida was, until my mother got irritated and said I told you already, she is your grandmother that's who she is, she was gone for a while, now she will live nearby and come visit us all the time. I asked but where was she all this time mama, where was Frida until now, why was she not here with us earlier? My mother did what she often did when she didn't like a question, she looked straight ahead as if she hadn't heard a thing and walked away.

The cuckoo bird called out again, then the Gypsy girl called for empty bottles, all familiar sounds returned, and Frida got up to leave saying she would be back. A sadness came over me, like it was the end of something important that was never going to happen again. I said: "Aunt Frida will you come back to see me?" For some reason, even if my mother said Frida was my grandmother, she felt more like an aunt and it felt more natural to call her aunt Frida, she seemed younger than a grandmother. Frida laughed, which seemed utterly surprising as she didn't seem like the kind of person who would even know how to laugh, but her laugh was both happy and sad and made her look so much younger, almost like my mother. It felt like I already had an aunt, but nobody ever told me about her. Frida said I had an aunt who traveled everywhere and never got tired, she watched over me. I had no idea what that meant, who that aunt was. I thought Frida was talking about herself in the third person, that she was the aunt watching over us, since I started feeling better with my chicken pox as soon as she sat down next to me and touched my forehead.

I said: "Aunt Frida, can you come with me outside to play hopscotch?" And that made her laugh again in a sad way. She said: "your mother used to play hopscotch when she was little, and we lived far away." I became very curious about that because I never imagined my mother as a little girl playing hopscotch and jumping and doing childhood things. At that very moment though there was a shift, a movement of the atmosphere in the room, the air became heavy and visible, almost like water and we were breathing it in without a problem. I was sure it was the delirium of my chicken pox fever. I didn't care, it was like a film with us as the main characters: mama, Frida, tata and someone else who looked like mama but was much younger like a child version of my mother, thin and spritely in a white dress and long curly reddish hair. We had an entire gathering of people in our room, my other grandma Victoria embroidering a blouse with blue thread, my other aunt, Lila, and several other people I didn't know sat down on every chair in the room. Only mama and tata stood up behind the chairs as if posing for a photograph. The girl that looked like the younger version of my mother wasn't clear in her contours, she seemed like a creature made of water and air, someone you would meet in a dream, yet she directed everybody else's movements. It all lasted a few moments, yet time didn't matter at all and just flowed over us. We sat inside a tableau and someone else was photographing us.

It was almost evening, only a thread of light came from the outside and my mother said: "turn on the light, it's dark in here." I asked my mother: "mama, am I dying, why are there so many people here in the room?" My mother laughed in an embarrassed way, she kissed me and said: "of course you are not dying, nobody is dying, you are just a bit delirious from the fever. But look, you are already better; the fever has gone down a bit, you'll be fine." Eventually everything became ordinary again though it felt like something monumental had taken place, like someone's dream had cracked open and we had all been sucked up in it and spat back out. I knew we were never going to be the same. My mother and father acted just like before, as if nothing at all had happened. Frida got up to leave and said: "I'll visit again, don't worry, I'll come when you are feeling better." I didn't worry, I was just curious why she had never showed up before and it was only when she got up to leave that the word "grandmother" which my mother had pronounced earlier, when she said, "she is your grandmother," meant that she was my mother's mother. That notion appeared to have a monumental importance because I had never even thought of or questioned the idea of my mother having a mother. It had never been brought up in our house as if my mother had been an orphan and never even knew who her mother was. I fell asleep after Frida's visit and when I woke up, I felt much better, the chickenpox was almost gone, there was no Radio Free Europe playing and no cigarette smoke coming from my father's room. My mother came into my room smiling in her gray and fuchsia dress that I liked so much. Something new had started. My mother said that soon I was going to get better, and she would take me to the park with the ferris wheel, the Russians were not going to invade us, for sure.

Over the following year Frida visited us often and every time she did, my mother had a special kind of wakefulness, as if suddenly everything became clear and worthwhile, very different from her usually absent-minded, distracted manner. That made me love Frida, my newly discovered grandmother, even more. She brought a lightness and an ease in our home, touched by a twinge of melancholy like you wanted everything to stay as it was and you couldn't because time never listened to you. Occasionally, in her presence, the other presence moved around us leaving a trail of sadness and of things unfinished, untold. This shifted our sense of time and space and made our memories of things and events simultaneous with the present. There were memories of trains going to unspoken places, of the disappearance of someone dear, an image from a blissful afternoon in a park with fanfare music passed by again and again like a record on a broken turntable. It all held the intensity of years, but when everything ended, I realized the hands of the clock had barely moved a few dots.

When summer came again the following year, my mother announced we were going to spend a week at the seaside and Frida was coming with us. It was the happiest news I had heard in a long time. The Russians hadn't invaded us, the stores had food, my father's job was stable for a while, and no secret police were following him. At least not that I knew of. While at the seaside, we went to the beach at odd hours: either very early or at sunset because Frida couldn't stand the strong sun, and she liked the mixing of colors on the water at those in between times when day and night mingled with one another.

The first day at the beach Frida almost drowned. A sliver of sunset melted into the sea with orange and violet streaks, like the water was a huge bowl of candy. A feather of a song, a piano sonata trickled unexpectedly from somewhere, from one of the villas near the beach. I thought I heard Frida say: "it's worth living just for this, for a moment like this." But then she touched the water, stroked it, and seemed to remember something. She walked and walked and glided into the colored water like she was never going to stop. My mother called out in a voice that didn't seem her voice but the voice of a seagull, a gust of wind. She said mama, what are you doing, come back. Frida needed that call to wake up and turn around and say my mother's name Zoe, Zoe, like a discovery of life itself. The colors of the sea, all the colors, the violets, fuchsia, orange and all the other reds lifted off the water, colored birds with enormous wings.

The beach filled with people wearing the colors that lifted from the sea: women in colorful skirts swirling like colored smoke. Everything and everyone took on a new, different color. Frida sat on the glowing sand, golden, too golden to be real, and chatted in whispers with the ethereal women: one was bright pink, another yellow, another was a mixture of reds, and they all surrounded Frida with love, caring for her with little gestures and wings of color. Everybody talked at the same time, everybody quivered in the sunset, there was a fire too, a fire like a fountain of cool light and Frida said suddenly in a louder voice: I understand, I understand, you don't have to repeat, one is gone, one is living in the mountains, one is a wing of smoke over the sea and the rest of the earth, there is still a breath of her left to wander. It all sounded too complicated to understand and follow, like a secret language. Then Frida called out a name in a quiet way, without a voice, a voiceless call, only her lips moved and curled around a name with long vowels. The next second all the colorful smoke people with violins and tents and fire melted and vanished. The sky and the water remained silver-gray, and we were all sitting on a white sheet on the sand: my mother, my grandmother Frida, my father Florin, my aunt Lila. We were all sitting in a circle on the sand having an evening picnic. A man passed by selling corn on the cob and another man passed by selling small fishes called guvizi. My father bought everything, the corn on the cob and the guvizi, and my mother even smiled at the sight and smell of the fish. A woman came a little later selling a Turkish drink made of oats and barley called braga. She was Turkish, like the drink.

Frida was the center of everything like a goddess who ate small fishes and drank the delicious Turkish drink in memory of something important, she was both the memory and the person remembering it. I told my mother: "mama, we should always come here in the summer and eat guvizi and drink braga, it's so much fun, and Aunt Frida should always come with us." But when I said that everybody went quiet like they had turned to stone and nobody seemed to notice or hear me, as if I wasn't there, as if I didn't exist yet and this was all happening before my time, in another life.

After Frida's spell passed, because I was sure it was a spell she made, my mother said: "let's go home, it's getting chilly, mama you are going to catch a cold." She said that like nothing unusual at all had happened. I finished my corn on the cob as fast as I could and drank the braga drink. We should all have been happy, but I wasn't sure if happy was the right thing to be. I didn't remember Aunt Lila coming with us on the train, but I was glad she was with us too, it felt right to have her and Frida nearby, like we were almost a full family but still waiting for someone else. We walked back to our rooms at the peasant houses in the twilight and I thought how nice we are all together staying with the peasants who cooked for us every night and my mother didn't have to worry about finding things to eat in the stores or cooking them on the tiny stove. Bucharest was far away, we still had one more week to spend at the seaside.

During the remaining time at the seaside, Frida and my mother spent almost every minute together as if making up for something that had happened before: a big separation with tears and a convoy of people. I seemed to have a special understanding of things in the salty air, shrouded in the candy colors of the sea at dawn or sunset, the liquid blues enveloping everything during the day. Aunt Lila and my father spent their time together like spectators of the main show: the Frida and Zoe show, a dance with a mysterious past in which someone had been sacrificed, some had been martyrs or heroes, and many had been villains. The villains in Frida's and my mother's story were not communists, but a different group from before and during the war. After the rainbowed picnic afternoon on the beach with the strange guests, my father and Lila talked a lot about their father, about a woman called Mitzi, and the beauty of their orchards before the war which the Russians and Communists had pillaged, destroyed and in the end completely taken away. There was talk of something important left at the house with the orchards, and something that looked like a fight between my parents with Frida saying, "it's no use now, don't argue about the past you can't change it."

I asked one evening out of the blue: "what happened with my other grandmother, Victoria the one with the fairy tales?" and everybody fell silent as if I said something wrong which I did all the time anyway. "Go make a sandcastle, Corina," was all that was said to me whenever I mentioned things and people I wasn't supposed to. "A castle with shells and algae ornaments on it, here are the pail and shovel to do that." I made six, ten sandcastles a day, lined them up on the shore like soldier castles, with white and black shells for decoration and slippery bright green algae surrounding them like gardens. One night I heard my mother scream in her sleep in the peasants' room where we all slept on several beds. "Breathe, breathe, I can't breathe Carolina, Zoe, I can't breathe, let me go." My mother was both herself and another person in the dream. And another night when my mother cried, I saw a smoky shadow gliding around the room, then sit on one of the chairs like a guest made of yellow smoke. She looked familiar even though immaterial. I had seen her another time in Bucharest when I was playing hopscotch on the sidewalk in front of our building, a boy had complained to my mother I was cussing too much, my parents' friends who were schizophrenic had visited and read our futures in the coffee dregs. But now she was sitting in the chair at the end of my mother's bed like a normal person reading a book. She was of indeterminate age; she could have been nine or thirteen and occupied a place in space like a real person.

My mother stopped crying from her dream as if the presence sitting on the chair brought an end to her painful dreams and answered her wish. I sat up in bed and saw that Frida was sleeping in her bed unmoved and I thought I was asleep too and just dreaming that the yellow presence was visiting and reading a book. She spoke to me and said don't worry, I'm not harmful, I'm just passing through, I'll come again. I said: I'm not worried, what's your name? I heard her giggle at my question as if I had said a joke. She said you can only see me in the dark, in the light I'm transparent, and indeed she made a place for herself in the darkness of the room. I asked her: what book are you reading? and she said: it's not important, it's from your grandfather's library from the orchard house. She wasn't a ghost presence but more like a drawing that had come to life: you could see the contours of her slender body and long curly hair falling onto her shoulders. The yellow smokiness inside the contours was like someone had filled her in with watercolor, like a bit of a sun ray got lost inside of the drawing in a gentle explosion. While she was there it felt like finally our family was whole. I saw the sliver of the new moon in the window of our room and when I looked back to the chair at the foot of my mother's bed she was no longer there. The chair was empty in a way that made it look lonely. The night inside the room felt lonely like a sad song. The sea made tiny sounds of splashing as it touched the shore, it sounded refreshing. When I woke up that morning everybody was gone from the room, and I could hear them talking and laughing in front of the house.

Frida was laughing and telling a story from her youth of horse drawn carriages and violins, and a circus. Nobody except for her in the group was alive at the time of the story, early in the century, before the war. She said before the war twice like a tiny refrain. There was a moment of embarrassed silence when she said that, like she wasn't supposed to mention anything with the word war in it. My father mentioned something before the communists, his house with the magnificent orchards, before the Russians. You could mention before the Russians and before communists but not before the war it seemed. He told his old stories of lost bliss that I knew by heart. Lila mentioned Mitzi, a doll, and a servant. I knew the doll, and I knew it was hidden inside the box underneath the sofa bed in our apartment.

Then my father mentioned a time when he fell from one of the orchard trees and broke his leg. But when my father started his story, my mother became agitated and told him to shut up, abruptly and almost with meanness. I didn't know the story of him falling from the tree. It happened the spring following the winter when he dove into the frozen pond of his town to save his friend from drowning when they were skating and the ice broke. I jumped in after my mother's interruption and said tata tell the story of when you saved your friend from the frozen pond when you fell through a hole in the ice. Everybody froze again like the ice of the pond when I mentioned that. There were allowable and non-allowable stories that morning, stories from before the war, from during the war, from after the war. The stories were creatures in themselves that you could take in like a pet. Once someone brought up a particular historical time and a story, it played itself out in a tiny silent movie, with the voice of the person telling it like the narrator. The peasant woman who owned the house where we stayed brought us warm milk with cocoa and chifle, bread rolls that she made and at that point I didn't care about the allowed or forbidden stories. I just focused on the delicious breakfast, the kind that I never got to have in Bucharest.

You could see a chip of the sea like a broken piece of glass from where we sat on the veranda of the peasant house every time there was a breeze and the big willow tree moved one way or another. The sea was a sparkling blue jewel that morning through the branches of the willow tree. I wanted to hear the story of my father falling from the tree in his orchard and insisted, tata how did you fall from the tree? We were playing hide and seek in the trees, that's how, the words seemed to fall out of my mother's mouth of their own will, without her meaning to. A shadow scene of children playing in an orchard, a young boy and a young girl chasing each other… no, two girls, two similar looking girls in light colored dresses and a boy in short overalls running among the blooming trees. The boy is climbing in the tree, one of the girls is climbing after him, the other girl is left on the ground swirling, dancing, taking off like a cloud. The images of the story fluttered their way between all of us as we sat around the table on the peasants' veranda. The light blue chip of the morning sea sparkled blindingly for a second between the branches of the willow tree.

A puzzling and fleeting realization came upon me that my parents had known each other long before they met in Brasov at some party in the bad times of the Stalinist fifties, and that the story of my father's broken leg involved my mother and someone else that we were not allowed to mention. There was another girl, a lost girl, someone who became a bird, a shadow, a cloud that kept returning. Frida was no longer laughing, her story of the circus and the violin and the horse drawn carriages melted away like the foam of the sea waves touching the shore. She stared at something in the distance, something familiar. I understood also that Frida had seen the sea before, and it was a lie my parents told me that she had never seen the sea. It felt like the other time Frida was at the sea was part of the forbidden stories.

I looked around me at the table and my own family looked like a circus family: aunt Lila smiling in a crooked way as if she had lost her train of thought in the middle of a funny story, my mother Zoe with a grimace of sadness like she wanted to be happy but couldn't, my father's melancholy as if listening to the violin in Frida's story. Everybody was caught in a pose, a badly posed picture or a picture taken by surprise in the middle of telling forbidden stories before, during, after the war, transplanted from a different landscape. All the landscapes were mixed up: an orchard at the sea, a frozen pond in the middle of the burning sand. And a picture with people badly missing from it. I didn't want to think of the stories anymore and ate greedily the chifle with butter and jam, drank the hot cocoa in small sips trying to remember the taste for when we were back in Bucharest and wouldn't have anything as delicious as that to eat for breakfast.

After breakfast Frida performed a small monologue from one of her plays, your grandmother was a famous actress, my mother said. I had no idea that Frida was ever an actress of any kind, but she transformed herself into someone else in a second on the veranda of the peasant house, moving with quick steps on the clay floor like a timid ballerina, talking in a higher voice, then a lower voice, many voices that were not her own. It was all about acting the mother role in a play. "It's Pirandello, my mother said proudly." I had no idea who Pirandello was either but felt slightly embarrassed by Aunt Frida's performance on the veranda as if she had stripped herself naked. Aunt Lila sat in her chair with her head down and looked like she was crying but I couldn't tell for sure because she never once looked up at Frida. My father was smoking a cigarette and stared at Frida through the circles of smoke with great interest, like he cared deeply about the character she played. He was the only one who seemed to follow the words. When she finished her monologue, Frida bowed in front of us. She was all flushed and looked languorous, and flirtatious.

That morning my family didn't feel like my family any longer but more like a group of visitors from a different world. A common past with a common memory tied them all together and I was not in any part of that world. The peasant woman had stopped on the veranda to watch Frida's performance and was crying at the end of it, holding another tray of food for us. I wondered where she got all that food, different breads and puddings, fruit, and marmalade. I cared about the foods more than about Frida's performance. For a little while I was scared that everybody would go and leave me there as if I didn't belong with them. The sun was moving up in the sky and the sparkling chip of the sea was becoming a deeper blue, the breeze stronger with a bit of a frightening touch.

The afternoon of Frida's performance there was a big storm, and the waves of the sea reached so high they flooded the road which separated our house from the beach. Frida became very mellow and lay in bed for the rest of the day. "She is not feeling well," my mother said later that evening. I thought I saw my mother cry in a corner of our room. My father went to comfort her and whispered something in her ear.

They talked in whispers for a long time. Something seemed amiss and wrong for the rest of the evening. The happy time at the beach was over, I was sure. The next morning, we had to return to Bucharest, and I threw a crying fit saying I don't want to leave, why can't we just live there by the sea, I don't want to go back to Bucharest, I hate it there. My mother held me and told me things were not so bad in Bucharest, we had a home, and I had to go to school. I was starting second grade. Wasn't I excited about going into second grade? I wasn't a bit excited; I wanted to live by the sea, with the lady peasant who made delicious cakes and had so much food. My mother laughed at my words and said we would come back next year. My family felt foreign and strange again, as if they were pretending to be my family when they were really someone else's. Everything moved quickly in separate images, a slide projection. Now we were standing on the veranda saying goodbye to our host Maritza, it was the first time I had heard her name. Thank you so much for everything Miss Maritza, everybody said. And Maritza said: it was wonderful, come again next year, bring the little one, the sea air is good for her. The next slide was Maritza giving me a package with her cakes to have on the train, that made the departure easier. I held on to the package of cakes with both hands like I was holding a baby. Next, we were waiting on the train platform like a group of pilgrims, all lined up in our summer clothes, straw hats, holding our luggage and staring at the tracks. I only held the package of cakes.

The Long Journey from North to South
June 1941

The next thing Frida knew after she walked straight into the waves with all her clothes on and holding her suitcase, she was lying on the sand and a group of women and children were squatting around her and staring at her. They cheered when she opened her eyes. One of the children was pointing to her hair, a woman went inside the tent and brought a wet cloth, and she started wiping Frida's face. She realized she was smeared with her own vomit, and all the water she had swollen. She didn't ask to be pulled out of the water; she didn't ask to be saved. She had found her salvation, and it was refreshing, and it tasted salty. They didn't have to bring her back to life. The people around her spoke a different language with clusters of hard consonants and brief stops like hiccups, it could have been Turkish. Maybe she had miraculously ended up in Turkey, she wasn't sure whether there was a war in Turkey, maybe the Turks were kinder and didn't crowd people on trains and trucks and slaughter them like cattle. One of the women lifted her head and made her drink from a cup, a refreshing lemony drink. She spoke to her in the foreign language as if expecting Frida to understand everything. The sound of the foreign language sounded comforting; she needed comfort more than understanding. The woman gave her clothes that she picked up off the floor of the tent, a colorful skirt, a white blouse with wide sleeves and tied a scarf around her head.

Another woman came who spoke to Frida in a language that she understood and that wasn't Romanian, but the secret language she and Gabi sometimes spoke with each other. She told her the Russians were bombing the hell out of the port and there were deportations here, too. However, an SS officer had saved a whole bunch of people from being deported and sent to the camps, herself among them, she was hiding with the Turkish and Gypsy people. He was an anomaly among the German officers. The woman had also lost her husband and one son, but her other son survived. Frida told her about the twins being left in hiding in the care of friends, but she wasn't sure anymore if they hadn't been seized in the raids, and her husband was taken away from under her very eyes. She shouldn't be alive, she said. "Yes, you should," said the woman, "I'm sure your daughters are alive if you put them in hiding with that family." She spoke as if she knew the family, as if she knew everything that Frida didn't know. There seemed to be a secret familiarity, as if the woman knew Frida from a long time ago, she was hiding that fact now and trying to appear as a stranger. It worked because Frida had no idea who the woman was despite a nagging feeling that they had met before. That they knew each other more than just acquaintances. But she didn't care.

Dusk was falling. They heard explosions in the distance, they always bombed at night, the woman said. Then again, as the woman spoke, an inflexion in her voice and tone reminded Frida of someone she had known long ago, before they put people on death trains. The woman was Jewish too, from Iasi, the city farther north where they were killing them by the thousands in the streets or putting them on the trains of death. She and her husband owned a millinery shop in town and on June 26th soon after the first Russian air raids, when the killings started in town, her husband and son were shot dead right in front of the store. She happened to be inside the store with her other son, Sebastian. They hid in the basement, and when the SS officer came into the basement looking for survivors and saw them, he pretended he hadn't seen anyone and yelled back to the others waiting in front of the store to stop looking, there was nobody down there. She and her son waited in the basement, until a relative came looking for them, took them to the smaller town up north and put them up in his house. They stayed there for a few days with his family until he was able to get false identifications for them and put them on a train to the south.

That was how she had gotten here and why she hid with the caravan of Gypsies and Turks on the beach. By now Frida was certain she knew the woman, that she had known her for a long time and couldn't understand why she talked to her like a stranger. She could have even been family. Or maybe it was only delirium from her endless journey and almost drowning. Her brain must have been filled with too much salty water and her heart with too much grief for her to recognize anyone or understand anything.

"I didn't want to be saved either," the woman said with wildness in her eyes. She found the group of Turkish and Romanian Gypsies who moved along the beaches with their carts and tents, escaping the purges. They put up their tents on small beaches farther from the port, in the coves next to the brush and the thistle fields, made their fires during the day to cook the food and put them out at night during the bombardments. When it's not the Americans it's the Russians. I prefer the American bombs, they are more civilized, the woman said and smiled as if making a joke. Frida asked the woman if her son was with her, where was he, but the woman kept quiet. It was better she didn't know, just in case they got caught and tortured, it was best if she didn't know anything.

Frida understood and asked no more questions. She was struck by such sudden exhaustion that she couldn't keep her eyes open, and she lay down on the sand. Then she was suddenly shaken by what felt like a strange current, as if she were being electrocuted. Her face became translucent and glowed eerily in the light of the setting sun. Her shaking stopped and she stared at the sea with a fierce fixity. Her face made a grimace, almost like a smile. She was surrounded by a thin yellow wind, a curl of golden smoke. The next moment it was gone. "One of my girls is still alive," she said. The old Gypsy woman who was sitting on the floor of the tent and stirring the soup in a pot looked up and said, "sure she is, they both are, but in different ways." Frida came out of what seemed like a trance and appeared calm, almost happy.

"I knew they would do anything to save my girls, maybe they are still in their house. We spent beautiful days together before the war, our children played together, there was music, even dancing. Gabi was alive, we danced in the park under the gazebo. At the house there was a Victrola and they played "L'Elisir d'amore." There was an Italian soldier, a maid and a doll named the same funny name. My two girls played with their children in the orchard, they had a lovely orchard, Zoe and Carolina loved the orchard. I don't know which of the two is alive though, it doesn't matter, maybe both, maybe it's a mistake ..." Frida went on talking in an uninterrupted flow of sentences as if she were on stage playing one of her parts from her theater days. She and the woman seemed to refer to the same family that hid and saved Frida's children but the woman pretended to not recognize the similarity between the descriptions: the Italian soldier, the girl talking to her doll, the Victrola playing Italian songs. The Gypsy woman kept stirring the soup and muttering a string of deep sounding words, a song, or a prayer.

One of the Russian bombs hit close by, it must have been close because they felt a powerful burning wind blow over them. The rest of the men, women and children came into the tent and crouched on the tent floor in silence. The women were holding the children, protecting them with their bodies. "It's the Russian bombs again, may all the Russians suffer the fires of Beelzebub" another woman said into Frida's ear. "How do you know it's the Russian and not the American bombs?" she asked. "Because they stink and they sound like hell," the woman said and laughed. Though it seemed incomprehensible to her own shattered self, Frida laughed too, crouching like everybody else on the sand of the tent, smelling the salty dry earth, tasting it, shaking with each blast, and hoping one would fall on her and instantaneously crush her into oblivion.

The woman's name was Sofia Marcela Kunovicis. She whispered it into Frida's ear just like she had whispered the curses against the Russians. She uttered the name several times as if wanting to make a point, to awaken a memory. Frida didn't really care, but in the deafening sounds of the bombing and the blazing explosions she found her name funny just like almost everything else about her and wondered why she had to say her full name as if it mattered, as if she was introducing herself in a formal way. Under the bombs, in the tent of a group of Turkish Gypsies on the beach, Sofia Marcela Kunovicis was whispering her name and Frida knew she would remember the name forever yet not know what to do with it when so much else had been lost and forgotten. Part of her had been obliterated and her past, her conscience, her memory splintered into myriads of pieces that no longer matched each other and no longer formed the portrait of who she once was. Knowledge and memories didn't matter anymore. Only that moment on the sand, in the tent mattered, and even that was somewhat superfluous. Her mind was focused on the next steps of her journey, and she clung to the hope she would find at least one of her girls.

When the bombings stopped, the night grew thick, the sand scorched her throat. Carolina and Zoe appeared to Frida gliding on the bridge of the moon across the sea. Carolina's face was turned away and moving towards the horizon yet fiercely alive, more alive than the living, like a different kind of creature made of wind and light. Zoe was looking directly at her mother and moving towards the beach with slow tiny steps like a ballerina walking a tightrope. Sofia talked softly against the wind, yet her words were clear. Zoe was being carried on a train, passed from loving hands to loving hands, she was carried in a blanket and put on the luggage rack, she didn't move, she didn't breathe, as if she was dead, they didn't find her, she got to a safe place, yet the other one kept breathing but was dead, there was not enough air where she was. "Your friends did the best they could." Who was Sofia Kunovicis, how did she know such things? Carolina glided towards the moon, a tiny silhouette of wind and light, immaterial, waving at the moon, drinking the moon light. Zoe tiptoed towards the beach, walked on shore, played in the sand, the moon held her in a silky net of light.

Frida woke up early in the morning on a bed sheet laid on the sand inside the tent, flanked on each side by the women and children who inhabited it. At first, she had no idea how she had gotten there and who any of these people were. The next moment though, memories of the previous days came upon her in a flood. She had acquired important knowledge, and she had to stay alive for one or both of her daughters.

She remembered a woman called Sofia Kunovicis and looked for her, but she was nowhere around. She realized Kunovicis had also once been her name, in another life and thought the coincidence was funny. How often two women with a last name like Kunovicis meet up on a beach under bombardments by Russian air raids? She brushed away her curiosity, it wasn't important. Who cared about their last names and coincidences? She got up and crawled over the sleeping bodies to get out of the tent. The beach was empty, and the water emerald, green, with algae and jellyfish along the line where the waves broke with soothing splashing sounds. Even though it didn't look like it, war was raging just a couple of kilometers away, she felt war in the air, in the smokey particles that seemed to still carry traces of the Russian bombs from the previous night, the smokiness on the horizon, the silhouettes of the dark war ships lined up in the distance where the port stretched like a sinister island. She recapitulated everything in her mind about what Sofia Marcela Kunovicis had told her or that she thought she had told her. She wasn't sure anymore whether that information had been imparted to her by the strange woman or whether it just miraculously slid into her brain. She chose the former. It was Sofia Marcela, she knew things about her family, she held important information about her daughters and now she was gone.

A girl being carried in a blanket and thrown on the luggage rack, traveling southwest to the Carpathians - that image was so alive in her mind that she was certain of its truthfulness. A sign of survival, for one of them at least. How does one choose between one's two children, who had decided to make that choice for her, for them, why one and not the other, why one and not both? The important thing was to find her, them, she didn't know how, she was stuck on the image of the girl wrapped in a blanket, carried by someone to the train station, placed on the luggage rack, taken to a town, a place, a safe house, somewhere more peaceful, where no bombs fell like rain. Zoe, Carolina, the last she had seen them was when she and Gabi dropped them off at their friends' house one morning in the spring of 1941, and Tudor had said "don't worry, we'll take good care of them." That was a long time ago, they must have grown, or they must be dead. Grown or dead, those were the only two alternatives that floated through her mind as she stared at the dark silhouettes of the warships in the distance.

Frida walked on the beach for a long time away from the port. She walked through the cool salty water now, stepping on shells, algae, jellyfish, her feet were inexhaustible, she could have walked for years until she literally dropped dead. A memory plays itself like a scene in a play: Frida and Gabi are hiding in a basement one day, in a baker's basement, a good family. There are some of those too, there are those who won't hand out Jews to the Nazis or kill them with their own hands. They are in a different town. They had taken trains to a town where Tudor had sent them with a letter. They go from the baker's to a priest's house. The priest is singing hallelujahs and spreading incense everywhere in the house. Then it's a professor's house with walls covered in shelves filled with books, then a welder's house, the burning iron smells clean and sharp. There are children, one burns himself on the hot iron and screams for hours, the smell of burned flesh smells nauseating. They take another train and end up at night in a northern town and realize when it's too late that it's the wrong town.

Orders have been given there to round people up. There are local militias made of citizens, they put people on trains or on trucks, one or the other, take your pick. Their contact told them to get out of there as fast as their legs could carry them. Yes, but how? Someone along the way had misguided them, it wasn't by mistake. Frida had carried wigs in her suitcase from her theater days, now that proved useful. She takes out the two blonde ones, one male one female. They go into the train bathrooms and come out as an Aryan couple. They spend the night on the bench in the train station. Somewhere there are bombs falling, American, Russian, it doesn't matter. The night guard at the station greets them in a friendly way. It pays to be blonde, it's a good thing to be blonde in this war. At dawn they take another train to where their contact sent them, and they get off in a town almost at border with Ukraine. They rent an attic room and live there for a while. It isn't clear anymore for how long. It could be weeks or months, time got stuck somewhere on one of the trains and it feels like it is always the same day, the same exhausting day made of running, hiding, sleeping, waking up, starting over. Then somehow, they end up full circle almost where they left several months earlier, right in the middle of the danger all over again. She doesn't understand who is guiding them and why they are moving in circles. Gabi must know. He must have arranged their entire escape, and every step must be a necessary one. He is not telling her, to not frighten her but also to protect her of course.

Frida was by now running through the waves chasing her memories, the scenes playing in front of her eyes, she had no choice but to follow them through the waves, the sand, the blazing morning sun, every form of nature and weather. There was something very valuable hidden in those memories like a secret key in a secret box. If she could only open the box and get the key, only the box also needed a key. She needed to find the key that opened the box that held the key. She ran on the wet warm sand and the live yet immaterial version of what happened to her and Gabi during the last year shimmered in front of her like broken pieces of a movie roll floating in the air.

Frida ran back to the tent as if needing to catch a train, there had been so many trains. Everything happened on trains those days, maybe the key to the secret box that held the secret key would show up in a train compartment. She moved into a new realm of overlapping realities. Something was guiding her, or someone rather: the frail silhouette made of golden smoke, gliding on the bridge of the moon. Halfway to the tent that was hidden among brush and thistles she knew for a fact that Carolina no longer existed in the material world, she would never be able to hold her and feel her tiny frame in her arms. Zoe would have to make do for both. Bones and flesh mattered, the quiver of life, the heart - they mattered. It was what she was still fighting for, running after, like in a dream within a dream.

She remembered a scene in the attic room in the afternoon of that year not long ago, that summer, or rather the scene remembered itself — someone else was telling her story and projecting it in front of her. Gabi stood in front of the tiny window almost touching the ceiling with his head. It seemed like he was not just randomly watching outside but that he was expecting something, watching for someone, for a sign from someone. He stood motionless in front of the attic window while she lay on the mattress to rest, there wasn't much to do in the tiny attic room. She had no books, no knitting to do, no parts to play. Their lives had been a long string of shabby secret rooms, moving from hiding place to hiding place, moving on trains, occasionally a car, often on foot on side alleys or dirt roads in the countryside. For the first time since they were on the run, that afternoon she felt desire for Gabi as she watched him stand straight in front of the tiny round attic window, the afternoon light glowing on his naked torso.

There were bombs over the entire region the previous night. She didn't care about the bombs, she didn't even know why they kept running anymore, maybe they should have just let themselves be caught and shot or blown up by a bomb. It almost looked to her that Gabi made a sign to someone in the street. She called his name, and he was startled, he had a happy smile on his face. For a moment she had the crazy thought it was another woman. She had a twinge of jealousy which she didn't even recognize as jealousy because Gabi had never given her any reason to be jealous, being madly in love with her. She called him again, he felt her desire and walked to the mattress, lay next to her. He touched her, caressed her thighs, the entire length and width of her small body, lifted her gauzy peach colored skirt, unbuttoned her lacy white blouse. The afternoon June sunlight shone and caressed both of their bodies like a feather, merciful and delightful, almost cool, almost lacking heat, a cooling liquid light. He whispered how much he loved her, that they were going to be fine, she moaned and laced herself around his torso with a fierceness she had thought was long forgotten. They made love slowly as if they had all the time in the world. A siren shrieked outside, and they didn't care, the sound of a truck came and went, and they didn't care, maybe trucks carrying people to their deaths. She wanted to hold him and feel him inside her, around her, enveloping her like a vengeance in the eerie June light sliced by sirens. Now, as she ran through the waves back to the tent, the scene played out with devastating clarity. Frida almost felt Gabi's hands on her breasts, stomach, thighs, she ran through the cooling waves knowing he was dead, knowing Carolina was dead, knowing Zoe was still alive, knowing Sofia Marcela had something to do with saving her daughter or knew something about where she was.

When she got to the tent everybody was outside sitting around a new fire drinking a sweet cool malted drink made of millet, the Turkish braga, they offered it to her, and she drank it in big thirsty gulps. She asked for Sofia Marcela Kunovicis. The women had a moment of hilarity not knowing who she was talking about. Was this woman a friend, an acquaintance, a character in a story, was she of high birth? She must be with a name like that. She had no idea what it meant to be of high birth, and she laughed at the expression that sounded archaic to her, from a different world or a story book. All she knew was that her own birth origins had been a source of misery and a curse for her entire life, as long as she could remember, since the times she lived in another country, somewhere in a country with a fierce revolution and a brutal counter revolution. It could even be the country that was throwing the bombs right then, a country she and Gabi had once ran away from on some rusty filthy train, an eternity ago, maybe in another life.

A young girl who must have been Zoe's and Carolina's age ran inside the tent and came right out with a folded piece of paper and handed it to Frida. She said "here, she left this for you, the woman who was hiding here with us, she left this, she said to give it to you, she left before dawn." The old Gypsy woman came out of the tent and told Frida she was going to find her girl. How did she know with such assurance Frida wondered, and remembered in that same second, that after they made love that last time in the attic room, Gabi told her the girls were safe, he said the "girls" not the "girl." How did he know, why was everyone hiding things from her? The Gypsy woman said the "girl" in the singular. All the note provided was an address in the city of Brasov in Transylvania, nothing more but an address written in elegant perfectly shaped handwriting. What kind of person hides with a group of Romanian and Turkish Gypsies in a tent in the brush on the beach and has the patience and calm to write a note using their best handwriting? She had to go to the address apparently. "You must go there," the Gypsy said. "Here have some more of this braga, it will make you stronger." Frida had a desire to swear at everything and everybody and at God and the whole universe. Maybe she didn't want to get stronger, maybe she wanted to be a heavy corpse at the bottom of the sea eaten by fish and wrapped in algae, that was what she most wanted really.

Instead, Frida picked up the tiny purse with her false documents that had miraculously survived her almost-drowning episode, put on her worn out sandals and was ready to leave. The old Gypsy woman called after her and handed her a handful of gold coins. Who carried gold coins in those times anyways, like in some old fairy tale? "Here, to have for the road," she said, "and here this little bag with food to have for the road." This also seemed like a scene from a play she once performed in, a fairy tale of a woman who gets hopelessly lost and ends up knocking at the doors of strangers, they let her in, and they show her the way to the important place where she must meet someone who will save her life. It was a funny thing that the plays she performed in before proved themselves of some usefulness now, who would have though it! "Travel by day," the Gypsy woman said, "they blow up trains and stations by night, here tie this scarf around your head, your red hair is too obvious, say you're Turkish." Frida obeyed quietly everything she was told like in a trance. Only she didn't know one single Turkish word. Why was it better to be Turkish anyways? One of the men in the group drove her in the covered carriage to the train station and told her to take the next train going north on the first platform, to not ask or talk to anyone. Her life was run by strangers, and she didn't question it for a second. She moved effortlessly in this new reality protected by an immaterial veil of light, a degree removed from the reality of the war, a degree removed from her own reality, scenes from her life occasionally flickering in front of her eyes, a traveling mirage.

The trains were almost empty at that time as if most people had disappeared. Maybe they had. A lonely passenger getting on occasionally, staying for a while, getting off, there must have been a lull in the waves of refugees. She stayed on through the blazing morning, the afternoon sun, the setting sun, the sea disappearing into the plains, there were even sunflowers. Who was going to make any use of sunflowers in times of war and furious bombings? Then, the train stopped for a long time at the Bucharest station. She remembered she had to leave and take another train northbound towards Transylvania. She got off and was surprised to see the swarming of civilians and soldiers on the platforms. She didn't know which way to go for the next train. Luckily, she heard a couple point to the train going to Brasov and she followed them. She had once been in a couple and had a family, a full family of four that sat at dinner tables and ate dinners together and even took leisurely walks in the park at the other end of the country. It was a big country after all, it took hours and days to cross it and everywhere someone somewhere was looking for refuge in one corner or another.

Whether you wanted to or not, that war forced you to know the country and travel like mad, nobody stayed in one place. Her thoughts moved faster than she could think them, they seemed to think themselves and move through her mind with restless flutters. Somewhere in a house, her daughter Zoe was waiting for her. Maybe the couple in front of her going in the same direction had a child too. They were a nice-looking couple judging from the back, dressed elegantly and with a dignified posture. They walked arm in arm. She followed them to the same train car and to the same compartment. Sharp train whistles and thick curls of smoke followed trains leaving the station. The Gypsy woman had said not to travel by night because they were bombing train stations, but what choice did she have? She didn't care about obliteration anyways.

In the train compartment she sat across from the couple and noticed the woman had been crying. They were younger than her, they both looked exhausted, maybe they too had been running for days and weeks. The man took off his hat and uncovered a full head of black curly hair that looked much like the woman's. Maybe they were not a couple, but brother and sister. They were quiet and stared out the window for a long time without saying a word. She had never traveled to that part of the country; the train got much fuller, and the compartment filled with all kinds of people carrying lots of luggage. It became completely dark outside, and the compartment was barely lit. She felt sleepy but afraid to fall asleep in case she missed her stop. The breathing of all the people in the compartment formed a warm wind and made it hard to breathe.

Frida must have dozed off for a few minutes despite all her best efforts because suddenly there was blinding light from the bulb in the ceiling and the train conductor was asking for tickets and identifications. She handed over her false documents and realized she didn't have the ticket for this stretch of the trip. In the rush of changing trains in the crowded Bucharest station she had completely forgotten. The man in the couple across from her pulled out a ticket other than the ones for himself and his companion and handed it to her smiling with the words: "Here it is Irina, dear, sorry I forgot to give it to you earlier, how absent minded of me." Irina was Frida's false name on the false papers given by the man in the elegant suit who drove her and Gabi to the train station in northern Moldavia which seemed like centuries ago, though it was less than a full week. She was shocked by the man's knowledge of her alias and his gesture. He must have seen her name when she showed her papers.

The conductor stared at all three of them for several seconds in silence, it felt like a long time. It felt like something was going to happen, an explosion, a derailment, the end of life on earth. Instead, all the conductor said was "you should carry your ticket on you, madam," then he checked everybody else's tickets and left. Frida stared at the man who saved her by miraculously producing a ticket out of his pocket as if he had it all planned. Now that she had lost half of her family everybody on earth wanted to help her and the sky rained miracles. She laughed and heard the raw hoarse sound of her own laughter in the stuffy silence of the smelly train compartment.

For a millisecond, Frida had a wild desire to kill everybody and saw each person sitting there next to her as a corpse that she herself had slaughtered. The mysterious couple that could be brother and sister, lovers, or incestuous brother and sister, with their throats slashed and their black curly hair falling all over their white faces, caked with blood. The old woman with a white straw hat over her white hair with a bullet in her head, the peasanty looking mother and son in worker's clothes and with ruddy faces, stabbed right in the heart. A bloodbath whose sole author was herself, just like in one of her stage performances, long ago when she was a respected actress and had a happy family with a loving husband and two beautiful twin daughters. In that play she was the victim of a jealous man turned serial killer. In this play she was the serial killer taking revenge on the whole world. She felt no gratitude toward the man who smugly produced the train ticket out of his pocket, nor toward the Turks who had pulled her out of the water, nor toward Sofia Marcela Kunovicis and her know it all arrogance like she was a seer or someone's Fairy God Mother. Maybe the train she was on was also a train of death only slightly more comfortable and while everybody thought they were traveling to some safe destination, they were in fact being taken to a slaughterhouse somewhere in the Carpathians. There were no safe places anywhere, certainly not for her and her people.

She had a dream in which Carolina and Zoe played in the orchards on Tudor and Victoria's property, the cherry, apple, and apricot trees were in wild bloom, a symphony of foamy rosy and white flowers. It was a day in May and her girls wore wreaths of golden flowers on their reddish curls, they looked like angels. Tudor and Victoria's children were playing hide and seek with her Zoe and Carolina. It was their turn to hide. A wind started that almost shook all the trees clear of their delicate flowers until the trees looked almost barren like in winter. It was winter in the summer, there was nowhere to hide because everything was barren. A screechy Victrola was playing the same Italian love song over and over until it became unbearable, and an Italian soldier appeared from behind one of the trees with a rifle. He said I'm an Italian soldier who deserted, I'm a deserter, they are going to kill me anyways, I'd better just kill myself before they do it. He offered Frida his rifle and asked, would you madam, would you please kill me, here you only need to press this trigger over here, see, once you do it once you can keep doing it over and over again, it's no big deal. She followed the soldier's instructions exactly. Before she shot him, he said see, the Italian soldiers are kinder than the German ones, they are better dancers too, we are not so bad after all. She pulled the trigger and there was a silent shot. Before she knew it, the soldier was dead on the grass between the cherry trees. Zoe and Carolina came running to her and said in tears, mama why did you do that, didn't you see it was papa, why did you shoot papa? And Frida said it's better this way than him being taken on the trains like everybody else. I did him a favor, he was going to die anyways, but I saved you two, nobody is going to take you away from me ever again. I had to do it, it was either him or you, I chose you two. Carolina and Zoe melted into the bare trees, and she was left alone. There was a quiet wind, everything was frighteningly quiet. The whole world was muted, and sound had simply disappeared.

She woke up sweaty and saw she was alone in the compartment; everybody must have gotten off. Then she started in a fright, she must have missed her stop. She went out in the hallway and saw the dark-haired couple standing and kissing in the hallway. She had a sickening feeling seeing them kiss, it seemed incestuous. Who cared if brother and sister were lovers as well, when they were going to die anyway? She remembered they were also getting off at the Brasov station so she must not have missed her stop. She didn't care anyways, she did everything with inertia, someone else was guiding her movements and choices.

Her station approached. She knew it because the couple stood in front of the door waiting for the train to come to a complete stop. When it did, she realized that only the man was getting off and she gasped. They kissed on the steps; she held his hand for as long as she could while he went down the steps. Frida trembled as if electrocuted: it was the same damn thing repeatedly, people's lives being torn apart, slashed in two, it was as if seeing the ghosts of her and Gabi of several days earlier on the train station in Bukovina. Only nobody was grabbing this man away from his lover, it seemed like a voluntary and needed separation. It distracted her from her own disasters to worry about the life of that couple, someone else's misery. She was not alone but part of an entire population of wretched people.

It was dusk again and she found herself in Transylvania. She lived her days awake and tense from dawn till dusk, hopping from region to region and gliding like a ghost through throngs of soldiers and refugees, predators and prey, and everything in between. She had no idea what to do next. It was as if it was not her, Frida, living her life anymore, but someone else inhabiting her body and impersonating her. She was a character in a drama and an actress was playing her. She had once played the role of the mother in Pirandello's *Six Characters in Search of an Author*, and it became her favorite role. The same suffering and the same gestures of suffering played themselves out repeatedly, grinding into her flesh, guiding her steps.

A woman with a baby tied to her back bumped into her, a soldier pushed her aside, she was squeezed in the crowd and almost lost consciousness when she felt a strong arm pulling her away from the mass of people. It was the dark-haired man in the couple. Nothing seemed strange anymore, she just let it happen. "I'll take you there, it's complicated, you would get lost for sure," he said. Then he leaned over and whispered in her ear: "don't look around you, just take my arm and follow me." Frida had a feeling of gliding slowly into a fluid realm, an in between space that had a different consistency and was a deviation in time. Following the unknown man was walking through tracks of time. Time was space and she was moving through its gelatinous corridors. She followed the man as he had asked, but it felt like he was following her too, and that she was following another presence stronger than both.

They walked on side streets with small stone houses, streets that were quiet in a sinister way, cries and bombs seemed shrouded in a forced silence. Then the streets became narrower and steeper, the air cooler and the smell of resin pungent and surprisingly soothing like a healthy drug. Good and evil merged and quivered in every drop of air and were shrouded in the beauty of the dark forest at the foot of the mountain. They left the road and walked for what seemed like a long time on a tiny winding path among pine trees, oaks, and ferns. Frida felt an unexpected burst of energy, and the memory of all the events of the past week acquired a crystalline clarity and coldness, a film of her life and what happened to her. A silent movie, sad but remote, a ride in a black car, a separation on the steps of a train, a husband she once had and loved who was now gone, two daughters she once had who were now one, a walk on the sand of a small beach, a cool darkness with fish and algae, a woman posing as a Gypsy Turkish woman who held invaluable information telling her you will find your daughter, your daughter in the singular, even though she had twins.

The memories were dislocated images separate from her yet physical and concrete, simulacra that appeared and disappeared in the resin smelling dusk of the forest. She no longer held the man's arm but walked in lockstep with him with unexpected lightness. It suddenly became dark, night fell like a giant bird from the sky, ruthlessly. The man said to hold on to him, he couldn't use a flashlight or matches because of the curfew, the Russian raids were going to start anytime. An explosion lit up the sky in the distance, a fire rose from the north like the tongue of a dragon. The Germans are setting factories on fire, maybe the wheel bearing factory, the man informed her. Frida didn't really care at all about which factory the Germans or the Russians set on fire or whose bombs lit up the sky. The climb in the dark of the forest stepping on pine needles and dry leaves felt as unreal as everything else that had happened recently. Only now the dream smelled fresh and had a sweet pungency, a sweet-smelling dream that meant to take her to her daughter, in the singular. And the singular made the dream instantly smell sour and heavy. At an unexpected point in the road a house emerged with a wooden door and two small windows with just a tiny sliver of light coming from behind the curtains. Other than the light coming from inside, the house seemed lit by a gentle haze of light surrounding it, a golden yellowish haze like a filmy thing you could touch or could feel dripping on your skin.

Everything from then on unfolded with a painful, new normalcy, like trying to make do without a leg or an arm, a mutilated normalcy of small gestures that carried with them all the burden of a terrible loss. Somebody opened the door from the inside as if they were expecting them. Frida and the man stepped inside, and she stumbled on the rug at the entrance, she would have stumbled on an empty floor as well. She was breaking from tiredness and a gaping hole in her being that spread from her heart to all her organs and limbs. She thought she heard a bird of the night call outside, a night cuckoo bird or maybe a bat. The person who opened the door was an older woman wrapped in a shawl with her hair in a bun, like someone in a story, a classic fairy tale of lost children. Here my dear Frida, this way please! The woman spoke to her directly with knowledge of her and her past.

She opened a side door to a room. Zoe was sleeping with her head slightly tilted to one side, her red curls spread on the pillow appeared to light up the room, a low burning cool fire. It seemed there was almost a smile on her lips, and Frida wondered how she could see all those details in the darkness of the room. The darkness had a smooth glow to it that shaped itself around the objects and people in the room. There was a faint crack like a branch breaking inside Frida's heart, like her heart was a small tree with branches reaching out and cracking one after another, cracking and twisting, a life of torment, a perpetually breaking branch. She felt Carolina's absence like a presence and finally understood and accepted that she was gone but that a sliver of her still roamed through passageways of time, asking for something, giving something, in a perpetual dance of yearning. A leaden tiredness overcame her, and she lay down next to Zoe like they had never parted. She held her and fell asleep almost instantly, with the sound of a faint voice calling her mama, a sound she hadn't heard in almost a year. Zoe's body had grown. In the sliver of wakefulness before sleep Frida thought my girl has grown, she is taller. Had Carolina grown too, was she still growing there wherever she was?

Frida's Death
Bucharest Fall 1970

That autumn after we returned from our fantastical seaside journey, Frida fell terribly ill and died before Christmas. She lay in bed for three months, getting thinner every day, she was melting from a mysterious illness that devoured her from the inside. My mother took me to her tiny apartment at the end of a vaulted alley and we sat by her bed unmoving for what seemed like a very long time, maybe hours. Frida opened her eyes occasionally. At first, she gave a puzzled look as if she didn't recognize anything and anybody, then she looked at us and her eyes lit up with a tiny smile when she saw me. She talked only in whispers and very rarely. My mother sat next to her and held her hand looking straight at a point on the wall, her eyes shining fiercely with tears she didn't want to let flow down her face.

Occasionally on those visits, the golden hazy presence that sat in a chair one night in our room at the seaside, would glide into our space and linger near us for a while, a breath that had lost the body breathing it. One afternoon on one of our visits, my mother took me right after school, I thought I heard Frida whisper "I can't wait to see Carolina, I can't wait to see her again." There was a strong shifting of air in the room, a sudden vacuum inside which we couldn't breathe for a brief scary second. I gulped for air and the next second it rushed in, an impatient windy air that returned to the room as if it had been stolen. I saw my mother lay the entirety of her body over the length of Frida's body. Dusk was sliding into the room, a flock of swallows rushed by the window, and the pigeons on the roof across the street fluttered and made gurgling sounds before sleep. The golden airy presence swished by almost touching me, then it all became unbearably quiet until I heard a wailing sob from my mother like I had never heard her produce before. I felt awkward and my body felt excessive, too heavy, and too hard in the tiny room.

Frida did something surprising, like a jolt of electricity had traversed her body and she received one last burst of energy before slipping into the next realm. She sat up and for a few seconds she looked beautiful, younger, glowing. She unbuttoned her nightgown and took off what looked like a necklace, a chain, with something hanging on it. It seemed of utmost importance. She gave the chain to my mother and whispered something in her ear. It felt like Frida could not die until she revealed the meaning of the necklace to my mother because her breathing was getting incredibly agitated, and she kept asking her to promise something. I tried to intercept the whispers. I had always been good at eavesdropping with all the secrecy going on in our house. I thought I heard the word for key, that the thing hanging on the necklace was a precious key that my mother must keep until she found the box or door that it opened. I imagined a secret room either with enchanted beings and sparkling jewels like in some of the fairytales my mother read to me, or a horrifying room with corpses and bloody human remains like in the story of Blue Beard who killed all his wives and hid their corpses in one room. The last wife, though, manages to call her brothers and they save her at the last minute and kill Blue Beard.

My mother's body shook. All I could see was her back. It looked like silent sobbing. Then my mother nodded as if to say yes, promising Frida something important, that she would find and preserve the contents of the room/box opened by that special key with her life. I was sure Frida said: "with your life," and my mother repeated after her "with my life." Then Frida lay back on her back, with her head perfectly situated on her pillow. I thought then that Frida knew how to die beautifully, just like in the theater, just like she had pretend-died in one of her plays. Only this time it was for good, and she wouldn't stand up for a final bow and applause. The golden airy presence in the room swished by one more time and flew out through the open window like an invisible swallow. My mother had the necklace Frida gave her around her neck when she turned toward me. I couldn't see the object hanging on it as it was tucked inside her blouse. It could have been a key or a precious diamond. I had no way of knowing nor did I have the disposition to explore the possibilities in my head because my mother's face was changed, transfigured, glowing with tears, touched by a special light, almost like a smile. My mother never smiled, she was either serious and severe or laughed in a timid way. Maybe that was why I couldn't really discern whether the light on her face came from a smile or something else, a magic force. Maybe both.

I don't remember us ever leaving the room where Aunt Frida who was my grandmother spent the last days and moments of her life, but hazy scenes from that evening still exist. My mother and I rushing home in the dark, with my mother saying we have to tell your father, we have to tell Florin that Frida died, as if there was a possibility that my father would be kept in the dark about his mother in law's death. It was also strange that she never said my mother died, but "Frida died." There were a couple of phone calls, a few sobs in the darkness of our apartment, whispers and shuffling across the apartment floor.

My parents were looking for something important in the dark, something that needed to be found with some urgency, but they were having a hard time doing so. I told you it's in the desk drawer, no it's it not, I never put it there, maybe we lost it, maybe you never brought it. There was an important object or document missing apparently that needed to be found the very evening of Frida's death, but it was never found. It could have had something to do with the necklace and the object, possibly a key. hanging on the necklace that Frida gave my mother in her very dying moment. But I wouldn't know until decades later, during the last day of my journey to my father's town with his mythic house and orchards.

After that evening Frida melted away from our lives like she had entered it: tiptoeing elegantly and inaudibly, like the swishing of a party dress. I missed her terribly for many months and sometimes I talked to her before going to sleep, with a strong sense that she could hear me. I felt the hazy presence near me whenever I did so, and sometimes I did it on purpose just to see if I could invoke her, it was my fantastical going to sleep game. Then slowly I forgot Frida and it felt like she forgot me, like she finally merged with the darkness and quiet she always seemed to long for while still alive.

Bucharest. Spring and Summer 1957

Victoria let in the person who knocked at the door quietly, closing the door inaudibly while speaking in a normal voice, not too loud, not too softly. Florin and Zoe continued to eat as if not paying attention to the guest who entered the apartment wearing a light gray jacket and an equally gray fedora hat. Florin was caught by a coughing fit, his tuberculosis had returned with a vengeance, and he needed new treatment, mostly he needed to be away from the hot stale air of the capital and in the cool air of the mountains up north. Victoria showed in the guest and asked him to please sit at the table and eat with us, here have some soup, lentil soup, it's healthy. She stressed the word healthy as if it was a code word, which it might be. The man thanked her and sat down at the table next to Florin, accepted the bowl of soup, started eating from it quietly.

Everything flowed seamlessly. It was all in the gestures, nothing in the words, a play of pantomime with lentil soup. Victoria, Florin, Zoe and the mystery guest were sitting down eating the soup, a siren screeched in the distance, a neighbor slammed the glass door to the entry of the building. Then it was quiet again with only the sound of their spoons against the soup bowls and Florin's coughing fits. The man stopped eating, took off his hat, ripped the lining inside it, took out an envelope and handed it to Florin. Victoria started clearing the table noisily, as if with deliberate loudness. Zoe took one last spoonful of the soup almost disgusted with it and stared outside at a sparrow chirping on a branch in the chestnut tree in front of the window. The chestnuts were in bloom now, as were the linden trees, she didn't care much about the letter hidden inside the lining of the fedora hat of their guest.

Florin opened the envelope slowly, laid it on the tablecloth next to him and started reading it while lighting a cigarette despite his cough. Zoe said, "you are insane, you and your cigarettes, can't you see how sick you are?" She said it with a smile as if joking, half absentmindedly the way she said just about anything. She took a quick look at the letter and her attention was drawn to the words "airplane," "landing place," "passport." She had no idea, she didn't care, but Florin seemed to care a great deal. As did Victoria who, after clearing up the table, decided to turn on the radio full blast. She hardly ever turned on the radio at all, since she didn't want to hear all the lies of the Party as she often said in a whisper looking around her to make sure no secret police informer was hidden in a corner of her room or in the icebox, you never know! But luckily there was no news, just a sentimental melody about acacia flowers in a lover's hair. Zoe almost laughed to herself while Florin read the letter, coughing, and smoking. The thought of acacia flowers transported her somewhere else.

The guest stretched out his hand for the letter after Florin finished reading it and set it on fire inside the ashtray on the table. The paper burst into quick flames which they all stared at in silence as if at a small miracle. When the last flickers in the ashtray died out, the guest stood up and walked slowly toward the window and looked outside from behind the curtains. It seemed he was watching for something or someone or hiding from someone. He acted startled and pulled back inside the room, afraid to be seen. Zoe and Florin sat at the table, gestured for him to sit down again, which he did anxiously. Victoria came back from the other room with a jar of candied walnut preserve and started serving little portions of it in small crystal bowls. It was all in silence, a silent film, a pantomime of secrecy and fear, of planning for something dangerous and forbidden. The cuckoo bird called out again, what seemed like an almost cheerful call in the otherwise heavy and sticky afternoon.

They heard a car start its engine outside and drive off at high speed. The clinks of spoons against crystal bowls were the only sounds in the room, a way of measuring seconds before something catastrophic, though the thick walnut preserve seemed to be the only preoccupation in the world of the people sitting around the table. The silence heavy with awkward gestures and a strained pretense of normality made the scene appear almost comical on the June afternoon, like a failed joke to which someone forgot the punchline and that needs explaining. The sugariness of the preserve filled the air too. In the absence of sound there was a thickness and a queasy sweetness in the air, a crooked memory of times forever gone. A shared moment of nostalgia for a better time that was forever gone and replaced with eternal misery. Zoe smiled, misery meant nothing to her, she had already lived the worst of it.

The guest whispered he had to leave, it was late, though it was not clear what he was late for. He gulped down the last of the preserve and drank the full glass of water in one breath. Florin accompanied him to the door, while Zoe and Victoria remained sitting, staring at the tablecloth. A span of time passed unnoticed, dead time. Florin was sitting at the table again. Then the sound of a car speeding by was heard again, screeching. A smell of blood and death filled the air, a bad draft of catastrophe. A dead body was left in the middle of the street behind a speeding Black Volga car. Zoe knew it was a black Volga, she recognized them by their abominable screeching sound, she had heard it before. Florin got up from his chair and walked towards the window, he wanted to see with his own eyes, but Zoe stopped him in an eerie voice that was almost a shriek: "Don't, you don't want them to see you." Then she whispered: "he's dead of course." "How do you know?" Florin whispered back. Another sugary song about tulips started on the radio, everything was all about flowers, life was a flowery meadow in their country. "I just do."

Victoria turned off the radio and sat down in her worn-out armchair, the only one saved from the old house. Zoe and Florin sat back down at the table, she took his hand and held it like a promise of tenderness. They felt the weight of the dead body lying in the street even though they never saw it. The smell of blood mixed with the linden trees reminded them of a time captured in a photograph with fanfare and a gazebo somewhere in another life. An ambulance shrieked nearby, probably to pick up the body, an "accident," so many accidents happened in the flowery meadow of their socialist republic. Florin grabbed Zoe's hand over the starched tablecloth and whispered to her in between drags from his cigarette, exhaling curls of blue smoke. He looked straight ahead at the painting of the person walking through a field of snow. "We are going to leave this hell hole soon, it's all arranged, next week." Zoe said nothing, nodded and smiled a dreamy smile as if already imagining for herself a life outside of the hell hole.

That week, Florin and Zoe moved in slow motion, quietly, preparing for their escape. Zoe never asked what was written in the letter that had been set aflame at the dinner table, but she knew the man who brought it was one of the organizers, if not the main organizer of a group escape by plane, with fake passports and a landing place that was not a hell hole. And that man had been killed in the street in front of their apartment building the afternoon with the syrupy acacia songs on the radio, minutes after he had visited them. She had no idea who he was and didn't ask, she didn't want to know anything more than she strictly needed to. She had no idea either how one day that week Florin came home with two passports that had their names and pictures on them. They looked completely real to her, and she wouldn't have known anyways as she had never in her life seen a passport. All her border crossings had been lawless, in darkness and whispers. Memories of days spent in a wardrobe-like space inside a wall an eternity ago flickered only rarely in her mind, images from someone else's life that she refused to recognize as her own. She and Florin made all the preparations in absolute silence with the radio blasting throughout the day moving about Victoria's apartment like nothing special was going on. Florin came and went in a flurry of secretive errands while sentimental songs about the beauty of love in the countryside or patriotic songs about the glory of the communist party poured through the hot June air of the apartment.

On the last Sunday of the month, Florin went out in the morning without saying where he was going, returned in less than an hour and whispered to Zoe to get ready because their plane was leaving in two hours. She put on her gray and pink polka dot dress, one of the two summer dresses she owned and closed the small wooden suitcase with some of her most important belongings carefully picked from the scarcity of everything she owned: her gray suit, her blue grey linen dress, a green sweater and her one pair of dress shoes. As she was about to close her suitcase, Florin thought he had noticed a bright blue item of clothing and was startled. It looked like a blue sash he had once held in his hand as he was hiding inside a tiny cabinet inside a wall in their old house. A swallow flew inside the apartment by mistake and swirled hysterically close to the ceiling hitting itself against each corner of the main room. Zoe picked up the beige trench coat she had forgotten to pack and flailed it in the direction of the swallow until she guided it towards the window. The bird darted towards the indifferent blue sky in a flash. Something was too blue, the outside too quiet, the music too loud.

Then it all shifted again. They were each sitting on one of the chairs in the living room, only the chairs were moved away from the table and turned towards each other. They sat looking into the thin air as if it contained a palpable thickness and they were trying to discern beyond it. But there was nothing beyond it, everything was right there within reach, an entire family scene from long ago happening in synchronicity with the present day. Mitzi the maid and Mitzi the doll were both there, sitting quietly and staring in the distance. Mitzi the maid was holding a baby called Gino and the doll was held by Lila. The same Victrola song that Father Tudor played went on and on, heartbreakingly, exasperating: "L'Elisir d'amore," stretching over time, melting the years into one continuous fluid substance that held both the past and the present next to each other in glorious simultaneity. A good snake was ticking inside one of the walls, a German soldier was bleeding on a pink sofa and a young girl was absent when she should have been next to her twin sister: tricks of history swept the good and the bad together in a cruel wave. The absent girl was stuck in the crack between the past and the present, inside an impenetrable wall, wailing softly in disharmony with the Victrola song. Zoe shrieked and broke the spell, it all dissipated like smoke, a fragile crumbly balance, like a seesaw in its brief moment of perfect balance.

"Let's not go," Zoe said. "It's our only chance," Florin said. "To die," said Zoe. A wind, the same soft fluffy palpable wind as before swelled around them and through them, filtered through the irreparable crack in time. The present was longing for the past or the past couldn't reach out to the present. The space, the crack left in between the two, was what created the dizzying confusion of realities. Carolina was wailing quietly in a whisper; a feather of sound wishing to exist more solidly or be extinguished forever. "We can't go, they'll catch us," said Zoe in a contained scream like everything else of hers, contained, rounded, no cracks or leaks of emotion. Victoria stood in the middle of the room straight and proud, a simulation of Queen Mary in her youth and whispered: "She is right, listen to her, she is never wrong, you know that." Florin looked sad, defeated, like life was ending. Zoe had never seen him like that and almost gave in. For a moment she wanted to lie to him and overlook her premonition of the future that surged inside her veins and her flesh once in a great while ever since, ever since … A quiver with yellow sour fragrances and flutters of blue winds descended over her, someone else was whispering from inside her veins and her heart. She needed to lie and make empty promises to Florin so he wouldn't crumble into a pile of ashes and nothingness like the ashes of his cigarettes in the overflowing ashtray. "That's not true," she said softly like a lullaby, "there will be another time, the right time, it will happen, I promise, this is not the right time." She uttered promises like verses, like a poem with rhymes and cadence to make them weigh more, to soothe Florin's despair and prevent him from doing something foolish.

Zoe had been right. The evening of their planned escape three people trying to flee to France on a carrier plane were caught and arrested for questioning. Florin and Zoe were supposed to be part of that group. The three people were never heard of again, they were swallowed in the bottomless pit of communist arrests, interrogations, and murders. Zoe never asked Florin if he knew who those people were. What did it matter anyways? They couldn't be saved no matter what. Her intuition of the energies that decide destinies served her right again.

During the days that followed the failed escape, the arrests, and the disappearances, an eerie quiet, and a semblance of normality settled over Florin's and Zoe's lives. Victoria carried on making jams and preserves in the communal kitchen overpowering the burnt cabbage smells with the fragrances of boiling rose petals and forest berries. "Just because we live in Communist hell, everything doesn't have to stink of rotten burnt foods," she would whisper to herself as she gathered the ingredients for preserves from different corners of Bucharest where she hid them over months of slowly storing away leftovers or findings on the black market. War time habits of surviving on almost nothing at all, only roots, crumbs, always came in handy. "During the war it was better," she also sometimes whispered to herself as she produced a cinnamon or a vanilla stick from behind a cushion or from the back of her letter drawer. Lila visited them sometimes for dinner when Victoria was able to miraculously produce a full dinner out of almost nothing and when she opened one of the newly prepared rose petal preserves. Lila always knew when her mother opened a new jar of preserves somehow and made her appearance accordingly. She now worked as a screen writer for children's films at the cinematographic studios in Bucharest and despite the shortages, the disappearances of people in black vans, the hopeless dreariness of the times, she was always cheerful and her appetite healthier than ever.

Whenever Lila visited, a light nostalgia for times long gone whisked through the air. She brought uncanny combinations of smells like jasmine and mothballs, because Lila was always wearing something she had kept with fierceness from the old house: an embroidered handkerchief, a sash, a lace collar she attached to whatever drab dress she might be wearing, giving it an air of elegance. The four of them would sit around the oval walnut dining room table while Lila told stories about a new film for children she was working on, a young pioneer girl called Veronica, and her many valiant pioneer deeds. There was always a tiny strain of tension between Lila and Zoe, or maybe a quiver of complicity, one couldn't quite tell, as no mention of the past or even of any prior knowledge of each other was ever made. Surrounded by his mother, wife and sister, Florin rebecame his charismatic self, talkative, even making jokes, almost forgetting where and how they lived.

There was something particular about Lila's visit one such afternoon, as if she had something in store for them, a secret gift, a bit of surprising news. Indeed, she did. After Victoria opened her jar of miraculous rose petal preserve, Lila opened her bag with a big smile: "I found Mitzi," she said producing her childhood doll, now with a lazy eye and matted braids. "Was she lost?" asked Zoe quickly, almost in a hiccup, as if she didn't mean to speak but the words came out unwillingly. "I never thought I would find her again," she went on, not hearing Zoe's question. "I looked for her everywhere, and where do you think I found her?" Everybody stared at her in expectation. They now knew it wasn't just about Mitzi the doll but about something else and that Lila was speaking loudly for potential secret ears, the tapped telephone wire or worse. There was a knock at the door. Zoe looked out the window which she had a habit of doing in moments of tension and indecision. She thought maybe they would have some respite, and she had been wrong to think so. Lila answered the door like she was expecting someone. A woman with braids rolled on top her head in a white summer dress accompanied by a stocky blondish man with glasses stood in the door motionless. Victoria let out almost a scream, but a quiet bizarre scream, not like her voice at all: "Mitzi, what are you doing here?" Lila went quickly to the door and pulled them inside, closing the door behind them. They stood in front of the door as still as before. "Mama, aren't you going to ask them in, they've come a long way," said Lila almost playfully.

A big secret was still in store. Zoe removed herself from the scene. Situations in life were often just another scene for her, like at the theater. Like in her childhood, when her mother acted in her plays in the little provincial town up north and Zoe and the sister she once had, would both sit mesmerized staring at their mother utter her lines and move on stage in incandescent colors, a vision they couldn't take their eyes off. Their mother always placed them in the last row, and they sat rapt, holding hands until she came back to take them at the end of the show. "You were beautiful, mama," they always said in unison. "Thank you, my darlings," she always answered. Together with the memory of her mother's theater days, Zoe had a vision. Sometimes her mind worked like that in parallel ways, combining memories with unexpected visions of people and situations like an amalgam of sites and experiences in her life. Her vision was of a woman and a child walking through the snow on a country road coming towards her: the woman wears a round fur hat like a Russian hat and the child wears a beret that looks like a military beret, too big for his head. They are trying to get to her, but the snow is too deep, and she can't help them. They are covered in snow, they drown in the mounds of snow and all she can do is hold on to a fence of a house for dear life. She is in front of an old house somewhere in the north of the country in this vision and the country road leading to the house has become unpassable. This vision could also have trickled into her psyche from someone else in her family, maybe her parents. The chain of losses and separations, of endless journeys and missed chances in her family history formed a common history that crossed the boundaries of individual lives and collectively possessed them. It was her access to that world of ancestral experiences that also gave Zoe an intuition for the future and an understanding of unearthly realities like the one happening right then in front of their eyes.

Zoe turned away from the window, stared at everybody in the room with blank looks and said eerily: "They are not alive, can't you see that? Don't let them fool you, don't look at them. Lila, what got into you, why did you bring them in?" Lila started crying like when she was little during the war and after her scarlet fever: "They were roaming the streets, they were looking for us, I had to bring them in." "You were always a tricky girl, Lila, always," Zoe said sadly, without resentment "Are they dead then?" asked Florin. The room became another realm. Everything was possible, and he found it entirely normal to ask such a question about the unexpected visitors. If they were dead while paying them a visit in the middle of the day, it didn't shock him. The linden smells, the hot air in the room, the syrupy melody on the radio, all acquired a watery consistence, a palpable glow they now moved through with slowness and deliberation. It was an out of body journey. The woman that Victoria called Mitzi a minute earlier and her male companion were still standing transfixed in front of the door. "Are they dead then?" Florin repeated the question. "No, not really." Answered Zoe, as she was the only one that knew. "What are they then?" "They are something else, that's what they are." "We have a story to tell you, it won't be a minute," said the woman with the braids who was supposed to be Mitzi the maid. Her voice sounded remote, an echo returning from far away. "Sit down and tell us then," said Victoria. Everything that was "something else" had become normal and they all sat down around the table waiting for the story.

The woman whom Victoria called Mitzi started telling the story in a voice that sounded like an echo of someone's voice. "When your father died, and the Russians took over, Kosmin here asked me to marry him after he became well again. He was wounded if you remember and we took care of him as well as we could, he bled on your parents' sofa if you remember." Mitzi's voice became more hollow and remote as she kept repeating "if you remember." The scene she just mentioned came to life. Kosmin was bleeding on the pink armchair, Victoria was caring for his wound. Mitzi helped with dressing the wound and German soldiers were knocking at the door. Tudor opened the door and spoke firmly in German, he took out a book from his tall bookcase, he talked to the German soldiers until they left, and Victoria and Mitzi finished dressing the wound. Then they helped him to the cellar where other people were hiding, a widow with two children, a neighbor whose house was bombed out of existence. The house with the orchards had become a refuge for deserters and runaways. After the Germans left, in came the Russians.

The narration unfolded at fast-forward speed, skipping entire chunks of history, mixing up episodes in one disorderly puzzle, and stopping at particular moments like a derailing train that forgot its stops, rushing through scenes or staying too long and forgetting to leave. The moment with the Russians was a long stop. "Kosmin married me," Mitzi said that several times, as if it was the most important part of the story, that they married after Tudor's death. "He was made to join the Russians, then the Party." "Who made him?" asked Florin. Everybody around the table stared at him like he had made a grave mistake. But Florin was stubborn and needed to know, it was important to know who it was that made you do things like join an army or a party or a group of killers. He lit a cigarette, and the fire of the match dissipated some of the thick yellowness of the air, its watery consistency, making a clearing.

Mitzi resumed the story; she was the only one talking. She herself was made to join the Party, and Florin asked again who made her join the Party, she didn't answer. "I never joined the Party," he said, but Mitzi moved on with her story despite Florin's interruptions. They were given cooperative land and a house, she said, it was better for them, their lives were coming together, they were practically happy. The way Mitzi said the word "practically" sounded like a joke in her mouth, like she had no idea what it meant, just repeated it because she liked the sound of it, as Mitzi's vocabulary had not exceeded the elementary school grammar book. Until one day when they realized about the killings, and the arrests, and the disappearances. Florin laughed bitterly and said it took him half a minute to understand what took them years. He too was arrested, he had disappeared for a while too, he was taken to basements and beaten for information, friends of his had disappeared for good. His words had a metallic sonority that traveled around the table and woke everybody from their stupor, from the dazed state in which they listened to the story of a dead-not-dead, something else kind of person with yellow braids wrapped around her head.

Mitzi persisted in her story, it was a bombardment of stories, and the air had become intolerably hot, a thin lava flowing over them. "We tried to flee, we tried to turn around and escape," continued Mitzi stubbornly. "Kosmin knew a pilot from the war, they had flown German planes together, he too had joined the Party to make up for his German allegiance during the war, and because he was a pilot, they used him and didn't kill him, they used him for their jobs, their different jobs around the country. The man was given a mission in France, he had to go after someone, he wasn't told what and who, he was just given a mission to take a package to someone in France. He told Kosmin about it because he was planning to defect and not come back. Kosmin told you and tried to get you on the flight, because he owed your father his life, he owed it to his father, to your father, the same thing, he was your half-brother, if you remember. Kosmin was your father's son from a different marriage. From his marriage to Sofia. And Sofia was Frida's sister. Your father was first married to Frida's sister, Sofia. Now, do you understand? That's what we came to tell you. Farewell." Florin got up and the lava like air dissipated. A blinding clarity burst into the room. Mitzi and Kosmin had disappeared. Zoe got up from the table and looked out the window. Two shadows were crossing the street, one with braids, one with glasses, and she thought it funny that one of the shadows wore glasses, as if it mattered.

The Departure
Bucharest, Vienna, Roma, Paris, September 1985

My parents did not find out about what happened to Gabi and the truth about the pogroms until the night before our departure. By mistake. After the war, weakened by tuberculosis, chain smoking and the communist purges, Florin did his best to put his past to rest and focus only on the present, miserable as it might have been. And truly, as long as he was with Zoe, nothing was ever hopeless. If she was near him radiating her luminous absentmindedness, her otherworldly lightness, her irony and the light of her deep green eyes, nothing could ever be hopeless or utterly miserable. Even misery had a glow of beauty next to her.

We had packed everything for our big trip ahead and were tiptoeing and whispering around our apartment like thieves. Those were the last hours in the apartment where I had grown up, where I almost fell out the window once as I watched the secret police officer patrolling in front of our building waiting for my father, where I had had my miseries and joys, my dreams, boredom, scares, where my parents laughed, loved, fought, whispered hundreds of secrets, the apartment with the sofa box that contained a life's worth of secret mementos. The idea I would never return to that space gave me a sense of vertigo, so deep was the sorrow slashing my heart.

We were saying farewell to everything, and our whispers were heavy with tears and heartbreak. They were heavy rocks that fell between us with quiet thuds. "Did you remember to take the pictures?" "The money?" "How about the medicines?" "And the addresses?" All hidden in secret packets in our clothes or secret compartments of the big suitcase, inside the three-layered bottom prepared by my parents over months of meticulous cutting, sewing, gluing. Addresses we had to go to for help once in Rome and once in Paris. Medicines for my father's rheumatoid arthritis because where are we going to find doctors and money to pay for doctors if he is going to have one of his debilitating crises in foreign lands? Of course, foreign currency for basic survival, obtained in great secrecy from one of my father's foreign students. And black and white pictures of our lives. Only two or three in color. One of me on a park bench with my father on my first day of school, on a glowing September day. I am hugging my father and wearing a huge white bow on my head like a Christmas gift. He is laughing and has one hand around my shoulder lovingly. We both look happy.

The black and white pictures reveal all the periods of our lives, from all the way back to the house with the orchards, the sepia images before the war, the early communist images after the war, the late communist images after the occupation of Czechoslovakia all the way to the present. We don't care about the most recent photos; we leave most of them in a big box inside the sofa box. The famous sepia photograph of the four adults and four children against the background of a gazebo in the municipal park of my father's native town is at the very top of the package of pictures. The photograph of Grandmother Victoria wearing her Queen Marie hairdo of rolled braids and her delicate embroidered traditional blouse comes second. A picture of my parents in the winter in the big park with the Ferris wheel against a landscape of snow with me in the background building a snowman stands to this day on my dresser in my American bedroom as a constant reminder of my parents' faces, their love for each other and the landscape where I come from.

We all look happy in the pictures we are taking with us at great peril, if they are found by the customs police they will immediately know we had planned a permanent escape. Why are we even leaving then? I think during that last sleepless restless night. Because of everything in between. That's why! Because of everything in between the happy pictures, everything that is not happy and is filled with all the badness of our lives in this part of the world and all the unbearable secrets and sorrows we have gathered over the decades, I answer myself. I also pack one of the photographs of myself next to the man I once loved with a hopeless love. I pack the gauzy greenish summer dress sewn by my mother which I wore inappropriately on my first date which consisted of a hike in the Carpathian forests, and which still has small holes where it tore against tree branches and rocks. Scraps of life and memory tucked inside secret pockets and compartments, pockets which only leant us an illusion of safety against the customs police. They would slash any layered bottoms of any suitcase in a minute if they had any suspicions about us and our luggage.

Out of the blue my father starts crying and searching for something desperately. He is searching everywhere: behind chairs and books, sobbing in gulps like I hadn't heard him since I was a little girl one night and I woke to the sound of his sobs for the death of Grandmother Victoria. It's a clear night with stars shining fiercely over communist Bucharest, with all its wretched lives glowing in the nakedness of poverty, with the nightmares of another gray tomorrow under a demented dictatorship, with all the reckless people planning escapes like ours, dreaming of a better fate drowning their misery in sweaty embraces to forget the hunger and the fear. It smells of heated pavement and crushed mulberries on the sidewalks, a late summer Bucharest smell that has rubbed off on me and entered my skin forever. The neighborhood cats are meowing in heat as they used to during my childhood. My mother stands in the middle of our apartment detached as always, while my father gulps for air and turns everything over in a mad search. All our suitcases and bags with their secret compartments filled with delinquent cargo are waiting in a corner bunched up together like a sad group.

My father opens the sofa box and searches every dusty corner of it, doesn't find what he is looking for, slams it right back, pushes the sofa in the middle of the room and then he stops. Mitzi the doll is lying face up on the floor with her one lazy eye closed and stares out of her one round eye at the entire delirium of our pre-departure frenzy, with sinister fixity. My father picks her up and calms down, throws himself in a chair. "I had to find her, we couldn't leave Mitzi to the secret police," he says, and I almost hear the beginning of his merciless irony.

Indeed, little did he know the truth that his irony held that night. Or maybe he knew it all along and that was precisely why he went on a rampage to find her that night. He was preparing the doll for its long voyage by trying to wrap her in an old sweater when I saw him palpate the doll's belly as if for a checkup. I remembered him telling stories of Lila cutting up the doll's belly for surgeries or demonstrating what was going to happen to Mitzi the servant when she would have her baby Gino. I also wonder why Aunt Lila isn't keeping the doll herself. Maybe she doesn't want to be reminded of all the miseries and traumas of their past, the unbearable loss of the house with the orchard, and so many of the people who inhabited it.

Suddenly my father produces an explosive "aha" sound like he had found the secret to eternal happiness. He takes off Mitzi's dress, opens her belly and pulls out an endless roll of paper with tiny writing filling every square millimeter of it. It all looks freaky and obscene, like a sacrilege, but my father manifests what looks like deep satisfaction at the discovery. I am overcome by tiredness and start panicking that I only have six hours of sleep left before a long voyage where we will be on a train for 24 hours crossing the border into Hungary and then into the free world of Austria. It's more than regular tiredness from the days' events, and more like a desire for death and forgetfulness. Everything ahead of us seems too formidable and difficult to overcome, and I'm exhausted already. I want to sleep for a hundred years and wake up in San Michele looking out at a cobalt-colored sea and houses with red flowers hanging over their balconies. All the drab mess around me in the tiny apartment where I feel like I have wasted the entire existence of my youth waiting for miracles that never came and for a magic red balloon to take me away from it all, looks pathetic and suffocating.

My father starts reading something off the tape worm-like paper filled with minuscule writing in trembling whispers like a chant to the dead, a mourning chant to all the dead and the undead in our immediate and extended family. My mother sits next to him looking over his shoulder. The pink armchair we got from my grandmother Victoria's apartment after she died, which came from the house with the orchards, appears filled with a presence of ethereal consistency. Once at the seaside in the darkness of our rented room in a peasant's house, in the sound of my family's various forms of breathing, after Grandmother Frida displayed a most unusual theatrical performance in the salty air, under the full seaside moon, such a presence appeared to me sitting in a chair like it was the only place in the universe where that presence could rest its immaterial body. If it could be called a body. There was a lovely transparency to it, with delicate contours, a painting of filigreed silvery charcoal lines, filled in by a child's dexterous hand with colorless watercolor, the color of smoke and of the beginning of sunrise, of all the in between moments of day and of life. She now conversed with me in a language of silence, dripping thoughts and words inside my soul with an invisible dropper.

We were all going to leave at dawn as planned, we were going to succeed, it was all going to work according to plan. Leave it all, leave it all behind, you've had enough of it, you have no choice, I believe she said. I remember saying as I was falling asleep that night on the eve of our imminent and irreversible departure that you always have a choice. We always have a choice. Words, just words invented by living adults, the presence was saying, contradicting me with a soft firmness like that of a friend you've known your entire life, like a loving relative who has watched over you and dares to contradict you when you are wrong.

As I was falling asleep, I experienced a few moments of utter clarity of thought and understanding. I heard my father's chant reading the missive hidden in Mitzi's belly about the ominous day of June 22nd, 1941. The date was repeated, two girls were hidden in a secret compartment. Another ominous day came soon after on June 28th. A man called Gabi that I had never heard of before, was put on the trains of death and separated from Frida. I wasn't sure if the letter meant the same Frida that I knew for three years as my grandmother, though who else could it have been? How many Frida's were there in our family and circle of friends? None. There were purges in the streets of Iasi, one of Sofia's sons was killed in front of the millinery shop, she was brought over to the house with Gabi's help right before he disappeared. Tudor and Victoria hid and saved everybody in the house. If only Gabi and Frida had gotten on the train a minute faster, a minute earlier, they would have both been saved.

I had never heard of a woman called Sofia in our family, or of many other people who were shot and massacred and hanged on hooks in abattoirs. Then when I was just on the cusp of sleep, or maybe I was already sleeping, I thought I saw my mother take something that could have been a necklace off her neck and place it inside Mitzi's belly in the place of the crumpled paper. A memory of long ago lit up. I am sitting in a chair by Frida's bed as she is dying, and my mother is on the bed next to her. Frida takes off a necklace from underneath her nightgown. The necklace holds something that is not clear to me, it could be a key, a cross, a locket. A key most certainly, because among the whispers I hear words like "box" or "room" and I may never be sure which, or maybe a box inside a room. Frida is dead and my mother cries over her body until sundown when we leave to tell my father what just happened. My parents mentioned the importance of the necklace, but again I wasn't sure whether the word "key" was ever pronounced and if it was about opening something with crucial documents about events called pogroms. I wasn't sure whether the scene and the conversation took place in real time in the room during our last night in Bucharest or in my mind, my imagination, my memory.

A siren screeched in the Bucharest night. I had no idea what pogroms really meant, I was a university student studying literature, and I didn't know an important word in the vocabulary of my native language. I had no idea what all that whispering about a piece of paper hidden inside a doll's belly really meant either. It didn't matter to me. The presence in filigree contours and watercolors sitting quietly in our pink armchair, our only armchair, spoke her words of silence into my sleepy mind, how it doesn't really matter, it's all in the past, you will come back one day and solve it all, she said. My parents were like statues in the Bucharest night before our grand escape, my mind melting into merciful sleep.

When dawn came my mind was sharp and ready, filled with a painful yet delicious clarity of what I was about to do and why. A magenta-colored sunrise glowed over the houses and buildings on our street, the five-hundred-year-old church where I had been baptized, the hospital where I got stitched by a brutal doctor when I cracked my head open in the school yard, the building with the huge cracks from the '77 earthquake. I was never going to see any of that again. Under the magenta sunrise it all looked beautiful and utterly sad, even the earthquake cracks, like a merry cemetery with my childhood and youth all buried under the dusty pavement and potholes.

Our train to Vienna departed on time and we managed to put all our luggage with all its secret pockets on the racks in the compartment. Our lives were neatly packed and zipped up. As the train was leaving the station, I kept thinking of the word "pogroms" that had somehow gotten in my head the night before our departure. I would have to find out the true meaning of that word later. Once we settle in the free world, then I can expand my vocabulary. The crossing of the border from Romania to Hungary was easier than we had expected, with only one scare. The border police rummaged perfunctorily through our luggage all the way to the bottom of the big suitcase and never asked to look inside our smaller bags, one of which carried Mitzi with her sleepy eye, her belly all torn up from the previous night's intervention and possibly a precious key hanging on an old necklace. I had no idea what happened to the paper tape worm with the writing on it that my father read so fiercely while I had my hallucinatory experience with an otherworldly presence sitting in the armchair next to my bed.

The customs officer touched the bottom of the suitcase with its three layers hiding all sorts of illegal objects and materials, of which the foreign currency was the most dangerous. Visions of the three of us taken off the train in handcuffs and spending our lives in communist misery with no end in sight passed at a dizzying pace through my exhausted sleep deprived brain. My father lit a cigarette from his precious package of Kent cigarettes, which in themselves were something of a delinquency. Maybe he thought that was going to distract the customs man earnestly searching through our luggage. The famous story that circulated in our family about my father's friend who tried crossing the border with a suitcase packed with dollars, getting caught, and having a stroke on the spot which left him a paraplegic, crossed my brain like a tempest, and surely both my parents' minds. But the customs policeman was satisfied with the search, told my father we were in a non-smoking compartment, that he had to smoke in the corridor if he wanted to and opened the door to leave. My father handed him the pack of cigarettes which the officer took with no hesitation touching his cap as a thank you.

Our one-day passage through Vienna was a chaotic carousel through majestic parks with marble statues and voluptuous swans gliding on the mirror of lustrous ponds, busy boulevards with elegant baroque buildings and stylishly dressed men and women wearing clothes we had only dreamed of during our decades of communist deprivation. From that carousel ride, one landmark alone stands with some clarity above all others: the St. Stephen's Cathedral. Its Gothic lacy stone ornamentation looked to me like an oversized version of the sandcastles I used to make by the shores of the Black Sea with the special technique I acquired of squeezing wet, pasty sand through my fingers over the solid rounded walls made with my collection of sand pails, thus creating curly surfaces and towers that looked like cathedrals and castles I had seen in books of fairy tales. That was the only thing I could think of as we stood in front of the formidable work of Gothic architecture and place of Catholic worship.

We stood in Vienna for a while marveling at the cathedral with our collection of small and big bags and our one bulging suitcase that carried everything from sepia photographs of my great grandparents to rolls of dried salami stuffed between our clothes for all weather, and rolls of dollars, marks and liras hidden in the pockets made by my parents over months of meticulous preparations. Before I knew it, we were in another train compartment trying to fit all our luggage in the racks above our heads and hoping we would be the only passengers to travel all day and all night all the way to Rome. Once in Rome, a Romanian immigrant doctor was going to put us in touch with other Romanian immigrant former dissidents in

Paris where a Polish immigrant with some important connections would help us move on to our final settling place in the Western world.

It was not at all clear what our final destination would be, and I never asked. I was nineteen, I had torn myself from everything and everyone I knew, from a love I had thought would last my entire life and with whom I had dreamed to one day escape together to that sparkling Mecca of the Western world. Although I had dreamed of escape for almost as long as I could remember, it was happening in a way that entirely contradicted the ways I had imagined before, and my entire being felt bruised and numb. I had fallen from a height, from the window of our old apartment on the pavement, on a new and unrecognizable pavement and every part of me felt the shock without yet feeling the pain. I was alive and it was all that mattered.

Several times during our trip to Western paradise my father suffered attacks of asthma and emphysema, and his rheumatoid arthritis was starting to show its sharp claws. His face conveyed a particularly pained expression which I hadn't seen even during his most difficult secret police and communist ordeals, while my mother's face on the contrary expressed a calm and serenity that was also new to me. And the face I saw when I looked at myself in the foggy cracked second-class train mirrors of the smelly bathrooms looked like a stranger's, a frantic person on the run. My blonde reddish hair was sticking up in all directions, my eyes were blood shot from the nights spent on train seats and train station benches. A wild look of disorientation mixed with excitement appeared in my eyes. It was a face drugged by the anticipation of the encounter with the Western world mirage, also grimaced by the shock of brutal displacement from everything familiar. It was suddenly me and someone else that was never going to be me again.

In Rome we met with other Romanians who had fully settled lives among the dizzying carousels of mad traffic and luscious fountains spouting water from all orifices of majestic statues. An elegant older man who said he was a doctor and long-time friend of our family, though I had never seen him in my life, took us to fancy restaurants where he praised the pizzas and pastas with great effusion as if they were his own restaurants. He gave us precise information, names of people and places to go to, phone numbers to call. He seemed to have been prepared for our arrival as brand-new refugees floating in the thick blur of confusion and disorientation. He spoke to us like we were his children with short orders and ironic comments about our new life in the Western paradise in between delicious meals he offered us in restaurants with views of famous cathedrals, marble statues and elegant avenues swarming with Italians parading their Italian made fall clothes and shoes. My father's face was becoming grayer and sadder with each one of those curt and self-confident remarks from the doctor friend of the family, though he braved it with big fake laughs and pats on the doctor's back occasionally. His body was also giving in to the shock of the uprooting from the country he had loved so much despite the long line of catastrophic events and mistreatment he had suffered in it since his teenage years.

There were still shreds of brilliance and color my father grabbed onto for his own survival and sanity. The incomparable orchards of his youth illuminated in their halo of rosy blooms in spring, carrying heavy sugary fruit in the summer, were the most precious among such threads. His limbs were becoming more swollen by the hour from the outbreak of his rheumatoid arthritis, his eyes hollower and wilder from the painful void of the loss he had just suffered. My mother on the other hand listened carefully to all the instructions from the benevolent doctor who knew the entire Romanian diaspora of that part of Western Europe and took notes and telephone numbers in a small address book bound in red leather I had never seen before. While my mother was a bottomless box of surprises growing more down to earth and practical by the minute, my father was sinking into despondency and despair.

After we were put up a few days in the doctor's luxurious apartment in a suburb of Rome, we boarded another train in the direction of Paris. There, we were supposed to meet with other important exiles who in turn would help us move along in our newly started journey of exile. The most important was meant to be the meeting with a Polish lady who apparently held crucial information for our future. It all sounded vague and tricky to me, exhausting and hard to achieve, spoken in an alien language of Western bureaucracies. The words of political asylum, immigration, sponsors, returned often over pasta dishes with mussels and steaks the size of which I had never seen in my Romanian years. I ate with a voracious appetite everything that was offered to me and shamelessly asked for more, large deserts of Italian tiramisu and multicolored ice creams, to the great delight of the doctor who winked at me occasionally and complemented my eyes and my hair, saying I could be a model every time I said I wanted to be an academic. You can be anything you want in the West my dear, he said and winked lasciviously over the pasta con vongole.

I stayed awake throughout the entire day and a half train ride through the Alps going into France. The full moon sprinkled its rays over the train windows and cast a silvery gauze of light over snow covered mountain chains in the Western night, opening inside me all the closed-up spaces and scars of lost love and lost country. It was merciless and irrevocable. An acute pain was splitting me into two distinctive halves that were never going to be made whole again. The alpine chains were beautiful but foreign, the moon was the same moon but shone with an alien glow over the thick pine forests and jagged crests.

I saw myself, the young woman I had been up to that point in my life, running into the arms of my lover on a late summer night under a shamelessly red moon in the fragrance of pine trees and marigolds. Corina, the girl with the name of a Roman courtesan and blondish red hair, was running across sleepy courtyards and deserted streets into the arms of a brooding dark haired Romanian man for the last time, under a red moon, amid the equally brooding Carpathian chains. The man and the mountains were made of the same substance, bitter-sweet, tasting of tree resin and forest berries, smelling of pine needles and humid earth. The arms of the man circled around her, and she melted inside their warm nest. The moon was wicked and raw, she felt his warm hands glide over her arms, her thighs, over every inch of her body in the Romanian night in the Carpathians where he laid her on a bed of leaves and pine needles and loved her with the sweetest caresses she would ever receive from any other man. The white crests of the Alps glowed with a matte light and swished by the train windows in quick sequences like a fast-forwarded movie.

My parents and I arrived in the Paris train station Saint Lazarre on a gray morning and descended with our clunky luggage in a daze of exhaustion and a blur of foreignness. Rome had been the candy at the beginning of our journey, the vacation part filled with fancy pizzas and afternoon strolls on its monument filled avenues under the guidance of our mysterious doctor "old friend of the family." Paris was the awakening to what was in store for us, to the hollowness that would fill our hearts for a while, to the disconnected sets of moves, actions, choices that seemed to be taken by someone else in our stead and that often left us befuddled in the middle of a crowded French street. My father's illness worsened by the hour as he walked under the gray Parisian drizzle, his limbs more swollen and his gait heavier. My mother wore an awkward new smile like she knew it all and she was slowly becoming someone else: a French woman with a sure gait who instead of surprise at her new surroundings experienced a sense of recognition like she had seen it all before.

We were met at the station by the Polish woman who was our main contact established by the Romanian doctor in Rome. She was a kind and solicitous person who spoke softly and slowly as if worried she might scare or upset us. Her French sounded like a brand of elegant Russian. She explained to us we were going to stay in her apartment for a few days and start our formalities for political asylum. Once that was set in motion, there was nothing else to do but wait for the immigration visas to come through. Then the refugee organization might find us lodging in some refugee quarters, if not, we could stay with friends of hers, Polish immigrants. She was walking ahead and looking backwards to talk to us as we trudged our luggage over the Parisian sidewalks with no idea where we were going. Iconic Parisian sites I had learned about and seen in my French language textbooks or in French films that were broadcast in our television programming, passed by us as we rode the bus through the center of the city. Then the bus went through poorer looking neighborhoods.

A few fleeting images in fast moving sequences like a kaleidoscope remain from our first weeks in Paris under the guidance of the Polish woman by the name of Paulina Kalinovska, visible through a veil of drizzle and whipping gusts of wind that pierced through our thin clothing with no mercy. We stayed in her tiny apartment in a massive tenement building at the edges of the city, which seemed to be an area mostly of foreigners from Eastern European and North African countries. Pungent smells of different types of stews reached us in the damp apartment together with lively cacophonies of Slavic languages, Arabic, and heavily pronounced French from balconies with vividly colored clothes hanging on lines across the inner courtyards. Foreigners and refugees from around the world merged and cohabited in crowded apartments in what seemed like a transitional condition of fidgety waiting for something better, a larger lodging, a visa, a permit of some kind, a job, or the arrival of a relative from another country. Children ran around unattended, earnest in their intense playing and shouting until a heavy silvery dusk fell over the area.

It all seemed familiar yet distant like echoes from a former life or from someone else's life. It was the chaos and poverty that made it familiar, while the relentless and noisy flow of life and languages spoke of something new, a different kind of life, one of possibilities in the absence of surveillance and fear. It must have been freedom, I thought. It was indescribable and felt both exhilarating and terrifying, as if looking down into a multicolored abyss. Poverty had many colors in the western world, and it was also part of that coveted freedom. Our Polish host came and went at odd hours and sometimes didn't come home for the night. When that happened, a new refugee from Russia, Poland or Czechoslovakia would occupy her room, come, and go, have a loud phone conversation, prepare a strong smelling dish with cabbage and fatty meats and be gone the next day. It wasn't clear what we were waiting for and for how long we had to stay with Paulina Kalinowska in that tenement building. My mother sometimes had whispered conversations in French with her in the kitchen late in the night, while my father wrote in a small notebook, smoked incessantly, or attempted to relieve the stiffness and swelling in his limbs with tepid baths, walking around the apartment or standing on the balcony and watching the flow of the multicolored humanity.

A dinner in a tiny French restaurant in one of the old Parisian neighborhoods, with Paulina and a Romanian couple, a scrawny chain-smoking woman and her white-haired husband in a tweed coat seemed important and directly related to our future as well as to my parents' past, in particular my mother's past in a different world. There was talk of manuscripts, escapes, defections, a journey to the south of France, and a small Spanish town by the Mediterranean where a man called Gabi had arrived during the war, committed suicide, and left important documents and a manuscript. It must have been the same Gabi I heard mentioned during our last night in Bucharest, the psychedelic night of overlapping realities with an otherworldly presence staring at me from our pink armchair. Not everything was about communist history but about another history, one that seemed at least as bad. There was talk of members of a group called the Iron Guard and events from that part of history that seemed to have had a direct impact on my mother's previous life, from when she was a child and a teenager.

Other than the organization that helped refugees from Eastern Europe, Paulina Kalinovska ran yet another organization that gathered documentation, testimonials, letters, pictures from those times and the massacres that took place in my blessed native country at the hands of Romanian fascists. It came back to the unrecognizable word of pogroms which I had not yet a chance to look up in any dictionary though the more I heard it the more I understood it had to do with sinister realities. More sinister than anything I had yet heard of, witnessed, or experienced. That much I understood though I still had no idea how much that history involved my own mother and how it had changed the entire course of her life. It would be another three decades before I delved into that part of my parents' history. Now, in the French restaurant with the Romanian dissident couple and our unrelenting host Paulina Kalinovska, I only caught snippets of conversations and disjointed meanings mostly because of my state of disconnection from everything and everybody else around me including myself.

I wanted to get somewhere final where I could start my own life, whatever that was going to be. Despite the material abundance of everything around me, and the lightness of what must have been the freedom of the free world, it all felt like I was trapped inside my parents' story and their labyrinthine past. I felt no connection to that past and no real empathy, for it was all wrapped in indecipherable mysteries, traces of lost documents and stories of unknown people who were long dead. Only a brief mention of my grandmother Frida and a terrible train ride during the war, as I was chewing on the elastic texture of some much-praised French snails, drew my attention once but the conversation swiftly changed to the topic of Romanian dissidents abroad before I could gather any more meaning.

One image towers above all others from our disoriented but eager Parisian days. It was a dinner at sunset in the famous restaurant at the top of the Eiffel Tower where Paulina Kalinowska invited us one evening. It was at the end of a long day of meetings with unknown Romanian former dissidents and émigrés. The conversations about possible government collapse in Romania, a former famous head of the Secret Police and Ceausescu's right-hand man's defection to France, more manuscripts, radio programs at the Free Europe station denouncing human rights abuses in Romania, all bored me to tears and made me feel superfluous. Nothing concerned me and my future and neither did it seem to really concern my parents' future except in an indirect way.

It was the first day the sun shone since we had arrived in that much talked about city of Paris and it felt like something in our trajectory was going to change, and an important decision was going to be made. For the first time my view of

Paris, after many days of relentless rain, exploded in magenta and scarlet colors of a sunset that took my breath away and made me feel that it had all been worth it. The endless rides and sleepless nights on clammy train benches, the fumbling through Parisian neighborhoods always getting lost and feeling we didn't belong, the days and nights in the humid and smoke-filled apartment of Paulina Kalinowska with the comings and goings of transient refugees. It had all been a preparation for the dinner at the top of the Eiffel Tower bathed in the scintillation of a fuchsia sunset.

For the first time during that evening, over a dinner of steak frites, buttery lettuce and a peach desert in a crystal cup, I heard my parents mention something from the tape worm paper that came out of Mitzi's belly filled with scribbles of great importance for our family history and discuss at length with Paulina the fate of the man named Gabi. To my great shock, this man turned out to be my maternal grandfather. I had never heard my mother speak at any length of her father, except for a few furtive mentions of a different life, from a childhood that didn't seem to belong to her, and in which her mother Frida and her father whose name I had never heard before, lived for a period of time in the same town as my own father and his family with their mythic orchards forever blooming in candy pastels and producing unparalleled fruit like a lost Eden.

As twilight melted into night and the city burst into a myriad of lights like overcrowded stars, stretching around us in our suspended restaurant, Paulina Kalinowska produced a large envelope that contained an abundance of documents and papers of great importance and related to the information found in Mitzi's belly. It also contained three passports to America with our names and pictures on them. The several unpleasant interviews we had endured in drab offices with irritated clerks and police earlier during our Parisian stay, now made sense. It all led up to this, and we were not going to settle in France. When I had finally caught a glimpse of the epic and iconic beauty of Paris and was ready to drop my entire Romanian self from the top of the Eiffel Tower into the sea of lights at my feet in order to start a French life, we were yanked into the unknown by a mysterious Polish emigre who seemed to have great interest in our departure and in us settling at the other end of the world.

By the looks of my father, it seemed he was as surprised as I was by the news of our impending departure, new passports, the huge leap into a world he had no desire to experience, as he dragged his swollen limbs and shattered soul from one Parisian sidewalk to another. There are important things you must do over there, Paulina said at some point as we sipped the last of our coffee at the end of the dinner, and it's better for you, there is no more room for refugees here, there is nothing for you here, she added. That last part hit me like a merciless hammer. For the first time I heard her speak in full sentences about our situation and not in halted half phrases and what seemed like a code language. For the first time I had a sense that her relation to my parents was deeper than just that of an acquaintance in whose arms we were sent by the benevolent mysterious doctor in Rome who seemingly mapped out our future for us, except for the small detail of our moving to a different continent.

We were puppets in the hands of inscrutable émigrés with secret identities and they all had some investment in the future they set for us in a concerted transnational effort. Of the three of us, my mother seemed the most alert and in tune with everything that went on and entirely ready for the dizzying journey ahead of us. As for me, I suddenly didn't want to immigrate anywhere. I regretted my decision to follow my parents instead of finishing my university studies and started missing our overcrowded tiny apartment with its sofa box hiding half a century of family history and bizarre objects, with its walls of books, stretching across centuries of world literature, art, and philosophy, its small but precious collection of prewar furniture from the house with the orchards. As we left the restaurant and the elegant waiters that looked like concert pianists bowed with overly polite bonsoir messieurs dames, I was determined to find out what was in the precious envelope and decipher its formidable secrets as soon as we arrived at Paulina's musty apartment.

Once in the apartment, I sat down on the ratty sofa in what could have been called a living room and stared at the vaguely shaped Parisian roofs outside the tiny window. I was in a state of utter confusion and indecision and wondered what the rest of the evening was going to bring, not to mention the rest of my life. I waited for my parents to fall asleep so I could search for the mysterious manuscript or documents and understand why suddenly we were being catapulted across the ocean into that big America that seemed as alien and foreign to me as the moon on which heroic cosmonauts landed in my very lifetime, less than two decades ago. My parents seemed to have the same idea as I did and sat down on the other drab sofa in the room staring into nothingness until Paulina asked us all whether we wanted tea. I had no desire for tea or anything except for some clarity about my future.

I heard myself say why are we going to America now, what is there for us, I thought we were staying here in France? Then I believe I also said I am not going to America; I am staying here. I noticed it had started to rain again, and the Parisian roofs glistened in the night. I realized I had become accustomed to those roofs and to the feeling of being in Paris, in the small amount of time I spent here. To my great surprise, Paulina, who just then entered the room said very well then, stay with me for a while longer, you can go later. My parents did not object, which seemed the strangest of all. I didn't understand whether later meant in a month or in a year or five years. I had had it with my parents' secrets and their incomprehensible past filled with horrors of all sorts, ghosts and documents hidden in a doll's belly or in the apartment of a secretive Polish émigré living at the drab margins of Paris.

That night, none of us slept. We didn't even try. We sat on the sofas in Paulina's living room and talked about the future, a total anomaly in my family whose only obsession seemed to be with the past. Bits of the truth came out and I learned in the humid Parisian night that my father was part of an underground movement of dissidence against the Romanian government that stretched from my native and now forever lost city of Bucharest all the way to Miami, Florida where we were all meant to go and connect with an important contact. The contact was a former highly ranked Securitate man, turned émigré in France turned anarchist in America. My mother on the other hand, was on a parallel mission to find out the truth about her father's escape from a pogrom and his last months or year in the south of France or Spain or both. He had left bits and pieces of journal pages and notes taken during his last months of life with various resistance members during the war. One of those people defected to America after the war and was now part of the anti-communist transatlantic group.

However, the most important journal that Gabi had written during his exile in the Spanish border town was still to be found. It could have been that this mystery man in Florida had left it at some point with Frida soon before she died but now it was nowhere to be found. This important individual now living on the Atlantic bathed shores of the United States of America, had been part of both the slim anti-fascist resistance during the war, and, after the terrible fifties, of the anti-communist one, if it could be called resistance. So much formidable and unexpected information poured in from my parents who suddenly decided to share their mind-boggling secrets in chaotic and overlapping strings of sentences that my head turned and felt slashed by painful throbs.

I had no idea who the people who had conceived and raised me really were. They seemed like strangers with incomprehensible pasts involving atrocities and underground movements of different sides. Only a few things were clear in that heavy smoked filled air and damp Parisian night in Paulina Kalinowska's apartment — that it was a true miracle we had all crossed the border untouched; that my parents' lives were in danger; that my maternal grandfather whom I had never met had spent the last months of his life in a Southern French town and after crossed into Spain and died there all alone by his own hand. I said I wanted to see those famous manuscripts and notes too that night. I wanted to hear all those stories, since they involved people I was also related to, like my own grandfather. But my parents said absolutely not, we don't want you holding any dangerous information period, it would put you in danger too. Then I said I am not coming with you to Florida in America, period. When my parents tried to protest, Paulina came in through the glass door out of her bedroom as if she had been listening all along, and said ça va, ça va, ne vous en faites pas, elle peut rester ici avec moi un temps, elle peut nous être utile ici, it's all right don't worry, she can stay here with me, she can be of use to us here.

I had no idea at that moment in Paris, in the apartment of an unknown Polish émigré revolutionary of sorts, what and who dictated our destiny, where our own choices started and where the pressures and choices that were made for us by history and by those who wanted to change history, ended. But it suddenly seemed adventurous and exciting, and I wanted to be part of it, whatever it was, whether government coups or searching for important manuscripts that dated back to the beginning of World War II. Eventually, I fell asleep on the sofa in Paulina's living room utterly confused, and terribly excited all at the same time.

When I woke up the next morning to another gray Parisian day choking from the cigarette smoke and wondering where I was, my parents had already left to catch their plane to Florida in America. I burst into copious tears for the first time since our departure on the train to Vienna carrying our pathetic collection of bags and one big suitcase with secret compartments. The feeling of irremediable loss, the regret of the unsaid goodbyes choked me. Paulina brought me a large cup of café au lait and said here drink this, you'll feel better, get dressed, we have places to go and work to do. I listened to her. Through sobs and gulps of café au lait I started my new life in Paris.

Atrocious June Nights
1941, Northern Moldavia

The three men who leave the house in the small Moldavian town on the night of June 22nd soon after the Russian bombardments started, arrive in the city of Iasi before dawn on the night train. The town is quiet in a sinister way. On their walk from the train station to their destination, they understand why. Corpses lie everywhere in the middle of the streets, on the sidewalks, some dead from gunshots, some unrecognizable from burns and mutilations. Blood and raw flesh are strewn along the road in repugnant patches and puddles. Mounds of indiscriminate objects spread along the sidewalks displaying a barbaric ravage through houses and lives: torn pieces of furniture mixed with bloody clothes mixed with torn sacks of foods, flour, or cooking oils. Every once in a while, one notices an object left intact in the pillage on top of the mounds: a child's doll with its full dress, hat and ruffles, a crib with the baby covers and tiny toys inside it and the glaring absence of any baby.

The sight of children's objects and furniture is most unbearable. The intact objects which must not have been of much value to the savages who authored the pillage and massacre render the spectacle more sinister by contrast. The heat enhances the stench rising from the cadavers and makes the air unbreathable. The three men walk in heavy silence, with handkerchiefs covering their mouths, doing their best to keep walking without stumbling or fainting, at times having to step in between or over the corpses, over entire families bunched up together in the throes of their last agonizing breaths. Parents with a small child curled up between them sucking his thumb, a girl holding a doll to her chest, the parents stretching an arm over the girl's body in a last gesture of desperate protection.

The men keep walking until they reach the desired address. It's a millinery shop that like all the other shops has been ravaged with savagery. Women's hats lie in a pile in front of the store, some of them bloody and squished under brutal steps. Amid the hats are two corpses, one of a man the other of a young boy, maybe ten or eleven. The father is lying with half his body over the boy's body protectively.

A rooster calls from one of the neighboring houses in the early hours of the new day like a huge blunder of nature, if anything can be called a day anymore instead of an eternal night. It's a miracle there is any life left, be it even that of a rooster. Two of the men take off their summer blazers and place them over the two bodies covering the gaping wounds and their faces.

Flesh and bodies melt in the evil night, illuminating the night, begging for daylight to never arrive. All three men rush inside the store, step over hats and two more bodies of young women exposed obscenely, most likely store employees. They rush through a back door, down a flight of wobbly stairs, call for Sofia, many times in semi whispers, Sofia, Sofia, are you here, are you alive, where are you? In a corner of the basement, they find a woman crouching, trembling, with her arms around a young boy and producing a wailing sound song of sorts, a lullaby that seems to be singing itself. More hats, women's fancy hats with colored feathers and bows stare blindly on the hat stands, the plaster heads appear with a creepy aliveness in the semidarkness of the basement, a tiny lamp is still flickering over one of the sewing machines.

One of the men goes over to the corner and holds the woman calling her "sister." He then calls the boy Sebastian as if telling them their own names because they are both speechless. Maybe they have even forgotten their own names or how to utter anything altogether. All three men are helping the mother and son to get up and move toward the back exit with soundless motions, slow and far away, in a different world, in a different life. The woman says we must get them, they are in the front, they were working late yesterday, we must get them. The three men are avoiding giving any answers and information or mentioning the fact that the people she is talking about, her husband and other son, are dead in front of the store. They don't want to deter the woman and child from their escape. They say no, no, Sofia, they'll come later, let's go now, the train will leave soon.

There are not many cars yet, it's only 1941, people travel more by train and horse drawn carriage still. Only the rich Romanians and the Nazis have cars in this area. Sofia says let me put my hat on, as if that was of great importance and she puts on one of the elegant pink hats with feathers off one of the plaster heads. Otherwise, she wears black as if prepared in advance for the mourning to follow. The group of three men, a woman and a teen boy walk against the walls of buildings, sometimes stepping on more bodies. As they walk in the direction of the train station she says, what happened here, did the war start, have there been bombardments in the area? One of the men, the one who called her sister earlier notices that one of her cheeks is slashed by a deep wound like that of a blade or a knife, he takes out his kerchief and hands it to her to place it on her cheek, she says don't worry, I'll be fine, the bleeding has stopped. She asks again about her husband and her other child. They are coming later, the men say. She wants to return at some point during the walk and says we should have buried them, we shouldn't have left them unburied in the street, because really, she knows everything that happened only her mind is racing between different flights of reality, memory, broken images of yesterday's events, a stubborn refusal to believe the truth and the equally stubborn flood of images drowning her.

The streets are tunnels of darkness reeking of death. They reach the train station just at the point of dawn when a blade of crimson sunrise slices the horizon and sirens, raids, gunshots are heard in the distance in the city they leave. The five of them occupy a compartment in the train that goes back to the town with the house belonging to a family called Angelescu, a family with a son Florin and a daughter Lila. The house and its orchards are something of an oasis in the darkness, a lit tunnel for escapees. The woman asks the man called Gabi: she says Gabi how is Frida holding up? And he says Frida is waiting, we'll leave soon too, she misses the girls, but Tudor has hidden them, and they will cross to the other side soon. Possibly Bulgaria and from there to the West. Very soon, it will be alright, he says without fully believing himself that all will be alright. During these days that are like nights anything can happen from one second to the next, most of it rather atrocious. They whisper heavy words that fall like bullets in between the clicking of the train wheels. Everything reeks of blood, the words, and the clothes and even the pink hat the woman Sofia is wearing reeks of fresh gore. They will clean up once they get to the house one of the men says. It's not important says Sofia, cleaning up is not important, saving the boy, that's all that matters, she says and falls asleep with her head against the windowpane. Her beautiful face with the bloody slash shines in the reckless crimson of another dawn in the new apocalypse.

After the expedition to save his sister-in-law, Gabi returns to Frida who waits in the attic room where they have been hiding in expectation of a sign for their escape. They knew of what had happened in Bucharest, the forests, and the abattoirs where many had been butchered, their bodies hung from trees or hooks meant for the slaughtered cattle. The wait becomes more intolerable by the day, in the gooey heat of their attic room, in the sounds of air raids, bombs and sirens. They feel the presence of the hounds in green shirts like the hunted animal feels the approach of their predator. The evening of June 23rd, a man in an elegant white suit and fedora hat takes them to the train station in his car, one of the few in the region other than the Nazi ones. Frida and Gabi are restless as they cuddle in the back seat of the car.

Something in their flesh and hearts is telling them the escape plan might be derailed and that these might just be their last minutes together. The man drops them off with specific instructions, how to move confidently arm in arm through the throngs of people who are trying to get on the trains. He gives them their tickets and all necessary documentation for the rest of their journey all the way to their final destination, which is supposed to be abroad, in a town by the sea south of Romanian Black Sea beaches, in Bulgaria. For a few seconds they have flashes of fantasy of the two of them finally away from the purges on a deserted beach looking at the sea. The girls are running to the water. Both, in their white cotton dresses — a vision of peace and happiness in the mellow reds and yellows of a sunset by the sea.

Frida and Gabi follow the instructions obediently once they get out of the elegant car, each carrying a train ticket and false papers as Irina and Vasile Angelescu. They are strong Romanian names, Christian names with their own saint days. The train station is a blustery nightmare of sweaty, demented crowds carrying all their belongings in large sacks and suitcases. Who needs belongings when one is on the run from a national massacre? They both think that as they try to make their way through the ruthless throngs without getting separated from each other. The man had warned them, he said don't let go of one another no matter what, he also advised they each carry a small piece of luggage to not draw suspicions. There are also groups separate from the refugee crowds who are supervised by SS soldiers and men in green shirts waiting to place them on the train farther on a different track. Frida and Gabi notice those groups are kept together with ropes around them just like the cattle and goats that are transported on yet another train. They keep moving through the crowds and make good progress getting closer to the desired track.

Frida notices the real Angelescu family with their belongings, carrying fewer than most. The boy sees them as he gets on the train steps and makes a gesture of recognition. The father pulls him back onto the train, but the boy is stubborn and sticks his head back out and his eyes search for them, watches them as they move closer to their train headed to the south, to the sea where they hope to arrive. The train whistle announces its impending departure. Frida and Gabi are a few steps away from the train. A man from the crowd calls Gabi, and he makes the mistake of responding to the call and turns around in the direction of it, though the man who brought them there told them to be careful and not respond to anybody. He said move through the crowds as if you were deaf and blind, and the only thing you see is the train you have to get on. It's one of the people inside the roped-up group, maybe a friend, maybe a distant relative. A man in an Iron Guard green shirt followed by an SS soldier runs after Gabi. Frida and Gabi are almost at the train steps, the man in the green shirt catches up to them. Gabi pushes Frida on the steps, she doesn't want to go, she clings to him. Her elegant hat falls off and he places it back on her reddish curls like it was the most important thing in the world. He pushes her again and whispers something in her ear. They kiss on the steps of the train; he holds her body in a rushed embrace.

The man in the green shirt tears him away from Frida's embrace under the attentive gaze of the SS soldier who seems to be coordinating the entire operation. Frida remains on the train steps. Her face is soaked in unstoppable tears. Somebody pulls her back from the inside of the train and closes the door. The train departs and disappears under its own whitish clouds of smoke like under a magician's trick. Its merciless whistle sounds like a trumpet of doomsday.

Gabi is led to the group behind the rope by the man in the green shirt and another SS soldier. He hates the man who signaled to him with the entirety of his being like he has never hated anyone in his life. If it hadn't been for his call, he would be next to Frida on the train right now. He hates himself too, for not following Tudor's instructions to the last detail and for his millisecond of inattention. For having allowed himself to be tricked. There are traitors everywhere, he thinks, among all people, and his people are no exception. Like an insult to all the injured humanity on that train platform, an orange moon bursts through the clouds and casts a shameless light over the crowds with sacks and animals and crying children, over the crowds that are herded by SS soldiers onto their death trains, over the soldiers themselves, over the men in green shirts. The moon does not discriminate or choose favorites. The air smells of linden flowers, of blood and sweat and derailed destinies.

Northern Moldavia, June 2015

I extend my stay in the town of my father's childhood indefinitely because I am determined to enter the entrails of our family history and put the last pieces of the puzzle together. "And then what?" Manole asks occasionally, hearing my thoughts, always. After the sanziene days with all their whimsical fantastical events and creatures, there is a quickening of time and of the movement of the light, the days are getting visibly shorter as if somebody is cutting them bit by bit with a pair of cosmic scissors. "I don't know what Manole, I'm not thinking that far ahead, I just need to settle this whole history and then I can go back to my children and my mother," I say breathlessly trying to entice Manole to open up the story again and allow it to spill itself out until my heart settles in a comfortable place and I can return. "But what if you have returned already? What if this is your real return?" Asks Manole.

The weather has spoiled, and the days have lost some of their dazzling light since I fell into the arms of the local police and since I fell into a hole in time inside a mysterious sepia picture within a dark tunnel in my family history and my country's history. See, this is your country here, that's what you are thinking, do you call it your country over there? Manole only refers to my life in America as "over there" and my conversations with him are mostly half monologue, half a strange combination of spoken and unspoken lines, as he sometimes answers my thoughts before I articulate them out loud. It's a cloudy evening with purple clouds hovering over the town in the east like the menace of a storm and the air is stuffy as it waits to burst open into wind and rain. "You ain't seen any of them storms over here yet, there is nothing like it." Manole laughs like it's the biggest joke in the universe and he calls out for Lulu, whom I haven't seen in a couple of days. I have been wondering where he has disappeared or whether he even exists, and he might not have been a creation of my imagination.

But Lulu comes out wearing a pair of Nike tennis shoes and a T-shirt with "I 💚 New York" on it. I almost gasp at the wildly anachronistic sight. "Where did you get that T-shirt, Lulu?" I ask as soon as I see him. "My mama and papa done sent it to me," Lulu says like it's the most natural thing in the world that he gets an I 🩶 New York shirt in the middle of the Romanian boonies from his parents. "Where are your mama and papa Lulu?" I ask in utter puzzlement and feel tiny drops of cool rain on my arms and head, unusually cold for the still warm day. There is a separation between the elements themselves, water, earth, sky, trees. They each seem to be on their own, splitting nature into its different parts. And me who had always thought out here in the deepest of Romanian countryside all is one harmonious whole, nature, and humans with one another, and all the elements of the universe unified in a perfect totality.

American strategies of idealizing or stereotyping faraway places must have seeped into my blood as well, although now that I think of it, I don't remember our lives in communism containing much of this perfect totality and harmony between humans and the surrounding elements. Much of nature, trees, forests, much of the land had been ruthlessly destroyed by all the forced nationalization of everybody's properties, demented and rapid industrialization. And for all the disharmony in the lives of the population, we might as well have had the elements themselves at war with one another. "From the place on the shirt, that's where!" says Lulu and I have already forgotten what we were talking about because my thoughts are disjointed from one another and from my own self. It's a piecemeal world.

Since I stare at him like I have no idea what he's talking about, Lulu goes on to clarify: "My mama and papa, they sent me the shirt from this place written on the shirt, that's where they live, and they are going to get me to live with them over there pretty soon. They say this city where they live is as big as our entire country and one building holds more people than our whole town. I don't know how they don't crumble to the ground, holding so many people in one single building." I have to pinch myself truly to make sure I actually exist in this stormy moment in the little town in northern Moldavia.

"Your parents live in New York?" I ask and look back at Manole who at this moment seems entirely removed from the scene and is staring somewhere in the direction of the orchard where a female presence with an old-time parasol in a long peach colored dress and a blue hat is walking between the trees. I stand up wanting to go in the direction of the strange, out of time and out of place looking woman, but Manole violently pulls me down on the bench and says: "Sshhh, don't bother

her, she'll leave soon, she always comes at stormy times, let her be." I wanted to know my family history and now I'm learning it but am no longer sure whether I want to delve much deeper into this search. I am being sucked into realms I don't even believe in, but they must believe in me. The woman turns slowly towards me, and the air becomes a vortex that absorbs me. She has a blurry face, almost with no features, a face made of fog, but the rest of her body is clearly defined like a perfect drawing or photograph. An overpowering wind like the eye of a tornado catches me and from there on it's all a fantastical story.

On this side of the so called orchard, closer to Manole's house, a ferocious storm is blasting into us, a tornado of some kind, pushes us and throws us on the ground, then lifts us off the ground as if to throw us to high heaven and Manole mouths something to me as he is flown around by the overpowering wind, hurricane, tornado, who cares what you call it. It's black and yellow like no other storm I've seen or heard of in human history. He is mouthing to me to stay calm and not fight the storm. Don't fight it, and strangely enough his words reach me and disclose their meaning like a magic fruit cracking open inside my brain, in the entire madness of this Romanian weather. Manole's silent words are the only stable comprehensible things. I listen to him and don't fight the storm, it would be pointless anyway, it's getting harder to breathe and whether I fight the storm or not, it feels like I will suffocate from the strength of the wind blasting in my face and choke on the barrels of water flowing from the sky.

In the meantime, the farther portion of the orchard looks quiet as ever: a picture floating impassibly in a zone of complete calm, dislocated from the rest of the landscape where I am being devoured by a vicious storm of apocalyptic proportions. I don't fight it. I am pushed around, lifted off the ground as are Manole and Lulu who seem to almost enjoy themselves like they are riding a wild roller coaster and in the quiet picture at the other end of the orchard, the same woman in the peach-colored dress, blue hat, and parasol walks calmly in a protective haze that hides her face. The storm stops just as abruptly as it started and in that second the face of the woman becomes clear, and she looks uncannily like my grandmother Frida whom I only knew for a short period in Bucharest. She had appeared and disappeared in our lives like a meteor, between the time I was seven and ten years old.

In another flash I see an image of myself and my mother in a tiny room by the bed of a dying person. My mother is crying profusely next to her body. She is stretched out on the length of the bed next to the dying or dead person, because really, she looks more dead than alive. A second before she dies, my grandmother Frida, because she is the one dying in this picture, takes a necklace from around her neck with slow movements and puts it around my mother's neck, making her swear she'll keep it with her life. Now in this colored vision of the woman dressed in peach and blue that I see from a distance as I lie on the ground in the eye of the storm, I see clearly my grandmother Frida. She is younger, more beautiful than the way I knew her, moving slowly as if nothing else existed in the world but this moment in the universe where she walks among plum and cherry trees with a blue parasol and a blue sash. There is always a blue sash in her story, it must have a symbolic value, but I have no idea what. She wears the blue sash like a turban now, as if she had time to rearrange it on her head.

In another liquid second, a woman in a long black dress appears softly in the very back of the orchard, more like a dark gray, the color and consistency of a shadow but in very precise contours. She looks like a widow character. The two women hold each other for a second, embracing as if they had found each other after a long separation. There is a resemblance between them, and I have a distinct feeling they are sisters. The storm is softer now, the winds have calmed down, but a thick curtain of rain still falls irrepressibly. It is truly a curtain, it's not even falling but just standing: a curtain of water that separates us from the scene of the two women, one in rosy peach and blue and the other in black. When I look at Manole through the sheath of rain I see he is crying, which on his toothless face looks like laughing. There seems to be no difference between the two. That's the last I see of Manole because I lose consciousness.

I wake up on the ground in the middle of the night under a brilliantly starry sky and have no idea where I find myself. It's déjà vu, I seem to have woken up on the same ground not long ago. I feel the earth around me, and I instantly remember a brutish storm and Manole's face crying or laughing hanging in the eye of the storm like a Cheshire Cat. I have come to expect anything and everything from this place and I pinch myself, run my hand over the length of my body and on my face to assure myself that I am me, and whole, and still made of the same recognizable flesh. While still lying on the ground and staring at the brilliantly lit night sky I try to remember my life and my reason for being here in this moment, to make sure I have not entirely slipped outside of myself and become someone new. I know I was born a few hundred kilometers from this spooked place here, in the capital of this country and that I don't live in any longer. I've been gone for a long time, and I have children and a living mother far away on another continent.

I know that I have come here to find the truth about my father's story and the story of his house with the orchards, it's all about my father, but also about my mother. It's an entangled story that involves the living, the dead and the in between. The people I have met here, namely the old Manole, and the young boy Lulu are inextricably bound to this story of my family in unfathomable ways that I haven't quite figured out yet. I have not entirely lost touch with myself though I feel as if I have slipped into a parallel tunnel of time and history, and I am not going to recover my full grasp of reality and life until I get to the bottom of things. Literally to the bottom of the tunnel and find out what happened with Frida during the war. Who is the widow woman in a grayish dress? Who are Manole and Lulu and who are the people making a film with a story that resembles too eerily what I know so far of my own family story?

More characters seem to emerge and bloom from this zone of my father's past every day and every night. An entire convoy of sad and whimsical people who refuse to melt and disappear into a definitive darkness and silence. They are waiting for something very particular to happen and roam restlessly in an uncharted space that is neither fully life nor fully death. A dog is barking somewhere distantly, and a rooster is crowing nearby. The stars are pale. I feel a panic about the coming of daylight, as if I only have clarity of thought at night, on the humid earth, under the star-studded canopy of the Romanian sky. Because this sky feels different from the sky of my "over there" country — it feels familiar, directly tied into my molecules.

I fall into a deep slumber at dawn with the rooster's crow, sliding into a dream of extreme clarity that doesn't at all feel like a dream but like the sharpest reality. An explanatory dream in which the characters that have emerged and appeared to me recently in their various forms visit me in the Bucharest apartment where I once lived with my parents and recount to me their story. I am their interrogator, and they walk in one-by-one acting and revealing their tale. There are three Mitzi dolls on the sofa where I sit for the interrogations and part of the puzzle of this dream is that I have to guess which one is the real Mitzi doll, because only one of them is real, the others are duplicates or simulacra of the original Mitzi. One of the three Mitzi dolls carries important information inside her and the key to our family past. First appears a woman in mourning with two children, the oldest a twelve-year-old boy by the name of Sebastian, dressed in traditional peasant clothes that are too big for his scrawny famished body, and the other one is an even younger boy in a full suit, with vest and scorched white shirt and tie, like a miniature adult man. He has a bleeding gash right in the middle of his forehead.

Everybody looks famished and speaks in anemic voices that are barely audible with the exception of the boy Sebastian who has a screechy voice, and he explains that their mother is in a state of shock from the death of her husband and younger son. She is a widow he repeats as if I wouldn't understand that by losing her husband, she became a widow. Her husband was killed in his native town in front of the millinery shop that their family had owned, together with their youngest son. Her husband had deserted from the eastern front where he had been fighting for a while. I ask in my dream well why did he have to fight on the eastern front on the side of the Nazis? And the boy Sebastian with the screechy voice answers because he had no choice, he was made to, he was drafted by the Nazis, don't you know Romania was on the side of Nazi Germany? I say I know, I know, but he could have refused, there is always a choice, and he says no there isn't, sometimes there isn't a choice, and he would have been killed one way or another, you know nothing of that war. And anyways he deserted and paid for it, are you pleased now?

In the dream the boy Sebastian is growing under my very eyes. He explains that his mother, being Jewish, had to hide during the Nazi raids and the big pogrom of 1941, even though her husband had fought on the side of Germany. I say wait a minute, your father was Jewish and fought on the side of Germany? And he says: stranger things than that happened during that war, my father was not Jewish, only my mother was but there were Jews also on that front and there were Jews fighting on both sides, and there were Jews massacred all over this area by good Romanian Christians. Or they were put on the trains of death and never seen again. Dying in battle on either side was better. And then Sebastian says something puzzling in my dream: my mother and I hid in the basement of our millinery shop and sat there waiting all night until your two grandfathers came for us at dawn. In the end, we were saved by your paternal grandparents who hid us in the cellar and in different compartments of the house. It was a damn good house with all of them secret places like it were built on purpose to hide fugitives in that terrible war. Only after the war my mother died in '57 in a Stalinist camp in Siberia. She escaped the Nazis to die by the communists. She didn't care, she wanted to die after she lost her son and husband. She helped people escape to the other side, and when she tried to escape by herself by taking me along, they caught her and sent her to Jilava and me to re-education camp. Sebastian's testimony ends there in my dream, but a full crowd of other people are waiting their turn to testify in the trial of my family's life story. They talk to one another, practicing their lines before they testify in front of me because it turns out in this dream trial, I am the judge who has to decide their fate and also to decide who the real Mitzi doll is.

A woman who says she is Mitzi the servant comes to the stand which is in fact my father's old walnut desk with the glass top that I always did my homework on. This is a family trial, and it all happens amid family furniture. My grandmother Victoria serves everybody walnut preserve, her specialty. Walnut trees have many uses in our country, you can make durable furniture and delicious preserves out of them if you use them efficiently. I hear myself say in my dream oh my god, oh my god, what a mess, I'll never be able to get to the end of this story, it's all a bloody mess but who cares, whatever. I say all this in English so that the people in the room don't understand me but the boy Lulu appears from the back of the room wearing an I 🖤 New York T-shirt and says to me, he says: yes, it's a darn messy story but it's your story too and you got to hear it to the end if you want to understand anything about this place and your family and your ancestry. Lulu speaks in English like an old man though he is only ten years old and wants to give his testimony in English, but I say no, this is Romania and you have to speak Romanian, it's the official language. Then Lulu starts his story in Romanian because he is perfectly bilingual just like my children back in America.

Lulu speaks a literary kind of Romanian like a nineteenth-century poet, almost in verse with archaic lines taken from Romantic poetry, at times even in rhymes because he says the language will disappear if it's not spoken in its full complexity. He uses words such as complexity. I say forget about the history of Romanian language now, we don't have much time, or the dream will end, and I must find out the truth before the end of this dream, just hurry up please and tell me the truth about yourself and this whole complicated family story like a labyrinth. At the word labyrinth everybody in the room panics and starts talking gibberish, only Lulu goes on in his poetic Romanian speaking above the general din and he says: I've waited for you for a long time, Corina. I start crying in my dream because I wish I had returned earlier. I'm always a minute too late for everything and so many people have waited for me for a long time here in this remote faraway town with so many secrets and murders. There weren't just murders, there were some good deeds too, Lulu says as if he heard my thoughts or maybe I said my thoughts out loud, it's possible. There is no difference between thoughts and spoken words anymore in this trial dream, everybody hears your thoughts. Then what's the point of thinking or of talking anymore? Exactly what I always said, says Lulu. Now you see what they all had to go through, they lived with thought listening machines, that's how the Securitate functioned, with special machines invented by the Russians and produced in America by a joined KGB CIA operation, that listened to people's thoughts and then sent them to prison and camp for re-education until their thoughts were the correct ones. That's how dictatorship survives, and America is just as bad as Russia if you want to know the truth, only their standard of living is better. I tell Lulu I don't want to hear his political ideas. I have no need for his opinions, I just need to know the truth about my family, just say it already, or the dream will end.

And that is when a middle-aged woman wearing a red scarf on her head enters the room. Everybody stops talking and looks at her. It's Mitzi the servant, finally, she has arrived. Lulu jumps up from his chair and goes to greet her saying: hello, grandma, only he calls her bunica by the Romanian word for grandma, and behind her is a stocky looking man with glasses and a balding head. Grandma and grandpa meet Corina, she's come all the way from America to uncover the story of our family and to find out who is buried in the back yard. I told her it's a complicated story, but she is very curious, she wants to know because she's writing a book. Everybody writes a book in America. Mitzi the servant doesn't seem to hear him though, and she looks through everything and everybody like she is from another world. They are dead, they can't hear anything, Lulu says, but I talk to them anyways, because it's good to talk to the dead, you never know when they might come back to life.

This is all nonsense, I say in the dream, all I wanted to know was which one is the real Mitzi, which of these three is the real Mitzi doll, the one who holds important information inside of her. At that exact second, the dream ends with all questions unanswered, and I find myself in full daylight lying on the ground, soaked in sweat and blood. Manole and Lulu are next to me on the ground trying to revive me as if I had died or fainted. I see everything and everybody in a daze. I am not very sure whether I am still in the dream, if I woke up or I am dreaming that I woke up. The fruit trees and flowers around me look too perfect to be real, bursting with ripe fruit and brilliant colors like a story book.

Manole seems younger and Lulu somewhat older or maybe it is just my demented state of mind that makes me see everything different from what it is. I also have no idea why I am soaked in blood and why I don't seem to care. Manole pours some cold water on my face then proceeds to wipe the blood off my face and neck and shoulders as if a scene like this happens every day. "You hurt yourself against some rocks when you fell down from the storm, you'll be alright." I panic about the blood and about the fact I don't seem to be able or strong enough to get myself up from the ground. The earth is pulling me towards its center, towards the places of the dead, the places where the dead are buried in this so-called orchard, in which fruit, ghosts, and corpses all coexist. "Manole, I had such a weird dream, what's going on …" "Of course, you did," Manole interrupts me, and he laughs with the same toothless laughter cry as during the savage storm of sometime ago, his Cheshire Cat laugh. "You sleep on this earth here and you are going to get all the dreams of the dead too, the dead are going to talk to you for sure when you sleep right here on their territory." "Oh, that makes sense," I hear myself saying as I get up with difficulty and I stagger in a completely faint, dizzied state. I almost fall all over again but Lulu who helps stabilize me and sits me down on the bench under the plum and cherry trees in front of the house.

I look around me and the landscape looks different again. The orchard trees grew and multiplied overnight, you can no longer see the cars parked all the way at the end of the back yard, just heavy branches hanging with dark red cherries, purple plums, bright red, and yellow apples. The air is heavy hot and perfumed to excess and the sun mercilessly shines while cuckoo birds and turtle doves call sweetly to each other. Yet despite all the sweetness there is a feeling of death and ghostliness everywhere and the strangest thing is that I have come to accept it all. "All this is normal over here, it's how we live," says Manole again. "The dead are all around us, they are restless and unavoidable." He is not kidding, indeed the orchard is filled with light treading feathery beings, phantoms of a time long gone, caught in a thin fissure between past and present, like a hair line crack in a wall through which you can see all the neighbors' lives even when you don't want to.

A red-haired girl moves in a yellowish haze with a sweet hollowness in her eyes which would be sinister if it wasn't also harrowingly sad, a deep wailing frozen in eternity. She swirls in figure eights in between the trees that sway with the heaviness of their luscious fruit. Sour, bitter, and sweet cherries, dark mauve plums bursting with honeyed juices, bright yellow and red apples like we are in the garden of Eden. Fruit is not just fruit here, it's mystic nourishment for the eyes and the flesh, feeding the living and the dead. The woman in the peach-colored dress with the blue parasol appears from behind one of the trees, as does the widowed woman in her dark mourning dress. It's all a continuation of the vision before the dream I had at dawn while bleeding on the wet ground. It's a miracle I haven't died of pneumonia and blood loss or concussions to my head already. Only it's neither a dream nor a vision, but a different kind of reality that is imperiously asking to be recognized, acknowledged. The figures seem to say here we are in total and undeniable coexistence with all you flesh and blood arrogant living, without us, you would be dead. Now it feels like our lives depend on the good will of these woodland orchard embodied spirits.

The girl in the yellow fog is in the center of everything, it all revolves around her. She comes nearer and she looks frighteningly like a younger version of my mother, while the woman in the peach-colored dress is a younger version of Grandmother Frida. A woman's voice says this part of history has remained untold and it must play itself out to the end while Corina is here. Yes, Corina is here, didn't you know that? She must know everything. This part of history needs to be revealed, it has been hidden for too long by people who didn't want it to be known. We will never rest until our history is illuminated. A rustling and shuffling through leaves are heard and more people appear from behind the trees. They were a part of the trees and now gently separate themselves from the thick trunks. A German soldier, and an Italian soldier, a plumpish woman with dark braids rolled around her head, they are all part of the convoy of people from the elsewhere. They are airy, light, and yet not without consistency, a translucent consistency as if made of water. I am sitting closer, very close actually. I am part of the circle, a watery circle made of watery beings. I am the only one hard, opaque, heavy, and bleeding.

Life can be such a drag, I think unexpectedly. Here is how it was! I hear a voice say and it seems to come from the red-haired girl in the yellow haze. The voices are melodious, also aquatic. Maybe the afterlife is all made of water, I think. It was like this, she repeats. Your grandfather was a good man, he risked his life to save our lives. She is swirling and transforming herself into different shapes. Our mother and father had to leave us with your family. My parents parted at the station the same day your family went into refuge by the Danube. Our mother got away, and she traveled by herself from the north to the south, through a system of escape, through a chain of people who were helping us. Everybody was not bad, you know, there were good people like your grandparents, but a lot were bad and killed us in the streets, burned our houses, hung us in abattoirs and slaughterhouses with signs that said, "kosher meat."

Her story is one continuous uninterrupted wailing confession that also sounds like a song that could last forever. There are no interruptions, no breaths in between the words and her dance is a hallucination of colored clouds in which she sometimes takes the shape of a girl with watery melancholy eyes. You see how restless I am, she says almost like a joke, I am doomed to continuous movement and transformation. I can never rest, it's the worst curse, Corina, you have no idea. It can only end when your mother returns to rebury me or burn me to ashes, or find my body, I can't even remember very well whether they ever found my body or not. I can only rest when your mother Zoe, who is my sister, brings the key to the secret box and reveals our story to the world. She holds the key. Then I can rest and disappear forever. That will be delicious to finally rest. You know your mother is the other side of me, don't you? I'm a restless air creature wandering across the world, everywhere and nowhere. That time when they came for us, she tried to save me, she tried to give me her breath but there wasn't enough of it, and it was too late. I was born different you know, I shouldn't even have been born, a mistake of the universe, it happens every once in a thousand years.

By now my head aches with a migraine of the century and I'm still bleeding, but my blood is a refreshing substance cleansing me. I feel it flowing on my neck and shoulders like a river and wonder why Manole did not put band aids and gauze on my wounds to stop them from bleeding. All the airy people in the orchard are looking at me as if expecting something from me. Your grandfather gave Zoe to a man in the network who gave her to someone else, and so on, until she was well-hidden in some secret woods in the mountains and your grandfather helped our mother Frida escape through the network with false documents. I am buried here in the garden, and so is our mother, and some others too, lots of dead are buried under these trees, they grow well from our blood. The cherries are red, and the apples are sweet. So much sweetness comes from blood. I wake up in a bed in a small room with large windows looking out into a garden, with a bandage around my head and a feeling like I am no longer myself. Manole feeds me a syrup he says is for the headache.

The Trains, the Sea
June, July, August 1941

Gabi was lucky that it started raining with a fury equal to the heat that had plagued that bloody part of the world for weeks. There was a moment of inattention on the part of the guards, and he had enough life left in him to take advantage of the moment. On the train he slept for most of the time in a stupor. While the others were begging for water and for food, he cared for nothing and just slept. The brutal separation from Frida worked on him like a drug. He had a hard time staying alive, food or no food, but one thing he knew for sure was he didn't want to die on that train. The taste of her mouth in the last torn embrace on the train steps lingered on his lips for a long time in the stench and agony of the crowded train. For the first time in his life, he had the impulse to kill someone and it was neither the guards nor the SS soldiers that he dreamed of strangling with his own hands, but the man who had called him and given him away at the exact moment he and Frida were about to get on the train together. He wasn't even sure who the man was, where they had met or known each other in the past, only that they had once been near one another in a city in a different country long before the war. Once on the train, Gabi moved as far away from him as possible, in an area with small children. Some were asleep, their heads dangling in the exhausted arms of their parents, others were screaming vigorously and uselessly formed a compounded wailing, a dissonant song, almost beautiful in its agony. The heat and the stench on the train were worse than the hunger and the thirst. It dug into your skin and brain mercilessly and splintered your will to live and act to smithereens.

Gabi remembered days long ago with hunger and stench, far away in a different world, in another country, yet like this one. He was a young boy, and the world was breaking at the seams, governments and czars were collapsing in oceans of blood. Maybe he had read all that in a history book, he wasn't altogether sure anymore. Yet something in his gut told him it had been real, and he had been part of another bloody scenario long ago, with huge throngs of people fleeing, killing, or being killed like insects on the sidewalk, being thrown off trains and shot dead in the streets. He knew Frida even then, he had always known Frida, she had been part of his heart and his flesh forever. At least she was safe now, riding the train he should also be on. Everything happened on trains these days, whole destinies crushed or saved, masses of people moved from place to place to their death or escaping to freedom in the screeching of train wheels, in the deafening clamor of train whistles. A child defecated on the train floor next to him, a mother screamed finding the baby she held lifeless, an old man with a crazed look collapsed and froze, dead.

Gabi felt he was going to lose consciousness any moment but the remote memory of another train ride long ago, with people fleeing something ominous and unforgiving, a general massacre, kept him awake. Clinging to a memory of survival kept him awake, even though for a few seconds he thought he was melting into a black pool of stench. The scent was palpable and suffocating him. He held on to the memory of the other time in a train filled with crowds carrying their belongings in large sacks with fowl and children running around in indiscriminate masses. Frida was near him fleeing too, then. They were fleeing together. Somebody had been stabbed to death, somebody else thrown off the train, but Frida was next to him and someone else too, someone he knew well.

They had always been fleeing. She was a translucent otherworldly presence with flaming red hair and despite the gore around them she laughed and recited verses from a Russian poet, a Russian playwright, a play with cherry orchards. That was how she kept up her spirits and his, until the train arrived somewhere else, in the country they were fleeing to, reciting lines from a Russian play in which some characters argued about selling or not selling a cherry orchard. The plot of the play seemed ridiculously frivolous and yet completely necessary and even tragic once you understood all the relations between the characters, their splintered dreams, and crushed aspirations. She knew then she was going to be an actress.

The train he was on now in this atrocious present, in which the stench was worse than the hunger and the thirst, stopped briefly. There was a deafening burst of thunder. In the opening of the train door, he saw the skies slashed by brilliant zigzags of lightening and in the same second it started to rain with unrelenting fury. One of the guards turned around for a moment to push the dead man on the floor farther away and the other one was distracted by the thunder and lightning and looked away. Gabi crawled on the train floor to the door opening and dove through it outside headfirst like a bird plunging into the sea for fish. He rolled down the embankment, on the drenched grass and earth for what seemed like a long time, a liberating fall into the abyss. The image of Frida as a young girl playing parts from a Russian play about orchards in a train filled with people on the run, crying babies and screeching fowl filled his mind to excess. He fell asleep almost instantaneously in the ferocious rain as the train to hell crawled its way ahead on the screeching tracks and picked up speed to an unknown destination. His last thought before falling asleep was that he was sorry to not have had a chance to kill the man who called out to him in the station before he and Frida could escape safely together on the same train.

He is not sure whether he is awake or dreaming, he is drenched in rain, he delights in every heavy drop on his body. Everything happens smoothly, with the fluidity of dreams, as if someone else were guiding his moves and his trajectory through a vast and variegated nature. Now he is running, now rolling down an endless hill, now walking by the side of fences, forests, on deserted roads, on roads that are not deserted, merging with large caravans of colorfully dressed people traveling in covered carts. It's him and not him. At times he forgets that Frida is not with him, and he looks for her around him, behind him, she must be walking behind, absentmindedly reciting lines from a play with orchards. There is a bloody revolution raging somewhere nearby and the two of them barely escape together with someone else and with a man who helps them cross frontiers into another country.

At other times on this endless journey of walking, rolling down hills, riding horse drawn carriages with colorful people speaking a different language, the truth pulsates in his brain with atrocious clarity of every detail. The way he placed Frida's hat on her head before he was yanked away by the SS soldier, the unbearable stench in the train car, the lifeless baby in the woman's arms, the soldier kicking the body of the old man on the floor, the godsent thunder and lightning, the dive into the rain through the door opening, headfirst.

The image of his two girls is too unbearable to contain, so he shuts it down whenever it rushes into his overheated brain. It seems he has been traveling for days, and time is irrelevant. He moves in the rhythm of the light, to the cadence of light and dark rolling one after another. At some point he hears another language that has a peculiar familiarity, the language during the first escape of long ago when Frida recited her dramatic lines, the language in the train from the time of the revolution. In that train of long ago, Frida and him, are running away from that language, its people, and their ruthless killings. Now he is back in that same language he ran away from for dear life decades ago.

The soldiers look different too, they seem less angry and more exhausted than the ones who were chasing after Frida and him only a few days earlier, though equally vicious. Or was it months ago, or years? Time is a viscous gel in which he drowns, and he has no idea whether he is moving forward or backwards in it. He understands only one thing during this never-ending free fall in time, history, memory: that he must keep running and moving through space. And space is all that matters now, pushing past it so he can get as far away as possible from the trains of death and the soldiers and the men in green shirts who pile thousands of people like him and Frida on those trains when they were not massacring them in the streets and hanging them from abattoir hooks and forest trees.

Gabi thinks he might have come to the wrong country though, one that he already ran away from long ago in the demented chaos of a revolution and pogroms. They were supposed to arrive in the neighboring country to the south not the north, Frida and him. They were supposed to reach the Black Sea shores of the country next door to the south, reach a particular town where Queen Maria once resided in the summers of her youth, meet other people in a shelter by the sea who would help them farther south and then west to the safer countries, as safe as any country could be in those times. It was all part of a well-planned escape through the special network which passed fugitives from hand to hand, house to house, country to country like burning packages. A thread of his past he already ran away from is pulling him back like a damnation.

At different moments throughout his hallucinatory progress through spaces, runaway crowds, fields covered in corpses, deserted ghost towns, walking, riding more trains, carts, even a boat, occasionally being fed by a kind runaway, or put up in someone's house to hide and sleep for a few days, an occasional presence clings to him and envelops him like an embrace, a boon, a veil of hope and possibility. It feels like the painfully familiar presence of someone incredibly dear that he lost some time ago. This presence, this fluttering of wings and smoke next to him, around him, is guiding his steps and the direction of his journey through the hell of a grotesque humanity on the run. Faces and voices pass by him in a perpetual cortege, or so he thinks, as it is really he who passes by myriads of unknown faces, hearing the cacophonous clamor of voices all calling for something, wailing about something, begging for a piece of bread, a cup of water, shelter to spend the night.

He has no idea how he even manages to find himself inside a plane roaring its way through dark clouds above an earth in flames. There are other people that seem fugitives like him and talk to him in a mixture of languages that he understands, in languages that are familiar and whose words he recognizes though once the words are strung into longer utterances their meaning collapses and breaks down into little pieces, into tiny animals crawling on the floor of the plane. He is aware that his consciousness is a few steps removed from him, he may even be hallucinating, someone on the plane might have given him a special cigarette or drink that is causing this splintering of his consciousness and his self into two separate entities. It is a liberating feeling. The earth is a sea of flames, and he pierces through dark clouds like no others he has seen before, clouds of rain, sky clouds but also clouds of dark smoke rising from the burning earth. The entire universe is bursting into flames and that gives Gabi a tremendous sense of joy, to see both earth and sky burning to ashes. Let it all burn to ashes, it's not worth saving, he thinks.

The people on the plane are wearing regular clothes, not soldier's clothes. They are kind to him, they are trying to speak to him and make him understand something important in two different languages: the language he was speaking with Frida right up to the last moment of their separation and a secret language that he only spoke with her occasionally for some special occasions, or holidays. But he no longer understands that language anymore. Languages come and go from his brain. Words grow or fade into empty sounds. The plane shakes and seems to be thrown around by powerful winds. The men on the plane are tying a kind of package on his back and trying to explain something about jumping off the plane with that package on his back. It will open, it will make you land on the beach, you will be alright, they say many times in a row. It sounds almost like an exciting thing, he has no fear of jumping from anywhere into the largest abyss, he has already been free falling through time, history, memories of bloody revolutions, fields covered in mutilated bodies, caravans of people running away in compact multicolored groups mixed with animals of different kinds.

The men on the plane are giving him instructions on how to operate the package on his back, but again the words fly away, and their meaning splinters into flocks of birds, there is no way he can grasp these birds that are important words flying about in the roar of the plane engine. Suddenly the earth is no longer burning underneath, there is no longer earth, but an endless expanse of water. Maybe he has reached the other side of the universe, where there is no longer solid matter, but just fluid blueness in which you float aimlessly. You must jump now, jump, someone is yelling in his direction, and he can't grasp the meaning of "jump."

One time long ago he had two girls who jumped rope and laughed in a space and time that was not covered in flames. There was once a woman named Frida with red hair like a setting sun that jumped next to these two girls showing them how to use the rope and turn it this way and that way and jump over it in a special kind of flight. An unbearable heaviness that resembles acute pain in a region of his being that is not altogether solid and physical overwhelms him at the image of the red-haired woman flying over a rotating rope. He doesn't understand this game at all, but his entire being is torn apart by the image of her and the two girls jumping, flying over a moving circle, he wants to do the same, fly and jump over a moving circle.

You must jump now, he hears someone saying again, it will open, after a while. Landing, running, all sorts of words are being thrown in his direction until he feels a hand push him over the edge of the plane and before he can take another breath, he is flying in a solid vertical plunge. Everything comes back to him with insufferable clarity. It was better before when his mind was wrapped in a thick fog, there was no pain of this kind that tears you into many pieces from the very inside out. He remembers the last months of hiding with Frida in the tiny attic room, the wait for something, for someone who was going to save them, the hour of love in the bed in the tiny room soaked in the afternoon light.

Her body, her thighs humid from the afternoon summer heat and from desire, her red curls spread over the pillow and her closed eyes, the consistency of her body in his arms as he is holding her and converging with her in fluid trepidation, a tiny moan, a whisper, a blooming of the flesh into something else material and immaterial, a bird, a flower, a cloud. Her sweaty body in his arms. He can taste the salty sweat of Frida from that last quivering embrace during his vertiginous descent through the smoke from the burning earth. Then there was the ride in the elegant black car, he and Frida were going to a place by the sea, they were going to be together and get the girls later. That later is now in this free fall through an acrid acid air. Now he can finally distinguish between the elements, the air, the words that he is thinking, the image of Frida on the train steps again and again, as he hurtles through the salty air.

The package on his back opens and he is now gliding over the blue expanse of water. "Later on" is now, and all he has of Frida is the still fresh taste of her last kiss on the train steps, the train is slowly moving away and she is standing on the steps in her pink hat, someone pulls her back and closes the door. He flies aimlessly through the sky above the useless immensity of water. What does he care about water and war, and revolutions? He never even properly said goodbye to her, in simple worn-out words, like goodbye my love, take care of yourself, I'll see you later. They hold hands, their fingers are still touching as the train slowly moves away, someone is calling his name, a soldier pulls him away, her face is covered in tears, and he is helpless, the train door closes, and he finds himself behind a rope with a crowd of other wretches like him.

He has no idea why he is still alive. Something inside his body is shaking him violently, unstoppably and he realizes he is crying in large sobs. He had forgotten what that was like, his salty tears are filling his mouth, his loneliness is as vast as the entire expanse of water beneath him. He hits earth not water though, he hits the wet sand near the water with a thunderous thud. He stretches his arms and feels the wet sand on one side, the water on the other, the fluffy foam of the waves like an embrace. The smoky presence that has been enveloping and guiding him for a while through the hallucinations of his voyage moves through him like a gentle wind. The image of one of their girls blooms in front of him and all around him and that's when he is sure he has lost that girl, that she was lost in the process of being saved. The salty fluffy waves caress his hand like a careless consolation.

Corina's Notes
September 1972, Bucharest

One afternoon in September of 1972, after the summer of our colorful seaside vacation filled with delicious Turkish foods, an older man dressed in a perfectly tailored suit showed up at Frida's door in the tiny apartment in the tiny alley where she had been living for the last two and a half decades and handed her a small package. It contained a black pair of pants, a gray pin striped shirt, an old watch, and a voluminous handwritten manuscript. The man said these belonged to your husband, Gabi Angelescu, they were found on a beach in a town in Southern Spain at the border with France, as if that precise detail of the location where the objects were found mattered. Frida was at first reluctant to take the package and mistrustful of the man, since many years earlier a similar scenario happened when another man appeared at her door with a similar claim of bringing her Gabi's watch and wedding band, without shirt and pants though. It was the manuscript that made her decide to accept the package, when she recognized Gabi's small, elegant handwriting with occasional nervous lines and deviations as if his train of thought had dissipated and he was just drawing shapes on a page.

The man refused to come in when she invited him and in that second of his refusal a momentous recognition happened of a time, she had long wanted dead and unremembered. It was the memory of a wretched train ride in the night, of a young man and a young woman sitting in the train compartment across from her. The man handed the conductor a ticket in her stead and called her Irina. At the time she had thought the relationship between the man and the woman sitting next to him was a strange one. They went in the train corridor and embraced each other, the woman's back was against the glass door but the man who was taller looked straight at Frida during that embrace and uttered something, mouthed a string of words. At the time she had thought he was whispering something to the woman, a priceless secret or passionate love words, but now seeing the man standing in front of her she finally understood them and realized those words had been for her and they had saved her life, if saving it was worth. Take the next train to the sea, that was what the man had mouthed to her while he pretended to whisper love words in the woman's dark wavy hair.

They were companions working in the resistance of those days, the small and thin layered resistance that was rescuing Jews from the pogrom. Standing outside her doorway, as the man touched his hat with his hand as a polite goodbye gesture, Frida had a powerful desire to utter the words to him: take the next train to the sea. She whispered the words once and then again uttered them in full voice. The man showed no emotion hearing the words, except for a tiny fleeting smile that crossed his face and made him look younger, almost as young as he had been then on the train, thirty-one years earlier. She said thank you, the man said it was the least I could do, your husband had prepared for the best and the worst. Frida took the manuscript with one hand and held out her other hand. She then realized he was missing three fingers. He smiled again, a bit wider this time and said I was lucky, others had it much worse.

Frida spent the entire night reading the manuscript which was really a journal collection of letters that Gabi had written to her from his last places of refuge, a village in the south of France at the border with Spain and then the first Spanish town at the border with France. He died, like he had lived, at crossroads, between borders. She never knew that Gabi lived for another full year and escaped the death train. The first man who had brought her the would-be wedding band with the story of being Gabi's friend from the train and of the vow the men apparently made to each other about contacting the other's widow, was the same one who had called out to Gabi in the station when he was about to get on the train with Frida. He was a Jew helping the SS at the price of his survival, there were such specimens as well, indeed you saw everything in those times, including SS soldiers who saved some of the Jews.

Frida understood that from the journal, from Gabi's description of him. Not only had the man not become a friend of Gabi's during their ride on the sinister train, as he had claimed, not only had he made up the story of the SS soldier who gave Gabi a glass of lye to drink instead of water, but the man himself had done exactly that to one of the prisoners on the train. He had also asked Gabi to give him his wedding band in exchange for water. Gabi asked him to first taste the water to make sure it wasn't poisoned like the other glass that had killed the prisoner. The man did what Gabi asked with a grin as if saying I can't believe you mistrust me this much. Gabi gave him the wedding band as he didn't care about any possessions even if they spoke of his former life with Frida. At the point of that exchange, in the smelly darkness of the train, Gabi didn't recognize the man as the one who had called out to him in the train station and who had been responsible for his deportation on that train to hell. He wasn't looking at anyone in those moments, being in a state of consciousness not too different from a semi coma. All that happened in the nightmarish stench of the train right before a thunderous storm started which allowed Gabi to escape through the opening of the train door and jump headfirst through the torrential rain. As she read his hallucinatory narration Frida wondered why the man who had betrayed Gabi ever bothered to bring her the wedding band and make up the story of their brief friendship on the train to hell. Maybe it was remorse, she told herself.

Gabi had crossed entire regions of the country by foot, in refugee convoys or by himself, walked across lands scorched by fires and bombs, towns where the population had either fled or had been killed, rivers, forests, mountains, all the forms of relief, rural and urban areas, all in a daze, in a state of semi consciousness driven by an inexplicable urge to get somewhere with no war and no SS soldiers. He crossed parts of the eastern front by night at the light of bombs and air raids. He realized he spoke Russian fluently and got the help of a Russian soldier who drove him in his tank farther west. He was further helped by a Ukrainian family who put him up for a week to rest and recover his strength. Help was surging his way like he was the hero of a fairy tale whose steps were guided by benevolent forces and beings. He had no desire to live, yet something or someone kept pushing him forward and guiding him like a miraculous wind of life.

I believe our Carolina is alive and unalive at the same time my beloved Frida, he wrote in a letter. He wrote that he felt her breathing, her immaterial presence near him at times, so near, he said, that I could almost touch her, hold her, but she always melted into air and the air became palpable and sour and then there was a merciful forgetfulness that overtook me. I am convinced it was our unalive, undead daughter who helped me survive and guided my steps through the most unimaginable sights. Things that I would have thought impossible before, now seem normal. I moved through them like a sleepwalker but at the same time with a limpid consciousness noticing small details, with maddening precision like the shoes on a corpse lying disfigured in the mud, the colorful dresses in the Gypsy caravan with whom I traveled for a while, the wrinkles on the face of the Russian soldier who saved me, the taste of bread in the house of the Ukrainian family. I had no idea why people helped me and gave me shelter or took me in their carts or tanks, but I was moving through everything as if through water, in slow motion, guided by a beneficent presence. The yearning for you and the girls never relented, I couldn't bear it any longer, and when I was finally safe in a beautiful town by the sea, (remember how much we had wanted to get to the sea?), it became worse than ever, and not even the beneficent presence of our lost daughter could alleviate the pain slashing my gut.

The manuscript went on in meandering lines of memory and narration, sometimes with excruciating detail at other times with large gaps of information, in no chronological order. It also depicted atrocious scenes of mass murders and tortures in the city of Iasi, north of my father's native town and the house with the orchards, from the summer of 1941 just days prior to the time when he and Frida attempted their escape. These scenes, sometimes written with photographic details, came back with relentless fury throughout Gabi's journey across devastated towns and unlikely rides in caravans or tanks, even ships. They were woven with the cinematographic depiction of his equally improbable flight in a war airplane next to French resistance men and his forced descent over a southern French shore in a parachute.

At times Frida had the feeling that Gabi's narration glided into fantasy and imaginary happenings that he wrote in the throes of a delirium of the mind and body. But then suddenly a sentence of luminous clarity and lucidity legitimized the startling truthfulness of the writing. There was one such long meandering but limpid sentence that emerged all alone in the middle of a page, written in beautifully formed letters like a deliberate and unbearable farewell to the world and especially to his beloved Frida. It said I have seen too much of the worst there is to see in the world and a tiny but shiny bit of the best which almost rivals the worst but not quite. I can no longer bear the loneliness, the horrifying images, and your absence. I shall die alone in this Spanish border town where I have been welcomed but where nothing makes sense any longer.

The sentence appeared randomly written in the middle of Gabi's retelling of his journey since their brutal separation on the steps of the train in Northern Moldavia and was followed by events that came before his arrival in the Spanish border town. However, when Frida arrived at the very end of the manuscript, to the very bottom of the very last page covered in writing, she realized Gabi must have run out of space to write precisely that last most important sentence. He must have leafed back through the notebook pages and found a page that had been left blank by mistake and that was where he wrote his last words of the memoir, and most likely of his life: in the very middle of his recounting. The sentence was also written in Russian, unlike the rest of the narration, written all in Romanian.

Frida spent the entire night reading the manuscript and after that she fell ill of an unknown malady. She never recovered from the illness and died on a fall afternoon in her tiny Bucharest apartment off a hidden alley, in the arms of her daughter Zoe and in front of my own puzzled ten years old eyes. I was losing the grandmother I barely knew but grew to love for three years of my life with the passionate love of a lonely granddaughter lost amid the sea of secrets that her parents moved through daily. In the parting letter that Frida left on the table in her tiny room she expressed the wish to be buried in the earth behind the house with the orchards, near her daughter, as she was convinced that Carolina was buried there in that earth filled with fruit and corpses.

Nobody knew of the manuscript that Frida received and read in the last month of her life, until years later when a mysterious man called my parents in Florida saying he had an important package to deliver, it was of utmost importance he said, could he stop by to give them the package. I was living in France at that time, in a tiny studio apartment near the Gare Saint Lazare. The proximity of trains seemed to have been deeply inscribed in my destiny and my family's. I had stuck with the decision made on a late autumn day in the damp apartment of Paulina Kalinowska to not follow my parents to America, at least not right then. My mother woke me up with a call at dawn startling the hell out of me in my fitful sleep, triggering as always memories of catastrophic news and events from all the years of surveillance and precipitous deaths of family members from my days in Romania. She seemed to always forget or simply disregard that we were separated not just by the immensity of an ocean but also by several time zones.

Since night or early dawn calls were usually about deaths from what I could remember of my childhood and youth, the first question I asked was what happened, who died? In my mother's usual refracted way of answering direct questions, she just said we received an important manuscript, the manuscript, your grandfather's manuscript, repeating the word three times like a magic spell. Manuscripts were a big deal in our family, almost as big of a deal as orchards and stories of people on trains. I asked her which grandfather, since I hadn't met either of my grandfathers, having both died well before I was born. And the only grandfather I had ever heard about in our Bucharest apartment was Tudor, my father's legendary father, owner of the famous orchard. He was the one who hid people during the war, then died of pneumonia in the nightmarish summer of Aunt Lila's scarlet fever, the draught, the famine and the Russian tanks that drove through the small Northern Moldavian town and the entire rest of the country.

My mother answered in her slightly irritated tone that it was her father's manuscript. He had written a memoir during the last year of his life in southern Spain and a man who had known and spent time with him there was in possession of that precious manuscript. Somehow this mystery man had survived all these years, and was still in possession of the manuscript, after it had traveled some more, moved through other hands, then back into his hands and now it was in my mother's own hands. It was a hugely important manuscript she said, that contained information of historical importance.

I had hardly ever heard my mother speak so clearly and straightforwardly about anything that had to do with her side of the family and their past. I told my mother I never knew that her father was Jewish, she said yes, Corina, both my parents were, your grandmother Frida barely made it during the pogrom of 1941, but tata never did. I froze holding the phone in the thinning darkness before another gray dawn in the city of lights, in my tiny apartment. It was the first time ever I heard my mother mention her own father and say the word tata other than when talking to me about my own father. Again, I felt I had no idea who I was and who the woman who had given birth to me really was. A stranger with a formidable box of secrets that she kept locked up for my entire childhood. Now that she was several thousand kilometers away, and we were all part of the so-called diasporas on different parts of the globe, she decided to open it up over a phone conversation at the cruel crack of dawn. When I asked for more details, my mother shut down again and changed the subject in her typical fashion of diversion. I had no idea why she even bothered to call me with the news of the traveling manuscript if she wasn't going to talk more about it, connect it to our lives, make me understand who we were and who she had been all those years since the war.

But then she did, in her own roundabout way, circling cunningly around the true motif of her call yet offering bits to me in codified language, as if we were still under communist surveillance with tapped phones and secret police following us. Which it turned out we sort of still were. The Romanian secret police had orders to follow abroad certain refugees that were deemed "dangerous material" by the government because they engaged in anti-communist activities abroad. She asked me to come to the States and join them, your father is very lonely and misses you terribly, she said, never mentioning anything about her missing me. Then she became brutally direct. He almost got killed in an assassination attempt by the Securitate, she said casually as if she was talking about the weather in sunny Florida, an unexpected storm, or a heat wave.

I burst out laughing at her sentence, so unlikely and weird did it sound, thinking maybe my mother had finally slipped into the state of madness I always suspected she kept in check for my sake while living in Romania, and now it finally took complete hold of her. But no, it turned out that indeed, my father's friend who facilitated their sponsorship and arrival in Florida, had been playing the double agent game for some time, a bona fide Mata Hari. Only he had been careless and got shot dead at the dinner table in his own beautiful Florida home, only minutes after my father had visited him and received yet another important manuscript from a dissident writer "back home." I had a fierce desire to burn all the bloody important manuscripts, and a surge of anger rose in me so violently that I hung up on my mother. Then I called back apologizing, crying over the phone, after which she hung up and never called back.

Later that day, I called my Parisian émigré fairy godmother Paulina Kalinowska and told her I wanted to join my parents in their sun and danger filled Floridian life. It had been three years since they left her apartment before dawn, sparing me from tearful goodbyes. Paulina took the news calmly with no emotion the way she took all news and events and said she had to get to work to get me a passport and visa to the States. A month later I was on a plane to Miami for the next portion of my immigrant adventure.

More Manuscripts
June 2015, Northern Moldavia

In my family there are manuscripts about manuscripts, stories within stories, hidden inside compartments within compartments, within an entangled labyrinth of lives. This is what I find out from Manole on day seven or fifteen of my visit to my father's native town. Time gallops or stands still at will and the pages in the calendar on the wall of my room in the so-called bed and breakfast where I stay for the duration, seem to be out of order or moved back and forth. One day the page for June 23rd is torn out, and the next day is June 28th, and another day we are back on June 22nd, the Sanziene. I have come to accept the irregularities and the bizarre movements of everything from trees, day, and night to the hours of the day, to the living and the dead, the mixture of categories of existence, human and natural.

One day I visit the house at number 18bis hoping to find the final clue, the exact chain of events and the mystery behind all the entangled destinies that started or ended in that location of soulful trees. Manole takes me to the basement of the house. We go down another set of stairs into what looks like a basement within a basement, a series of chambers whose sizes and entries and exits are deceiving. One moment you think here you are, this is the cellar where mother Victoria hid her preserves and roots during various refuge expeditions, German occupation or Russian invasions, and the next moment you open another door that goes down another set of stairs into another chamber that looks like a cellar where Mother Victoria kept preserves and hid people on the run. In a corner of cellar number three, Manole points to a wardrobe and makes a sign that I should open it.

Turn-of-the-century dresses and hats enveloped in a seventy-year-old film of dust quiver on wooden hangers and stands. It's a deep wardrobe, almost like another room. Manole points to the bottom of the wardrobe, underneath the dresses to an enormous wooden box and signals to me to open it. Today seems to be Manole's silent day, he talks to me in gestures rather than in his slow modulating sentences that often mark the passage of time. The box contains a mountain of manuscript pages written in different handwriting, some of the pages are crinkly and yellow, others seem almost recent, only two or three couples of decades old, which is recent for out here. I am determined to spend the rest of my stay in this town reading every single one of these pages that may just offer me the final understanding of everything that happened here.

I wonder why Manole didn't think of taking me here earlier, instead letting me ramble through painful days of uncertainty and various forms of agonizing travel between dream and reality, not to mention time in the local jail, weird storms, and bodily injuries. As I settle on the floor in a cozier corner of the cellar within the cellar of this unfathomable house, a deep sense of familiarity rushes over me. Like I've been here before and the place is welcoming me as an old friend. Because here places and rooms, objects, and trees have the unheard-of ability to react to the presence and movements of the humans that inhabit or touch them. Maybe I was here before, only that I entered from a different side, at a different time of the day and in a different state of mind. I stop thinking about it and let myself just be in the womb-like space underneath the house with the orchards, with the certainty that more will be revealed to me. I focus anxiously on the mountain of paper in front of me.

The people on my father's side of the family wrote down everything they experienced throughout their lifetime, almost like a duty. In times of peace, but mostly during wars, revolutions, atrocities, famines, droughts, floods, pogroms, government takeovers, dangerous escapes. They took notes, wrote journals, letters, or memoirs. They wrote on loose pages, cheap notebooks, leather bound fancy ones, even on table napkins and toilet paper, in a frenzy of recording everything and not letting any episode of their lives go to oblivion, in the hope someone someday will look for them and read them. I must be that very someone, I think as I turn pages that crinkle and crumble under my touch, and that have dates as early as 1917 and 1920, long before the war years that obsessed my father. Sometimes the same story is told differently, as it may be told one time through the voice of my aunt Lila, another time written in the stern hand of Grandfather Tudor, and another time in unknown, unsigned and unidentified aerial writing, elegant and artistic, as if the person writing was more interested in the shapes of the letters than in the meanings they conveyed.

I feverishly leaf through the century old treasure of notes and manuscripts breathing in the dust they produce as if it was fresh air. Manole stands in a corner of the cellar inside a cellar inside a basement space like a guardian watching me. He occasionally moves his finger like an admonition or says things like you have to handle all this with care like they are live beings, or they will turn to dust under your very eyes. Indeed, they do, some pages are so old and brittle. I am afraid to turn them for fear they will turn to dust, and I will lose priceless knowledge about the demented convoluted journeys of my family. I say Manole, can't we somehow take this upstairs so I can read it leisurely, at length, in peace, this will take a long time to go through all these pages. He laughs his toothless smile that also looks like a cry because today he is not wearing his dentures, and he says Corina you have to exercise patience, a lot of patience, and read it all here, you can't take it anywhere, or it will dissipate and turn to dust, is that what you want? I try to object and say but Manole, this will take days, weeks maybe to go through all this, I object. And he says, indeed it will, we have all the time in the world, what else have you got to do, isn't this why you came here for? Yes, Manole has a point, only I don't have all the time in the world, I have to return to, I have to return …

Everything becomes a blur and I'm not sure where I have to return to. Don't I have children and a house and a job and a partner, and a mother still out there, out there … Out where? I seem to hear echoes in the cellar within a cellar which suddenly metamorphoses into a living room, a salon, a bedroom, a hiding place, a dancing hall, a kitchen, a hallway, a cellar again, a hanging basement that is both underneath and above the ground. It takes all the shapes and allure of any possible room that has ever existed. Now I'm crouched over the mounds of crinkly papers yellowed by time, now I am sitting in a fluffy velvety armchair looking out at the orchards in the back. Now I am sitting on an old chest filled with more letters and journals and memoirs about wars and revolutions and camps and pogroms and dances in the twilight, dances under the moon or in the orchards. Again, and again the orchards and the dances, sprinkled among every possible atrocity in the book of atrocities! Testimonies are mixed in rushed disjointed narratives written sometimes by sure hands sometimes by trembling hesitant hands that wanted to inscribe their so-called story for eternity and then hide it from the curiosity or avid inquisitiveness of informers, soldiers, officers, neighbors, Russians, Germans,

Romanians. Droves of people searching for something in this trembling mound of desperate writing.

I try to follow one thread at a time, like the thread of the story of Zoe and Carolina and their hiding during the Nazi purges in Romania, the story of their parents Gabi and Frida, a mysterious elegant couple who ended up ravaged and torn apart in an atrocious misery of death trains and failed escapes. Or the thread of the story of a woman whose name I hadn't heard of before, Sofia Marcela Kunovicis and her son Sebastian who barely escaped the 1941 pogroms in the North and lost half of their family to those pogroms. An uncle named Kosmin who was my grandfather's mystery son from a previous marriage. The bifurcated story threads of Mitzi the servant and her soldier husbands, the Italian deserter Gino with whom she had baby Gino, and that same Kosmin who fought on the side of Germany. Why haven't I ever heard of any of these people? I ask myself out loud moving maniacally from document to document. You are going about it all wrong, Corina and if you don't calm down and take it one life at a time, you'll lose it all, everything will crumble, they will all dissipate and go back to where they came from.

I have no idea what Manole is talking about but as usual I sense there is great wisdom in each one of his remarks and I'd better listen to him, weird and otherworldly as all this has been. Manole has after all led me to some important clues and guided me through some of the most astounding experiences of my life. Then I realize all of these are not stories. Stop calling them stories this and stories that, somebody says, it must still be Manole though it sounds like a different voice now. They are lives, these are real lives unfolding and running their wretched course under your very eyes Corina, in very diverse handwriting that takes on the characteristics of every individual, just like life does, yes just like the lives of people. When you get that straight once and for all, that's when it might all become clear and unfold and live itself out under your very eyes. I am now talking to myself out loud, but it sounds like it is also someone else's voice talking in my voice. I've seen and lived stranger things since I've been here, nothing surprises me anymore. Just let it be, Corina, just let it be, stop searching for the story, look for the life, stop trying to find the meaning, the thread, it will find you. It always does. I try to follow the advice. I let the pages come to me, move of their own will, I barely touch them. I have spread the different bundles of papers on the dusty floor of the cellar, gently, like babies who are sleeping, and I don't want to disturb them. I have woken up all the ghosts, spirits, memories and there seems to be no turning back now. I must follow and pursue this road to a rough and demented past whether I like it or not.

There is Russia in 1918, somewhere in the north, not quite Russia but almost. It's Ukraine, with the city of Kiev, only the authors of these pages still call it Russia. The big revolution has already ravaged through every corner of the city. Now there are mini revolutions here in the North. There are massacres within massacres, this one is called a pogrom. A man who has returned from some holy place in Greece named Athos, is helping some young people, practically children, to get away with fake documents. They are trying to get on a train late at night to cross the border, they are a rowdy group, and they don't even understand the danger they are in. The man who is saving them is called Tudor. The ones he is trying to save from both fascist and communist massacres are Gabi, Manole, Frida, and Sofia.

There are others whose names I don't recognize, an entire group on the run. I wonder who is writing this story, who is the author of this narration written in a small leather-bound notebook, almost elegant like it was given as a gift to write a diary on sunny days that are not in times of war and pogroms. I have a vague memory of running into that word at some point in my life, and I didn't know what it meant then. It was long ago in a situation of escape, when my parents and I were on the run from our country which is this country right here, and my father found important documents or letters hidden inside a doll's stomach. One of the young women is reciting lines from a play she has read or acted in, it's a play about a cherry orchard and although the entire group is crowded on a night train on the run from a combination pogrom Bolshevik revolution, she doesn't seem to mind and entertains everybody with her acting. The writing differs from story to story, sometimes within the same notebook or even on the same page, as if this was a collective collaborative project.

They are not stories, they are lives, Manole keeps saying and I say I get it Manole, let me read in peace, they are lives, yes, but they are still written down here in this colossal mess of notebooks and loose pages and diaries. The lives are moving around the space of the cellar now like a live performance, talking and reliving themselves in a mad carousel of grief and runaway episodes. A lot happens on trains again, and then in fields and streets with massacred bodies strewn on the sidewalks of a city in a country in the north called Ukraine but also Russia. It is 1918, a year after the stupid Bolshevik revolution now, but some groups are still massacring other groups of people. They just can't get enough of killings in this country. Tudor is a protector of the group; he traveled all the way from the country in the south which is this country right here where I'm sitting on the floor of this weird cellar with the lives of people from my family living themselves again in all their agonies for my benefit. Or maybe for their benefit too, so they can exhaust their undead lives once and for all and find eternal peace. Tudor has come expressly to save these people and get them false identifications so they can pass the border controls from Ukraine back into Northern Moldavia. He has come expressly from this place in Greece on a mountain with a famous monastery. He gave up his religious training and returned to Ukraine via this country here, only to help Gabi and Frida and Sofia and Manole. It's not clear what the relationship with them is yet, and what his interest is in taking these people out of their revolution and pogrom ridden country and why it is he has those resources, the power, and the desire to go through all that.

Gabi and Frida's parents were all killed, in the revolution and the pogroms. There were massacres from all sides. Gabi and Frida were not good communists, and they were Jews, the writing says in a corner of a page in a different notebook, the runaway from pogroms notebook. The train they are on is filled with an entire humanity from peasants and their animals to factory workers in overalls, to men and women in attires that were once elegant as if they are landowners on the run, to students from the university of Moscow with berets and pamphlets, to soldiers in Russian uniforms, because we are also at the end of a war. It's July of 1918 and World War I is in its last breaths of ravaging and killings. We live in a conglomerate of violence and horror. Someone wrote the word "conglomerate" in small, elegant letters. How do we survive all this, where do we go from here? A tireless writer also wondered in the same notebook.

I am no longer sure whether I am hallucinating all the quivering lives, the shadows, the movement of the air around me, the human breaths exhaling and inhaling their past with their last energies across an entire century, or whether I am being hallucinated by these lives and am a figment of their imagination. I realize I am writing everything down in the little notebook with the picture of Marilyn Monroe on the cover that I brought over from where I supposedly live in America. It's as if I need to add my own life to the lives written on the crinkly notebooks and diaries, as if my story is writing itself, though according to Manole I can't call it a story. I am also copying everything like mad, hungry for all the lives opening for me out of the yellowed manuscripts like butterflies coming out of puffy hard-shelled cocoons.

I keep searching through the books in frenzy but also trying to be very careful with the brittle pages, so they don't turn to dust, which some already have. With each notebook I finish reading, the lives around me quiet down and then resume their agonizing quivering with each new set of pages or diary. The year 1918 is an important year in the history of my family. At this point I can call them ancestors, it's almost a century ago and I thought World War II was as far back as I would need to go. The disorderly nature of the chronologies and the retelling makes me dizzy as I keep searching for a key to everything: where it all started, and how these lives were caught so brutally in the worst of the worst of every possible historical apocalypse of the past century.

I know Tudor is my grandfather, and I have no information whatsoever from my father about anything that goes as far back as World War I, but it's all here in the mound of yellow brittle paper in a cellar within a cellar, hidden from any possible pillage and invaders who would have gotten tired before they had a chance to discover this corner of a labyrinth underneath the house at 18bis. Tudor must have already been in his thirties then, since from all accounts of my father he was an older parent, in his mid-sixties when my father was born. He would have already lived a full life by the time of the train crossing into Northern Moldavia. What was he doing on the train running away from both enraged communists and rabid Jew haters in the year of 1918, at the end of the Great War, in the company of these young people who didn't even seem to care about who and what they were running away from? And it hits me that maybe Tudor and his young protegees might not even have been born in Romania, but Russia, that they could well have been Russian Jews who didn't adhere to the Bolshevik madness and were caught between the horrors of two purges. And what was the relationship between all of them, and who is Sofia?

I see that Manole is still standing in the same corner watching my every move with shiny eyes which in the semidarkness of the cellar seem like cat eyes. The air is stuffy and the presences, lives, beings made of particles of undying memories of a long gone past are coming and going in hallucinatory traffic. I have gotten used to them as one gets used to just about anything in this world. Russian names are sprinkled on some of the pages, some in red ink, like streaks of blood. It's not clear whether they are names of people, of groups, or of localities: Novgorod, Severeski, Glukhov, harsh consonants like steel train wheels on their steel tracks. A few lines later I realize they must be names of places they are running away from. "The peasants, the Red Army, the Haidamaks, they are all after us and killing us in the streets, our houses, the rail stations, we have to find the right train to get on and get away. We move through blood and smoke like blind people. Someone is coming to help us. We are running but also waiting." There is no indication of the authors of the records, but these lines strike me somehow that they must have belonged to Gabi, and I have no idea why or what it means to both run and wait.

The air in the cellar is moving like warm winds swooshing this way and that way and the words "we are running and waiting" become alive, in large letters moving across the ceiling of the cellar like an advertisement. The words "the peasants are the worst" are repeated, like an admonition against peasantry. A throng of smoky shadows swooshes by, a youngster with a beret and a young girl in a pink hat are at the very end of the throng trying to keep up, they are holding hands like they are tied together for life. The pink hat shines through the heavy blurriness of the air. "We make it on the train at the very last second, there are corpses on the platform, we have to step over them to get on the train. One corpse is a small child dressed in red overalls; his head is smashed. We are on the train together."

The writing shines on the page like it's on fire and I hear Manole from somewhere nearby whispering to me to turn the page before it's late. I ask too late for what? Manole comes over from his corner and turns the page in a fury. You ask too many questions, always, instead of just seeing and living everything, you'll never get to the end of it at this pace. I see Manole's face is covered in tears. I've never seen Manole like this and I don't ask. I don't ask any questions. I move on to the next page and the next. The word Haidamaks keeps turning around in my head like a tumor, an evil set of sounds that blast inside my head. The Haidamaks killed Jews at the stations of Sarny and Korosten. I have no idea who the Haidamaks were, but I imagine them as angry large, bearded men in uniforms carrying axes and guns. Manole is now moving away from me, and the chaotic pile of manuscripts is agreeing with me as if I guessed an important riddle. He doesn't say anything, but I feel it in the way he shuffles his feet and the movement of his shoulders that he acknowledges my guess to be correct and it strikes me at that very moment that Manole must have been there in that city, on that day, on that platform, in that train, that he must have been part of the group who barely escaped from the Haidamaks and their axes. He must have been the fifth person together with Gabi and Frida, Sofia and Tudor. Novgorod, Severeski, Glukov, Sarny, Kerosten — wicked sounding words that toss in my head at their will, trying to imprint themselves in the matter of my brain with no hope of ever leaving it. Some of the writing must have been that of Manole himself, woven in with that of Gabi and other hands in this collaborative effort to keep the memory alive.

There are leaflets and ordinances with dates of March, May, June of 1918, all written in Russian. The thick black Cyrillic letters glow on the yellowed papers, some of the Russian I was forced to study in school comes back to my overheated and crowded brain. Who would have thought it then, when I was a rebellious teenager in an ugly communist uniform resisting the imposed study of everything, that I would ever use a language forcefully drilled into my brain, in order to decipher orders to eliminate Jewish populations in remote areas of northern Russian empire or leaflets on the one-year anniversary of such abominations? The names of gangs and groups responsible for the purges stand out on the yellowed papers with aggressive thickness and boldness as if still screaming their right to kill and pillage and eliminate over an entire century of more miserable and atrocious wars, camps, dictatorships. The Grigoriev led groups, the Petliura and Zeliony gangs, the Terek Cossacks. Then there are names of provinces and localities where the pogroms took place, and some are doubly names of gangs and of localities: Petliura, Pereiaslav, Belaia Tserkov, Fastov, small provinces in the region of Kiev. There is a call to arms of something called "The Universal," it's a call for a "people's government without Communists and Ukraine for the Ukrainians."

On a torn newspaper page sit the words "Bolsheviks are Jews, communism is their work." I mouth out loud most of the words I read hoping to better understand the killers and oppressors who later in the century also devastated my father's house, and the entire country I had the misfortune of having been born in, who made camps for every possible group of people they deemed dangerous or undesirable. The air around me vibrates in cold waves as if the season suddenly changed and we are in a winter of the soul and of the mind, a freezing of feeling and of the flow of thinking. I am shivering and Manole comes over again and makes an angry sign to me to stop muttering the words, to stop uttering, forming words and syllables that invoke indescribable deeds. I startle and keep quiet, keep moving my hands deeper in the pile of manuscripts, papers, journals, leaflets, letters. Another persistent thought returns to me about Tudor. Who was he really and what was he doing on the train of that day in July, running away together with a younger group of people from chains of atrocities on top of atrocities, the spectacles of mounds of desecrated human flesh across city streets, houses, apartments, fields, every inhabited corner over entire regions?

I say, Manole, I'm so cold, what's going on, and who was Tudor, why was he there on that train, how did he know Gabi and Frida and this Sofia woman, and what were their relationships with one another? Manole is crying again, and the air becomes warmer. I even feel a soothing balmy breeze coming from somewhere, I have no idea where, since there are no windows, and we are inside a compounded cellar system. Keep reading, he says, and I pick up a random sheet of paper that looks like a letter in small, even handwriting that starts with "Dear brother Tudor" and is signed Manole and in it there is a plea to return from the monastery in Greece urgently and try to save them, meaning him Manole and Gabi and Frida and Sofia from the killings of the revolution and the pogroms. They are caught between both the revolution and the anti-revolutionary pogroms. The letter says "this is the worst of all possible worlds, the end of the world, an inferno within an inferno, we are in great danger from all sides, the Bolsheviks, the anti-Bolsheviks. We are hiding wherever we can, in basements, attics, fields and forests and are on the run almost day and night. The girls are exhausted, they will die soon if we don't leave here and find refuge, a home, clean water, a bed, peace." A shivering and shimmering of the air around me like an illumination startles me to death for the hundredth time that day afternoon evening. Who knows how much time has passed or not, and who cares? All rules of existence, time, space, the living, and the dead are nonexistent or entirely overturned, mixed up in an unstoppable motion of energies, traces of souls, contours of bodies, echoes of voices. A carousel of the restless dead and their memories.

I get up from the place on the floor where I have been reading the mind boggling and heart-rending testimonies and records and go to the wardrobe in the corner to look at the dresses and suits and hats in the hope that I will recognize who they belonged to, and where their owners wore them, in what circumstances of their lives. The pink silky dress that looks too short for the period, almost like a flapper's dress, too tiny for a grown woman, too large for a child, for some reason I am sure it belonged to Frida. I already see Frida on that train in that compartment on a nefarious June or July day on the run and wearing this feminine entirely out of place dress, carelessly acting out lines from her favorite play, Chekhov's the Cherry Orchards.

The Last Manuscript and the Death Game
Romania 1957-2015

There were things that happened in the aftermath of my parents' failed attempt of escaping to France in the fifties, that nobody ever knew, not even my mother. My father was arrested again, taken in the middle of the night by two men in the notorious black van that did the rounds in those times yanking people out of their sleep and communist misery to place them in the compounded misery of a political prison or put them out of their misery altogether. His manuscript was different from all the others. It was written in stark clear sentences that followed the events in chronological order. Having gotten used by then to the chaotic mixing of temporal lines, the coexistence of past and present and the random narrations overlapping each other or moving in unpredictable back and forth dances, the linearity of my father's recounting appeared bizarre. He was taken from home on July 22, 1957, and kept for only one week after which he was released. That meant nothing compared to his previous arrest of several months or to the yearlong arrests of others who had been deemed "dangerous" and "inimical to the victorious forces of the socialist revolution." But those seven days determined the entire rest of his life from then on.

In the damp semidarkness of a basement cell my father had been given the regular beatings and blows of all political prisoners of the time. But again, that was little when compared to the rest. Within the span of those brutal days that he was kept in the dungeon-prison for political detainees, my father was summarily given the death penalty. He was sentenced to capital punishment by a makeshift group of judges on grounds of "high treason and counterrevolutionary activities against Country and Party." He writes this very clearly and unsentimentally in the notebook that I am holding as I am myself sitting on the floor of a basement cell in the house of his birth and childhood. "On July 25th of 1957, I am sentenced to death by firing squad. The execution is expected to take place tomorrow at dawn. I am not afraid, never was. I am thinking of Mother and of Zoe. What will they do, how will they cope?" Unlike the other manuscripts which are on loose sheets of paper or written in leather bound notebooks designed to be used as diaries or personal notebooks, my father's tale of imprisonment and execution is written in a school notebook on lined pages. By the time I get to this last manuscript at the bottom of the colossal pile I am sweating profusely in the cool cellar. I don't see Manole anywhere, he has evaporated into thin air, which wouldn't surprise me if he did. Nothing surprises me. My father's notes written in the school notebook do leave me speechless and breathless though. If I had stopped being shocked by the vivid negotiations between the dead or the undead in their demented apparitions and chaotic flights through the space of that cellar, I am shaken out of my wits by the stark tale of my father's weeklong imprisonment that concluded with a death sentence.

What I wonder about the most is when was it that he wrote these notes, were they taken in prison, at the time of his detention, were they written days, months, years later like an autobiographical novel? I look carefully at the notebook, its make, the discolored thin brown covers, the pages that look yellowed by time but not to the degree any of the others do, not crinkly, not brittle. There is no date of the make of the notebook and no date on any of the pages written clearly in my father's steady and carefully formed handwriting. I am not in a hurry to go further into the recounting to find out by what means he eluded the death sentence. I have a nagging fear about what I may find out. Whatever it is though, a good thing it was he eluded it for I would not have existed had that execution been carried out. Atrocious thoughts cross my mind. Demented thoughts like the entire pile of manuscripts put together cross my mind, the kind that only horror and science fiction films indulge in. Thoughts like what if I don't exist and am a fiction of someone else's imagination? Or what if both my parents are ghosts from the time of all the purges and I was their daughter then, and so what does that make me other than the ghost child of these two ghostly people haunting the Romanian territory with indefatigable energy for decades? The energy of the dead!

What a joke and a superficial manner of thinking to believe it is the living who have energy! It's the dead who have more energy than the living. This is the most important lesson of my entire journey to the bottom of my family's frenzied ramblings through history and time. I delay as much as possible turning the page to find out how my father escaped the execution by firing squad. I prefer indulging in the notion that I may be a dream in someone else's dream or a rambling ghost from before the war. I am sweating and shivering at the same time and instead of thinking that the awkward combination of sensations is due to the shocking information that my body is being made to digest, as well as to the dampness of the cell itself, I prefer thinking that it is because as an undead person I experience all the sensations simultaneously. And, that all the whimsical presences that I have encountered over the days spent in my father's town and on his former property, are the real living creatures while I am the dead or the undead one frantically searching for a place and a body inside which to rest for all eternity.

Manole appears again suddenly in his Cheshire Cat manner to nudge me and to say turn the goddam page. I resist Manole's urging this time for as long as I can. I make an enormous effort of memory, trying to conjure in my mind the course of my entire life up to that point in a desperate attempt to find the hard reality of my existence, of who I really am, dead or alive. The pinching myself test doesn't convince me, maybe the undead rambling around the spaces of the living can also pinch themselves and experience sensations, maybe they have their own kind of carnality and physical existence. I make huge efforts to delve into my memory believing that if I can trace a coherent line of existence, a cohesive past that led me to this moment, then I can prove to myself that I exist on this side of the world: the side of the living.

My brain pulls out of its murky waters the thread of my past from the times I was a little girl in the matchbox apartment in Bucharest living with my parents a life of daily anxieties, yearnings and occasional moments of excitement and passion. The time I almost fell out the window, the endless hours of watching the movement of the quiet street and yard out of the window of our apartment. The daily secrecy of my parents translated into more whispers than into loudly uttered words and created a permanent buzzing or swooshing sound in our miniature apartment. The cats in heat mewing all night long in the summer outside our window. The sofa box filled with bizarre objects and documents that dated back to World War II. The cobalt vase that broke to smithereens when two secret agents, a man and a woman barged into our apartment and had a fist fight with my father. The death of Grandmother Frida when I was ten or eleven. My mother's burnt foods and the unpleasant smells that filled the apartment. The petunia, linden, jasmine smells that came in through the windows of our apartment in the summer mixed with the stench of rotting garbage from the trash shoot. The afternoon wailing calls of the Gypsy woman asking for empty bottles. All the sounds and smells that marked my childhood and pre-teen years.

I visit the restless teenage years when I left Bucharest and the premises of that suffocating apartment every chance I got, for the city up north where my aunt and cousins lived and later, the love story with my brooding prince charming of the Carpathians. That entire love affair and its irremediable heartbreak gleams for a second in my memory in the bright shades of its short-lived glory: a colored page in a book of black and white pictures. The departure to the Western World at dawn with a bunch of suitcases filled with forbidden objects and documents spread throughout secret compartments. The days in Vienna, Austria and the ornate St. Stephen's Cathedral, the days in Rome and the delicious discovery of freedom among magnificent churches and fountains. The first days and weeks in Paris under the guidance of Paulina Kalinowska, and my parents' departure to the United States, one gray Parisian dawn before I got up to say goodbye. The dinner at the top of the Eiffel Tower offered by Paulina Kalinowska to me and my parents, the night of the mysterious envelope that contained our passports and much more, the sea of lights of the city at our feet and my sudden infatuation with it. My three years in Paris giving private English lessons to French children and French lessons to Russian and Polish immigrant children and running errands for Paulina Kalinowska for causes and secret operations I never fully understood: picking up false papers from such and such a person that lived in a dark apartment in a shady neighborhood and meeting another person on a park bench to give them the fake IDs. Going to some other address in a bloc in a suburb of Paris to hand over a sealed envelope to some family from Poland or Tunisia. I never asked Paulina what was in the envelopes, or whose fake IDs they were, I mechanically fulfilled the tasks like a job and even got paid for it.

I went back to the early morning of my mother's call with the news that my father had almost been assassinated during the assassination of his double agent Romanian friend in Jacksonville, Florida. My departure to the United States one October day and the arrival in the stuffy muggy air of Florida. The first sight of the Atlantic Ocean and my parents watching me watch the ocean in complete awe, as they had already gotten used to the sight. The move to New York and the years of schooling, the New York grayness, and smelly metros, the first marriage, the first child, the second marriage, the second child! Moving out of the city to a small university town in upstate New York. My father's death one frigid January day after I had already moved out of New York City into the country. The years of motherhood with husbands, the years of single motherhood, work, book writing, translations for extra money, teaching language classes to refugees from all over the world for extra money. So much for extra money.

And then, in the two thousand tens, one summer day with smells of honeysuckle and freshly cut hay in the back yard of my American house — the sudden need to return to my father's famous house with the orchards and the decision to do just that during the following summer. The departure on a hot and humid June day, my mother waving goodbye at the New York airport as if we were parting for good. The arrival in the little town of my father's childhood and the visit to the wrong house, to the house next door filled with bizarre and incongruous conglomerates of objects and decorations. All the mind-boggling events, discoveries, happenings, and people, alive or less than alive, that have filled my several weeks in the town, up to this moment here as I am sitting buried in century old manuscripts, letters and documents. It seems to me like a clearly delineated life: a few large brush strokes of destiny and personal choices across five decades, across two continents with no filled in colors, no texture between the lines, just the large brush strokes. At that point I decided I was the one alive, and I could turn the page to my father's notebook.

The two or three weeks in this town here in the north of my native country feel more real and fuller than the entire lineup of events and existential brushstrokes of before. I turn the page, come what may. I must know the full raw truth about everything, if such a thing even exists.

My father has written entire interrogations in his notebook like a play, as if he had copied dialogues from a book of dialogues about interrogations in the time of the Communist purges in Romania. An interrogation about the plan of escape to France takes up a couple of full pages written like a one act play in the notebook.

"When did you first meet Parisot?"

"In October of last year."

"Was this meeting by chance or had it been arranged?"

"It was arranged by France."

"What was discussed at this meeting?"

"The possibility of an escape to France. It was about a clandestine departure of a certain Ghitulescu."

"Was the second meeting arranged just like the first?"

"Yes, it was."

"What was discussed on this occasion?"

"The possibility of an airplane that would take several people. Ghitulescu proposed to Parisot even the place where such an airplane could land — a place I don't know myself. He said he was going to leave with his daughters and others."

"Who others?"

"I don't know."

"What did Parisot say?"

"That it was almost impossible to find the plane, for the landing you needed special conditions which was hard to accomplish on such occasions."

"Where was the plane going to go after all the passengers were on board?"

"To Yugoslavia or to France, I'm not sure."

"And you, what did you say?"

"The same thing. I was against it."

The interrogation goes on for another page with short questions and quick answers like a ping pong game. I am intrigued by the fact that one of the people involved in the escape plan was named France. Or maybe it was a code name. I'll never know. I try to imagine my father in the situation of his arrest, in the basement cell in 1957, under the blinding lights of some interrogation lamp. Part of me is in awe at the adventure of it all, the planning of a real escape from the country by plane. My parents were recently married then, they were both planning for it and were caught, or someone in their group was caught and my father was obliquely associated with the escape plan. I wonder what my mother was doing in those days. Was she waiting for my father in a state of desperation and agitation, or was she in her usual state of distracted indifference? And of course, somebody informed on them, it was what always happened, they had a mole in the group who must have sold everybody out for a leather jacket or a pack of foreign cigarettes. Or maybe they had also been threatened with the death penalty, one Romanian threatening another with the death penalty or torturing him to death.

Those were my people. If they had been capable of burning Jews alive and hanging them on abattoirs during the pogroms, what would prevent a miserable wretch of a penniless country boy come to the city during the massive industrialization period to inform on everybody he could, his own parents included? Nothing.

After the dialogue, which seems to me like part of a playscript for a movie, comes my father's forced statement, and declaration of intent. It appears to be forced because it starts with "I, of my own volition and uncoerced by anybody." I knew that any statement in those times claiming to be "uncoerced," claimed that precisely because it was coerced. "I, of my own volition and uncoerced by anybody, assume the responsibility from now onwards, to help the Communist Party and its revolutionary causes by providing information on individuals who act against the interest of the Party and the welfare of the Popular Republic of Romania, on a regular basis." The language is wooden and clumsy. It was the language forced out of my father and which he carefully and faithfully transcribed for future generations to see, for someone in the future, for me to see. Then follows a list of names that he "assumes the responsibility" to inform on. The statement goes on: "In exchange for such services the Party has generously commuted my merited sentence of capital punishment, an action for which I will remain grateful and indebted for the rest of my life."

The entire space in which I find myself, the cellar basement room, whatever it may be called, is spinning rapidly with me in it like a carousel yanked off its hinges and gone wild. I vomit on the floor of the basement next to the mountain of manuscripts. I cry over the notebook in violent gulps. Manole yanks it out of my hands and says stop crying, your tears are making the ink of the writing run, this is an important document. I tell him I don't give a shit about the ink running and melting into a boiling furnace for all eternity. Manole tells me I'm a spoiled idiot and I don't understand what people had to go through in those days, what people had to do to survive, it was life or death, don't you get it, what would you have done, Miss Self-righteous judgmental American writer, hm? Ask yourself that question first and then judge and vomit and cry! This is not a rhetorical question and Manole actually makes me ask myself this question, he tells me go ahead and ask the question out loud, I want to hear you say it.

I cannot resist anything that Manole asks me to do so I go ahead and ask myself out loud the very question he feeds to me like: "What would I, Corina Roxana

Angelescu have done, were I to choose between being executed by the firing squad or becoming an informer for a while?" He adds the modifier "for a while" and explains that later in the sixties my father got out of the pact, he stopped providing information and made a written declaration to the Secret Police authorities that he was no longer willing to continue the repugnant activities, or he would commit suicide. In addition, Manole says, he was just pretend informing, he was giving information about trivial and unimportant activities and conversations, stalling, and never really informing on stuff that would have gotten anyone arrested or in trouble. Most likely he was being informed on about his unenthusiastic informing. Manole goes on and on, but I am no longer listening.

Scenes from my childhood and youth return to my singed memory and appear in a completely different light. Everything I had thought was one thing, now must be reinterpreted because as it turns out it was in fact another thing. The asthma attacks my father had on a regular basis when I was five and six and seven, must have been caused by the torment he must have felt from doing what most repulsed him about others. The sinister couple of secret police who barged into our apartment one summer afternoon and engaged in a fist fight with my father, which led to the breaking of the precious cobalt vase, must have happened because my father refused to go along informing on people. The mention of his friends Bogdan and Simona and the book or manuscript that my father was accused of having written or wanted to send abroad must have been connected with his denunciation of the pressure exerted on him. For all I know it could have been about this very manuscript right here under my very eyes. Somehow my father or someone else of great trustworthiness must have kept and stored this precious manuscript that there could very well also be a copy of in the center for the study of the files of the secret police. All the subsequent secrecy in our apartment, my father's continued demotions from his teaching jobs, the whispering late into the night, must have all been connected with this crucial moment in my father's life, when he accepted to collaborate with the secret police in exchange for his life and then when he stopped serving them.

The manuscript I had heard of then during the fight, and that supposedly had been taken by my parents' friends, who were going to transport it over the border on their way to crocodile hunting in their African adventure, could have been this very manuscript right here. It's just that it never made it across the border then.

This manuscript and sending it across the border, was his redemption from the years of self-hatred and disgust with the world and mostly with himself. At times he might have well wanted to be dead, to have taken the firing squad straight on instead of being a collaborator. His intensified smoking and drinking over the years were a form of slow suicide. Or not, and I will just never really know. All that I know is right here under my eyes in my father's carefully formed letters on the lined pages of a notebook.

The assassination of his Florida friend must have been directly related to this double game my father had played, probably like thousands of others who exchanged their freedom or their life for the shame of collaborating with the system they despised, precisely because they fought against that system. But then again, I'll never know for sure. Manole guesses my thoughts as always, comes over from his corner at the other end of the cellar and sits next to me on the damp floor as if he was still a young man. For all I know he could very well be an ageless ghost of the past. He says it doesn't matter, Corina, this is how it was, you can't change anything now, it's all in the past, your father was a remarkable courageous man, he just wasn't ready to be killed by an execution squad in his thirties, and that's that. Or you wouldn't be sitting here with me, if he had chosen otherwise.

I know all of this of course, but in Manole's voice it has more weight, it sounds truer than if I were to just say it to myself. And how do I know for sure that nobody got in trouble from my father's informing? You don't know, Manole answers, you must live with this and trust that what happened had to happen and there was no other way, that your father did the best he could do in atrocious times and situations. And the puzzle of all puzzles remains: how did this live bomb of a manuscript end up here in this cellar, back in my father's house with the orchards? That's a question for another day Corina, Manole says, you've read and learned enough for today. How does he know, what's enough and not enough for me? And who is this Manole character anyway?

A haunting image and a slew of queries dig and settle inside the messy chambers of my mind. I see my father inside the sinister cellar where everything changed for him. Did he think of his orchards then? Did he call for his mother, did he dream of Zoe, did he remember Lila and her forever Mitzi doll, carrier of so many secrets? A man hovering over him with a smirk and asking him something along the lines of: "What will it be Professor, the firing squad or life next to your Jewish beauty?

You choose, you can't say we are not humane and don't give you the freedom of choice." I recreate his image as I sit on the damp cellar floor of his old house. He found himself in a much more sordid cellar. In the dampness of that basement, Florin thinks of the orchards at their most glorious splendor. The orchards in the spring have always been his place of refuge, his fantasy of choice and his salvation. He is holding a greasy pen that was forced into his hand by the Securitate man and for a moment he is tempted to let it all go. Life, that is. He is tempted to let go and a delicious sense of liberation washes over him. There will be orchards on the other side too, he is sure of it. There will be blue skies, magenta skies, all the colors of skies like the flowers popping out of the tight buds, like the fruit swelling from the pastel flowers into an orgy of sweet fleshy shapes. He is a millisecond away from saying it's fine, let the firing squad come, there will be orchards, there will be skies, go ahead, I'm not afraid. He who has never been afraid, he continues to not be afraid for himself and plunges deeper into the orchard ecstasy like a thirsty swimmer plunging into the cool waves of the sea under a torrid sun.

The man with the smirk says: "What will it be professor, what will it be?" His mouth is crooked, and Florin thinks he notices a greenish spit lining up the man's mouth. Maybe he is hallucinating. The man's face changes shapes and becomes a dog's face, a snake's face, the face of the Iron Guard man who barged into their house during the war looking for Zoe and Carolina. Aren't you worried about your red-haired beauty, professor? Who knows what might happen to her in these uncertain times? The man's face becomes his father's face and for the first time he experiences terror at the sight of his own father's face. Everything has changed, everything is upside down. Sweat and tears are dripping down his face until they turn to waves, and he drowns in his own sweat and tears. Everything is possible. What if even his own father collaborated with the Nazis to save the family, what if his own sister collaborated with the Secret police to save the family? What if everybody collaborated for the sake of saving each other and everybody is tainted and broken?

The image of Zoe the way she looked at the party where he first saw her, met her, re-encountered her in the fifties, standing in a corner by the window at the party is a star in a starless night. She was wearing a red polka dot skirt that flared up and a loose silky blouse. He noticed a pair of emerald earrings sparkling from under the waves of reddish hair. He remembered that he had found one such emerald earring on the upstairs landing of their house when he and Lila were secretly watching and eavesdropping the mysterious comings and goings that went on in the middle of the night. Zoe turned her head towards him as if she had been waiting for him all that time. She smiled. Now only in this damp basement does he realize she smiled then. It was as if the sun had risen on her face and the entire world was suddenly bathed in light not because of the sun but because of Zoe's face which had become the sun. Now only when he must choose between the firing squad and the life of a collaborator, between Zoe's suffering and possibly her death at the hands of men like this one standing right here hovering above him like a bile spewing monster, does he understand fully the significance of that encounter. There is nothing he wouldn't do for her. She is the only one in the entire rotten world who is steadfast, incorruptible, always shining even in the darkest night. People like that occur only once in an era like a comet. It would be easy to let go of himself and take the firing squad full frontal. He would merge with the pastel flowers and the fleshy fruit of his childhood orchards. But it's Zoe who calls him to make this hardest of all sacrifices and he is ready to take it upon himself.

Florin, the proud and recklessly rebellious young man always with a cigarette in the corner of his mouth, lecturing with devastating charisma to adoring students under Stalinist skies, is sitting in a metal chair forced to the death of the body and the death of the soul. Which one will it be? He who has never compromised on anything. Maybe he thinks he can have both, save his body and save his soul too, through cunning. Tricking fate like some version of Sisyphus or like the forever adventurer Ulysses. He agrees, he wants to get back to Zoe and he cannot let himself die while his mother is still alive. He owes it to his two guardian angels and the beloved women in his life. He thinks of literary heroes who tricked evil enemies and got away with their lives from the most unimaginable situations, cyclops, unfathomable storms and voracious monsters, the devil himself.

He takes the pen handed to him and writes the statement dictated that yes, he will inform on "enemies of the people," he will "support the cause of the Party in its road towards the final glory of the Communist future." They are only words on a paper, he'll find a way to trick them, others have done it before him. At least he and his family had not been strangled to death or sent on the trains of death like Zoe's sister and father had been. Things can always be worse, he thinks as he writes: "I assume this task by my own volition and uncoerced by anybody." He signs the statement. Two hours later he is released into the heavy linden smelling air of Bucharest of the year 1957. I see my father walk on the wide Boulevards of a late July day with his brisk steps, his head up and dragging from the cigarette in the corner of his mouth like it was indispensable air for survival.

I realize my body is shaking as I sit on the damp cellar floor. You are channeling the spirits of your people, Corina. It is Manole speaking words of wisdom again from a dark corner of this lugubrious space in the bowels of the famous house. It strikes me that Manole must be a hundred years old, or more, how is he still alive? How could he be my grandfather's brother and still be alive? I try to make all sorts of calculations in my mind trying to figure out what Manole's age must be, even if he was ten or twenty years younger than his brother Tudor, how could he be alive if he was a young man or a teenager during the Bolshevik revolution? Someone must be lying in this whole story of ransomed lives and of lives on the run from ferocious deeds. Maybe Manole is not the Manole of the letter to Tudor asking for help in the hell of Jewish purges combined with communist purges in Russia at the tail end of World War I.

And if anybody is lying it must be Manole right here guiding me through all this madness. He must think of himself as God of the Past of the Angelescu family at 18bis, holding all the keys to that formidable Past worthy of historical novels and avant-garde films. Let it be, Corina, years and age don't really matter, he says again, as if he had heard my thoughts, or as if my thoughts were being uttered out loud without me even realizing it. I feel immensely exhausted like I have myself lived a hundred years. I am seized by a deep longing for my home over there, a longing for my two children and my house in the American Northeast, because that is where I live now, in a beautiful home facing the Adirondack Mountains that are splendidly raw in the light of the sunset. Only in the earth of the Adirondack Mountains are buried Indians of variegated tribes and pilgrims and adventurers of a hundred countries and nationalities. My life is over there where everybody that I love lives.

Maybe I too fell into the valley of tears like the young man in the famous Romanian fairy tale, only in reverse way or even twice. I returned to my native country and my father's native town, house, and orchard, thinking I was going to find secrets and stories that would set me free but instead I am more and more trapped in the coils of a past that keeps opening into more secrets than I could have ever imagined. One secret door leading into another and then another, an endless tunnel of intertwined destinies and the people that lived them. First, I must have fallen into the valley of tears as I got struck with insufferable longing for my native earth. Then somewhere during the days spent here I must have stepped again in another valley of tears and got struck by the burning of a second yearning, for the places I had run away to thirty years earlier. I'm doing a slalom kind of race from one valley of tears to another with expanses of "life without death" territories in between.

Until you have things straight and complete with all the people and happenings here in this place, Corina, your life over there will never be fully real, says Manole suddenly as I am trying to order my thoughts. I don't know what "fully real" means anymore, how can Manole talk about real and "fully real" as if there were degrees of reality? I hold my father's manuscript to my chest, then I leaf through it again as if saying goodbye to it, as if this manuscript was itself a living creature, and from it falls a blue silk sash. It is thinned out and its color faded by time, but the softness of the silk is remarkable, like no other item of silk clothing or accessory I have ever touched in my life. I hold it and caress it greedily. Maybe this sash is the answer to all my desperate queries, to my voracious curiosity, to my endless desire to know what happened in those times and how it happened and why.

A door opens in the cellar, in a place of the cellar I had no idea there was a door. A shimmering figure in yellowish whites gracefully dances her way to the place where I am sitting next to the mound of papers, holding my father's notebook in one hand and the blue silk sash in the other. She exudes a fragrance of times gone by, of silk dresses and feathered hats soaked in lavender and mothballs from winter months. She whispers words that are also a lullaby. Finally, Corina you found the blue sash, I've been looking for it for ages, you keep it as proof, you hear me, it's important proof of what happened that day. She stops so close to me I could touch her. I try to touch her, and she melts into the damp air with no sound, like she never existed. I am pretty sure she was right here, that she expressed relief for the fact I found the famous blue sash, proof of some awful deed in some secret chamber of this house where two girls were once hidden from the Nazis and only one came out alive.

Manole reappears in the shadow, in a corner of the cellar. In a plaintive voice he says Corina, Corina, do you see how empty and painful it all is, how unbearable and unresolved, everybody rambling here in a state of perpetual restlessness, only your mother can bring it to a stop so we can all rest. She holds the key. I am struck by Manole's use of the pronoun "we" this time, for the first time, instead of "them" which is what he has been using all along. It is the first time I have heard anything about a key. It must be a metaphorical key, like the key to understanding, the key to the secrets of family stories. I feel heavy and out of place, in the margins of knowledge and understanding, trapped in perpetual ignorance like the dead who are trapped in perpetual disquiet. I run out of the cellar, hungry for the daylight.

Zoe's Return
July 2015

During the week following my voyage through the mountain of manuscripts in the cellar within a cellar of my father's old house, I call my mother daily, sometimes twice a day, begging her to please join me in Northern Moldavia, to the town of my father's birth and childhood. And isn't it your town also, mother? I ask her during the conversations, as I have never really known where my mother is really from. The story always changes. She is from this one town in the North, not really from my father's town but nearby. Oh no, she is from a city in Transylvania, much farther, but still up north. Everything that is clear cut with most people, such as place of birth, dates of birth and childhood, is vague and ambiguous with my mother and it changes continuously as if she was many people in one. As if she came from another planet. Like the photo of her as a tiny toddler on an empty street in an unknown location. It could have been another country, another planet indeed.

My mother won't hear of the journey down here. She once told herself she would never return to this country when she left more than thirty years ago, and she has kept her promise. As for returning to this area, that was sealed and decided more than half a century ago, she would never return. Why would she break these promises now? I try different methods of convincing her, by logic, by emotional blackmail about how desperate and confused I am amid all the tumultuous information and unearthed lives. Nothing works, she just says I told you not to go, why did you put yourself through that, you should have just stayed in your home and worked on your books and spent time with your children who miss you. She turns the guilt card right back in my face, we are masters of that in our family. I even bluff and say mama what if I'm not coming back, and she bluffs right back at me and says then don't, and what's going to happen to your children? She has a point of course, even though they are grown children she knows I'd never put so many thousand miles and an ocean between us for longer than a couple of months. Besides I'd never just stay here in this godforsaken corner of Northern Romania populated by the most ungodly creatures and leave the life I built over there and my two beautiful sons who love me more than plums and whom I love more than all the fruit of the world. But I know we are all stuck in this labyrinth for now. We are entangled in the knot of our family story, and nothing will move forward for us if we don't disentangle it, make peace with all the dead and the undead, understand and accept even the most incomprehensible of deeds that took place here, in this house and in this orchard.

When I mention the manuscripts, particularly the last two ones about my father's journey to the bottom of communist hell and the blue sash that fell out of it, I feel my mother's resistance melt. Two histories of terror, two slivers of memory, one enfolding the other: the thinned out feathery sash folded inside the severe lined notebook, a stubborn embrace across histories of wars and regime changes. From the magnitude of the puzzle in the form of thousands of pages of record taking, diary writing, storytelling and memoirs, kept in the cellar inside the cellar of a basement guarded by Manole the ageless man like a Cerberus at the gates of hell, I emerge empty and blank like an unwritten page. I must rewrite everything in the book that I thought was my life, my past and myself and emerge as someone else but also the same, the true Corina Roxana Angelescu.

I emerge as a daughter of survivors of two compounded horrors of history, descendant of fugitives from pogroms and concentration camps, death sentences and forced betrayals, trains of death and revolutionary massacres. Not to mention related to unearthly presences, undead individuals who have been rambling among fruit trees for decades, in haggard or frothy shapes, searching fiercely for the eternal peace of death. I had never imagined that death could be such a sought-after thing, such a desired destination. During one of the conversations with my mother, I remember Manole's mention of some key, and I mention it in passing. That it is only this key that can open the last of the mystery boxes. I make up the words "mystery box" because I don't really know what it is that it opens. But that is when my mother finally decides to get on a plane and take the journey back to the realm of her origins and undead relatives.

I return to the inn where I have been staying for a couple of endless weeks and get ready to travel to the city up north by the airport. It is also the city that was once soaked in the blood of pogroms, whose actual meaning I discovered while a doctoral student at the American university where I studied in the nineties. Those streets carry many of the names of the very authors of such bloody events, apparently considered heroes by the twisted conscience of the people I come from. All the rest of the world has long ago torn down names and effigies of fascism from public spaces, yet my people proudly display such effigies and names with pride, for the whole world to see. After having absorbed the accounts of the unlikely lives and afterlives of the people in my family dating all the way back to the bloody Bolshevik revolution and the compounded misery of the two wars, I feel more distant and revulsed than ever towards my own people and the country I come from. No wonder my mother never wanted to return, now I get it. But what to do with all the shreds of bloody histories and unfinished lives that roam around this part of the world and that for all we know are disrupting cosmic order as well as our own lives and nights? Maybe that's the reason why my mother has been suffering from insomnia for decades, maybe that's the reason I have been torn with inexplicable longings and anxieties for years. Our psyches are torn to shreds by the fidgeting of the dead. By buried stories that need to be brought to light so that our undead relatives can reach the soothing darkness of eternal sleep. The insomnias of the dead are our ordeal.

I return to the house at 18bis because I want to see Manole before picking up my mother from the airport in a day. I find Manole sitting on the bench in the back yard under the crown of the cherry tree that fed me its divine cherries a few weeks ago on my arrival. Lulu is kicking a ball against the back wall of the house and wearing his I love New York T-shirt. It all looks the same as several weeks ago, at the time of the Sanziene festivals when I first arrived here eager to delve into the stories of my father's past and his famous orchards. Time slips from under my conscience again and I am no longer sure whether any time has passed since then, whether I am arriving here for the first time and whether everything I have experienced so far hasn't just been a weird dream. There is a swaying of the trees and all their branches without the presence of any wind.

Manole looks up at me and greets me warmly like he is happy to see me or like he sees me for the first time. They are here again, working inside, is all he says. I have no idea what he is talking about and given the events of the past weeks it could be anyone visiting, a family member from a century ago, a former Securitate member gone rogue and become "good" neighbor, a former Nazi soldier turned humane, or a former Romanian soldier turned rabid murderer. The film people, they've returned for the filming, they must have heard your mother is coming. I have no idea how some obscure filmmakers with pretenses of avant-garde artists might have heard of my mother's arrival in a day, and why they should care. But at least now that Manole talks to me in a way that illustrates some contiguity in events and lines of memory, I am reassured that everything that has happened has indeed taken place in time and space and that I have been here before many times talking to Manole, watching Lulu kick his ball against the back of the house, acquiring knowledge of my family's history and the beings that populate it.

Of course, I remember the film people, I tell Manole, why would it matter for them if my mother is coming here or not, what do they really know of all this Manole? I ask insistently. And as usual Manole answers calmly and cryptically, oh they know plenty, just you wait and see. And I say proud of my biting irony Oh, I can't wait to see what's next in this film of my family's life, maybe the spirits of General Antonescu or Stalin himself are going to show up any minute now dancing the tango with each other. Don't joke with things like that Corina, Manole admonishes. Alright, far be it from me to joke around right now, on the eve of my mother's return to the house where some horrible deeds of some seventy years ago propelled her to the very other end of the world and where a team of so-called movie makers play with simulacra of my family's histories. The movie director comes out of the house for a minute to smoke a cigarette and greets me enthusiastically as if we are buddies and have some complicity with each other. I don't greet him back but instead turn around and leave the yard in a huff and decide on the spot to return to the inn where I'm staying in the hope of some much-needed clarity of mind and thought.

Clarity never occurs. I decide to walk around town to know it better and realize I haven't yet done that at all since my arrival. Everywhere I go people stare at me like I am an apparition from another planet. I feel their stares burn the back of my neck and whenever I turn around, I catch people moving their heads quickly pretending to mind their business, tending to their garden, sweeping the front steps of their shops, or sitting at a table in the one café in town. There seems to be a sustained and continuous whispering moving through the streets, that follows me everywhere I go. People must know things I never will about all that went on long ago in this idyllic nook of the country with its sweet rolling hills and resplendent orchards. The family at number 18, the one in the wrong house, must have spread news all over the entire town, of my being an American spy on the prowl for stories of the past, but mostly greedy for properties and orchards. Since the government created the law of "retrocedare," returning properties to former owners whose properties had been confiscated by the Communist authorities, new owners of old houses were jittery about the arrival of an old owner asking for their former houses, lands, apartments back. These people staring at me in my passage through town must all think I have returned to claim my father's ancestral house. Let them, it might even be true.

My mother arrives tomorrow and most likely the second she sets foot in this curious town that was once swept by every imaginable human and natural catastrophe she'll feel everyone's stares and whispered gossiping behind her back and will want to disappear at the speed of light and never return for an entire geological era. But I should not make any presumptions yet about anything regarding my mother. On my way back to the inn, it occurs to me that my father's other worldly existence seems to be settled forever although he is at the center of everything, and I have only recently unearthed important portions of his life story. No traces of him have materialized in any apparitions or presences of the kind I have had the pleasure to cavort with for the past month. Nor have Grandmother Victoria or Grandfather Tudor. These are the solidly dead in my family. The peacefully dead forever in my family. Good for them. My father is buried in the earth of that "over there," a standard ugly cemetery of the kind he hated, his remains held in the Adirondack mountains in America. My grandparents are buried right here in the earth of their orchards. Lila is in the Bucharest cemetery in the company of uncles and aunts on Victoria's side. Children and parents are spread across different corners of the world and separated from each other in their otherworldly existence. These most immediate family members are spared the ordeal of perpetual wandering in the spaces of the living. I don't get any of the rules of otherworldly travel if there are any. But despite the torments of their lives on earth, my father, his sister, and their parents must have found the cocoon of eternal slumber. They have fit in the perfect groove of deadness. As I return to my inn under the inquisitive looks of the townspeople, I experience profound joy at this thought and return a wide smile towards the town, like a vengeance.

My mother appears in the small provincial airport sharply dressed in white pants and a navy-blue blazer, moving briskly through the crowd of travelers, and looking straight ahead with clear intent. When our eyes lock gazes, she smiles her irresistible smile that brightens her deep green eyes while my eyes bubble with tears. For a moment I think of all the separations and encounters at train stations and airports that our family has experienced over the decades, and they are in the hundreds. I feel dizzy at the thought, as if a wind of goodbyes and hellos sweeps over me with the force of a storm. Before I know it though, my mother is next to me, and we embrace like it has been ages since she dropped me off at Kennedy airport in June. It feels like ages indeed and her small body feels fragile and brittle as I hold it in the crowded provincial airport. Before there were trains, now it's airports, I hear her say softly. I remember the picture of her in the white ruffled dress on an empty street next to a house sitting crookedly behind her. How many ferocious histories, partings, separations, a few reunions, and more partings have swept through her life and weighed on her petite frame?

I burst into tears as I hold my mother, and a profound sense of recognition and familiarity I had been yearning for ever since I was a tiny toddler in our Bucharest apartment, washes over me. As if I have finally found my mother, my true mother, Zoe whose childhood and adolescence were sliced by war, escapes, living in hiding, unbearable losses, then more escapes and resettlements. Zoe, who mysteriously appeared at the party where my father was invited one evening in the Transylvanian city where he taught, wearing a red polka dot skirt and a white blouse, who my father married on a May Day in the terrifying fifties in the city where I was born. As if finally the two women, Zoe of those times and my mother who always burnt our dinners in the minuscule kitchen of our apartment, who smoked absent mindedly as secret police thugs ravaged through our apartment, or who carefully prepared me for school in the morning pursing her lips as she straightened my uniform collar or as she watched me gulp hot cocoa for breakfast, had finally merged into one and the same person. It took that long.

I wipe away my tears as I know my mother dislikes sentimental moments and guide her towards the airport exit through the throngs of Romanians recently arrived from their vacations abroad or Western tourists who decided to take a tour of vampire and Dracula country on their summer vacations, avid for "exotic" sights and experiences in these backwoods of Eastern Europe. We take a taxi from the row of taxis waiting at the airport exit and ride in silence for a while. I notice she doesn't look out the car windows at the city we are crossing or at the rural landscape of rolling hills once we leave the city on our way to my father's mythic birth town. She stares straight ahead of her, unmoving, like a statue. At some point she closes her eyes, and I think she has fallen asleep after the long flights, layovers, and more flights as she has travelled all the way from New York City to Paris, from Paris to Bucharest, and from Bucharest to this remote corner in the north of our blessed native country. But she isn't sleeping, she opens her eyes wide and stares at me as if seeing me for the first time.

"It has been seventy years. Seventy years and some," she says abruptly and closes her eyes again like she doesn't want to remember or recognize anything around her. I take her hand and hold it for the rest of the trip. It is sweaty like I have never felt my mother's hand. My mother's hand is crying all the tears that her eyes do not. When we arrive at the inn she also refuses to look around with any curiosity or recognition. I take her through the back entrance so that she doesn't have to greet and talk to the talkative and curious inn keeper, a plump woman in her sixties who crosses herself every two words she utters. We sleep in the same bed that night and she cries in her sleep, most likely from an onslaught of nightmares just like she used to when I was an anxious child sharing a bed with her in our tiny Bucharest apartment.

The next day my mother is up way before me. She is drinking coffee that she must have made in the coffee maker in the room and staring out the window. She is wearing a simple but nicely tailored beige dress with tiny black polka dots. The bright sun of this early July day floods her face and makes it appear almost circled in a halo. I want to tell her everything and ask her about everything but am worried that words might break the balance and lightness of this moment in the morning sun. Unlike so many of the moments and episodes I have lived so far in this town, which contained more than just a twinge of unreality and often felt downright fantastical, this moment right here keeps me motionless and transfixed by its striking concreteness. It feels deliciously and overwhelmingly real, warm, plump, brilliant. This is going to be the day, I tell myself. The day when all secrets will be revealed and the lives fidgeting throughout thousands of manuscript pages will come to rest, when all the restless presences roaming around will find peace and we can return to our homes in America and live happily ever after.

My mother turns around and looks at me with a limpid look and says all right, let's get this thing over with. I startle from my shortly lived indulgence in the sweet reality of the moment and ask her what it is that she wants to get over with. She answers everything, this whole rotten story of our lives, let's go. I am startled out of my wits as I have never in my life heard my mother speak with such determination and bitterness combined. My mother is a never-ending carousel of personalities, foolish me to think I had gotten to the essence of the woman in the sentimental millisecond when I held her in my arms at the airport. I don't know what to say. I mumble a string of incoherent sentences about a box of manuscripts and people buried in the back yard of my father's old house and weird stuff going on around the house and this old man Manole and his grandson Lulu and my mother tells me to stop talking, let's just go, alright!

We walk through the town to the house at 18bis with my mother looking straight ahead of her like a woman on a mission. The townspeople stare at us two red haired women in our Western clothes and shoes walking briskly to our mythic destination of the house with the orchards. I have no idea what's ahead and what we will find at the house, but as we get closer, I am filled with trepidation and anxiety about what may occur once we get there. Will Manole be waiting for us with his toothless smile and Lulu kicking his ball against the back of the house? Will there be doomsday storms and undead beings roaming around in period dresses and blue parasols, what? And how about the orchards, will they be swaying gently in the summer breeze dropping delicious plump fruit to the ground, or will they be shaking in some ungodly wind and whispering about the dead buried at their roots? My mother doesn't seem to care a bit, she just keeps a steady pace, entirely unconcerned about any of that, except to get something over with.

When we get to the house at 18bis there is music, people milling around in the back yard, and a film crew unpacking equipment and setting up as if ready to shoot a scene. The trees in the patch of orchard are quiet, expectant, not a leaf budging. The music is scratchy, resembling a record playing on an old turntable and the needle getting stuck on the 30's song Tango della gelosia. There is a strange alacrity in the air, people are quivering with excitement, the women are wearing chiffon dresses in the style of the ones I found in the wardrobe with the box of manuscripts, in the cellar within the cellar of the house. They look like oversized flowers waiting to be picked, their beauty appears contrived and overdone, a colorful simulacrum. Some couples are dancing the tango to the music, most likely rehearsing for the scene to come. I am becoming more anxious that my mother will just wish to turn around to the inn and then to the airport and all the way back to her studio apartment in New York where she always claimed to feel more at home than anywhere else in the world.

Instead, she walks around the place like visiting a museum, with interest, even curiosity. I see the director whom I met on my first visit to the house when he was shooting a scene with fake plums and women like statues in a museum sitting around the table with labels on their chests. He is walking out of the house and when he sees my mother, he comes right over to greet us like an old acquaintance. This reality feels more unreal than the gallery of restless spirits and smokey presences gliding around the property at dusk ever felt. How could my mother be at ease in such a simulacrum world and on top of everything be acquainted with the director of this pretense of an avant-garde film? I am restlessly looking around for Manole in the hope he will save me from the unease and burden of dealing with the unwelcome film crew and their pompous director. I miss his wisdom and dry irony and realize I have become accustomed to and fond of him like a father figure friend, and something else I can't explain. Someone like a necessary and caring guide showing me the way through the underworld of my family. But he is nowhere in sight, nor is Lulu, wearing his I♥New York T shirt and kicking his soccer ball against the back wall of the house, or feeding me divine plums. The landscape feels arid to me despite the luscious costumes and sentimental thirties tango music.

I stand baffled against one of the majestic cherry trees carrying the last remainders of the years' fruit production, when I hear my mother calling the film director Sebi, the diminutive from Sebastian, and I see them hugging like old friends. He is a short man in his sixties with a dark beard and receding hairline, who gesticulates a lot so that he almost gives the impression of being taller and bigger than he is. I hear him say how nice to see you Zoe, after all these years! The expression "after all these years" sounds artificial and out of place. I don't understand which years, why is it nice that he sees my mother after many years, and how many years exactly? I am falling into another trap puzzle, another rabbit hole, gliding through a watery mirror of a past I cannot comprehend.

Secrets Revealed
July 4th, 2015. Northern Moldavia

The day of the filming, behind my father's old house, my mother takes me and Sebi the film director to a room where nobody knew there was a room. We stand in front of the tiny door that looks like the door to a children's room, and I see my mother search under her polka dot dress and pull out a silver necklace with a locket hanging on it. She opens the locket by turning it a few times like dialing a code. She opens the locket and inside is a tiny key like no other key I have ever seen. It is round and thick almost like a tiny tube with a double set of key teeth. With it she opens the secret room. In the movement of my mother taking off the silver necklace the image of Grandmother Frida making the same gesture on her death bed and putting the necklace around my mother's neck lights up in me with a dizzying force. I try my hardest to excavate through my memory and remember more. I can't remember anything except for these two related movements. I know there must be something else.

I have a vague sensation like a bit of knowledge that is buried deep inside your brain, and you can't get to it. The bit of knowledge blinks in my brain to tell me that the Mitzi doll is also involved in this complicated key operation. The Mitzi doll has been present forever in this labyrinthine story like a traveling metaphor, only entirely concrete. She has carried Lila's scribbled notes that recorded the family's stories day in and day out throughout the war years and maybe past that until one day when she landed inside the sofa box in our Bucharest apartment. And she could have carried this very mysterious key right here. At some point in my life, I also witnessed the hiding of this necklace and key inside the Mitzi doll only I can't reach that memory. I am jolted out of my brain excavation by my mother's nudge and her saying what are you waiting for, go in, it's all in here. I have no idea what is supposed to be in here.

It is a corner room with no windows, or whose windows have been walled in, and from the inside of the house appears like a closet, or an insignificant efficiency. But once you enter it, the secret room is relatively spacious, triangular, so it fits snugly in the corner of the house. It is a room like no other I have ever seen. It once was the Angelescu family's secret hiding space for refugees, fugitives, deserters on the run from either the German or Russian armies, or both. But mostly on the run from the SS and Iron Guard men between the years of 1940 to 1944. It had been built by Grandfather Tudor when he returned from Russia, shortly after the Bolshevik Revolution, I suppose as a premonition of when it would serve a purpose, mostly that of hiding people on the run from armies, government officials, regimes, genocidal groups, who knows? It smells of burnt church incense. The air is stuffy though not overly hot like the rest of the house, it keeps a relative coolness and has an almost cozy feel to it.

My mother moves around the room at ease as if she knew it like the back of her hand. Which most likely she does as it turns out it is the very room where her sister Carolina and herself had been hidden for months in 1941 during the worst of the Jewish pogroms. Her sister disappeared on June 22nd of 1941. Literally disappeared. My mother is relating the events as if guiding us through a museum, coldly and unaffected. Until she goes to the corner of the corner room, taps on it as if knocking to check if anyone is inside, then leans over and pulls a tiny string that sticks out on the floor like a lost object. When she does this, a tiny door opens into a secret space the size of a small wardrobe.

It was here we stayed for months, Carolina and I, she says as if it was not a big deal. Sebi who by now feels like part of the family, and maybe he is, has stopped gesticulating and stands still listening to my mother without as much as a sigh or a syllable uttered. I peek inside and the space is all upholstered in red velvet; there are two Turkish cushions on the floor as if for decoration. It's hard to imagine that one person could fit and stay in there for any amount of time, let alone two people. Without saying another word, my mother goes inside the space and pulls the door from the inside so that again it all becomes flush with the rest of the room and the walls enclosing it. Sebi and I stand in the middle of the corner room looking puzzled with no idea how to react or what to say. There is nothing to say. My mother is providing us with a full reenactment of what went on in the months of her and her sister's hiding and we are the spectators. Maybe this is done for Sebi's benefit so he can use it as material for his film, maybe it's done for my sake to finally let me know how it all started, how the journey of my mother's life through the atrocities of history started. Or maybe it's all for her own benefit, so she can put it to rest and bury it forever.

There are so many people milling around in the story book of my family, most of whom I had no idea even existed. It feels like being part of a large ensemble play in which you get cast overnight and you have no idea what your lines are or what the lines uttered by your fellow actors are all about. Like the man Sebi, the director of a film project that seems to have been going on for several weeks and whose plot is all derived from the histories concerning my parents and their extended families on each side. It seems unreal that my mother would know this man from anywhere and yet she does. We wait in the small room in a state of frozen embarrassment for endless minutes. We are afraid to move because in the hollowness of the empty room, every move, word or creaking of the floor resonates with an uncomfortable ring, like a warning. It's as if my mother had disappeared inside the wall.

I remember a story by a nineteenth century French writer titled *Passe-Muraille*, or "the man who passes through walls," which tells the story of a man who possessed the unusual ability to melt through walls and pass onto the other side smoothly. Until one day he didn't, and he remained stuck in an enclosure of sorts forever. And his body rotted in there. So much for his passing through walls ability. I don't think my mother could pass through walls, but it feels like she just did. No sounds come from the secret room where she has walked in.

When my mother reappears from the hiding space she looks like a different person. Not changed or transformed. Different. She looks younger and her face has a strange fixity to it. Her eyes seem to bulge and are strangely shiny though not tearful. And she is holding a box she didn't have when she went in. She places the box gently in the corner of this undisclosed corner room and leaves it there. Her manner is freer, more animated. Something in her body has unlocked, which seems strange to me because I always knew my mother as a guarded person with small and restrained gestures. There is a mismatch between the looseness of her movements and the fixity of her look. She says let's leave this room, let's go outside and sit in the sun. She has never been a person to command action for others either, except for small commands about my duties, homework, and behavior when I was a child and teenage girl in Romania. And even then, it had always been with a level of distraction, as if she didn't care either way, whether you obeyed her or not. But now it's different and something in her voice says you have no choice

My Father's Orchards

but to obey her. Sebi and I follow her to the orchard, and both stand next to her under the arch of a plum tree whose fruit is still green, in the process of ripening. She leans against the tree trunk in a way in which she becomes one body with the tree, stretching her arms behind her around the circumference like a reverse embrace.

It was June 21st of 1941, the day of the summer solstice. As my mother starts to tell the story in a most nonchalant manner, I am struck that she refers to June 21st as the infamous day and not June 22nd. I don't interrupt her of course. But she must know already there is a discrepancy of one day. Which day was it? There were 14 hours and ten minutes of light she notes unexpectedly, in passing, like an important afterthought. Then she proceeds to tell us that the sun stood still for three days, and the length of daylight varied only by a few seconds between June 20th and June 23rd. Yes, she knows that's what happens during the summer solstice but that was not an ordinary summer solstice, and the sun literally stood still.

It was daylight for three days because of the bombs. And because of the sun not moving. American and Russian bombs fell over the region day and night. SS soldiers and Romanian Iron Guard men in green shirts ... Whole families with their children, sometimes massacred ... or sent on trains ... or burnt in public squares "as an example." The quick deaths were better than the trains ... Frida and Gabi had the foresight to leave us with the Angelescus knowing we would be safe with them, and that Tudor and Victoria would rather die than give us away.

Tudor had known all along it was going to come to that. He and his much younger brothers, Gabi and Manole and the sisters Frida and Sofia had already escaped the Russian pogroms that followed the Bolshevik Revolution. Russian peasantry rose against Jewish populations soon after the 1917 Revolution considering them the main culprits for the advent of Communism and massacred thousands across their formidable motherland, including Frida's parents, and the parents of the three brothers. They were all butchered inside their houses, by a group of peasants that called themselves Haidamaks, with bayonets, axes, and daggers. The children were in school and returned home to find their parents' massacred bodies in the front rooms of their houses.

The two families had been neighbors ever since they settled in that region, and they were like one big family living in a modest province of Kiev where they ran a printing shop jointly. The Haidamaks destroyed the printing press, crushed every bit of equipment, burnt all the books, and wrote on the walls in the blood of their victims, slogans such as "Jews are Bolsheviks. We will not be ruled by Juda's children. Death to the traitors!" A neighbor who was not a Jew and witnessed the massacre from his house but did not share the sentiments of the Haidamak peasantry hid the youngsters in his house for a brief period until Tudor arrived from Greece where he was studying at the seminary on Mount Athos. He helped all of them escape with false identifications.

My mother stops, changes position, and lets go of the tree. She is now walking slowly among the trees, like in a trance. She is reaching out to the farthest and most odious points in her own and her family's past. Which is my heritage, I realize. Something to tell my children back in "that" America as Manole once called it. And the past responds to her and tells itself, an enormous live creature channeled through my mother's frail body and voice. It becomes a fairy tale with gruesome happenings and some good deeds sprinkled in between. The trees rustle and moan, the air feels heavy with fruit fragrances mixed with the metallic odor of blood. The same blood that circulates through my veins, that was spilled on this earth right here under my feet.

I find out with great surprise that Frida's and Gabi's parents were from the town of Czernowitz, in Bessarabia. At the turn of the century their families had settled in Ukraine when Gabi went to study at the University of Moscow. Theirs had been families of travelers, nomads, and book makers. When one left, the whole family moved together. The places they exiled themselves, however, soon became worse than the ones they had run away from. In 1918 and 1919 Romania was better off than Russia and their earlier move had turned out to be a fatal error. That part of the world was all aflame, ravaged by war, revolutions, counter revolutions, camps, massacres motivated by ideologies of the left and of the right. People lived with their suitcases packed by their beds, then they picked up their belongings and fled again, ran across muddy fields covered in rotting corpses, got on trains without even asking for their destinations, settled for a while in makeshift habitations then ran again somewhere they imagined there would be peace and clean water. Bread was too much to ask for. Some even managed to pack a few photographs as proof that they had also lived lives that were not on the road with some semblance of homes.

The years between the two wars had been a respite for Gabi and Frida, their only happy years. They got married and moved to Northern Moldavia where they had heard life was easier and more abundant and Jews were accepted and even embraced in some communities. Frida found work as an actress and was hired by the local theater. Her talent, ethereal presence and flaming red hair shimmered on the small stage and drew many audiences whether she played in Romanian plays or in Chekhov or Pirandello plays. Gabi found work as a math teacher in the local gymnasium for boys. They had girls who looked like miniature versions of Frida and always caused a sensation in public due to their striking appearance and similarity. People always called them by the other's name or stood perplexed when they saw two of the same versions of pale red haired green eyed tiny girls in pastel dresses appear at a street corner or on a park alley like an apparition from a story book.

The three Abramovic brothers were now together for the first time since their childhood though they never revealed their kinship for fear of drawing curiosity about their Russian past. They treated each other like friends in the community and had occasional get togethers in Tudor's house. Manole taught literature at the local high-school and Florin was his favorite student with his sentimental and intense manner and flowery compositions. Florin had no idea his favorite teacher was also his uncle but looked up to him and his admiration only grew during the war years when he remained among the handful of teachers to not be swayed by the wave of fervent nationalism. The only person in the group who lived farther north and had very little contact with the brothers and with her own sister was Sofia Marcela. She had a mysterious past and liked the big city life where she had arrived during the twenties as a single mother of a five-year old boy named Kosmin.

In the summer of 1941, the Iron Guard men went rogue and killed women and children with impunity drawing even the General's admonishment not for any particularly humanitarian reasons, but because they created chaos. The Germans killed orderly and methodically, but the Romanian fascists had no method and killed "barbarically." That, the general could not tolerate, it did not look good for Hitler. On June 22nd, a group of the green shirts ravaged Sofia's neighborhood and killed her husband and one of her sons. She and her younger son Sebastian were hiding in the basement of the shop when the brothers Gabi, Tudor and

Manole came to save them on the night of the 22nd. Or the early morning of the 23rd of June, the exact dates remain still confused.

On the train ride to the Angelescu's provincial town Sofia prayed for her own death. At one point, waking up from her pained slumber, she attempted to jump out of the train. Had it not been for Gabi and Manole who held her, she would have been crushed by the train coming from the opposite direction — a Romanian Anna Karenina. Their late arrival in the house at number 18bis was watched by Florin and Lila with curious eyes and ears from the upstairs landing of the house with Lila of course recounting every move to her beloved Mitzi doll who was the witness of every single tragedy and apocalypse in their house. By the time they left at dawn and took the train to the Black Sea area with false identifications procured by Tudor, Sofia attempted two more suicides, one with Victoria's kitchen knife and one with rat poison. It was Victoria who saved her each time. After she forced an antidote down Sofia's throat and made her vomit every bit of liquid she held in her stomach, Victoria held Sofia for a long time in the kitchen and the two women cried in each other's arms over the never-ending string of calamities befalling their families from all sides.

In the chaos of her escape journey Sofia ran into a Turkish and Romanian Gypsy group on a wild beach only a couple of kilometers from the railway station on one side and the war ships on the other. From above it rained with bombs. There, on the white sands washed by the petulant sea, the colorful group formed an oasis for runaways from the pogroms and a point of passage towards the less dangerous areas in Transylvania. They welcomed Sofia's offer to join them in their efforts to save as many fugitives as they could from the ferocious extermination that was sweeping the country. Sofia remembered a similar time of massacres and the spectacle of their parents butchered in their own house at the end of the previous war by the rabid peasant group with a name like a raging tank.

There had also been a younger sister by the name of Ester. She was murdered the day of her parents' massacre by the counter revolutionary peasant group called Haidamaks. She was not yet in school. Sofia remembered Ester's disfigured face and massacred body holding a doll, lying at the entrance. A neighbor hid Sofia, Frida, Gabi and Manole for several days, maybe many days, she couldn't remember how many. Then Tudor came from Greece and in one of his miraculous moves, managed to get all of them out of the country. They traveled by train for interminable days. It seemed endless. Their whole life was going to be a ride on crowded stinking trains. Frida recited lines from a Chekhov play and was cheerful despite everything. Now they were running again from equally heinous groups, in an equally gruesome war. Maybe worse, and it was just starting.

When Frida met Sofia at the beach amid the Romanian and Turkish Gypsies, she was unrecognizable from the voluptuous blue-eyed beauty she had once been. She had cut off her wavy reddish hair, was emaciated and a ghost of her older self. Frida used to tell her sister she should have been the actress in the family, you are the beautiful one, I'm just the whimsical one, she would say. Traveling for endless hours on trains, her heart bleeding from the loss of her husband and daughters, Frida lost her sense of time, of herself and the world around her. When she arrived at the beach, she walked nonchalantly into the sea with clothes and luggage wishing for nothing more but to sleep forever at the bottom of that sea. She did not recognize her sister who kept repeating that her name was Sofia Marcela Kunovicis hoping her shell-shocked sister would regain her full senses. Both sisters had lost a beloved husband and a child at that point. It was a miracle they could even stand, talk, or go about any simple actions throughout the day. Unlike Sofia, who had her son Sebastian near her, Frida still hadn't found her one remaining daughter, Zoe. She had no idea what had happened to her other daughter, though she suspected it and felt her absence deep in her flesh.

Only three days earlier the two sisters Zoe and Carolina were still alive hiding in their secret chamber in Tudor and Victoria's house. The story gets told backwards to clarify the dates. The confusion of days is harrowing. It turns out the date for the Sanziene celebration is June 24th and not 22nd. And the summer solstice that year was June 21st and not the 22nd, which was written in one of the many manuscripts hidden in the cellar. People around the globe had just started to consider the days of solstice and equinox as calendar markers. Some newspapers of the time stated the sun stood still between June 21st and 24th. For Frida, Gabi and Sofia, the sun and the planets, the crackling of time in its passage — it all stood still and was caught in a sinister glow like that of a cosmic floodlight.

On the day of the summer solstice in 1941, on June 21st Carolina and Zoe were hidden in the secret room but not in the tiny compartment in the secret room, where they only went whenever they heard the sirens or when Uncle Tudor gave them a sign to hide because of raids and round ups by SS soldiers and the

Iron Guard. That day they didn't hear anything until it was too late. When they heard loud steps on the stairs the girls moved towards their hiding place. Only Zoe made it inside, while Carolina lagged by a second, just like she had at birth, when she surprised everybody with her appearance a couple of minutes after Zoe's birth. Two Green Shirts and an SS soldier barged into the room and grabbed Carolina. The Romanian Iron Guard men first violated her, and the SS soldier strangled her with the blue silk sash that had fallen from Zoe's dress. They divided their labor, some raped, others killed. Some did both. Zoe watched the scene from a crack in the wall of their hiding space and when they were gone, she rushed to her sister trying to resuscitate her, but her body was limp. She breathed into her mouth with the full force of every molecule in her being until she fainted over her sister's body.

Around the same time the air raids started, and bombs were dropping like hail. The house next to the Angelescu's was hit by a bomb and crumbled to the ground with the people in it. When Zoe came to, Tudor was carrying her wrapped in a blanket. He rushed with her to the train station, where he put her in the care of a young man from the resistance. Tudor placed her in his arms on the steps of the train, seconds before the train took off, like a precious package. The man who took the package that was Zoe, was the same brooding young man who two days later would appear in the train compartment when Frida was running away under the name of Irina Angelescu. Ferocious separations were written in our family's history: twin sisters torn apart, children and parents torn apart, husbands and wives torn apart. Some halves survived, others perished in violent acts, murders, or suicides. For some, a second too late or too early had meant the difference between life and death. Sometimes death was better. Surviving was not everything.

The man who saved Zoe and took her from Tudor's arms on the fated night of June 21st to 22nd, 1941, passed her to another couple traveling north to Transylvania. Was it June 21st or 22nd though? The exact day is murky and it's not clear why. When referring to the night of June 22nd, was it the early morning of that day following the night of the 21st?? Or was it the night from the 22nd to the 23rd? And why is that of crucial importance? Gabi came to the Angelescu family the day after Carolina was killed or "disappeared." Maybe hours. Tudor opened the door and the two brothers whispered in the June night standing in the doorway. The two children, Florin and Lila had woken up and were listening at the top of the stairs. Lila must have been recounting to Mitzi everything she saw and heard as usual. She whispered the scene almost as it was taking place, in real time, from the upstairs landing like watching a theater show from a balcony row. Florin was with her only a few steps away. He found an emerald earring on the floor and remembered it belonged to Zoe. Or was it Carolina's? He couldn't remember. Gabi asked Tudor to see the girls and Tudor stalled. He tried to distract his brother and told him they are fine, the girls are fine, don't worry. Let's go, we don't have much time. The only reason Tudor would have prevented Gabi from seeing the girls would have been if Carolina had already disappeared and Zoe was on the way to the train station. There were no girls to show.

Zoe was passed from hand to hand, in the same blanket that Uncle Tudor had wrapped her in, even though it was summer. The people in the resistance chain carried her like a bundle instead of letting her walk on her own. Even though eleven years old, she was tiny and thin, barely weighing fifteen kilograms and they thought that the bundle version was the safest one so she didn't draw attention with her long red hair. Then the young man who took Zoe from Tudor at the station returned the next day to the city up north and saw to the escape of Frida and Gabi which was the 22nd or the 23rd. And again, the two days are confused, which one was it really? It matters because if Gabi and Frida's failed escape happened on the 22nd, then they would have been at the station the day before the Angelescu family which all accounts contradict. Somebody pulled Frida inside the train and closed the door seconds after Gabi was grabbed by the SS soldier or the Iron Guard man. It had to be Tudor. But maybe not. It could have been someone from the underground too. This matters also because if it was the night of the 21st to the 22nd, then Zoe and her parents were at the same station on the same night without meeting each other, each in their own ordeal. Missing each other by seconds. The most critical seconds of their lives.

Maybe when it came to the precise dates the narrators were all unreliable. They were more concerned about recording and recounting the little details, the words they heard, the actions they saw then about writing down the exact day. Particularly since some of the narrators or record keepers were children: a terrified girl who talked compulsively to her doll to calm herself, and a timid, equally terrified boy who was in love with one of the twin sisters. And entire chains of events were recounted decades later by the man who had been the timid boy in love with one of the twin girls. He was now married to one of them. By the time he wrote his memoirs he had spent a couple of decades on the carousel of hardships and clusters of calamities with intermittent oases of happiness thanks to Zoe and the family they were creating.

From my perspective as the moody girl named after the Roman courtesan Corina growing up in our tiny Bucharest apartment, though secretive and mysterious, worried, and anxious, my parents did often look happy even amid the havoc caused by incessant surveillance combined with perpetual deprivations. There were often boisterous discussions, drinking and loud laughter in our house, when my parents' few bohemian friends gathered on the sofa with the secret box underneath, or around the big mahogany desk from the old house, drinking the lousy Romanian version of vodka, tuica, secretly listening to Radio Free Europe and whispering political jokes about the dumb dictator.

Within the span of three June days in 1941, indeed, the sun stood still and watched a massive conglomerate of atrocious events collapse on members of the same family. A sinister and irreversible carousel of life and death. A lot of death. Frida and Gabi were on the very cusp of that carousel, at the point of it moving upwards, only seconds before it came crashing down on their lives and crushed them forever. The man assigned to help them drove them to the station in his own car, reached the station and acted as their shadow, a guardian shadow. When he saw Gabi being yanked away from the train steps at the exact moment of embracing Frida goodbye, he almost intervened but then thought better of it. He would have been shot or taken away together with Gabi, and then he couldn't have helped anyone anymore. Instead, he went on with the plan to save Frida.

He got on the same train to Bucharest where he met the dark-haired woman who posed as his lover. Then, according to plan, he got on the next train to the northern city in Transylvania where he shared a compartment with Frida, traveling as Irina Angelescu. His plan was working. He thought that since Frida had not been informed of the next steps to take and the direction in which to move once she got to Bucharest, if he just locked eyes with her on the platform in a meaningful way, she would follow him, which she did. One of the two girls was safe as far as he knew, and one of the two spouses had made it. He and his group had saved half of the family. It was the best he could do.

The anti-fascist Romanian resistance was a thinly formed group, a minority among minorities, but those who belonged to it were fierce and fearless. They were helped for a while with resources and intelligence by the small group of Moldovan partisans during the early summer weeks of 1941. They used no names, left no traces, communicated only through messengers or in person. They were always on the move, walking, riding trains or driving one of the several old cars that they shared with each other according to need. But with the creation of the Transnistria governorate, the organization was crushed and most of its members executed later that summer. The dark-haired man who saved both Frida and Zoe had miraculously escaped that purge. But his partner and pretend lover would not be so lucky. She was swallowed in the ferocious wave of blood and hatred that swept thousands of people those days with hardly any trace documented in history books.

Back at the house on June 21st the family was taking refuge from the bombs in their underground shelter. The girls did not hear the usual signal to hide in the secret compartment, or Tudor had not heard the group of SS soldiers barging into the house, until it was too late. When he rushed upstairs to the girls' hiding place and found the dreadful spectacle of Zoe collapsed over her sister's body, he only thought of saving the surviving girl. As soon as he returned from the train station after having given the bundle that was Zoe to the man in the resistance, he rushed back to the secret room with the intent of burying Carolina that night. There was not a minute to waste, he couldn't leave the body in there, bombs or no bombs. Only that when he went back to the room, there was no body. The room was clean and empty as if nobody had ever been there. Only the blue silk sash was lying on the floor.

What do you mean there is no body, Grandmother Victoria asked in the basement under the thunder of shells and bombs? There is no body, I can't explain, Tudor said it must be somewhere; dead bodies don't just take off and disappear. Maybe she wasn't dead, maybe she survived and ran away, replied Victoria. Impossible, I checked her pulse, she was not breathing, Tudor insisted. Still maybe she was not dead. Or maybe she died only partly, maybe she died and went away. Yes right, you and your speculations about the supernatural. I guess we'll never know what happened to her, or to her body, or to her spirit. If there is no body, there is no spirit, concluded Tudor. There is still a spirit without a body, contradicted Victoria.

Lila repeated everything she heard on the pretext of recounting every day's events to her doll Mitzi. Then she wrote it down in her best and tiniest calligraphic writing and stuffed the paper with the story inside Mitzi's belly. It ended up being an endless roll of thinly cut paper rolls made of many strips of paper glued to each other and containing the littlest details of the family's events from the start of the war in 1939 until her scarlet fever in the draught and famine ridden summer of 1944. The roll of paper sat inside Mitzi's belly for decades until her brother remembered at the last minute, just before leaving the country for Western Europe in the eighties. He never told Zoe about it, just said he had to find Mitzi, she was an important "relic" and memory holder. He couldn't leave her in the bottom of the sofa bed for the communists to find and destroy her when they repossessed their apartment as they did with the houses of all those who were considered enemies of the people. Zoe, who often dismissed Florin's sentimental attachment to relics and memories, also dismissed the roll of paper coming out of the doll's belly. But at the last minute, seeing the dissected doll on the eve of their departure she remembered the necklace with the key she had been wearing since her mother's death. She had to decide which was riskier on their escape journey: to be found with the necklace and the secret key on her body or to have Mitzi discovered with the key inside her?

It wasn't clear why Zoe thought there was a chance the customs police would have found the necklace around her neck. They weren't doing body searches on the trains, but they were searching inside the luggage and bags. There were more chances of Mitzi being found in the suitcase than of the necklace getting found around Zoe's neck hidden underneath her blouse. Suddenly the feel of the necklace around her neck bothered Zoe. It choked her. Her body was forever tied to Carolina's body and had felt her sister's agony in the last seconds of her life when she was strangled with the blue sash, decades earlier. She took off the necklace and put it inside Mitzi. That was how the necklace with the precious key crossed the border inside the Mitzi doll that up to that point had only carried the documentation created by Lila. The doll's belly was a replica of a bottomless womb that carried dark secrets and objects, a sinister kind of pregnancy.

The stories written on the roll of paper didn't solve the mystery of Carolina's body. Had she died and been buried by someone else while Tudor was taking Zoe to the train station? Or did she survive, run away and disappear without a trace? There could also be a third alternative, that she was neither dead nor alive, that she had become an in-between being. She might have slipped in a crack between life and death.

Carolina was always special, unusual, like an apparition from another realm. She appeared into the world as a surprise and was born with strange signs that the local people thought to be of a different or even maleficent nature. The girls sometimes did almost starve as they spent their days hidden in the little room for months and the family was occasionally late bringing their food, particularly during bombs and raids. Another story circulated that the children born like Carolina, with their head covered in a kind of skin cap that had to be removed at birth, returned to earth a second time, having once lived and died a violent death with no proper burial. Let us not forget that many of the locals participated eagerly in the butchering of our people. Their backwards superstitions and prejudices led to countless acts of violence in this idyllic landscape of orchards and rolling hills.

There had been another girl in the family, a younger sister of Frida and Sofia. Her name was Ester. She was killed in the Ukrainian pogroms of 1918. Frida found herself on the train in 1918 traveling with the three Abramovic brothers reciting lines from a Russian play about cherry orchards despite the horror her family had experienced. Or maybe because of the horror, that was how she survived and helped the others survive and not entirely lose their minds. Becoming someone else in a fictional story was her way of surviving those times. There are no clear documents about the fate of the family at that time, it's too long ago, almost a century ago. All that was kept, the only records, are in the diaries and manuscripts. Both the Abramovic and the Kunovicis had been in the book printing business after all, they believed in the power of the written word. And they produced a lot of it. The names are confused in the documents, sometimes deliberately so. "Just in case" someone would ever find them and track them. They lived like that, on the run, almost their entire lives, they created codes and misleading paths not just in their actual lives but also in the recording of their lives on paper. "Just in case." Tudor and Manole had both changed their names from Abramovic to Angelescu, just like they adopted Christian orthodoxy, as a cover. Gabi, who was the third of the Abramovic brothers, never did change his name, he lived and died with his original name with the brief exception when he and Frida took the Angelescu name for the purpose of the escape on June 23rd. It did him no good since he ended up on the death train and died alone in a Spanish town yearning for Frida and his two girls, the beautiful family they once were.

I had never heard my mother talk so much in my whole entire life. It was a continuous flood of uninterrupted sentences that flowed for hours that afternoon. All the people in the flow of my mother's narration, including herself and her sister Carolina, were referred to like characters in a play or a novel. She referred to them by their names and not as Frida, her mother, Gabi, her father, Carolina, her sister, Tudor, her uncle, Lila, her cousin. And Florin? It felt like the earth stood still indeed. Or like the earth was slipping from under my feet and I was falling into a bottomless void. My mother Zoe had married my father Florin, who was the son of Tudor, who was her father's brother. That made Zoe and Florin first cousins. My parents were first cousins. Of all the things recounted, the discovery of this genealogical chaos and kinship taboo was suddenly the most shocking. Under all the fabricated identities, disguises, secretive family relations and name changes during times of revolutions, pogroms and wars, all the characters that were my immediate family two generations back had in fact fallen into an inescapable circle of forbidden kinships, that rolled back onto themselves in a semi-incestuous coupling instead of branching out into the world towards other families and kinships and worlds. It is likely that neither my mother nor father knew of this genealogical mess at the time of their encounter as adults and their marriage. After she was reunited with Zoe in the mountain house where she arrived late at night with the help of the mystery man from the train, it is unlikely Frida would have cared at all about anything else other than her and her daughter's survival. By the time Frida was living in the Bucharest apartment, she wouldn't have known that her daughter Zoe married the son of the man who had saved her. She didn't meet Florin until she first visited us during my bout with chickenpox when I was seven or eight years old. Or at least that is what I had to make myself believe to make this astonishing discovery bearable.

In between parts of my mother's recounting Sebi intervened and at times it all looked and sounded like a rehearsed play. Sebi interfered with questions or contradicting statements, which nevertheless sounded like an addition to the tales my mother spun as if wanting to contain all sides of the truth, of the real, the unreal and the in between. My mother was holding the album she brought out of the secret compartment. The afternoon was heavy, the air sticky and humid without rain. The crew and cast of the film were still in the back of the house, but all music had stopped, and everybody seemed to wait for something else. Something that had not been said or done but was expected to be said and done, and it wasn't clear what. One of the women in chiffon dresses walked over to where we were under the arch of the plum tree and started talking without any introduction as if it was all part of the plan of storytelling, of reliving the past, of opening the daunting box of secrets of the Abramovic/Angelescu and Kunovicis families and letting it all burst out in the full daylight like a flock of caged birds flying to freedom.

The Film Crew and More Secrets Revealed
July 5th, 2015, Northern Moldavia

A young girl was often seen roaming around the grounds among the trees. For decades, she would appear mostly at dusk, at the joining of light and dark, dancing her way among the trees, softly and lightly, a feather of smoke, visible but intangible. It's what local people say, how they saw her during the war, after the war and occasionally throughout the following decades until quite recently. She became a local legend, the neighbors became used to her and treated the phenomenon like any other occurrence, like the rain or the setting of frost. Some said she hadn't been buried properly and her soul never found the rest she needed, but those are just clichés and superstitions. She is not a cliché. She is not the sum total of superstitions and of the collective imagination. She is part of the local history. History and not story. She is claiming her life and the truth about what happened, how it happened and why it happened. She wants it revealed with all the precision of the most disturbing details. She witnessed all that happened here, among the fruit trees and inside every hidden corner of the house. They say she was born unusual, that she had returned from a previous life of another murdered girl and found enough space in the mother's womb to grow into a creature like the one already conceived, like a twin sister. She couldn't make it this time around either, she traveled across history from one atrocity to the next looking for the proper body, for the right life and death cycle, but she got it wrong every time. Or history got it wrong, repeatedly, the way history does and the way history keeps repeating itself under different guises, creating the illusion that it's a new history, when in fact it's just the same thing under different faces and different names.

As I am listening to the fantastical recitation of the woman in the peach-colored chiffon dress, I keep wondering about Manole and Lulu, whatever happened to them and why I haven't seen them at all since my mother arrived on the premises. He was the one who kept insisting that my mother should come to make everything clear, to stop the chain of unusual occurrences that have never stopped since the war. All the peculiar things that happened to me here have felt disturbingly real even though every bit of every second of those occurrences did not belong in the world of the hard, scientific, provable reality. And yet they addressed all the senses.

During the days of her visit to my father's birth town, my mother was a different person. She moved around with the lightness and agility of a young woman. Her usual distracted manner, like she was a visitor from another planet, had disappeared and she paid attention to every material detail around her, even listened when people talked to her and answered with pointed remarks. We visited the house every day and with every new visit my mother spun more of her, and her family's life events in the same uninterrupted flow with an intense urgency. The film crew and their director Sebi used my mother's memories to improvise and add to the film script and the film shooting which all seemed to be done on the fly, almost in simultaneity with the telling. He used local people as actors besides the international actors that danced the tango in the roles of Stalin and Hitler on the first day of my arrival at the time of the summer solstice. To make it more authentic, he said. Like the films of Felini, Zeffirelli or Visconti, the Italian directors of groundbreaking film waves, he also said.

In between mini lectures about film history and aesthetics, Sebastian or Sebi as everybody called him, revealed to me he was the son of Sebastian who was the son of Sofia Kunovicis, Frida's sister, who then was my mother's aunt. That made us cousins twice removed if my genealogical calculations were right. I gasped again at the realization of yet another genealogical conundrum. His grandfather and uncle had been killed in the late June days of 1941. His grandmother Sofia and his father Sebastian had been saved by the three brothers Tudor, Gabi and Manole out of the bloody apocalypse of those days. Sebi told everything matter of factly like recounting a random event, a quarrel between neighbors or a meeting with an old friend. Life and fiction, the real and the fantastical coexisted in a startling balance. I decided to not worry about the levels of reality or unreality any longer.

I took my mother to the secret cellar within a cellar that Manole had shown me, and I showed her the mound of manuscripts. Given all the unusual appearances and disappearances I was almost surprised that the enormous box was still there, as were the old dresses hanging in the wardrobe. The days that followed were magical. Not metaphorically magical, like very lovely and special days, the way one flippantly uses the word, but days with actual magic in them. The unexpected and unpredictable became habitual, and things we would have considered unreal before, now became ordinary. They were days populated with presences of a third dimension of existence, sometimes light and feathery, at other times cloudy and dark. They weighed on our souls from the grief and suffering they released from their spaces between the living and the dead. We had entered a sacred and secret passage of in between the living and the non-living and we accepted it as any other occurrence.

A cortege of light presences in period clothes fluttered and danced their way through the cellar. They were mostly faceless but not gory, and at times even the intimation of a smile could be detected on their faceless faces. There was always the young girl in the twenties dress and the woman in the peach-colored dress, there was the yellow smoky presence that even gave off a sour smell just like my father's accounts from his early journals described. There were also groups of presences waving heart wrenching goodbyes and then melting into a grayish smoke. So much was about farewells and goodbyes. My mother acted unphased as if none of it was any big deal or something that she was unaccustomed to. A few times she said memory is a tricky thing, you can't play with memory, or look what happens, it comes back to haunt you, you need to honor memory and the people and events in your field of memory. I had no idea what that meant but remembered the episodes earlier in the summer under Manole's "supervision" when we were visited by what he then called memory people, living simultaneously with us in the cracks between the past and the present.

Do we want these memory people to go on visiting us mother, or should we just put them to rest? I once asked during our journey through the multitude of handwritten and typed pages. We are not the ones putting them to rest, my dear, we have no control over them, they have to find that opening themselves, we are only facilitators of that opening. Of that opportunity for final and eternal rest. I understood nothing of my mother's language and explanations but the one thing that tugged deeply at my soul was her use of the expression my dear, which I heard for the first time ever coming out of her mouth.

One day the little girl that I had once been, playing hopscotch on the pavement in between gray communist buildings appeared at the house all plump and rosy with blonde braided hair rolled on top of her head. She moved around the trees in the orchard, approached the people in the film crew and asked them their names with a sass and confidence that I never possessed as a girl of her age. Or rather, of my age at that time in history. This young plumpish sassy Corina kept saying it could have been me, Carolina could have been me. Any girl could have been Carolina she continued, and so it could have also been me, Corina. More than any of the other apparitions, hers freaked me out of my wits to an unprecedented degree. My mother explained it to me all calmly like the most normal thing in the world. That there were phases of our lives that relived themselves, we called them "memories", but they were real spirits and shapes of people stuck in a moment in time, in the fissures between the past and the present. They relived that moment until we learned what we had to learn from the past and put it to rest. It happened once in I don't know how many hundreds of years when things got so out of whack in humanity that the past poured itself into the present and forced us to deal with it. Time was an illusion my mother said, she had read all the books of Stephen Hawking and understood it all. As I remembered, the books of Stephen Hawking dealt with the black hole theory and the origins of the universe, not ghostly appearances of younger versions of oneself. But she insisted it was all connected, memory, time, and the tiny place that humanity held in the unfathomable infinity of the universe.

This new mother I had who at eighty years old emerged like a new person, a force of nature and of mind who spoke clearly and eloquently about the most obscure and incomprehensible facts and events, left me speechless and filled with wonder. Where had she been all my life? But maybe that was the entirely wrong question to ask, and rather, I should ask myself why I hadn't seen my mother in her glorious power my entire life, behind the veil of absent-mindedness, of other worldliness, burnt foods, irritated short answers to repetitive questions? I should have noticed and treasured the moments of brilliance and levity we had experienced along the course of our lives ever since we lived in the matchbox Bucharest apartment through the chaos of our escape and immigrant life, the Paris weeks, the Florida years, the New York years. It sounded like material for a national geographic article, the only difference was that the crossing of spaces and regimes had been less important than the journey through our inner selves.

My mother writing a poem on an afternoon bathed in a honeyed summer light at the old desk that came from this house here, the tilt of her head, her dreamy expression turned towards herself. The ironic way she lit and smoked a cigarette during arguments and domestic squabbles like a queen rising above the tiny concerns of her subjects. The crisp self-assurance and energy she exhibited during our first gray days and weeks in Paris to the sound of Paulina Kalinowska's instructions and explanations. Like she understood everything at once. Which she did. The uncompromising rectitude about the Romanian double agent assassinated in his Florida home, the lucid way she talked about her father's manuscript she received from the mysterious messenger who came to Florida in the eighties. The way she circumvented the other side of history, her lesser known and acknowledged one, the Fascist history of pogroms and trains of death which had affected and twisted the course of her life much more than anything during the communist years. Maybe the entirety of my life had been headed precisely towards these days of rambling in my father's orchards, deciphering inexplicable mysteries and unspeakable histories and rediscovering my mother in the full glory of her vision and power.

The weather had settled into a crisp coolness unusual for this time of the year. It was soothing and delightful after the days of heavy heat, storms, more heat, humidity, and more heat. The tree branches perked up like they were suddenly paying attention to everything around them all while conscientiously working on the ripening of their magnificent fruit. I remember my father always saying that late summer and early fall was always the most colorful and succulent time, when the apples and the plums all ripened. He used the word succulent which is how I always imagined and thought of the best fruit. Manole and Lulu were still nowhere to be seen and I had stopped wondering about them. They would probably reappear unexpected as they always appeared as if emerging out of thin air or out of the ground magically.

One afternoon I asked Sebi about the film, why had he chosen to film it there, and most importantly why was he so set on turning the palimpsest of apocalypses in my family's history into a movie? The question left him surprised. As if how could I not understand that of course he was going to turn all that into a movie? To reveal all the hidden horrors that our people were responsible for but refuse to acknowledge. To offer a new perspective on the abridged history of fascism and communism in Romania, which seemed to be a phrase I heard the first day of my visit and laughed heartily at it. For him it was a matter of life and death, he said, not out of any artistic ambitions, but because his father, grandmother and uncle had both suffered unimaginable traumas during those years that needed to be revealed to the world. They had been saved by Grandfather Tudor, uncles Gabi and Manole, and Grandmother Victoria and he owed his very existence to them. It was mostly an homage to my grandparents he said, after which he left me in the middle of the orchard feeling stupid for having asked and not understood the reasons behind his obsessive film making project.

But then something astounding happened as soon as he finished his sentence about the importance of telling the world about the atrocities his family had suffered and the reasoning behind his film project. The group of film people or the crew that I saw occasionally on my father's property and who invited me to their bizarre party on my first day there, started emerging from behind the trees, from areas behind the house, and even from the house itself as if they were all going to an important gathering. They seemed to be rushing somewhere but also their movements and bodies moved in slow motion with deliberate, exaggerated gestures. They reminded me of the Latin proverb "festina lente" "hurry up slowly" which my father would sometimes use with me when I was a child to warn me against hurrying up too much. I never fully understood the meaning of the expression and now it appeared like the group of so-called film crew and actors were doing just that. There was a contained desperation in their movements, they wanted to get somewhere, but their bodies only allowed them to move so fast, which was in fact very slowly by any standards of regular human movement. It looked like an awkward ballet. Sebastian was standing in the middle of the orchard at number 18bis, and the group was moving towards him with this new hurried slowness. They were all moving into the area of the orchard where all the other ethereal presences had appeared to me in previous days. The woman in the peach-colored dress with the blue parasol was gliding in a dreamlike stroll. The air around me felt thick and palpable: it had an acidic consistency that stung my eyes. It was replete with the unearthly substance of restless souls.

Of all the presences gathered there, Sebastian seemed to be the only one made of solid matter, opaque and heavy, therefore alive. He was holding a notebook and a pen as if ready to take notes. I pinched myself to verify my own aliveness and opaqueness, the matter of my own body and wondered again for the umptieth time during that summer and particularly during the last days filled with an orgy of manuscripts, whether I was myself fully alive and fully awake. I was there and I was breathing in the full carnality of my being, so it felt. I stopped questioning it and took it for what it was. The afternoon light filtered through the heavy tree branches. The group of people gathered around Sebastian appeared in a transparency of otherworldliness and for the first time I understood or so I thought. From where I was, at the edges of the orchard, it did look like a movie scene unfolding slowly against the background of the voluptuous orchards. The women with the labels like museum artifacts that I had seen in the back room of the house on my first day there, were almost in a state of levitation, barely touching the ground, afraid of gravity, gliding on it as if on an ice rink. Sebastian turned around to look at me, to see my reaction of the bizarre gathering.

Out of literal nowhere Manole made his appearance in the middle of the group. Sebastian made a sign showing me Manole as if to say, see, here he is, he's been here all along, Manole doesn't go anywhere, he is here all the time, literally all the time, sometimes you see him, sometimes you don't, it's how Manole is, the keeper of the orchards, the guardian of the souls. Oh, I thought to myself in a kind of unspoken conversation with Sebastian, he is like Cerberus at the gates of Dante's hell, only kinder, and human. Then I thought with a kind of sudden and deep understanding: Sebastian talks to the dead, he is from here, half his family are right there in that airy group of would-be film crew, film actors and he knows their language. I'll never be able to do that, they'll never accept me in their midst. I'm a foreigner even to the circle of the undead presences from my family history. But maybe it's not all bad, being a foreigner to everything, because then you can travel everywhere, and everything is always new and old.

My own thoughts in my own conversation with myself stopped making sense. It felt like they were thinking themselves and they were thinking me into existence. The space in the center of the orchard, with the colorful watery group in pastels appeared suddenly like an abyss into which I gazed famished for understanding. It's a time warp someone said, it could have been Manole from the slow rhythm of his uttering, that's what a time warp looks like Corina, you are at the very edge of this very special abyss in time that is also space. What do you do with a time warp, will time and space ever be in sync with each other ever again? I wondered. Or said it out loud, I wouldn't know.

I lay down on the earth. I wanted to experience the full force of gravity to prove my aliveness. I touched the grass around me, then the dirt, and its roughness, the flowers in the grass and their delicate tendrils and petals. They all quivered under my touch like they were talking to me. Under that earth an entire population of ancestors throbbed and quivered and tossed in perpetual torment: family and friends of family, former fugitives, men, women, and children whose lives and deaths had been so abominable, and so out of any natural order, that the earth itself and everything else on top of that special fertile earth rebelled and disobeyed the laws of nature. Sometimes, the earth itself pushed those populations out of its entrails, the tree roots begged for freedom and pushed them to the surface to breathe. The earth was a minefield of unsettled stories. What had to happen for all to return to their rightful place, the dead with the dead, the trees with the trees, the living with the living walking among the trees?

I understood why Sebastian needed to make the film of the abridged history of fascism and communism and of our family. It came over me in a cloud dripping colors and shades like rain. It came over me in winds and breezes that enveloped and caressed me. The presences that moved and danced and wandered in the space of the abyss of the time warp in the middle of my father's orchard, pleaded to be given shape and consistency once and for all. The woman in the peach-colored dress with the blue parasol looked my way and the resemblance to my grandmother Frida shook me to the core. I remembered the performance she once gave on the veranda of the adobe house on the shores of the Black Sea from a play titled *Six Characters in Search of an Author*, when I was a morose and always hungry seven-year-old girl. The sea sparkled through the willow trees in the back of the house like a precious crystal, so blue that it was heartbreaking. I remembered how I felt then that Frida had a special presence on earth, that something she had experienced turned her into a different kind of being. That my mother Zoe too, was part of that same group of beings in my family whose past crushed them and from that rubble they emerged as a new kind of being, as if they had been thinned out and made lighter, of the consistency of feathers and clouds, only partly alive.

I repeated the title of the play by the Italian author Luigi Pirandello which Manole had also talked to me about. Your father was very fond of that play, and of Chekov's plays, in particular *The Cherry Orchards*, Manole had said then. I didn't think much of it then, but now it all acquired the dimension of a deep understanding. These too were "characters" in search of a home and a cohesive shape. Sebastian was the one to give them that home, because his parents and grandparents had traversed the realms of the living and the dead and emerged at the other end of the dark sinister tunnel on that June day in 1941 when my grandfather Tudor, my great uncle Manole and my grandfather Gabi saved his father and his grandmother Sofia from being butchered. He needed to fashion those forgotten yet tortured lives into a solid entity, into a crafted story that gave them voice and gave them permanence in the world of the living. Only then would they quiet down and find their resting place. The earth held me like a loving mother and lulled me to sleep on that last afternoon of my stay in the village of my father's birth and youth.

Final Return, Final Manuscript
August 2015, Northern Moldavia

It was August by the time we were ready to leave. My mother had spent hours in the cellar crouched over manuscripts. I wondered how much longer she would take. And then the image of the girl I had once been appeared close by in between two of the cherry trees that by now had lost all their cherries. She was holding a ragged doll that looked like the mythic doll Mitzi. The girl looked the same as before: plumpish, wearing one of my childhood favorite dresses, a blue and white ruffled dress with sleeves like bells and her hair was arranged again in the same perfect braids rolled on top of her head. I was crossed by devastating grief: a sliver of my soul had been sliced off me and separated forever. I had lost all connection with the little girl that I had once been, and she was doomed to be on her own, rambling through all eternity with her stupid raggedy Mitzi doll that hadn't even belonged to her. I never even played with the Mitzi doll, I thought. She always just sat inside the box under our sofa bed like a big secret that I was dying to decipher when I was the age of this plumpish girl impersonating me.

Maybe my memory of myself had just peeled off me and how things really once were, was very different from my memory of them. Maybe this memory incarnation floating around a film crew and a bunch of fruit trees from a hundred years ago was the real thing, the real me and how I once was. We had both been separated, torn off, sliced off each other forever like an apple cut into two halves. I reached out to touch her, and she faded the second I did so. I almost fainted from the sadness of the loss. I thought the film people were playing cruel tricks, she was part of the cast, and they were testing their special effects on me. Maybe I was also featured in their movie without giving them either permission, or valuable information about my own childhood, youth, past.

That Sebi and his damn film crew were a bunch of thieves of souls and memories. They were going to make money from our souls and histories too, while we would be bereft and irreparably broken for the precious rest of our lives. At least I was featured during one of my healthiest periods. I could have been living in

France or Germany for how rosy and plumpish I looked, not in Communist Romania with food rations and endless lines for every single necessity of life. I decided to look for my mother in the manuscript cellar as I now called it. Then I remembered the life altering realization I had earlier that very day, that the people in the film crew and the actors were only shadows and airy presences, traces of ancestors buried underneath the charmed orchards. I remembered that the film people were not film people at all, but rather souls searching for their equivalent in the lives of the living to imprint their gory, their tragic, their unbearable stories within the flow of our lives. They wanted to be given their due — undeniable palpable reality. This could also be a dream that traveled into my conscience as I had fallen into an afternoon slumber when I lay on the fragrant earth covered in the multicolored lives of wildflowers. The frontiers between dreams and the palpable reality around us were blurred. Because of course it was the most normal thing in the world to just lie on the ground in full daylight, instantaneously fall asleep as if under the influence of a potent drug and be transported into a dream world that explains every last hidden mystery in the incomprehensible maze of your family's stories and histories. I no longer wondered or questioned. I let it all happen like an inescapable wind, rain, sun, any other element.

As I followed the little labyrinth of staircases and secret entrances that led to other secret entrances and chambers, I started asking myself, why were we still here returning to the house every morning as if it was a job we now had? What else was there to do and find out? We still hadn't unraveled the big enigma of Carolina's death, disappearance, whatever it had been. We hadn't found out what happened to her body after the brutal murder that my mother witnessed more than seventy years ago from her secret cell and that changed and dislocated her sense of self and reality forever. But we had found out and clarified a whole lot of other things from our history. Truth be told I still had a hard time putting together the image of Zoe the ethereal girl in a white dress tied with a blue sash and the image of the mother that birthed and raised me and who now, in her eighties, was reemerging into yet another self of imperious power, self-control, and efficiency.

I found her sitting on the floor like myself a couple of weeks earlier, amid the mountain of manuscripts. She looked small like a girl surrounded by the piles of papers and notebooks and holding the blue silk sash in her hand — a precious treasure. The old album of photographs she held a few days earlier under the crown of a large plum tree was next to her. I sat down beside her and reached out for the album, curious to discover more unfathomable treasures and secrets. She caught my hand with startling speed and stopped me from doing so. Just wait, give it some time Corina, you are always so impatient about everything. This will take time, and you are not ready for it yet, she said softly and quickly, almost like a prayer. Stunned as I was, I moved away from the album wondering what new happenings and magical occurrences were going to take place in that spooked space again. The air was still. Everything acquired such stillness. It seemed we were no longer alive. We were just images in a photograph, pictures in an album ourselves. Maybe we had crossed on to the other side. Maybe we had always been on the other side and everything we had lived through had been an illusion, a dream of ourselves from that side. Feelings, thoughts, movements, breath, it all stopped. The immobility and emptiness of it all was astounding. We could start a new history, everything was possible. An empty field of snow waiting for the steps that would leave the first traces. The whiteness of snow was the only season. The whiteness of an unwritten page was the only reality. My mother and I were looking at the world from the frame of a black and white picture and it all looked like a huge mass of entangled wires, bodies, shapes, indistinct matter. I was with her on the empty planet in the picture where she wore a ruffled white dress on an empty street in an empty town next to a house the same size as her, and her eyes were closed like she was dreaming the entire bloody story of humanity and smiling at it.

My mother and I left the little town of my father's birth on August 15th with a colossal box filled with papers, notebooks, old journals, and manuscripts during a fierce storm of biblical proportions. On the last day of our stay, Sebi brought a wooden box which we filled with every single manuscript, notebook, diary, packages of loose papers tied around with string except for the items of clothing in the wardrobe. It was my mother's wish that we leave them. She said let them stay here in peace, where they belong and where the people who once wore them can find them. I thought my mother might have been ironic when mentioning the possibility of a group of dead people rambling down to the cellar within the cellar looking for their dress up clothes. But she was as serious as I had ever seen her. I let it be and let it go. Then Sebastian proceeded to wrap the box in saran wrap and said we should have no problem checking it in at the airport in Bucharest. By that time, we had read and gone through every piece of paper, notebook, manuscript or cut out from old journals at least twice. It appeared that some of the documents had travelled several times back and forth between the house in Northern Moldavia and Bucharest, and between Bucharest and the United States, only to come back to Northern Moldavia in convoluted and circular trajectories, passed from hand to hand, suitcase to suitcase, more precious than our family jewelry, than Grandmother Victoria's star diamond brooches and earrings.

On that same last day, my mother took me back to the small hiding corner room where she and her sister Carolina had spent their last weeks and days together. She held out to me the old album of photographs that she had taken out of the secret cubby the first day we went there with Sebi and said here, now you are ready for this. I had no idea why I had to be ready to look through an old album of photographs, and I was anxious we might miss our plane to Bucharest which was departing later that afternoon. It was still morning, yet time seemed again slightly out of whack as it often had during my stay which, from the initial planned couple of weeks, stretched throughout the entire summer. Everything seemed rushed and fast forwarded now. The minutes and hours rolled rapidly and unstoppably like pebbles down a steep slope. She said sit down and look through it, I must take care of a few last things. I'll come get you when we are ready to leave. Sebi is driving us to the airport.

I had no idea what things my mother had to take care of at the very last minute after more than a month of being there. Things felt out of sync, the suddenly cold weather, the reckless rush of the minutes and hours, my mother's slowness of movement. I felt out of sync with my own self, as if I were forgetting parts of me in various corners of that house like lost objects. A barrette, a sash, a hair clip, a photograph, a last thought, a rediscovered memory — all strewn throughout the house under a chair or stuck under an old rug. Only then did it strike me that the house we had spent so much time going in and out of during more than a month had hardly any furniture left in it now that the filming was finished, and the crew was gone. The real crew of the living actors playing the parts of the souls or characters gliding and floating through the air of the time warp in the back of the orchard, had left without us even realizing it. I had thought the house and everything in it belonged to Manole, that he had saved it from the sinister Secret police and spies.

Our steps through the house sounded hollow and our words reverberated with a haunting ring. I had nowhere to sit, so I took the two Turkish pillows from the hiding place and propped them against the corner of the room. Now I was ready to look through the enigmatic album. The room was dark even though we were in early morning and a brilliant sun was glowing outside. Only a night light was flickering timidly on one of the walls of the triangular room. I turned on the flashlight on my phone and noticed the leather cover of the album was peeling and was covered in scratches like it had traveled to the end of the world and back. Which very likely it had. I was paralyzed with anxiety. I resisted opening it as I feared I would see things I never really wanted to discover. A feeling of claustrophobic desperation filled me. I opened it. The first page was blank. I moved to the next heavy dusty page which was filled with small sepia photographs or cutouts from old photographs of faces I had never seen. Women and men in attire and hair dos from the turn of the last century. They all looked severe and gazed straight at the camera. It felt like they stared at me with unwanted fixity. They were neither happy nor unhappy, just serious, unmoved. Their names and dates of birth and death were scribbled on the rough surface of black paper next to each photograph. Some were faces of children in overdressed attire, the boys with bow ties, the girls in ruffled dresses, with bows in their hair.

One such photograph of a girl drew my attention. At a closer look, her face was almost identical to that of my mother from the photograph of her in a ruffled white dress on an empty street that looked either deserted or alien. Almost — the key to so much resided in "almost" realities, in the sliver that remained from the overlapping of an original with a lookalike reality. The years were 1910-1918, her name was Ester Kunovicis, and next to her death date the words "killed in the pogrom of 1918 by Haidamaks," were written in uneven almost childish handwriting. It could have been the other half of the photograph of my mother in the same white ruffled dress that I had once found hidden inside the sofa box. Except the years were out of sync and would have made my mother more than a hundred years old. Or it could have been that the picture I had thought all along to be of my mother as a small child, was in fact of Carolina. And Ester could have been the other half. This half right here. One girl replaced another and tried living again. Ester's soul returned in Carolina, but she didn't last much longer on this side of the earth either. Ester and Carolina were born and lived a couple of decades apart from each other. Of the three, my mother was the living one who had crossed a century in body and soul. It was like she contained the souls of her murdered sister Carolina and aunt Ester who refused to completely disappear into the totality of death until their past was fully reckoned, and my mother came to bring it all to rest. The sisterhood of the Kunovicis girls, one turned Abramovic, one turned Angelescu stretched across a whole century.

The air felt stuffier in the room. I wanted to close the album and stop what seemed like the beginning of an old photojournalistic journey into yet another a history of atrocities. How much more could I take? I had had it with atrocities. I couldn't take all the stories and new photographs of people killed in massacres and pogroms in the lineage of my family anymore. I wanted to find myself in the comfort of my home in upstate New York, if that had ever even existed, and hadn't been just a fantasy I had made up while living in that country in the back woods of the Balkan peninsula. I was arguing with myself in a bilingual conversation and wanted to close the album and get up and run, get on the plane back to whatever that "over there" other country of mine might have been. But I could not. A pressure, an unmatched force of gravity kept me from getting up and kept me from being able to close the album. I turned the page and from then on, the pages appeared to move with a will of their own, at a speed that gave me just enough time to see the faces and the scribbled notations next to each of them.

I stared at a gallery of stern faces and figures dressed up in period attire that changed with the years illustrating the passage of time and fashion. From the long-corseted dresses of the women at the turn of the last century to the twenties' flapper dresses, to the forties' pinstripe zoot suits for the men and pin up dresses and pencil skirts for the women. I kept asking myself who are these people, why are they featured in this album and why should I care? I wanted to go back to the picture of Ester Kunovicis but it felt like the album was resisting me going backwards. Forward was the only direction, through a lost humanity of well-dressed people killed in pogroms, camps, massacres, and death trains.

About midway through the album, a picture of a dashing man in a white linen suit with a white straw fedora hat by the name of Gabriel Abramovic filled almost half of a page. Below it, there was a smaller photograph of an equally dashing young woman in a twenties' flapper dress, very similar to the one I had seen in the wardrobe in the cellar and imagined it must have been Frida's. Indeed, the name

Frida Kunovicis was scribbled next to it. The years were 1908-1941, only instead of dead it said disappeared in the pogroms of 1941. My people had been very careful to cover up and hide the entire history of fascist massacres. I had been fed a mockery of a history during all my years of schooling in Romania, and it wasn't only because of the lies that involved the "glorious" deeds of the Soviet Union and the Romanian Communist Party with their "liberating actions." It was because of the even deeper cover up of the sinister and unleashed massacres perpetrated by the Iron Guard and the fascist governments during World War II.

Now, sitting on the floor of the weirdest looking room I had ever inhabited, leafing through an ancient and mysteriously preserved family album from a hundred years ago, the weight of that hidden history suffocated me. Literally, I had to gasp for air. I wanted to call my mother, but my voice perished in my throat. History was a living creature that demanded retribution and recognition. It pushed through layers of simulacra and lies like a fierce dragon breaking its chains and surging out of the cave where it had been locked up for decades.

My mother's face, or a face that looked like hers in different stages and versions, kept reappearing throughout the crinkly pages of the photo album that left a thin blackish powder on my hands like the ashes of times and people long gone. As did Frida's face, or versions of her face, from that of a little girl in braids, to that of a teenage girl in a flapper dress, to the versions of her aging face through her early thirties after which it stopped appearing. I was never going to finish studying that album and get to the end of it. A force inside it held me down to the floor leafing through page after page in a controlled frenzy and never getting to the last page. On one page there was only the photo of one family alone, a beautiful looking couple with two girls dressed in white dresses and dated 1939, the year that Germany invaded Poland. The date was scribbled in the same small uneven letters and next to it the names of Gabi, Frida, Zoe and Carolina Abramovic. It was my mother's family, my family, that Zoe was the Zoe that was my mother, turned Zoe Angelescu, the same name that Frida and Gabi had taken in 1941 under the false identifications given to them by Grandfather Tudor.

Frida became Abramovic when she married Gabi, but it seemed that her sister Sofia had kept her maiden name of Kunovicis even though she had been married to a mystery man who now, after my mother's revelations, was no longer a mystery, but my own grandfather Tudor. She had a son who survived the pogrom who in turn fathered Sebi the movie producer and director who had spent the entire summer working on his bizarre cinematographic concoction. Then Frida and Gabi changed their identities to Angelescu thanks to Grandfather Tudor to escape the June days in 1941. Only half of that family survived. In this precious album, Gabi is given as disappeared as well, which contradicts the manuscripts and the memoir. It was the memoir with the suicide sentence hidden in plain view on a blank page in the middle of the notebook that Frida received one late summer day in her Bucharest apartment from the man who had saved hers and Zoe's lives during those same June days.

Whoever put this album together hadn't read the memoir, hadn't found out the news that Gabi had escaped after being put on one of the death trains, and ended up in a Spanish village by the Mediterranean where he ended his days all alone. And then came the famous photograph of the two families: the Angelescu and the Abramovic-Kunovicis in their best Sunday dress, linens, silks, fancy summer straw hats and the four children in the front sitting cross-legged and almost smiling but not quite. Aunt Lila is holding her Mitzi doll to her chest like a cherished baby, with fierceness as if protecting her with her life from anyone who might wish to take her away. I had seen the photo before. I had a clear memory of it from long ago in my grandmother's apartment. A few times when I visited Grandmother Victoria with my father, I saw the photo on her nightstand and remembered how each time she rushed to put it away either in the drawer of the night table or on the top shelf of her big wardrobe, as if caught red-handed with something. Then everybody changed the subject and talked about the weather or the walnut preserve. Another time I found it inside the sofa box in our Bucharest apartment next to the one-eyed Mitzi doll. It was next to the torn photograph of my mother as a child in the white dress smiling to herself with her eyes closed. I wondered who had brought it back to the house and placed it in that mind-boggling album of people from a century ago with intimations of gruesome stories of violence scribbled in childish handwriting.

Manuscripts and photos in our family had a life of their own just like people. They traveled from house to house, city to city, country to country and right back to the house with the orchards like a final resting place for everything and everyone. One such manuscript was brought by a mystery man to Frida right at the door of her Bucharest apartment. She recognized him for being the man who had helped her get to Transylvania, on the most horrendous day of her life. It was the day when Gabi had been torn away from her arms by an SS soldier, on the steps of the train in the little town of my father's birth. There were the stories scribbled by Lila in tiny writing on thin rolls of paper and hidden in Mitzi's belly. There was the man who brought the same manuscript of Gabi's memoir to my parents in Florida in the eighties. The same manuscript that was brought to Frida's door by the man who had saved her in June of 1941. It could have been the same man only my mother had no way of knowing that when he appeared at her door in Florida in the eighties because only her mother Frida had known him. We would never even know the name of this mystery man, yet he had a crucial role in our family history, having apparently saved both my mother and grandmother and a couple of priceless manuscripts that over time had become like some holy grail of Romanian history. Or at least of our family history that turned out to be a miniature, a vignette of the larger history of the country.

Now I understood: my mother brought back to Northern Moldavia Gabi's manuscript to join the others in the treasure box of manuscripts and to share with Sebi for his film project. And even more importantly, to add it to the archives of the Romanian pogroms that someone was developing for the purpose of revealing that history. It was another reason why my mother's return had been so important and so desired by both the living and the dead. And then there was my father's notebook recounting his prison years, death sentence and escaping the death sentence by accepting the informer duties for a period. They had all been brought back and put together in the same box in the same cellar within a cellar. Somebody wanted all the testimonials reunited like a family, in the hope of a formidable reunion of the family members themselves, from all the realms of life and death.

Then came the most appalling part of the album: pages after pages with images of people massacred in the street, in empty fields, placed on trains or truck platforms, piled on top of each other like slaughtered animals. One photo of several dead bodies seemed to have been taken in the street in the very front of the house with the glorious orchards. Two of the bodies were women, two were small children, several others were men in civilian clothes. Bloody and mangled bodies and body parts stretched obscenely on the ground, captured in yellowed black and white photography by someone who really had in mind the importance of recording such facts. There was another body in the street in one of the pictures, at a distance from the others: that of an Iron Guard man in the typical uniform of the green shirts though the green was dark gray in the picture. I felt a sickening sense of joy at seeing the body of the green shirt and wondered who had killed him. Even tinier scribbling than in the previous pages covered almost the entire surface between pictures. It all felt sticky, bloody, suffocating, as if blood itself was surging out of the sepia photographs and the scribbled notes and was going to drown me and the entire house and street and humanity in its dark red viscosity. Everything was blurry and incomprehensible. I was reading the notes, yet the words failed to record in my brain as anything meaningful.

There were names of people I had not heard of but somehow it felt like I knew them, or like I should have known them. A child's body holding a doll that looked like the Mitzi doll kept me transfixed. It was a girl with a bow on her head lying on her side and holding the doll, while a little bit farther lay a woman with arms stretched towards the girl. The woman's head had been splattered on the pavement. Her stretched arms seemed to be in perpetual movement, alive in the picture. Behind the two bodies stood the stately front door of the house that I was in right then. The silhouette of a man standing in front of the door, captured in semi-profile and holding what appeared to be a rifle drew my attention. I looked closer, refusing to trust my first impression of the image. It was indeed exactly what I thought I had seen: a man standing in front of the front door of the house at 18bis, holding a rifle and watching the spectacle of massacred bodies on the street. From the position of the rifle aligned with the corpse of the Iron Guard man, it could be deduced that he was the one who had shot the man. The question of the person right there with a camera taking a photograph of that scene, seemed unanswerable and opened the door to another field of presumptions and suppositions. Gruesome as it was, I couldn't take my eyes off the picture as it offered a bewildering view of the reality of those days that had been carefully hidden from history books, news reports and records.

A luminous clarity washed over me: the man with the rifle was no other than Grandfather Tudor. The stature, the imposing profile and the white head of hair, it all matched the two or three other pictures I had seen of him, such as the famous one of the last glorious day in the municipal park in the summer of 1939. I then stared at the Mitzi doll look alike in the hands of the murdered girl: it looked identical to the one with the lazy eye hidden in the sofa bed box of our old

Bucharest apartment. In one of my father's diaries from that period, it was noted that Lila didn't have her doll with her for a while. So, she talked to an imaginary Mitzi doll, which at the time I read it, appeared even more bizarre than the dialogues with the real Mitzi doll. Then it suddenly reappeared in the story. Maybe cunning, playful, distracted Lila was behind the photograph.

I knew my grandfather owned a Leica, one of the first modern cameras available in Romania at the time. That knowledge sprung in my mind. I knew it because I had seen such an old camera in our old Bucharest apartment but never gave it any attention. It sat in a small drawer that was part of the bookcase where my father kept his hundreds of volumes. It was not unlikely that in the gory chaos of that day Lila would have taken her father's camera and started taking pictures of the scene unfolding in front of their house. The awkward angles of the pictures, the almost amateurish way that some of the people had been captured, some with just half of their bodies, or someone's random leg stuck in the corner of a picture, seemed to support the theory of Lila as the author of the photographs. Lila had turned out to be something of a miracle of ingenuity and cunning throughout the family history and a formidable keeper of events. Maybe the girl lying in the street had played with her earlier and Lila gave her the doll. And then she or Tudor took it back from the girl, which would have been cruel, to leave the murdered girl lying in the street without even her doll. Or maybe it just happened that there was another Mitzi doll in the neighborhood, and it happened to belong to the murdered girl. I would never know for sure.

I remembered an American film I had seen while in college at the special movie theater that showed foreign films in Bucharest: the entire action centered around a photograph and of the photographer blowing it up many times only to discover the very secret of a murder that had been committed. The movie was called *Blow Up* and I had no idea then that it was such an important masterpiece in the history of film making, one of Michelangelo Antonioni's most famous creations. The photograph of the massacre on the street named by the famous Romanian king who had united the three Romanian principalities and was taken in front of the house at 18b gave the clues to an overwhelming abundance of mysteries, murders and possibly even acts of bravery. Not to mention the mystery of the Mitzi doll and its many avatars.

One evening that summer, I dreamed of or hallucinated a trial in which I was supposed to guess in front of a severe, morose looking judge, which was the real Mitzi doll, and pick her from the three that were lined up on the sofa in our apartment. This trial dream/hallucination occurred while Manole guided me through the secrets of the house and its orchards, with its array of fantastical weather, temporal phenomena, and archaic phrasings. I was never going to make my way out of the labyrinth of my family's histories. One clue gets revealed and another one appears on its heels. It was a never-ending game of missed or secret identities and appalling deeds.

I wanted out of the room, out of the house, out of the universe of that sinister album. A sliver of blue sky, a sun ray, a fragrance of fresh hay, a dance in the moonlight. It was what my body craved for with ferocious intensity. I must have fallen asleep because I found myself soaked in tears and cold sweat, with my head in my mother's lap. "Now you see why I didn't want to return?" she said. Her words sounded like the sweetest lullaby in the world, of such tenderness I had never experienced from my mother in my entire life. "And also, why did I decide to return in the end?" Everything had its opposite, its double, its twin reality. That made me laugh and with the laughter came a refreshing sense of relief. Of wanting to let go. Of levity and lightness, after being dragged and kept to the ground by an unparalleled force of gravity that seemed to lie in the weight of the album and everything in that room that surrounded it.

The weight of the deeds that had once taken place in that space hovered above us, a merciless bird of prey. My mother stroked my hair and spoke with the same eerie gentleness. It flowed inside me like a drug and all I wanted was to sleep with my head in her lap for the rest of eternity. She brought with her the feel of blue sky, of fresh hay scent, of lilacs in bloom I had been craving. Carolina is finally at rest, she whispered. I thought I was dreaming but touched the hardwood floor and saw I was not dreaming. I touched my mother's hand as it moved over my hair and felt it quivering and more alive than ever. I was not dreaming. Maybe someone was dreaming me, and I floated at will in a watery universe morphing from one shape into another, from one substance into another. I was a cloud, a flower, a little girl holding a doll with a funny name.

She rolled through lives and history and embodied herself as Carolina, after she had been someone else, my mother recounted softly. She had been Ester, who was killed by people with names like tanks rolling over living bodies, the Haidamaks of 1918. She took space in real life and lived with us like a foreigner, someone from another world. Because she was. It happens once in a millennium, when history and humans go haywire and the order between the living and the dead is thrown off balance so badly that there is no longer a line of separation between the two. Frida did not know she had twins until she gave birth and realized that after me there was still one more being who wanted out of her womb. She was tiny and light like an afterthought, but she was fully embodied just like any other living being. She saved my life, she purposefully remained outside the hiding place to trick the men who entered the room and gave herself as a sacrifice. She saved your father's life in this house when the Germans barged in hungry for our flesh, she saved everybody's life when the Russians drove their tanks and barged into the house with their heavy boots and butchered your father's beloved dog. You might have encountered her while you were here too, the little of her that remained over the years, the feather of light who made everything quiver and change shape in her vicinity. She broke the barriers of memory between the past and the present and brought it all together in the same space, the living and the dead, the past and the present, an unlikely reunion of all who have breathed in one location. Her body was never found after the murder. Tudor buried someone else in the garden under the plum tree, a small girl that was killed right in front of this house, holding Lila's doll or a doll that looked like Lila's doll. He buried that entire family in the orchard, all butchered on this very street. He carved crosses on the trees next to the graves to mislead the Germans that they were all "good Christians" and had nothing to do with the Jews. Every sign mattered, they looked at everything and Tudor knew it all better than anyone. He killed the Iron Guard man responsible for the massacre in front of the house and buried him too. An entire humanity rests under these trees like an underground city of the dead. All but my sister Carolina. Her absence has been a living thing ever since, until now. By the time all this happened, I was already gone, wrapped in a blanket, and passed from hand to hand, from train to train, until I was deposited in a house at the foot of the mountains near where your father and I met a decade later. A woman took me in and cared for me until my mother arrived. I don't remember much of anything after that, all a thick blur of more journeys by foot, on train, secret hiding places, and my mother not letting go of me for one second. Sometimes she performed a scene from a play for me alone. In a train station or compartment, in a back room of a rundown hotel, in someone's back yard. She came alive wherever we found ourselves and became different people in different lives. Just for me, to keep me entertained during our hardest trials.

I thought I was back in my childhood, in our Bucharest apartment and my mother was telling me stories of eerie creatures traveling and circulating in space from the past and from the dead. Now she was telling me the story of her twin sister Carolina who had travelled from body to body to test the horror that was history and save an occasional life. My mother's life. My father's life, too. By doing that she had made it possible for me to exist. A swooshing wind visited us in the secret room, a final cleansing, a final caress. After that everything felt dazzlingly clear. Like we could start over.

And Manole and Lulu, where are they, who are they? Why did they disappear as soon as you arrived? My mother opened the album at the last page that I had missed and showed me a photograph of an older man with a fedora hat and next to him a teenage boy in a white T shirt with I love New York written on it. They were Manole and Lulu. Next to the photo, the same tiny handwriting as in the rest of the album said: Manole and Lulu Kunovicis, dead in the revolution of '89. Lulu was Mitzi's grandson from her second marriage with Kosmin who was the older son of Tudor from a previous relationship. From the union with Sofia Kunovicis, Frida's sister, who had been Tudor's first wife before he married my grandmother Victoria. She stubbornly remained a Kunovicis, to keep a thin thread of the lineage barely alive. Tudor and Manole had changed their names from Abramovic to Angelescu. Lulu's lineage was the only one written in yellow pencil on the black album paper next to the photograph.

My people wrote their life stories even in the space between pictures in photo albums. Even in yellow pencil, with whatever instrument they found that could scribble the lines of a destiny on a flat surface. My mother spoke again in whispers, exhausted from the journey of recent months. Lulu's parents had emigrated the very year of the revolution, months before it all started and Romanians killed their leader on Christmas day in the backwoods of Bucharest. They were going to bring Lulu to New York through the official channels of emigration only he happened to be in the wrong place at the wrong time with his great uncle Manole: in the middle of a piazza in a nearby city in the midst of a shootout between the revolutionaries and so-called terrorists. He was wearing his I love New York T shirt under his parka the day he and Manole died.

I had a hard time breathing again. The room was closing in on me like a prison. Manole and Lulu who had offered me the divinely tasting plums and cherries and guided me throughout the secrets of the house and of our past, through secret rooms within secret rooms, cellars within cellars, the journeys of the living and the dead, stories within stories, mounds of manuscripts, notebooks, and diaries! They were on the other side, of course, closer to Carolina than to any of us on this side of the universe, of time and space. What then had I been living since the day of the summer solstice and the Sanziene wood fairies' celebration? Who were the people next door? Who did this very house belong to? My mother said let's go, you've learned enough, we are going to miss our plane. Enough questions, she said. Sometimes you have to let go of knowledge and just be. It doesn't matter anymore. The dead are finally dead. Let them be. She said it like an admonishment. The sweetness in her voice had disappeared. We had to go, but shreds of our past still hung in the air like broken wings from birds caught in a ferocious tempest. Who does the house belong to, and the orchards?

The orchards are ours, my mother said, and the house too. Manole bought it when the State started allowing private properties in the eighties. He bought both houses at number 18 and at number 18 bis and rented the house next door to a family of farmers who turned out to be former secret police, relatives of the family who had bought the house from Grandmother Victoria in 1947. She meant the Soviet looking couple who spoke in short premade sentences in the Party line and leased the house for one month to Victoria until she could move to Bucharest with the two children. They had bought the house for the price of my father's coat. My grandmother asked them for a little more time to gather their belongings, the little that remained after the winter when everything went into the fire to heat the house and cook meals to save them from starvation. And to have the time to say all the farewells to the house that had breathed and existed like a living creature. The house that had witnessed unimaginable deeds and events, that had folded itself protectively around the doings of the living and the dead, resonated with the music of an old Victrola, and ticked with the quiet movements of a benevolent snake hidden in its thick walls.

I thought of the old gauzy flapper dresses in the wardrobe hidden in the cellar within the cellar filled with clothes and manuscripts dating back to the Bolshevik revolution and the equally sinister counter revolutionary pogroms that started the entire chain of events in the intricate web that was my family history. Carolina's blue sash, Frida's peach colored flapper dress, Manole's fedora, objects that carry heavy histories in their light fabrics. I should have kept them all and taken them with me to the city on Lulu's shirt. But there was always the following summer. It was comforting to know all those objects with a life and intricate past of their own would wait silently in the dusty wardrobe of almost a century ago.

Sebastian appeared out of nowhere, in a blue Dacia car ready to take us to the airport. The film was finished, he said. What an accomplishment, it wouldn't have happened without you, he said. Meaning my mother. She had arrived at the last but the right moment. Sometimes the last moment is the right moment, he said. Everybody seemed to always talk in riddles. The moments of clarity were so short lived, little puddles of light. Right before leaving the property though, Sebi turned off the ignition key and said: "Wait, I can't believe I was forgetting this. The most important of all!" I couldn't imagine any more room in our lives for anything more important than what we had already lived and learned.

The album — do you have it, Zoe? You cannot take it with you, it has to stay here. My mother had not packed the album with the rest of the manuscripts and paper documents, in the big wooden box, but put it in her small carry-on suitcase. Without a word, she took it out and handed it to Sebastian, a secret understanding swishing between them. "I was thinking that it would be equally important to make it known to the world out there. But you are right. You have to start here first, where it all happened", my mother said wearily. She was saying goodbye to the priceless album. "It's our most important document, people died trying to preserve this and hide it so that the truth can be revealed to the world at the right time," Sebastian said turning towards me. "Do you understand Corina, what this document could mean for the writing of the true history of this wretched country?"

There I was crammed in the back seat of Sebastian's blue Dacia car buried among boxes and luggage in total lack of understanding. "The truth about the pogroms, Corina, has been covered up for three quarters of a century. Sure, you can go and research all the communist documents at the Center for the study of the files of the secret police. But where in this country can you find any archive, any center with documents and files with proof of what happened to us in those years? You know where?" I didn't know where. I said: "I have no idea where Sebastian," and with the saying of his name the truth burst in my conscience." "Nowhere, that's where." Of course, there were no archives of the pogroms, and certainly nothing about the atrocities committed on that very street, and in that very lovely idyllic little Moldavian town.

"It's because they've been destroying documents and archives like mad," Sebastian went on. I didn't know who "they" referred to. During my childhood "they" always referred to the secret police, the party, the "rotten communists." We always lived surrounded by some kind of "they" of one side or another. It was true I had not heard of any "they" who were responsible for atrocities of the fascist kind during the war and the popular refrain was: "us Romanians were good to the Jews, we saved a lot of them." Whenever General Antonescu was mentioned during my upbringing was in praise and not condemnation. What that line really meant was we didn't kill all of them, we didn't hand over all of the Jews to the Iron Guard and the SS, we only exterminated half of them, aren't we so noble! What a lie I had been living for so long! "This album is gold Corina," Sebastian went on. "Who took the pictures of the corpses on this street"? I heard myself ask. Sebastian seemed bothered by my question and answered that it didn't matter, "what matters is that these photographs exist. I'd rather die than let them get into their hands. Here they are safe for a while, until the film release." He got out of the car holding the album like a treasure or a fragile child and gestured to us to follow him.

In the middle of that last day of our sojourn in the Moldavian town, my mother and I followed Sebastian in a miniature funeral procession. Because that was exactly what this remote relative of mine on my mother's side proceeded to do. He carried the album with the history in pictures of the atrocities suffered by our family and by others in the neighborhood, to a spot under one of the trees with the sign of the cross carved on it. He asked Zoe to hold on to it for a quick second. "I'll be back in no time," he said. He ran into the cellar part of the house and minutes later reappeared with an iron box, a strong box of sorts. He placed the album carefully in the box that happened to be the perfect size as if he was placing a miniature corpse inside a miniature coffin. Then he took out a key. It looked like the key that my mother had been wearing all along around her neck, only it was off its chain or necklace. I was immune to surprises of any kind. A key like no other key, that opened doors and secret boxes. A key to a most inglorious past that travelled across the world and back. He locked the box and placed the key carefully in the top pocket of his shirt.

"It's important the album rests here for a while, where she might have been buried," he said. He took out a Swiss army knife from his pants pocket and carved a six-point star over the cross on the tree. He proceeded to dig into the earth at the base of the tree with his bare hands until he made a hole big enough for the tiny "coffin" holding the photo album with the miniature history of fascist carnages perpetrated in our family. My mother instantly started sobbing like I had never seen her sob in my life. "Maybe now she'll find peace," she said between torrents of tears. The ground under my feet shifted, a tiny earthquake. A smooth breeze like the swishing of a silk dress fluttered by us and a dizziness came over me. I thought I was going to faint. In the smoky blurriness that formed around me I thought I saw again the face of the young girl who looked like my mother who looked like Frida who looked like the girl called Ester in the album. Maybe now finally the two sisters could become one and my mother could move on to the next chapter of her life: the rooted in the here and now chapter, the guilt free chapter. A dazzling brilliance spread over the entire space of the orchards, a sun so brilliant that trees, grass, flowers sparkled with a new light like they had been reborn. Which they probably were, at least for our group of three as we walked back to the street, to the front of the house at 18bis.

Sebastian drove on back roads alongside rolling hills, some covered with vineyards, others with orchards. Really mostly orchards heavy with ripening fruit like the ones that fed my father's childhood in the idyllic pre-war and pre-the long chain of catastrophes years. The leaves were starting to bleed into the reds and oranges of fall already and flocks of swallows and other migratory birds darted from the red tiled roof tops. A stork cuddled in a hefty nest on top of a chimney. In one of his diaries my father wrote that one could die from longing for those places where he was born and grew up. Now I understand why. Maybe he had died exactly of that longing one cold January morning. And when he called those places magic, he was not kidding, he wasn't even speaking in metaphors.

My father's spiraling life journey from the idyllic pre-war days to a gruesome war, to murderous regimes, to the rupture of exile, to his near-death experiences, to the move to New York which didn't make things any easier, and to his sudden death at the turn of the century, appeared in its full glory of tragic ironies and brutal falls from grace. Throughout it all the light of the orchards in spring, summer, fall, winter under all their changing colors, budding flowers, ripening fruit, dying leaves shone like a continuously shooting star. He had fiercely resisted the destructive forces around him, smoking his way through the war, the ferocious Nazis and Iron Guard, the brutish Russians and their forever tanks, through famine and terror, through unbearable losses of family, house, health, even dignity.

The star lighting his path had been my mother Zoe, with her red hair and greenish eyes. During the weeks before his death, in the small New York apartment on the Lower East Side where he and my mother lived since the early nineties, my father often returned to the war days almost with nostalgia. They had the house, his parents were together, and his sister Lila was alive. The orchards flared unphased in their petulant cycles of bloom, flower, and fruit, through the bombs and the raids, the floods, famine, and draughts. Manole, who as I have found out only this summer was also his uncle and his school literature teacher, opened the windows of literary wonder to him and praised his essays on Russian plays like *The Cherry Orchard*, a favorite. His eyes always filled with tears and stared in the distance with the fixity of someone who sees beyond the surrounding space, beyond the present moment, both into the past and the future, like a bifurcated road that thrusts its meandering paths into the universe. It didn't matter which path you took, you got to the same place in the end. The past was a soothing oasis for my father during the last days of his life, while the future offered the promise of a complete merging with the very essence of that oasis, an infinite and dazzlingly colorful cosmic orchard.

In front of the airport of the provincial town in Northern Moldavia I told Sebastian "See you next summer, I'll visit with the children," like it was the most natural thing in the world. We owned the house after all, not because we deserved it, but because it deserved us and wanted us back even if just for summer vacations from the city on Lulu's T shirt, the I ♥ New York shirt he wore on the last day of his life. Manole might have been right about this just as he had been right about so many other things: about the foreignness of the "over there" and the magic of the "over here," with its enchanted trees and their many entangled roots.

The End

Acknowledgments

I gratefully acknowledge the support of Washington and Lee University with summer Lenfest grants and the 2019-2020 sabbatical leave that afforded me time for researching and writing this novel.

I am extremely thankful to the Fulbright commission for the 2017-2018 fellowship which allowed me to perform extensive research at the National Archives in Iasi and at the Center for the Study of the Files of the Secret Police in Bucharest. I am equally grateful to the Dorot Jewish Division of the New York Public Library where I performed important research of the Romanian Holocaust.

I owe a large debt of gratitude to Evangeline Pappas for the assiduous and superb editing work she performed on my manuscript bringing it to a crisper and more polished form.

I thank my partner Hank Mierzwa for his unflinching support of my work and for giving me encouragement and valuable feedback on the early versions of the novel.

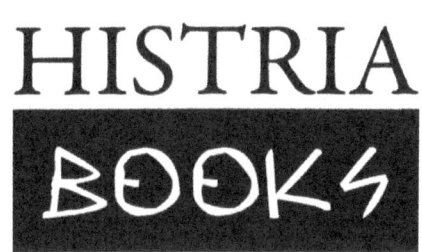

Other fine books available from Histria Fiction:

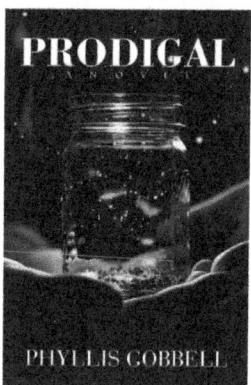

For these and many other great books visit

HistriaBooks.com